Beauty in The Ey

MW00879904

Beauty in the Eyes of His Beast:
The Pack

By

Natavia

SOUL PUBLICATIONS

Ammon

"What do you want me to do?" Saka asked.

"I want you to get rid of her and that pup," I said to him then he chuckled.

"That is an evil thing to do, Ammon. I will shame my ancestors," Saka spat. He walked around his small tent with paintings of snakes all over it. The snakes were black with red eyes.

"All witches are evil," I said to him.

"You may think so, but you know not all snakes are evil. One must see a snake and show fear. Why is that? Not all snakes are poisonous. Not all witches are evil until they give their soul to a demon, and even then, you still can't say they are evil. Greed and power can take over the best of us. It can make us someone we are not. Everyone battles demons, Ammon, even the purest soul. We all have something we want and will do anything for and you are one of those people who have many demons to fight," Saka said. He grabbed a sheet of rock with drawings on it then handed it to me.

I snatched it away from him. "What is this?" I asked as I read the drawings.

"My daughter's destiny. The man she is with is not you, Ammon. Why are you going through this? Why keep a woman who does not belong to you?" Saka asked.

"A witch is supposed to take an offer to get one in return," I said.

"I'm not a greedy warlock. I don't want anything from you," he said.

"I can offer you a life in Anubi with all the gold, diamonds, and gems. You will live a great life, instead of living in this shack," I said to him.

"I'm not a greedy warlock. I have all I want here. If I get rid of your pup and the jezebel you bedded with, that will change my daughter's fate and keep her from finding her mate. Naobi needs to see the true warrior she fell in love with. The jezebel is fate, Ammon, and the pup she gave you is fate too. That is your destiny and you should not interfere," Saka said.

"Very well," I said then walked out of his tent. I walked a few miles until I came across a village where a warlock named Musaf lived. The warriors in his village were cat shifters. They stayed away from Egypt. The cat shifters had their own territory and the wolves in Egypt had theirs.

The warriors danced around a small fire with their faces painted. One of the females had just given birth and they were celebrating. When they saw me they stopped dancing. I was a wolf on their territory.

"Who do you seek? You don't belong here!" the warlock, Musaf, said. He had the skin of a lion's head on top of his head. Two sharp lion teeth pierced his cheek. His face was painted white and he had a lot of markings on his body.

"I seek Musaf," I said.

"I am Musaf, what do you want? You are far away from home. I can smell the gold on you," Musaf said.

"I come in peace. I need a favor," I said to him. Musaf raised his stick up and the warriors continued to dance.

"What favor do you want from me? You are Ammon who is in love with a witch. She can give you favors," Musaf spat.

"This favor I don't want her to see. If she sees it, then she will leave me. I won't be able to give her a pup. Tonight is the night I mate with her," I told Musaf.

"What do you offer?" Musaf asked.

"I will offer you a life in Anubi when I go. I will take you with me if you shield Naobi's vision of my doings," I said to him.

"Naobi is a strong witch. How do you know she doesn't see?" Musaf asked.

"She is strong but she is still a young witch. She has not practiced seeing visions yet, but I must do this before she does," I said to Musaf.

"Come in," Musaf said. I followed him into his tent. He cut his wrist then dropped his blood into a cup. He started chanting then the blood boiled. After he was finished, the blood looked like wine.

"You should give this wine to the jezebel then she will die," he said to me.

"What about the pup?" I asked Musaf.

"The pup will live. The pup will be a great warrior. The pup will be shielded from Naobi's vision but the jezebel shall die," Musaf said then handed me the small, wooden cup.

"Before I go I will need one more favor," I said then dropped two red gems into his hand. Musaf held the gem up then smiled. He was a greedy warlock, the one Saka told me about.

"What do you want?" he asked.

"I must show a man that all snakes are evil," I said to Musaf.

"That portal will open soon," one of the warriors said to me then left my feast room. He brought me out of my daydream. Baki walked in. "Are you sure you want to do this? There has to be another way that doesn't involve Jalesa," Baki said to me.

"A great warrior follows his king. I have taught you that for many years," I said to Baki.

"Jalesa is a part of Anubi. Musaf is not a part of us and we should not give him Jalesa," Baki said.

"I need Dash to be stronger when I go through the portal. I can't take you because you have to watch over Anubi until I get back. Musaf giving me a stronger Dash in exchange for Jalesa is the only way because you cannot leave Anubi. Dash knows Earth more than I. I will do whatever it takes to bring Naobi back," I said to him.

"Jalesa doesn't deserve to mate with him!" Baki yelled.

"Raise your voice at me again, and I will have your tongue," I said to him.

"I was going to ask Jalesa to be my mate before she went to Earth and now I have to watch her mate with an old witch?" Baki asked.

"You were scared to talk to her. Who is at fault? After Musaf gets what he wants from her then you can mate with her," I replied. Baki's eyes turned yellow as he growled at me. He walked away angrily. The warriors came into the feast room. "We are going to bring Naobi back. Kill anything that gets in our way!" I shouted at my warriors. Kaira came into the feast room. I walked over to her, "What is it?" I asked her.

"I'm carrying your pup," she said to me.

"I know and it's a female. A female pup can't rule Anubi or become a warrior. I have no use for her," I said to Kaira.

"You bedded with me!" Kaira screamed at me.

"I'm bringing my mate back. You can't offer me anything. Do you have magic? What can you give Anubi besides pups? I'm going to get my mate back, so stay clear of me," I spat. Kaira growled at me then stormed out of the feast room.

Naobi

I paced back and forth in the basement in front of Keora's cell.

"When am I getting out of here?" she asked me.

"Shut up!" I yelled at her. She laughed.

"You must have watched something on your globe that you didn't like. If I were you, I would get rid of that thing," she said. A long black snake crawled into her cage then wrapped around her body.

"You make one more sound and it will swallow you like the filthy rat that you are," I said to her. The snake's red eyes glowed as it stuck its tongue out in front of her face.

"Please make it disappear," she said. I snapped my fingers and the snake disappeared.

"What's the matter, Keora? I thought you liked snakes," I said.

"Not that big," she spat.

"When I tell you to shut up that's what I want you to do," I said.

"Ammon is going to find you. You might be powerful but you are outnumbered. The last time I checked, numbers don't lie. If I were you I would take Garfield and go far away," she said.

"Garfield?" I asked.

"He's a feline just like your mate. How did you go from a black, strong beast to a prissy cat?" she asked me. I turned her into a deer. "You know my tiger is very greedy for meat," I said then turned her back into a person. Tears rolled down her face. "You are evil just like your father," she said.

"I can be but only when someone tests me, my dear," I said. I sat in my chair at my desk looking into the globe. Ammon was getting his warriors together to come back to Earth. Musaf was also a powerful witch. He wasn't a big threat but he concerned me. Musaf knew me more than my father did. Musaf showed me a few voodoo spells when I was young. Musaf would be a big threat if he could see visions, which gave me the upper hand. Our magic was different in many ways, but him behind Ammon wasn't good.

"I can help you," she said to me.

"Help me do what? Your heart is just as black as Ammon's beast. You are too selfish to help," I said to her.

"If I help you then maybe I will become pure again," she said.

"As much as I still love you, I can't trust you," I said.

"I have been mastering my spells for centuries. I have been studying every trick in the old, ancient spell book. I know more than you think," she said.

I stood up then walked to her cage. “That’s what make me not trust you,” I said to her.

“What do I have to do?” she asked.

“Shut your mouth and let me think,” I said.

“Musaf is going to open up the portal for Ammon and his pack. You and I both know that once that happens, Ammon and his pack can be trapped on Earth until he gets what he wants,” she said.

“I won’t allow that to happen,” I said to her.

“You are a very powerful witch but even you have a weakness. You are scared that you might have to kill Ammon,” she said. A tear slid out of the corner of my eye before I walked away. “Just give me the word, my queen!” she called after me as I walked up the basement stairs.

Kumba was in the kitchen preparing dinner. He was shirtless with his tiger stripes embedded in his skin. His broad shoulders and tall structure awakened something inside me. He turned around then smiled. “What’s on your mind?” he asked me.

“I’m worried about Ammon and his pack coming to Earth. I don’t want to hurt anyone from Anubi. We are all supposed to be like a family. Decades and Decades of traditions and caring for one another, and now it’s going downhill. I have to defeat people who are like family because of Ammon. The only way to stop it all is to kill Ammon and Musaf. If I kill Ammon, Akua will have to go to Anubi. If he goes to Anubi, his mate and pups will stay on Earth,” I said.

“Why would Akua go and not his family?” he asked.

“Usually when you go to Anubi, it’s because you lived for many years. It’s like a heaven without dying, and Akua would be forced to go because of his father. That’s the only way he can go before it’s his time. It’s not time for his mate or pups, yet and there aren’t any exceptions. If you are born in Anubi then you can stay in Anubi,” I said.

“Your world is very different. I come from a small village in Africa that worshipped all species of cats and, somehow, I was born one. I came over here with my parents to live the human, American life and that’s it,” he said.

“That small village which you lived in worshipped a man named Musaf. He was like a god to them and that’s why your people are the way they are. Musaf is your god and Ammon is the god of the Egyptian wolves,” I said.

“I honestly don’t give a damn about any of it. I am who I am and live how I see fit,” he said then smiled. That’s what I loved about Kumba. He wasn’t into his tradition like the Egyptians. He lived carefree and I wanted to experience it all.

“Ammon made a deal with a warlock. Musaf wants to mate with Jalesa. Jalesa is the only witch that can carry in her womb because she was once human. A warlock and a witch will make a very, very powerful offspring. Musaf wants Jalesa and Ammon will take her to him in return of having stronger warriors. Warriors as strong as my son, Akua,” I said.

"Fuck, Ammon. He and I can battle right now! You are my mate and I hope he doesn't think he can just come to Earth and take what doesn't belong to him. You never belonged to him. I waited years, Naobi, and I mean years, and now I finally have you," he said as his tiger eyes turned green.

"I always had a thing for cats. I even made one of my witches a cat shifter. She can shift to any animal but her animal is really her Mua," I said to him then he laughed. He picked me up then lifted me up in the air. "You are a giant," I said then he bit me gently.

"I love you," he said to me.

"I love you, too," I responded.

The doorbell rang and Kumba sat me down then went to answer it. Moments later, my son walked in with his mate and pups.

"Look who arrived for dinner," I said to them. I gave Akua a kiss on the cheek then gave Kanya a hug. I took the babies from her. "My heavens, aren't they heavy," I said.

"Just like their daddy," Akua answered.

"How was your honeymoon to Africa?" I asked them.

"It was great! It's so beautiful there and the villagers are very different yet welcoming. Oh, and let's not forget about Egypt, the sand is so pretty. I rode on a camel, and as soon as I hopped off, Goon tore into it like he was starving," Kanya said.

"I was hungry and I kept telling you that we didn't need to ride on one," Akua fussed then laughed.

Kumba handed Akua a glass of brown liquid. "Seriously, Goon? You are going to drink in front of your mother?" Kanya asked then he growled at her.

"I'm one-hundred-plus years old. I'm over grown," he said to her then sipped the liquid.

"What is that?" I asked him. I gave Kanya the twins back then reached for Akua's cup. "This isn't Anubi, Mother, one sip of that and you will be out. No amount of curse can get rid of that hangover," he said to me. I didn't quite understand him when he spoke but I sipped the liquid anyway. It burned my throat. "UGGHHHHH," I said then sat it down.

"Get me out of here!" Keora yelled from the basement.

"That's that bitch, isn't it?" Kanya asked me.

"She is locked away," I said.

"Good for her," Kanya said.

I should go down there and beat her evil ass, Kanya thought.

"Let's all just enjoy this time," I said to her. Kanya took something out of her bag then laid it down on the floor.

"Are you ready to study a spell?" I asked her then she laughed.

"It's a play mat for the twins. I lay them down on it and watch them lay on their stomach," she answered. Kumba and Akua were talking and laughing about something. Kumba took to my son better than I imagined. Akua had an attitude like his father and could be very stubborn. After Kumba fixed our dinner plates, I took one down for Keora. She sat in the corner of the cage with her knees bent to her face.

"Here is your dinner," I said. I made it disappear then reappear inside the cage by her feet.

"Just kill me and get it over with," she said.

"Adika is innocent. I created you two from the same spell. If you die, then so does she. What's the matter? Can't take a punishment that you created for yourself?" I asked.

"She created it all on her own," Kanya said from behind me. Keora stood up then walked to the bars.

"My, my, my, look what the wind blew in. Isn't it the prissy jackal," Keora said. Kanya's eyes turned gold then she charged into the cage. She reached through the bars to grab Keora's cheek. Kanya's long nails scratched Keora's skin as she grabbed at her face.

"ENOUGH!" I shouted then Kanya let her go. Keora fell down onto the floor. I blew into the cage to close Keora's cheek that bled from deep scratches.

"Her punishment is enough," I said to Kanya. I looked at Keora. "You will never learn when to shut up, will you?" I asked her.

"When you get me out of here then maybe I will," she answered.

"She needs someone to whip her ass," Kanya said then growled. Akua came down the stairs. "What's going on down here?" he asked.

"Hey, handsome," Keora said to him.

"Oh, it's that hoe," he said then chuckled.

"If I'm a hoe, then so is your mate. I know all about Xavier licking between her legs and her enjoying it. Oh, yeah, I was there. I have always been there. Even when you couldn't see me, I was there. How was it, Kanya? I heard you moan from it and you weren't thinking of Goon while doing it," Keora said then laughed. Kanya charged into the cage again. Akua pulled her back.

"Chill out, Kanya. You know this bitch is just messing with you. She is just bitter because her pussy wasn't enough to make me remember it," he said.

"Mama's boy. I wouldn't be surprised if Kanya is breastfeeding you too," Keora said. Akua's eyes turned blue then he growled. All of a sudden Keora fell down onto the floor into a deep sleep, her snores echoing through the basement. I smiled at Akua because he had been practicing his spells.

"Don't wake her up until we leave," he said then grabbed Kanya's hand as they walked up the basement stairs. All I could think about was what Keora called him. She stated he was a mama's boy. I have heard that term before and I knew what she meant. I guess I have been overprotective of Akua and for a very long time. Akua can handle himself and protect his family. I headed upstairs then sat down at the dinner table. "Goon, pass me the wine, please," I said to him.

"Are you calling me Goon now?" he asked me. His smile lit up the room.

"Everyone else does, so maybe I should, too," I said to him. When I looked at my son it was as if I was looking at Ammon. After dinner we talked for a while then Akua and Kanya started to get the twins ready to go home.

"Dinner was very delicious. You should teach my husband how to cook. I get tired of eating raw meat and grapes all the time," Kanya said then Akua growled to himself. I noticed he did that a lot when he was agitated.

"She is very ungrateful. I hunt the biggest deer for her then serve it to her, cut it up nicely on a platter with grapes and a nice glass of wine," Akua said then I patted his back.

"That's all in your tradition, my son," I said to him.

Kanya kissed my cheek. "Thank you very much for having us over," she said. Moments later they were out the door.

******

A bright flash came through the sky, brightening up our bedroom. I hurriedly sat up and watched another pass through the sky. I ran outside then headed to the woods. I ran until I came to the portal from Anubi. I wasn't expecting them that soon. A black paw stepped outside of the portal then the rest of Ammon's beast. Behind him stood almost twenty wolves from Anubi. The wolves had gold beads in their manes and gold bangles around their tails and legs.

"My beautiful queen." Ammon's voice came inside my head.

"You have no right on this land," I said to him.

"You've been so busy trying to become a jezebel and a human that you forgot about the rules in Anubi. I can step foot on any ground that my mate stands on," he said then growled at me. His ice-blue eyes stared into mine and his big, black beast walked toward me. I couldn't deny that I still loved him but it wasn't meant to be. I spent thousands of years with him and it was hard to let it all go.

"Let me live in peace, Ammon. You have another life back in Anubi and I have one here," I responded.

"My beautiful queen, I missed you so much," he said. His big beast pushed me, knocked me down. He towered over me then rubbed his bushy mane on the side of my face. The bushes shook followed by a roar. It was Kumba. Ammon perked his head up then sniffed the air because he sensed another animal.

"I smell your mate," he said to me. Kumba's oversized tiger leaped out of the bushes and landed in front of me. Ammon's pack growled at Kumba then circled around him.

"Kumba, please, there's so many of them," I said.

"Fuck that! This son-of-a-bitch is in the woods in back of my home, coming onto my mate!" he shouted inside my head. Ammon growled at Kumba then Kumba charged into

him, knocking him into a tree. The tree howled before it came crashing down onto the woods' floor. I put a block up to keep Ammon's pack from attacking Kumba. It took a lot of my strength to hold up such a big shield.

Ammon bit Kumba then Kumba's big tiger paw came down onto Ammon's snout, slicing it open. Ammon howled then charged into Kumba. Their beast rolled around biting and slamming each other. Kumba's tiger jumped up into a tree then leaped onto Ammon's back, slamming him face-down. Kumba's teeth sank into the back of Ammon's neck.

"Kumba, NO!" I called out. Ammon's pack started to charge into the shield I had up, and they were strong. Two of them got through the shield then attacked Kumba, but he fought them off. I turned them both to dust but more started coming out of the portal. One of the wolves jumped on me then howls could be heard from deep in the woods. They were my son's howls.

"Stay away, Goon!" I said into his mind.

"I saw a vision of you and Ammon," he responded then out of nowhere Goon's pack leaped into the ambush. Goon's beast was fighting and turning wolves into ashes.

Kumba was injured but he fought a battle of his own. Three wolves tried to take him down but his huge tiger wasn't easy to fall. Jalesa and Adika floated around in the sky sending bolts of lightning into Ammon's pack. It was a war zone between Anubi and the immortals on Earth. I watched before my eyes as my son tore apart his own people. Ammon's pack didn't have a choice but to fight because he was their god. A lot of wolves were killed that didn't want any parts of it. A tear fell down my face because our tradition would never be the same.

Kofi appeared through the portal then froze, looking confused. He didn't know whose side to take because he, too, was a warrior in Ammon's pack.

Three wolves attacked Izra's beast. Kofi charged into them then started to shred them apart. After I got my strength back, I sent some of the wolves back inside the portal then closed it. Ammon charged into Kofi then Akua charged into Ammon as the three of them rolled over a cliff then fell deep, down into a ditch. Kumba's tiger was drenched in his blood. He looked at me then collapsed. I ran to him but was knocked over. When I looked up, Dash was standing over me, his beast growling at me. His eyes glowed and I knew what Ammon meant when he asked Musaf to make his army stronger. He wanted it for Dash. He wanted Dash to be as strong as Akua. Ammon knew Akua was going to go against him; he was using Dash as his protector.

Dash tried to bite me but I moved out of the way. I sent a bolt of lightning into his body. It shocked him then he charged back into me. I disappeared then reappeared behind him. I sent him crashing into a tree. A wolf snuck up on Kumba, aiming for his neck, but I turned him into ashes. I couldn't turn Dash or Ammon into ashes because they were too strong. Dash tried to attack me again then Adika turned into a large snake. She wrapped her body around Dash's body, squeezing him until Ammon appeared from nowhere then attacked her. Izra and Amadi charged into Ammon. I crawled to Kumba then disappeared; we appeared back in our bedroom.

“I will be right back,” I said then teleported back to the fight. When I returned there were dead wolves from Anubi lying around in the woods. Ammon was fighting Kofi, and Goon and his brother were biting each other. I sent everyone sailing into the air to break it up then disappeared. We came crashing down in the basement of Kumba’s house. Everyone was naked when they shifted back to human form. I waved my hand in front of me then clothes appeared on their bodies.

“Damn it! I was just loosening up,” Izra fussed. Akua’s wounds started to close up and so did the rest of the pack. I knew their healing came from him. I hurriedly went to Kumba to heal him. I chanted over his body then pricked a small hole in my hand. I held the dripping blood over his mouth. When a drop of my blood went into his mouth he yelled as it pulled his skin together to close his wounds. Sweat drenched his clammy body.

“You scared me,” I said to him then he squeezed my hand.

“I’m your protector, Naobi. I will be less of a man if you had to use your magic all of the time to defend us,” he said. I had to figure something out because Ammon wasn’t playing fair. I needed to get rid of him without Akua having to rule Anubi, leaving his family behind.

Ammon

"What temple is this?" I asked Dash.

"It's my home," he answered. I looked around his temple and wasn't pleased.

"You lived in a hut?" I asked him.

"It's an apartment! This is all me and my mate could afford after we lost everything. I'm sorry I'm not rich and live in a mansion like Goon," he spat.

"Don't you use that tongue with me! I am still your king!" I shouted at him. He growled then walked away. He came back with a piece of cloth then tossed it at me.

"You got blood on your jewelry," he said. I walked around his hut to look around.

"We shall stay here until the portal opens again. Musaf has a spell over it until I bring him Jalesa," I said to Dash.

"I don't mind staying here. My pups are better off with my mother anyway," he answered.

"Your pups won't be able to stay that long. It's against Anubi's rules. You can't stay there until it's your time to go, unless you are born there," I replied.

"How do you feel about Kofi turning on you?" Dash asked me. He ignored what I said about his pups.

"One more word from your mouth and I will pull your tongue out," I said to Dash.

When Kofi, Akua and I fell off the cliff, I stuck my nails on the side to keep from sailing all the way down. Kofi and Akua did the same, but I managed to get back over the top before they did. The fall could've caused a lot of damage.

"What's the matter, Father? Are you mad that something is out of your hands?" Dash asked before I knocked him over while he was seated. I took my foot and brought it down on his arm. "Now, let's see how that will heal," I said then walked away.

"You are going to regret everything you just did," Naobi's voice came into my thoughts.

"No beast will live to tell the story of them bedding my mate! No beast shall defeat me because of my mate. I'm going to walk your precious Earth until you come home," I said to her.

"You are going to see a witch that you've never seen before," she gritted.

"And you are going to see a wolf fight a battle like you've never seen before," I answered.

Dash cracked his arm back into place. "Ancient muthafucka!" he said to me.

"I'm assuming you are speaking in sin," I replied.

"Look, nigga. I'm home now, and I can give zero fucks about your little fantasy home and stupid-ass rules. I can care less about your robot-speaking ass right now! You made a deal with that old, creepy nigga with the lion skin. I didn't make a deal with him so you can get the witch yourself," he fussed.

"You are a waste of good warrior blood. I made the deal for you to become stronger, but without that witch, Musaf takes it back. Do you know what that means? That means Akua is going to snap your neck like a stick," I responded.

Dash sat down on what looked to be a long chair. "You set me up," he said.

"I don't know what you are speaking on," I said to him. There was a knock at the door. "Who is that?" I asked him.

"A friend of mine. I texted him a few minutes ago," he answered. When he opened the door a tall man stepped in, smelling like an animal. He was a wolf from a different tribe.

"You look different," the man said to Dash.

"I was cursed—it's a long story but let's just say a witch hid my real identity from my father," he answered.

"Who is he?" I asked him.

"He is a friend of mine and he just moved back into the area. His name is Sosa," Dash said.

“Sosa? What’s the meaning of that name?” I asked him.

“Your father is a little coo-coo, and why is he dressed like that?” he whispered to Dash.

“He is from Egypt,” Dash replied.

“How is he a comrade of yours? He is from a different tribe,” I said to Dash.

“I did business with him is all you need to know,” Dash said.

I grabbed Dash by the throat then slammed him into the wall. “I am still your god and you will respect me,” I said to him. His comrade growled at me. “I shall fear no beast,” I said then dropped Dash onto the floor.

“His tribe is willing to help us,” Dash said as he held his throat.

“In exchange for what?” I asked.

“Your gold, of course,” Sosa replied.

“Do you know that wolves with Egyptian roots are stronger than an ox? What can your tribe offer me?” I asked him.

“My tribe is very large in numbers,” he said.

“I’ll leave it up to you. I don’t know this comrade of yours nor do I trust him. I will let you be in charge, but just know that if you fail me, you will become a memory. No pup of mine should fail and that includes you. I came to

Earth for my mate and I shall leave with my mate. If all fails then you shall feel the wrath of the Egyptian wolf god," I said to Dash.

Anik

"It was crazy last night. Wolves were everywhere fighting and biting each other. Amadi and Izra are mad at Adika and I because we came to the battle, but Naobi is like Adika's and my mother," Jalesa stated.

"Goon came home pissed off that his father came to Earth. It's only a matter of time before the big BOOM!" Kanya stated.

"I hope Goon's mother is okay," I said.

"Naobi is fine as long as she stays out of Anubi. She is happy with her mate and her new environment. The pack is going to do whatever it takes to make sure she is safe," Kanya said.

"What about that Kofi guy? He came back home with the pack last night. Dayo said something about him being locked out of the portal, his mate still in Anubi. I met him briefly then he went to his old room and stayed," I said.

"Kofi has a lot to take in right now. His mate is in Anubi and he went against Ammon, who is like a brother to him. He will come around after a while," Kanya said. We all made small talk as we walked toward Beastly Treasures.

"So, where are you and Amadi going tonight?" I asked Jalesa while Kanya unlocked her store. The rest of the staff arrived at ten o' clock.

"He didn't say, but he said it was a surprise. What if he wants to bed me? I'm nervous. I have never been with a man in this new life. When Naobi reincarnated me, I lost all memories," Jalesa answered. Kanya yawned. She and Goon had just come back from their two-week honeymoon a few days ago.

"You can go home and rest, Jalesa, and I can handle everything," I said to Kanya then she laughed.

"Pardon me. Goon wore me out physically and mentally. I don't think I have any of my essence left in me. I think he screwed it all out." Kanya blushed.

We walked into the store then headed straight toward the back. Jalesa turned on the lights to the showcases where the jewelry was held. I pulled the curtains back. Kanya eyed me. "What's going on?" I asked her. I already knew what she was thinking.

"How was it?" she asked me.

"How was what?" I replied.

"Losing your innocence?" she responded.

"It hurt like hell when he first entered me, but after a few seconds, the pain slowly went away. It was the best thing I have ever experienced. My body felt like it was floating. It was beautiful," I told Kanya.

"That's the part about sleeping with a wolf. It's amazing how it makes your body feel. I feel sorry for the women who will never get the chance to get pleasured by a werewolf," Kanya said.

A few hours later, the store was crowded. Izra started his own jewelry line and his gold bracelets with red rubies sold fast. Kanya advertised them on the Beastly Treasures website; the customers were all looking forward to the bracelets.

Moments later, Dayo walked in wearing black jeans and a black wife-beater with a black leather jacket over it. On his feet he wore a pair of black leather boots and he carried his motorcycle helmet in his hand. My hands started to sweat and my skin felt clammy. The attraction I had for him was unexplainable, his aura was enticing. The way his strong hands massaged my body and the way his tongue brought me pleasure caused my body to go through spells. My nipples hardened, so I closed my blazer to hide it. A dampness seeped from between my slit. I hurriedly rushed to the bathroom.

I splashed water on my face, my caramel, reddish-looking skin looked a little pale. I stared at myself in the mirror as my face changed. My lips darkened, my fangs protruded out of my gums and my eyes were a brownish-yellow. I almost howled but I hurriedly covered my mouth. Dayo's presence drove my wolf insane. I needed his thick and long member buried deep inside me. I craved his love bites and the high I received when he sank his fangs into my neck.

The door opened. "I will be out in a minute," I said, drying my face.

“You need a fix?” Dayo said then locked the door behind him. I backed away from him because I was ready to shift.

“We need to wait until we get home,” I said. Dayo walked toward me. When he got closer he pulled me to him. His tall body towered over me then he nuzzled his nose into my neck.

“I’m at work,” I whined. He ignored me as his hands slid up my legs underneath my black pencil skirt. A growl escaped his throat. “We need to wait,” I said, my voice trembling. My pussy throbbed insanely; I needed him as bad as he needed me.

“I can’t help it, Anik. I promise I will be quick. I just need to have a functioning day today,” he said. He pulled my skirt up above my hips. My scent permeated the air, which caused Dayo’s hazel eyes to glow. I still wasn’t all that experienced yet; he taught me a few things but I still found myself having thoughts of not pleasing him. I knew Dayo was a free wolf before he met me and he screwed any human he wanted to. I knew the women he had been with had experience and I still had none.

He moved my kinky hair out of my face then his fingers traced my lips. “Why are you scared of me, Anik?” he asked.

“I’m not scared of you. I’m scared that you will look for pleasure with someone else,” I replied.

“I’m addicted to you, not just to your body, but also to your mind. Your whole aura, everything about you, I crave. My beast doesn’t want nobody else. Feel how hard he is,” he said. He placed my hand on his huge erection. I looked down and he looked like he was ready to burst out of his jeans. My panties were coated with my wetness; they stuck to me. Dayo came closer to me then attacked my lips. I threw my arms around his neck then kissed him back. A breeze swept across my pussy lips when he slid my panties down. A loud growl escaped his throat. My shaky hands unbuckled his belt and jeans. He reached inside his pants to pull out his beautiful, dark tool. The veins that went along it caused my hormones to spiral out of control. I was lifted up against the wall. When his girth pierced through my slit, I howled.

"Goddamn it, Anik! You are about to scare them bougie muthafuckas out there," he fussed. I ignored him as I concentrated on the ache that formed between my legs. Dayo slowly grinded into my spot. *"Unbutton your blouse,"* his voice said inside my head.

I took off my blazer then unbuttoned my white, silk shirt. Dayo reached inside my bra to pop my breast out. His canines sharpened. His tongue flickered across my aching nipple then he gently sucked it. His dick went further inside me. I whimpered from the pressure. His girth was ripping me in half, but it felt too good to stop him. His teeth sank into my nipple as he lustfully sucked on it, which caused me to moan louder. I growled then my red nails sharpened; my wolf nails were red. I had red designs and markings on my body because of my breed. Dayo growled deeply as he licked my neck. My walls clenched around him then my body went limp as I had an orgasm.

"Come harder," he growled, viciously pumping into me. I howled out again as my legs shook from another orgasm. Dayo grabbed my wet panties that sat on the sink then stuffed it inside of my mouth.

"Take more of me, Anik," he spat, gripping my hips harder as he banged me against the wall. My beast was coming out; I snatched the panties out of my mouth. My teeth went into Dayo's neck.

"AAAAAAWWHHHOOOOOOOOOOOOO!" he howled as he grew inside of me. He swelled, filling me up; his dick jerked as he pumped his semen inside me. He buried his face inside the crook of my neck as he panted heavily.

After his dick swelled back to its size he pulled out of me. I slowly eased my shaky legs down onto the floor. I looked at his shirt and it was shredded with bloody scratches on his muscled chest.

"I need more," he said, staring into my eyes.

"No, I've been gone long enough. My panties are ruined," I said then I was hit with reality. I was at work locked away in the bathroom. Dayo smiled then reached inside of his pants pocket; he pulled out a pair of fresh panties. I took the panties from him. I wet a paper towel then put soap on it before heading into the stall to freshen up.

"I won't tell anybody about your hoe bath." He laughed.

"What is a hoe bath?" I asked him.

"What you are doing now," he said. After I cleaned off I stepped into my fresh panties then washed my hands.

"I want to take you out tonight," he said.

"Where?" I asked excitedly.

"You will see. Get back to work. I will see you when you get home," he said. When we walked out of the bathroom the customers and the other staff were frozen in place. Kanya and Jalesa were talking and laughing like everything was normal.

"What's going on?" I asked after I looked around.

"Jalesa froze them so they wouldn't hear the loud growls and howls that were coming from you and Dayo. They've been frozen from the minute he followed you into the bathroom," Kanya said.

"I had panties inside my mouth for nothing?" I asked then everyone fell out laughing. Dayo patted my bottom.

"I will see you later," he said to me. He looked at Kanya. "Goon should've left your ass in Egypt," he joked then she growled at him.

"Jalesa, stay a geek for as long as you can. If you start acting like Kanya, I will feel sorry for you. Her attitude is a bad influence," he said then Kanya playfully pushed him.

"I can't stand you," she said then giggled.

"What's a geek?" Jalesa asked.

"You and Amadi are made for each other because y'all don't know shit this day and age," he fussed.

"Get out of my store," Kanya said to him. Dayo pushed one of the frozen customers onto the floor. The customer was a white, older man; he was standing at the counter looking at the necklaces.

"DAYO!" Kanya shouted at him.

"He cut me off in traffic when I was on my way here. That's what his old ass gets. Let me leave out of here," Dayo said then walked out of the store.

Kanya pulled the older man up as blood drizzled from his nose. She hurriedly wiped his nose then Jalesa unfroze the customers. Everyone moved around back to normal. "I have a damn nose bleed," the old man fussed as the blood continued to drip onto his shirt. I felt bad for him because Dayo wasn't the nicest person at times. It seemed like all the pack brothers had a stubborn streak in them. Adika came into the store; she was running late. She had a saddened look on her face.

"What's the matter?" I asked then pulled her to the side.

"I just came back from the adoption agency. Izra threw a fit. He said I must be out of my fucking mind to adopt a human baby. He told me he didn't want a baby that bad and that I was getting on his nerves," she said.

"Find a wolf to carry the pup, so that it can be immortal. There are a lot of lone female wolves roaming around. Arya and I ran into plenty of them, but it will cost," I said to Adika.

“Izra will have to mate with one. I don’t know if he will do that,” Adika said then I shrugged my shoulders. “It’s just an idea,” I replied.

“It’s not a bad one at all,” she said then hugged me.

I left work at three o’clock in the afternoon to pick Arya up from school. I pulled our brand new, soccer mom van up to the building. Kanya thought it was a must we get one because of the twins and Arya. Arya walked out of the school giggling with a few of her friends. She fit right in with the human children. After she waved them goodbye, she got inside the van.

“I see you fit right in,” I said then kissed her cheek.

“I love it here; I don’t want to go back to our hometown,” she said.

“We will never go back there. As long as I have life in my body, we will never go back. That place is behind us,” I said to her.

“I don’t want them to take me from you,” Arya said.

“They will not find us,” I said to Arya. I lied to the pack about my real reasoning for leaving my hometown.

Arya and I ran away; her father wasn’t dead, but he was dead to us. The story of my family being killed was true. Arya’s dad was responsible. He was a part of another tribe; he wasn’t a Chippewa wolf. Chippewa wolves didn’t kill their own kind. Sosa wanted to mate with me when it was time for me to go into heat, that part was true. The real reason he killed my family was so that I wouldn't have anyone to turn to. He wanted me all for himself. I was the only female that had not bred yet in my tribe. I was the only pure one and he wanted me. I had enough of him when he was going to give Arya away to be groomed as an Alpha female. He was going to sell his daughter to another wolf, so that later on the wolf could mate with his daughter. His pack is full of vicious wolves. I had been a prisoner of his, a slave to him. I took care of his daughter, protecting her. I ran away the day a wolf came to our home ready to take Arya with him. I attacked the wolf and Arya's father before we ran away. I couldn't bring myself to tell my new pack my story because I didn't want them to turn their backs on us. They were my only hope because Arya and I had no one else. I will forever be grateful to Goon's pack.

"This is between you and I," I said to Arya.

"I promise I won't tell. Are you and Dayo going to mate? Will that make him my father too?" she asked.

"You are too grown, but yes that would make him your father. When Dayo and I have pups, he and I will become one forever," I said to her.

****

When we got to the house, Arya headed straight to the kitchen for a pitcher of water. We needed water more than we needed red meat. Our body temperature is higher than humans, which causes us to always be thirsty.

Goon walked down the hallway along with Amadi and Elle. They had small specks of blood on their faces from hunting.

"What's up, Anik? Where is Arya's bad ass? She thinks I haven't noticed she's been sniffing around my liquor cabinet," Goon's deep voice echoed through the foyer.

"Her father was an alcoholic and Indians suffer from alcoholism. I talk with her all the time about it but she has a craving for it sometimes," I said.

"I will go and talk to her," Elle said then called out for Arya. Chippewa wolves could sense mood changes; we could feel when someone was troubled. My grandmother used to sell her stones inside our small town. Many said that it helped with changes in their mood. I missed her a lot. Her throat was ripped out because she was trying to defend me the day I was taken away from my home. I could feel Elle's mood and he was sad. Something was bothering Elle though he hid it very easily. His thoughts were normal but his aura wasn't.

I went into the woods to hunt. I prayed over my catch before I chewed into its flesh. I growled and grumbled as the taste of fresh blood from my kill satisfied my hunger. After I was done, I hurriedly put my clothes back on. I went inside my room to take a shower. When I got out of the shower, I braided my hair into a braid that wrapped around my head. I put on a pair of leggings with a long-sleeve tunic top. I wore a pair of suede moccasins I made myself. I heard Dayo's voice coming down the hall. Seconds later, he burst into my room. "Do you knock?" I asked him.

"Do I need to? I'm a stalker, I keep telling you that. We are supposed to be sharing a room now, anyway," he said.

"Yeah, I know. But you are stalker, you watched me pleasure myself twice," I said. I stood up then kissed his full lips. His strong hands went to my bottom, his tongue into my mouth.

"Get a room, damn," Izra spat as he stood in my doorway, chewing on a cube of raw meat.

"Where are we standing, nigga?" Dayo asked him.

"Seriously, bro, you need to teach Anik how to kiss. I was getting bored watching y'all. I'm fittin' to take a nap now," Izra said then walked away. Dayo followed behind him.

"Keep fucking with me, lil' brother, and you just wait and see what I do to you," Dayo said to Izra.

"I'm not scared of you, Dayo. I don't understand why you think I am," I heard Izra respond to Dayo. I chuckled to myself as Dayo and Izra argued.

"The pups are asleep and if y'all muthafuckas wake them up," Goon roared at Izra and Dayo.

"Well, nigga, you ain't helping because you are louder than the both of us," Izra said.

"Don't start, bro, I'm warning you. Akea and Kanye are starting to resist naps," Goon said then yawned.

“Nobody told you to be a stay-at-home mom anyway,” Izra teased. Goon shoved Izra into the wall; the wall opened up then swallowed Izra whole. I was amazed at how Goon was catching onto his other side of being a male witch.

“Get me out of here!” Izra’s voice muffled. Izra banged on the wall.

“This is why I stay home because if I didn’t, you and Izra would fuck this house up so bad and then we all would be homeless,” Goon said to Dayo.

“Leave him in there,” Dayo said.

“Adika can get him out when she comes home,” Goon said as he headed toward the gym room.

“Come on, bro, I saw something! Something is crawling on me!” Izra shouted as he banged on the wall.

“Is he really going to leave Izra there?” I asked because I was worried.

“More than likely that nigga was serious about that. When Goon doesn’t get any sleep, he gets angrier,” Dayo said.

“Aye, bro, get Izra out of the wall!” Dayo shouted out to Goon. Even though Izra and Dayo didn’t get along, they still cared for each other’s well-being.

“Tell Izra five minutes,” Goon shouted back.

******

Dayo gave me a helmet to put on. “Where are we going?” I asked.

“You will see,” Dayo said before he put his own helmet on. After he pulled off, I gripped him from behind. I was afraid of riding on his motorcycle though I felt safe with him. The sun had set by the time we got to our destination. I looked around and a chill went up my spine; it looked to be a deserted area.

Dayo parked his bike in an alley; the buildings looked old and rundown.

“I don’t like this,” I said to Dayo.

“Trust me,” he said to me.

He grabbed my hand then we walked deeper into the dark alley. It reeked of human feces and rat urine. I hated how sensitive my nose was. I covered my mouth and allowed Dayo to take me somewhere that I was nervous about.

When we came to a dead end, Dayo lifted up a pothole. “Oh, hell no, I should bite you. What kind of date is this, Dayo? I know you are an asshole, but are you freaking serious?” I yelled. Dayo tossed me over his shoulder then jumped down into the hole, landing on his feet. Bright lights lit up the tunnel and the ground looked like bricks.

“What is this place?” I asked him.

"You will see," he said as he pulled me down the long hallway. At the end of the tunnel was a metal door with a big man standing by it. He nodded at Dayo then stepped to the side. Dayo opened the metal door. I received the shock of my life; there were humans in cages being treated like animals. Someone threw raw meat at one White guy and he ate it.

"What the hell is this?" I asked him.

"This is a club where humans act like animals. They don't know we exist. This is their imagination of us shifters and most of them are very rich. This is like a fetish that they have. The guy that was just eating that raw meat is a billionaire," Dayo said. We headed to the bar and one guy crawled over to me then licked my leg and started panting like a dog.

"Dayo, I don't like this," I said to him. Smoke came across the stage in front of us. Dayo grabbed our drinks from the naked bartender.

"What is this?" I asked him.

"Just drink it, Anik, trust me," he said. I drank the liquid that was in the cup. It tasted stronger than alcohol. "UGGHHHHH," I gasped. The strong, green liquid burned my throat.

"By the end of tonight, you will be a new wolf," Dayo said then downed his drink in one gulp. The thick, red curtains on the stage opened up. In the middle of the stage, there was a human biracial-looking woman wearing a wolf outfit. The crowd howled then a fake full moon dropped down in the background. The wolf woman seductively crawled around on the stage as the humans made sounds that were supposed to sound like a wolf's.

Another figure dressed like a wolf came onto the stage, but it was a man. The woman crawled to the man. When she got to him she sniffed his crouch area. For some reason, I was turned on. I watched how she released the man's dick from out of his costume. She hungrily took him into her mouth then slurped on him. Her finger went between her legs, which caused the crowd to howl louder. I wanted to howl myself because of how turned on I was; I had never seen anything like it. The woman costume was cut out around her pussy and butt area. I could smell her arousal for the man she pleasured with her mouth.

Sweat beads formed on my forehead as the show continued. My nipples were pressed against my shirt as the throbbing between my legs became worse. I felt moisture seep from my slit; Dayo got behind me then wrapped his arms around me.

"You want to cater to me like that, don't you?" he said inside my head.

"Yes, I want to make love to you like that," I replied back to him. The woman lay on her back then the man chained the woman down to the floor. The woman's legs were gaped open as the crowd stared at her glistening, wet sex. I wanted him to hurry up and penetrate her. A Black man walked out onto the stage and his dick was huge; his size was almost like Dayo's. I didn't know a human man could grow that hard. The crowd cheered on then flames shot up from the stage.

"What are they about to do?" I asked Dayo.

"They are about to mate," he responded. When the Black man got down on the floor and entered her seconds later, I wanted to scream. A slight moan escaped my throat then Dayo caressed me between my legs. It seemed normal to showcase our affection in the place we were in. He slipped his hand inside my leggings, his fingers caressing my swollen bud. I fell back against his solid chest. The sounds from the woman moaning as the man rammed himself into her, almost caused me to shift. The harder he fucked the chained woman, the faster Dayo's fingers worked inside my panties. I felt like I was about to burst. Dayo licked my neck before he bit me. I howled as my legs began to tremble. I almost fell but Dayo caught me. When I howled out from my orgasm though the humans seemed oblivious to the fact that I was a werewolf. Some even howled with me; humans are insane.

After I caught my breath, Dayo pulled his wet fingers out of my panties. There were two women hungrily eyeing him, one got down on the floor then crawled over to him. She grabbed his hand then licked my wetness from his fingers. She howled after she tasted me. I couldn't wait to tell Kanya and Adika what happened. Jalesa wouldn't understand. The woman grabbed Dayo's dick then I growled at her. She fake-growled back at me; she really thought she was an animal.

I growled at her louder then she backed away. She stood up and grabbed the hand of the girl that she was with before they disappeared into the crowd. Dayo ordered me another drink then he and I sat and watched three women lick each other's bodies on stage. Someone from the crowd threw a huge chunk of bloody meat at them. One of the women growled as she ate the raw meat. Dayo laughed. "This is like a comedy show. We act nothing like this," he said then shook his head.

"What made you come here?" I asked him.

"So you can see what type of sex I like and why I was sleeping with human women. I want you to understand this part of me. I like to get my dick sucked and I like for a woman to take advantage of me sometimes. I want you to learn, so that way you can never question me about my happiness with you. We are forever, Anik, and I want you to be happy with us. I don't want you to ask me if I love your pleasure. After tonight, you will fuck me so good that you will never doubt yourself again," he said then licked my lips. Dayo was complicated but I fell even more in love with him.

Elle

I watched her house from the woods. I wanted to howl out for her. I was in love with her years ago. It was the year 1940 when I met her. I looked to be only nineteen years old at that time but I was one hundred years old; I'm older than the rest of my pack brothers.

I met her while I was hunting in the woods and she was fifteen at the time, walking home from school. A group of White men followed her and threw rocks at her, calling her a "nigger" and a "wench". One of them jumped from a pick-up truck and was trying to rape her. I attacked the man and killed him. The group of men left their friend in the middle of the dirt road as they took off. They left their dead friend behind because my beast frightened them. She looked at me in horror and I could never forget how scared she was of me…

"What are you? You aren't just an animal. You have eyes like a human," she said backing up and away from me. She tried to run but she tripped and hit her head on a rock. She was out cold when I dragged her by her skirt into the woods. I sat and watched her; she had a pretty and extraordinary face. Her skin was dark, the color of the woods' soil. Her hair was braided down her head and she had a mole on her full, pink lips. As I watched her, I became amazed at how precious she seemed to be. She was perfect but she was a human. I shifted back then hurriedly got dressed; my clothes were hidden behind a tree. I heard

a truck driving up the road. I picked her up then hid behind a tree.

"Goddamn it!" someone said.

"Billy wasn't lying. That damn dog shredded Lester into pieces," someone else said.

"We got dogs that big?" another voice said.

"Apparently so. We'll have to hunt it and kill it before it attacks again," the man responded.

"This is by the old slave plantation. Eighty years ago one of those dogs killed everyone on the plantation. The myth was that it was a wolf. He was black with blue eyes and had teeth like knives. My mother told me the story when I was a little boy," one of them added.

"Maryland doesn't have wolves; maybe it was a coyote," someone responded.

"I know what I saw, and that dog was bigger than a wolf. He was brown and black and he had eyes like a darn human. I know what I saw and can't nobody tell me that was a dog or coyote," was the last I heard. I took off deep into the woods until I stopped at a lake. I laid the human down then ripped a piece of my shirt off to clean her wound. Her eyes fluttered as she lay in my arms.

"You are the wolf boy, aren't you? My grandmother told me about that old plantation. She said a beast roamed around it," she said. She stared at me for what seemed like forever.

"Do you talk?" she asked looking into my eyes, but I still didn't respond.

"How old are you?" she asked as I continued to wipe her forehead. The blood seeped through the tiny gash which caused me to lick her wound.

"Ewww, gross," she said then I laughed.

"It da only way," I said to her in my broken English.

"You speak differently. Where are you from?" she asked.

"I'm from Africa," I responded.

"What's your name?" she asked.

"Elle," I answered.

"Well, Elle, my name is Camille and I'm fifteen years old," she said as she stood up. I stood up with her. "You are very tall," she said looking up at me with her big, brown eyes. I touched her lips, tracing the outline of them. I never interacted with a human before. Kofi told me to stay away from them and to hide our identity.

She looked into my eyes. "Your eyes are the same as your beast," she said. She went into her brown leather sack then pulled out an apple. "Thank you, Elle. I don't have much to give you," she said. I took the apple from her then sniffed it. She covered her mouth as she giggled.

"I have to get going now because it's almost night. My mother will be looking for me when the sun goes down.

Blacks shouldn't roam the roads at night because a lot of negros have been lynched from it," she said.

"I must walk you home," I said to her.

"Okay." She smiled.

That was the beginning of our love. Every day we met by the lake in the woods. I followed her when she walked home to make sure nobody hurt her. She was the only human who knew what I was and it didn't frighten her. When she turned eighteen, she gave herself to me. I had the urge to mark her as my beast pumped into her body, but I couldn't. A wolf's marking bite can kill a human instantly. I was in love with Camille and I still loved her. She went away to college, but when she visited home, she met me by the lake. We spent hours at the lake and even nights. Years went on and Camille started to look her age and I still looked nineteen. I would never forget the day my life changed…

"I'm twenty-eight years old, Elle, and you still look the same as the day I met you. I want to get married and have children; I want to live amongst my people. I want to go out on dates," she said as tears filled her eyes. Camille taught me how to speak better English, she taught me a lot.

"What are you saying?" I asked her.

"I met someone and he asked me to marry him," she said then burst into tears. She wrapped her arms around me. "Oh, Elle, I'm so sorry. I love you, I really do, but we are so different. I will always love you," she said to me. Water ran from my eyes. I touched my face then looked at

the clear liquid that rolled down the tips of my fingers. I had never experienced that before. "Those are tears, Elle. You are crying because I hurt you. I don't mean to. But it's not fair and if there is a way I can be like you I will," she said.

"You make love to him?" I asked her then she looked away.

"Answer me, Camille! Do he enter your body too?" I yelled at her then she jumped. She backed away from me.

"Your teeth are sharp," she said. I was angry and on the verge of shifting.

"Answer me!" I shouted with a growl coming from the pit of my stomach. My beast wanted to attack her, so I took a few steps away from her.

"Yes! He and I make love the same way I do with you. What do you want me to do? Look at you, Elle! Soon, I will get old and then die! Don't you see? We are in different times because I'm aging and you aren't. I'm sorry, Elle, but I cannot see you anymore," she said. She walked away from me in sobs. I burst out of my clothes then ran into the deep end of the woods where I howled all that night...

I stepped out of the woods then walked to her window around the back of her house. I watched her from afar but I had a feeling she knew I was there. I watched her while she carried a child in her womb. I watched her and her husband run around the yard with their children. I watched her children have children. Time stood still for me as time for her went on. Her husband passed away a few years ago then her children and her grandchildren stopped visiting.

Human life came then it went, and when it did, you die alone. I lifted up her window then climbed through. I saw the light on from the TV in the living room. When I saw her my heart almost stopped; she was old and gray. Her glasses hung down her sunk-in face and when she coughed it sounded painful. Her shaky hands reached for a cup of water. The cup tipped over and I hurriedly grabbed it for her. She looked at me then pushed her glasses up.

"So you finally come after watching me all of these years?" she said then coughed.

"I've waited until you fully lived the life that you always wanted," I responded as I gave her the cup. She took a sip from what was left.

"The life I wanted wasn't the life I lived, although I'm glad my family came from it," she responded. I looked around the small living room. She had pictures of her family decorated on her wall.

"You still are tall and handsome. God answered my prayers because I wanted to see you before I die. I couldn't forget you even while being with another man. I loved another man for years, but I never was *in* love with him," she said.

"I felt it in my heart that your presence will no longer be here," I said.

"Come closer to me Elle, so, I can get a better look at you. I can't see all that good," she said.

I kneeled down in front of her then her small, old hands touched my face. Tears fell from her eyes. "My wolf man," she said to me. She gripped my hair then laughed.

"My great-grandson has these. He calls them dreadlocks if I can remember," she said.

"That's what we call them," I answered.

"You only look to be in your late twenties, if that. I'm ninety years old now. I'm getting tired of waking up," she said sadly.

"I have watched you for years, but I had to come in because it was a dark cloud over your house today. The sun is shining everywhere else but here. You are trapped between Earth and what you humans call "heaven". What are you holding on to?" I asked her.

"I'm holding onto you," she said. She wiped the tear that fell from my eye. "Truth is I died the moment I left you. Your love is so strong for me that it is keeping me alive. I'm not the only one that's holding on, Elle, because you are, too," she said.

"I can't do this," I said as I pulled away from her. I left her home then headed back to my house. When I finally got home it was late. I went straight to the kitchen for a pitcher of water.

I shut the refrigerator door and Anik was standing behind it in her house robe.

"Don't mind me, I'm thirsty," she said getting some water. I sat down at the kitchen island. Anik was still in the kitchen while I wanted to be left alone. She sat down across from me then grabbed my hand. "You are very sad, Elle, and if you talk about it you might feel better. You can't keep it in anymore," she said to me.

"I'm fine, Anik," I said.

"No, you are not because you are heartbroken. I want to know your story. I know everyone else's story but yours. I can feel your aura, so tell me, who is she?" Anik asked me.

"Her name is Camille," I stated.

"Okay, that's a start. Where is she and what is she like? Is she a wolf?" Anik asked me.

"She is at home dying because she's aged. She is stubborn but yet very passionate. Her smile is brighter than the sun and she is the most beautiful thing to me," I said.

"Oh, my, Elle, why didn't you bring her here? Is she going to die alone?" Anik asked me.

"I'm not ready for her to die, Anik. I don't want to see it nor do I want to think about it. I just wished that she was immortal so I wouldn't have to experience her death," I said.

"Why are all of you so damn stubborn? Death is a blessing to my tribe. We believe that once we die our soul will be recycled. You should know because Egyptians have the same belief; it's called Afterlife," she said.

"I won't see her again," I replied.

"But her spirit will be within your heart. If you love her you will feel her presence everywhere you go," Anik said then I smirked.

"You really have a good spirit," I said to her. She came around the island then hugged me. "Now I need to get dressed so I can sneak out," she said.

"Where are you going? You want to piss Dayo off? I can't cover for you, Anik," I said to her.

"I'm going to drive to Camille's house to bring her back here. You, my brother, are riding with me because I don't know where she lives. She will not die alone, Elle," Anik said then walked out of the kitchen.

Moments later, Anik came back with a sweat suit on. "Get your ass up, Elle," Anik said. I got up then followed Anik out of the house. She handed me her van keys. "Let's hurry up before Dayo wakes up because he will give me hell for being out late," Anik said.

"I will kick his ass if he does," I said then laughed. I started the van up then pulled off. An hour later, we arrived at Camille's house. I snuck back through her window and she was still in her same spot. Her eyes were closed and she looked dead; I was too late. When I got closer to her she coughed.

"Who is there?" she called out.

"It's me. Elle," I said.

"You came back," she said then coughed again. I picked up her frail body. I felt like I was holding nothing. "You are still strong, I see. You used to climb up the trees with me on your back. I was dreaming about that before I woke up," she said. I walked out of her front door then Anik opened the back door to her van for us.

"Is that your wife?" Camille asked when she looked at Anik.

"No, I'm his sister and my name is Anik. It's nice to meet you," Anik said politely.

"Is she a wolf too? I don't remember you mentioning any females in your pack," Camille said when I slid in the back seat with her.

"I'm new to the pack," Anik said then laughed. *"She is still jealous over you, I see. Aww, that's cute,"* Anik said telepathically.

"Your mate is starting to rub off on you," I responded then laughed.

****

An hour later, we were back home. "I can walk, Elle," Camille said. I put her down in the foyer then she stood up slightly hunched over. I grabbed her hand in case her legs gave up on her.

"Anik! Where yo' ass been? You didn't sneak out to go to that club, did you? I knew I shouldn't have taken you there," Dayo fussed as he came down the stairs. He froze when his eyes landed on Camille. "What in the hell are y'all doing with Harriet Tubman?" Dayo asked us.

"Bro, don't start no shit," I said to him.

"Start shit? Nigga, you took my mate out of our bed so y'all can steal people out of graves and shit?" Dayo fussed. I heard doors open. Seconds later, Goon came down the stairs on the opposite side from where we stood. "What is that noise?" he asked.

"This nigga and Anik stole someone, Great-grandmamma," Dayo fussed.

"This is Elle's soulmate," Anik said.

"Soulmate, my ass, more like guardian angel. I want whatever it is y'all smoking," Dayo said.

"Chill the fuck out, Dayo, I know her. Elle was sneaking around with her years ago," Goon said.

"You knew?" I asked him.

"I was hunting one day and saw you and her by the lake. I'm not going to say what y'all was doing, but you know what I saw," Goon said.

"He saw us making love, Elle," Camille said.

"She remembers? Damn, bro, you must have given her some good wolf loving," Dayo said then I growled at him.

"I'm going to take her in the room and let you all talk," Anik said. She picked Camille up then walked up the stairs with her; even the female wolves were strong.

Dayo and Goon stared at me. "I'm not going to lie, bro, that's some weird shit right there. I thought maybe she was just a fling but you found her after all of these years. I'm surprised she is still living," Goon said.

"Don't say nothing, Dayo! Not a damn word," I warned him because I heard his thoughts after Goon said he was surprised Camille was still living.

Izra came down the stairs. "Can someone tell me why Anik is carrying a dead woman? What type of shit is going on? Goon isn't practicing waking up the dead, is he?" Izra asked us.

Dayo pushed Izra. "Have some respect for Elle's mate," Dayo warned Izra. Izra laughed.

"This nigga actually said a joke that was funny."

"Bro, he's serious. She is human and she aged," Goon told Izra then Izra laughed even harder.

"Y'all smoked weed and didn't invite me? I could've pulled my dick out of Adika for twenty minutes."

"I'm ready to put this muthafucka's back in the wall," Goon said then Izra stopped laughing.

"Wait a minute, bro, seriously?" Izra asked.

"Yes, damn, does your brain ever work?" I asked him then walked into the kitchen to get a drink, as they followed behind me. Amadi came from the basement yawning.

"What's with all the noise?" Amadi asked.

"Long story," I said. I pulled out my cognac then passed it around so they could pour it into their glasses.

"Y'all woke me up so I'm down to listen," Amadi said. I told my pack brothers everything from the very first time

I met Camille, up until when Anik and I went back to get her from her home.

“I need another drink,” Izra said reaching for the cognac.

Kanya came down the stairs. “Goon, honey, I’ve been waiting for you to come back to bed,” she said then nibbled on his ear. He grabbed her bottom through her silk robe, squeezing it firmly.

“I will be there, beautiful. Run the bath water and I will meet you in there,” he said to her. She kissed his lips then said goodnight to us before she went back upstairs.

Goon looked at us angrily. “How dare y’all stare at my mate’s ass like that,” he said then we laughed.

“Excuse me, bro, but you just gripped that muthafucka and it spilled out from the side,” Izra said. Goon chuckled.

“And I’m about to go and make her howl and splash all the water out of the tub,” Goon said as he stood up.

“We can’t talk about pussy around Elle and Amadi. Neither one of them niggas are getting it,” Dayo said.

“I may not have the pleasure of entering her yet, but I have tasted the juicy, ripe fruit,” Amadi said. Izra gave Amadi dap.

“My fucking brother,” Izra said.

“Elle’s pussy expired,” Dayo blurted out. Izra held his laugh in but it ended up slipping out. Amadi tried to keep a straight face but he couldn’t.

“Fuck all of you,” I said which caused them all to laugh even harder.

“Take a joke, bro, damn. We talk about each other’s mates all the time. Jalesa disappears like a crackhead because one minute you see her and the next she done teleported,” Izra said. Dayo laughed until he had tears in his eyes.

“What do you think she stole, Izra?” Dayo asked.

“Amadi’s manhood because I’m not eating pussy without filling her up with my inches,” Izra said then the both of them fell out laughing.

“This is what happens when a beast is born without a brain,” Amadi said.

“Real talk, though, Elle. Why do you hate that we speak like humans but you are in love with one?” Izra said.

“Nigga, did you see that lil’ old woman? She doesn’t understand the human language now, either,” Dayo said.

“I’m going to bed before I shift and bite the both of those jackasses,” Amadi said then left the kitchen. Dayo and Izra both went back upstairs for bed.

Kofi came into the kitchen with his robe on. “What’s going on? Nothing has changed, I see. You all still like to keep a beast from sleeping at night. I heard Dayo and Izra from all the way upstairs and down the hall. Do those two ever sleep?” Kofi asked.

"I suppose not. How does it feel to be back home?" I asked him.

"It feels different with the females in the house, especially that little one, Arya. I find her beast to be quite interesting. She is very observant. I miss my mate but I'm glad to be back," he said then patted my back.

"What do you think is going to happen with you and Ammon? You went against your pack," I said to him.

"I honestly don't know what is to come with Ammon and his warriors. But I do know that I am to protect you all and I will do that even if it means going against Anubi. I've been with all of you for over a hundred years. I taught you pups how to do almost everything you know. You all became my pups and nothing will ever change," he said.

"Ammon is still on Earth, isn't he?" I asked him.

"According to Naobi he is, but Musaf has a shield over Ammon. We can connect to his thoughts but Naobi cannot see a vision of where he is hiding. We have to wait until the spell Musaf has on Ammon wears off. Unlike Naobi's, Musaf's spells are temporary because he is a very, very ancient witch. He is not strong like he was many years ago," Kofi said. After I told Kofi about Camille he looked at me with a surprised look on his face. "Humans can't cheat death and just know whatever happens is out of your hands," he said to me.

After I talked to Kofi and finished my drink, I headed toward my room. Anik and Jalesa both were sitting down with Camille. They excused themselves then exited the room when they saw me. I checked on Camille and she was asleep.

****

When I woke up the next morning, I checked on Camille. Anik was in my room giving her breakfast and a cup of my herbal tea. I slept in the guest room to give Camille her space. I checked on her all night to make sure she was breathing.

Kanya walked in with new night clothes. "I ran out to the store to get Camille some things. I'm sorry I would've met her last night but I kinda got tied up," Kanya said.

"You have a nice family, Elle," Camille said weakly. After Kanya and Anik left out of the room, it was just Camille and I.

"I need a bath," Camille said.

"I can get one of the females to help you," I said to her.

"I'm still the same woman, Elle. It might look different but you've seen me naked before. You treat me like I'm your great-grandmother," she said as she sat up. She slowly got out of the bed then I carried her to the bathroom. I sat her on the toilet seat then ran her bath water. I dropped a little oil inside the tub along with bath salts. When Camille took her clothes off she was nothing but old skin and bones. I could see her ribs and her breasts were like dried raisins but I still loved her. I helped her into the tub. She leaned her head back. "This feels good. Arthritis is a pain in the ass," Camille said.

"You don't have to be this way," I said to her as I watched her from the doorway.

"Maybe one the witches can help her, I thought to myself.

"What are you going to do? Bite me and turn me?" Camille asked me.

"I wish it was that simple but we cannot turn humans into wolves," I said.

"I know," she responded. "I don't mind death, but if there is a way for me to escape it to be with you again, I will. Help me wash my back then afterwards I want you to take me outside into the woods by the lake. I want to see the beast I have been dreaming about since the day I met you," she said.

****

My beast crept up on a deer then tackled it. My jaws clamped down on the deer's throat. I cut off its air supply to suffocate it. Once the deer stopped breathing, I tore into it. My beast savagely ripped the deer apart.

"Oh, my heavens," Camille said then coughed. She sat on a blanket with her back against the tree. She wanted a flower behind her ear. It took me back to our dates by the lake. She used to watch me kill and rip my meal apart without an ounce of fear. I knew then that she accepted my beast, which wasn't likely for most humans.

“You were hungry,” she said then laughed. I licked the blood from around my snout. Camille held her hand out so that she could rub my mane. My beast lay against her body as she patted me. “This is an amazing gift you and your pack have. It’s beautiful, almost like a fairytale,” she said. Then she stared at the lake. It was a beautiful morning; the sun shined down on us and the birds chirped.

“When I die just take me back to my home. There is a number by my bed I want you to call. It’s a must that you dial that number. Tell them that I am dead and then the rest will be taken care of. The funeral home will come and get my body,” she said. We sat until the sunset and the crescent moon peaked over the cloud. I shifted back to my human form then grabbed my clothes. I got dressed behind the tree because even though Camille had seen me naked before it was no longer the same.

“Are you ready to go back?” I asked her. Her eyes were closed and the night breeze blew her thinned, gray hair back.

“Camille!” I called out to her then jogged toward her. When I kneeled down in front of her I stared at her chest. I put my hand to her throat and there was no pulse; Camille was dead.

“It’s okay, Elle,” a voice said from behind me. When I turned around it was Kofi.

“How did you find me?” I asked him.

“I heard your thoughts, so I came,” he said as he looked down at her.

“She is gone,” I said to him.

“I know,” he said. I picked up Camille then grabbed the blanket she sat on. I wrapped the blanket around her body then Kofi patted me on the back. “Now you can live freely. She is in peace and so are you. You’ve spent many years watching her, knowing that the two of you had no life with each other. Just because you love someone doesn’t mean that it’s meant to be,” he said as we walked through the woods. Kofi walked with me all the way to Camille’s house, which was over an hour away on foot.

When I got to her house I lay her down in her bed. There was a number by her telephone and I dialed it.

“Hello,” the sultry voice answered.

“Hello, my name is Elle. I’m a friend of Camille’s and—”

“She died?” the voice asked sadly.

“Yes,” I answered.

“I will be right there. Give me twenty minutes,” she said then hung up.

“She has a big family,” Kofi said as he looked at the pictures on the wall.

“I know and she was all alone,” I said. Kofi leaned against the doorway of her bedroom.

“She didn’t die alone, Elle. She died with the person she was in love with. You came into her life for a reason and that reason was for her to not die alone. We all have a purpose in someone's life. You were her protector and that's why you always felt the need to watch over her," he said. I kissed Camille on the cheek then walked out of her bedroom into her living room. I sat down on the couch and thought about everything. Kofi was right. I felt more of a need to protect Camille than anything else. Kofi started to growl then his eyes changed. I stood up.

"I smell an animal," I said to Kofi.

The door flew open and there stood an ebony woman with glowing yellow-brownish eyes. Her face was ready to grow into a snout and her sharp teeth hung over her bottom lip. She growled as her body crouched and snapped as she was ready to shift.

"What are you doing here? What do you want with a human?" she asked me.

"What are you doing here?" I asked her as my neck snapped. My beast was fighting to come out, but I couldn't risk the woman I called, seeing my beast fighting in Camille's house when she arrived.

"I'm a friend of Camille's, and if you don't answer me, I will bite your damn dick off," she said then my beast calmed.

"I talked to you over the phone," I said to her then Kofi stopped growling.

"Are you Elle?" she asked me.

“Yeah, how do you know Camille?” I asked her. I have watched Camille over the years and have never seen her with an immortal.

“It’s a long story,” she said then walked past Elle and I. We followed her to Camille’s bedroom. The stranger sat on Camille’s bed and stared at her lifeless body. A tear fell down her face. “She was such a strong woman,” she said then kissed Camille’s cheek.

“What business does an immortal have with a human woman?” Kofi asked the stranger.

“The same business you two have with her. I don’t have to tell either one of you shit. I thank the both of you for being with her but now you two can leave. I have everything in control from here on out,” she said.

“Just who in the fuck are you talking to like that?” I asked her.

She stood up. “Is your beast challenging me? If so, we can take it there. I don’t mind fighting two male beasts. Matter of fact, I find it quite entertaining,” she said.

“Let’s just leave, Elle. We don’t take challenges from female wolves. Our breed will snap her in half,” Kofi said then walked out of the room. I took one more look at Camille then followed Kofi. The stranger growled until Kofi and I were out of the house.

“She was a straight-up bitch,” I said then Kofi looked at me.

“Such language coming from you,” he said.

"She is a female dog, and calling her a bitch is a compliment compared to the other words I have for her," I said to him. Kofi chuckled.

"I think the younger pups are rubbing off on you," he said referring to Dayo, Goon and Izra. Kofi and I shifted to our beast then headed toward the house. Our beast was fast; the hour and a half walk turned into fifteen minutes as we ran our way home.

Amadi

"Stop, Amadi," Jalesa giggled as we showered. I gently bit her neck again. I pressed my body against her; she was trapped between me and the shower wall. I kissed her lips then she kissed me back. "Why won't you take me?" Jalesa asked. Her arousal permeated the air; it almost caused my beast to come out, but I wasn't ready.

"It's just not the time right now," I said to her.

"I'm giving myself to you, Amadi. What are we waiting for?" Jalesa asked me.

"I'm not trying to hurt you; I cannot control my beast during intimacy. I told you I have killed someone before," I said to her.

"She was human and I'm not human. As soon as you bite me it will close up. I will not bleed to death," Jalesa said then she hurriedly washed up. She opened the shower door then stepped out. I rinsed off then stepped out behind her.

"Did I do something wrong?" I asked.

"When are you going to let that woman go, Amadi? I'm living in her shadow. You are afraid to enter me when I have an arousal. I have an ache between my legs that is driving me crazy. I'm ready to give you my body now and you won't take me," Jalesa fussed.

"You know, for you not being with a man in this life, you act like you have been with a few," I said. A force came like the wind, knocking me into me the bathroom shower door.

Jalesa was standing in my bedroom looking at me with anger-filled eyes then she disappeared. When she reappeared she was standing over me. "Be careful of your tongue when I'm careful with mine when I speak to you. Don't you dare refer to me as a jezebel," she spat. I heard the door to the basement open. Jalesa threw a towel at me, so I could cover up then she disappeared again.

"Everyone in the kitchen wanted to know if y'all were okay," Izra said standing in the doorway. I slowly got up, winced as I stepped on the small pieces of glass.

"Are you okay, bro?" Izra asked me.

"I'm fine, and do you ever fucking knock?" I spat at him.

"You cursing at me?" Izra asked surprised.

"My bad, I'm cool," I said then patted his back.

"Why were your eyes about to turn then? You almost shifted, bro," Izra said.

"Jalesa used a force that knocked me into the shower," I told Izra.

"I just knew her weird ass was kinky. I'm going to tell Adika to try that tonight," he said. I let out a deep breath because talking to Izra at times could be complicated.

"She was mad at me for not entering her," I told him.

"What is wrong with you and Elle, bro? He is sad about a woman who looked like one of our mummified ancestors. Now, you are getting your ass kicked because you won't fuck your woman? You know I thought something was wrong with Dayo but you two muthafuckas are questionable," Izra fussed.

"I killed someone. Why don't y'all retarded assholes understand that?" I spat. I was on the verge of losing my mind. I tried to keep my anger in but I fought with it every day. I stayed in my room on the other side of the house, making oils to meditate me.

"You bit a human, bro, big deal. I killed a few of them and I can't even remember when and who it was," Izra stated. The pack knew I killed a human but they didn't know the details behind the story. The human I killed was someone that was very dear to me.

"I couldn't control it; she was screaming at me to stop but my beast wouldn't allow me to shift back. I turned while inside her then her screams pierced my ears and I still couldn't control myself. I think I was possessed or something. I don't know but I wasn't myself. Do you know what humans call that now? They call it rape, and every time I close my eyes, I hear her voice crying and screaming for help. I bit her neck, purposely killing her, so she wouldn't tell anyone what I did to her. I did it to protect the pack identity. I haven't had the urge to enter another female since," I told him.

Izra hugged me tightly. "I love you, and if I never told you before, I'm telling you now," he said as he squeezed me.

“Put me down,” I said as I felt my back cracking. Izra put me down then patted my shoulder.

“You needed that but don’t tell nobody,” he said then I cracked a smile. I put him in a headlock when Goon walked down the stairs.

“Is everything okay down here?” he asked then my towel dropped.

“Ughhhhhhh, nigga! Let me up muthafucka your dick is ready to swing in my eye,” Izra shouted. Dayo came down the stairs behind Goon. Dayo looked at me as I stood naked with Izra in a headlock.

“Hey, bro, is it okay if I move in a separate house from the pack? I mean, it must’ve been a bad moon last night. Elle’s mate checked out and now these niggas are about to make love,” Dayo said to Goon. I let Izra go then he fixed his shirt. “Yo, don’t ever do nothing like that to me again,” he said.

“Izra probably was talking shit,” Goon said. I picked my towel up then wrapped it back around me.

“Always,” I said to Goon then patted Izra’s shoulder. Izra was the pest little brother that made you want to bite his throat. I was second to the oldest. Goon and Dayo was around the same age.

After I got dressed I headed upstairs and the house was quiet since the ladies were at work and Arya was in school. I headed to my oil room then locked the door.

“You are late,” the voice said.

"You are not real," I said to her then she laughed.

"It's guilt, Amadi. As long as you hold onto me you will always hear me," she said then she appeared. Her face was pale, her eyes lifeless. The hole in her neck had maggots crawling from it. I closed my eyes.

"You are not real," I said to her again. She wasn't there but I couldn't live down what I did to her because she haunted me. It was all my imagination but I couldn't control it. A part of it was because I couldn't let her go so easily; I loved her at one point.

"You want to fuck her, don't you? Are you going to rape her, too?" she asked me.

"STOP! I was young and it was my first time," I explained.

"You left me all alone, Amadi. You never came back for me. I loved you," she said. Tears dripped from her eyes then turned into blood.

"I'm sorry," I said.

"I am, too," a voice said from behind me. When I turned around Jalesa stood in front of me. I didn't hear when she came into the room but that wasn't a surprise because she never used doors.

I pulled her into me then squeezed her tightly, which caused her to giggle. "If I didn't know any better you missed my presence," she said then I kissed her lips. Jalesa threw her arms around me. She pulled me close to her bosom. I immediately caught an erection.

I walked out of the room with Jalesa by my side. I heard Goon talking to someone that sounded like his mother. We walked into the living room and there stood Naobi. Jalesa and I bowed our heads to her. "There is no need for that. Come over here and give me a hug," she said with her arms stretched out. Jalesa and I both hugged her.

"Is it private?" Goon asked his mother. I took Jalesa's hand.

"We can walk out of the room," I said.

"No, I came here to talk to the pack. I would've come sooner, but I had a few things to take care of. You all really need to know what is going on. Ammon wants Jalesa in exchange for power. I was the power behind his strength. Since I'm no longer in Anubi, he needs another source. He made a deal with Musaf in exchange for a witch that can give birth. Musaf wants a full witch child because a full witch child could be more powerful than I. Even at an early age the child would be more powerful than I am, and that's without practicing spells," Naobi said.

"He is going to take me back to Anubi to mate with Musaf?" Jalesa asked in disbelief.

"Yes, so that he can become stronger. But what Ammon doesn't know is some of Musaf's spells don't stick. He is a very, very old warlock. But what I do know is that his shield over Ammon is going to weaken. That spell takes a lot to hold and Musaf is too old for a spell that strong," Naobi said.

"We have to kill my father because Ammon is not taking anyone from this pack. Jalesa is Amadi's mate and

Amadi is my brother. I will fight Ammon myself," Goon spat angrily.

"He is your father," Naobi said to Goon.

"Ammon is nobody to me but a god. Kofi taught me everything I know. When I saw visions of my past life it was Kofi who was in all of them. Ammon is no father of mine. After I kill Dash, Ammon will be next," Goon said.

"This isn't good because Anubi isn't like this. We don't fight each other. We fought our own warriors nights ago because of greed. All of this mess is because of Ammon wanting power. He is putting his own people at risk," Jalesa said.

"The only way to defeat Ammon is if he gets what he wants, and that is me," Naobi said sadly then sat down. "I don't want to see my son fighting against his own people. Ammon may be a lot of things, but he is still your father," Naobi said to Goon.

"This is too much," Jalesa said.

"If Ammon dies then Akua will have to leave Earth and rule in Anubi. But he will have to leave his mate and pups behind because it isn't time for them to go. You only get accepted when it's your time. Kanya and the pups have years and years before they can go," Naobi said.

"That's his advantage because he knows Goon cannot leave his pups and mate behind. Even in death, Ammon will still have won the battle," I said.

"That muthafucka!" Goon shouted angrily, his eyes turning blue.

"I may have to go back to Anubi. I'd rather sacrifice my happiness for my son's," Naobi said. You could see in Naobi's eyes that even with a lot of power, you still couldn't defeat them all; she was giving up.

"Fuck that! We will figure this out. There is no way in hell I'm going to some fucking Anubi. This is my home, my mate, my pups and my pack is on this planet. I will burn Anubi down, and rip everyone's throats out before I rule without my pack. An Alpha never leaves his pack unless he is dead," Goon spoke in a roar. He was past angry and I could tell he wanted to shift because Goon always had a temper problem. The slightest thing pissed him off, especially if you woke him up. When we were younger we had to tiptoe past his door. I chuckled when I remembered the day we had to all jump on him because he was slinging Izra around like a rag doll. Izra blew a dog whistle in Goon's ear while he was asleep. He attacked Izra and there was blood everywhere, and still, Izra haven't learned to let him sleep.

"Ammon isn't your soulmate. If you go back with him then you won't be happy. There has to be a way to get Ammon to step off," Jalesa said.

"I will figure it out and I want you all to stay out of it. This is my battle, so from here on out let me deal with Ammon while he is on Earth," Naobi said.

Goon shifted right before our eyes then stormed out of the living room. You could hear him growling then the sound of the door crashing down echoed through the house.

"I will fix it. I noticed my son doesn't like to use doors and would rather break through them," Naobi said then laughed. She suddenly got quiet for a few seconds. “Did someone die around here?” Naobi asked then Jalesa told Naobi about Elle and Camille.

“Old witches can feel when death is present. I felt when my mother was dying and when I visited her home afterwards, I still felt it. The ones you love return to you so that you could go in peace,” Naobi said.

“Can you reincarnate her?” Jalesa asked.

“She wanted to die. Elle would’ve been hurt if she turned immortal and didn’t want that life. I will talk to Elle; I have a vision of where he is,” Naobi said then disappeared.

“Do witches ever walk out of a room?” I asked Jalesa.

“It’s so much easier to just disappear,” she said.

“I have a feeling that Goon is going to defeat his father to keep his mother from Anubi. There’s about to be more chaos because even though Naobi wants us to stay out of it, Goon isn’t going to listen. If Goon battles his father and the rest of his father’s pack, we will have to battle right along with him,” I said.

Later on that night…

“Look at you sleeping peacefully like you didn’t kill anyone. You are a murderer,” her voice said to me. Jalesa was snuggled underneath me as I watched her sleep peacefully. When Jalesa turned around, her neck had a chunk missing from it. I fell out of the bed.

“What troubles you, Amadi?” Jalesa got out of the bed as blood dripped from her neck. I backed away from her.

“It’s not real, it’s not real,” I growled.

“Snap out of it! You are having a dream!” Jalesa shouted. Her neck was back to normal.

“I can’t do this,” I said. I put on a pair of sweatpants and tennis shoes. I stormed out of my bedroom. I was headed for the woods. When I got there, I shifted then headed towards the lake. Jalesa appeared in the middle of the lake; she looked like she was standing on water but she was floating above it.

“I know you see her, Amadi. You only see her because you can’t move on. It wasn’t your fault because you were a young beast,” Jalesa said.

“I’m not good for you,” I said inside her head.

“I love you, Amadi, and you loving me back will be good enough for me. You can’t kill me the way you killed her. I’m going to give myself to you tonight,” Jalesa said then dropped her cape. She was naked underneath, her nipples erect. I shifted back from my beast. Jalesa floated over to me then landed on her feet. She pulled my naked body into hers then her hands touched my chest. She looked me in my eyes. “I’m nervous, too, but you need this. I’m giving myself to you so you can let it go. You need to prove to yourself that you can make love to someone,” she said to me. She pulled me down onto the ground then a tent surrounded us as silk, gold sheets appeared underneath us.

Something appeared over my eyes. “I can’t see,” I told her.

"All you need is to feel me. I don't want you to look at me and see her," Jalesa said. My hands groped her breasts. I leaned down then took one into my mouth. My fangs expanded when I slowly sank my teeth into her breast.

"OOOOHHHHH," she moaned. I massaged the other breast as semen dripped from my dick. I wanted to enter her badly, which caused me to howl. I felt myself shifting as my nails grew out. "I'm not afraid of your beast," she said. I lay flat on top of her then kissed her neck. Her wetness seeped from between her slit. I kissed her from her neck to her feet. I flipped her over onto her stomach then massaged her butt. My nails dug into her skin but she seemed to like it. Jalesa's moans grew louder then I kissed her shoulder then bit her again. Her arousal filled my nostrils and a painful like growl slipped from my throat. I could feel the sheet tugging from underneath us as she pulled it while I massaged her body. My tongue traveled down her spine back to her ass again. I bit her buttock then her body trembled. I spread her cheeks, welcoming her sweet scent. I nuzzled my nose into her pussy from the back then I stuck my tongue inside her.

"Amadi, it feels so good," she whined. I lapped up her wetness that reminded me of drinking from the lake. My tongue dipped in and out of her sweet hole then I curved my tongue to keep her wetness from spilling over. I wanted to enjoy the taste of her. I wanted to be full off of her. I wanted to make love to her body until her body trembled as if she were in fear. She started speaking in our original tongue from ages ago as her body released.

I turned her back over. "Relax, Amadi," she said then pulled me on top of her. I slowly entered her, stretching her open as her walls began to grip me. Her pussy reminded me of a snake during feeding because her muscles tightly squeezed me as it pulled me in. My hair pierced through my skin like needles and my ears grew out as it pulled the skin back on my face. I felt my snout growing out as I howled. Jalesa's body tensed. "It's a good pain, Amadi," she said as I continued to fill her up with all of me.

"It's so much," she said digging her nails into my arms. I tried to pull out of her but she pulled me forward. I slipped on the silk sheet and all of my dick went sailing into her. Jalesa screamed as I felt her hymen tear. *"I can't do this,"* I said to her.

"It's okay because you already took my innocence," she said. I lay fully planted inside her for a few seconds before I started moving. Her body relaxed as I moved in and out of her. I sank my teeth into her nipple, which caused her to squeal.

"Ammadddiii," she moaned. I pushed further into her then she trembled underneath me. I kissed then sucked on her neck as she wrapped her legs around me. I sped up my thrust that made her body buck upwards. Her nails dug into my back as I sucked harder on her neck. My teeth pierced through the sensitive spot on her neck. She screamed from my pleasure as her body convulsed. I went deeper inside of her as I bit harder, marking her.

"UUGGHHHHH," she moaned when I lifted myself up. I pounded into her spot over and over again until blood rushed through the veins in my dick. I was harder when I swelled up, filling her pussy completely up with my girth. Jalesa cried out and moaned as I slammed into her again; my size had stretched her completely open. Her body went limp then I howled as I pumped my semen into her. I swelled up more than before. As my dick continuously jerked and pumped seeds into her, it caused me to howl louder. My nails dug into her skin and into the silk sheets. I ripped the sheets into shreds because I couldn't pull out. The jerking wouldn't stop, which caused the pleasure to be unbearable. Jalesa moaned and her screams grew louder as her body rose off the ground. I lay inside her until I slowly went limp. I pulled out of her once the swelling went down then snatched the material off that covered my eyes. She lay sprawled out with long, bloody scratches that ran down her arm. She had a bite mark on both of her breast. I shook her but she didn't budge.

"Jalesa, wake up!" I shouted, but she didn't move. I started to panic. "No, this shit can't happen again. Jalesa, wake up!" I shouted again. I wrapped her up in what was left of the sheet then took off toward the house.

Moments later, I burst through the door, knocking it down on the floor. Anik covered Arya's eyes because I was fully naked. "Ewww, why does uncle Amadi have a snake?" Arya asked.

"Some snakes are harmless," Anik said then pulled Arya down the hall.

"What in the hell is going on?" Goon asked coming out of the weight room. It dawned on me in that moment that it was morning; Goon worked out every morning.

"I killed her," I said. I lay Jalesa down on the couch. Goon's face was expressionless, almost like he didn't care. "Did you hear what I said? I killed her!" I said to him.

"Bro, seriously? Jalesa is asleep. You fucked her, didn't you? Did you mark her? Did you swell inside her? If so, then let her rest. Kanya goes out like that all the time. I usually just run her bath water when she wakes up. A couple of drops of your oil then she is back to new," Goon said. Izra came out of the kitchen with a glass of orange juice. He smiled at me.

"You are a man now. Nigga, that right there is what you call the power of the beast," Izra said then peeked around me. "Her breasts are swollen; you definitely marked her," he said then walked upstairs.

Goon looked at me. "Was that your first time getting some pussy?" he asked curiously.

"You know it's not," I said to him then he smiled.

"Old man, Amadi. I knew you wasn't a virgin, but at times, you damn sure acted like one," he teased then I waved him off.

Kanya came around the corner. "Goon, what do I keep telling you about leaving the darn toilet seat up?" she asked. Goon hurriedly covered her eyes because I was naked. "I forgot beautiful but Amadi and I are having brother talk," he said.

"Why is Jalesa on the couch like that? Is she okay?" Kanya asked.

"Yeah, she is having one of your episodes," Goon stated then Kanya blushed.

"Ohhhhh, well, I'm going to go feed the twins," she said then laughed.

Once she was out of earshot Goon looked at me with a serious expression. “You have to get her pregnant, bro,” Goon said.

“Now?” I asked.

“Soon because Musaf, or whatever his name is, isn’t going to want her if she is pregnant. That would leave Ammon without a source because their deal would be off,” he said.

“She might not want a pup,” I replied.

“Once you mark your mate their body starts to crave it. She is going to want a pup. I don’t want my mother to go to Anubi and I’m not trying to kill my father because of it. But if killing him is my last resort then dead he will be,” Goon said with a flash of blue flickering in his eyes.

“What if we kill Musaf? Without the source, all falls down,” I said then he nodded his head.

“That’s not a bad idea, but we can’t just go to Anubi. Hopefully Musaf comes here,” he said then walked off.

I carried Jalesa to the bedroom. I washed her body then oiled her down. I pulled the cover over her after I lay her down in bed. “I’m not going anywhere,” she appeared in front of me with maggots eating on her. I was still allowing her to haunt me.

“When will you go away?” I asked her.

“You are the only one who has the answer to that question. I will go away when you stop thinking about me, but you can’t. I will always be around,” she said.

“I’m moving on,” I said to her.

“No, you are not. You are settling for what you think is real. This is not real, Amadi, and soon your eyes will see. I must go. I don’t want to wake up your sleeping beauty,” she said then disappeared.

Izra

"OOOOOOHHHHHH, FUCK! YES, BABY, RIGHT THERE!" I almost shouted as Adika had my dick down her throat. I gripped her hair, slowly thrusting upwards.

"Excuse me, but I have to ask you two to leave," the guy said to us. I was in the movie theatre while Adika was sucking me off.

"Wait a minute, muthafucka, don't you see my dick swelling up?" I asked him as Adika slurped on the tip of my head.

"Ohhh, shit, baby, right there. Hold it right there and jerk that shit off," I moaned.

"I'm getting my manager," he said. I tossed my bucket of popcorn at him.

"I wish you would hurry up and do it, so you can leave me the fuck alone," I spat at him. Adika and I were the only two in the movie theatre. The guy opened his mouth to respond but I growled at him with my eyes turning, my teeth sharpening. He hurriedly walked away. "Michael Jackson's *Thriller* muthafucka," I shouted behind him then laughed.

Adika sat up then wiped off her mouth. "Damn it, Izra. Do you not know how to act?" she asked me.

"Yeah, like an animal. What do you want me to do?" I asked Adika.

"Ugghhhhh," Adika said then we disappeared out of our seats. Moments later, we reappeared back in my car.

"Can you warn me next time?" I asked. She rolled her eyes.

"We need to talk," she said as she turned down my rap music.

"About what?" I asked her.

"A baby," she replied.

"Adika, for the last time. I do not want a baby. You think I want a human child? You and I will still look twenty and that baby will be old and wrinkled like Elle's mate, Camille. You want me to sit at the dinner table during family time, checking our child's pulse every minute, making sure he or she didn't check out?" I asked her.

Adika started purring. Every time she got upset she turned into her Mua. Her eyes were yellow with black slits in the middle and her ears pointed upward before her whiskers grew out. I pinched her cheek. "Hello Kitty," I called her then she scratched my neck.

"ARRGGHHHHHHH!" I shouted because her scratches burned my skin. I growled at her then yanked one of her whiskers off her face. Her face turned back to normal. She held her cheek.

"Oh, you want to go there?" she asked me.

"What are you ready to do?" I asked. I placed my hand over my dick because Adika didn't play fair. Adika's eyes watered then I started to feel guilty.

"I'm tired of pretending I'm happy. Kanya has pups then Anik is about to have pups and Jalesa is able to carry a pup. Everyone around us will have pups and I will have nothing," she said.

"You got me. Why can't that be enough? I don't want a human child. I will not have an attachment to it," I said to Adika.

"But China has so many children up for adoption," Adika said.

"China? You want a Chinese baby in a house full of a bunch of Black werewolves? You want Sushi to grow up then kill us? Chop our asses up then toss us into some noodles and vegetables? Do you know what Chinese people eat? They eat animals, and I'm not talking about chickens and pigs. I'm talking about cats, rats, and dogs," I said to Adika.

"It will adapt. Stop being silly because I'm serious," Adika said.

"Listen to us, baby. We are talking about it like it's a pet. We are different and we live in a world that they don't know exist. Humans are greedy and they know nothing about what we believe in. What if this human child grows up and sells us out for money? What if you and I get locked up in a cage in some high-tech lab, so they can cut us open? We are beasts to them, Adika. Humans fear what they don't understand," I said to her.

"Okay, what if you get another wolf pregnant and we raise the pup together? You will have a bond with it," Adika said.

"You want me to mate with another wolf?" I asked not believing her.

"It's our only way. Plus, the child can be immortal," she said.

"I'd rather you take my dick then me fuck another wolf. I love you, Adika. I can't see myself entering another wolf and giving her my pup. We mate for life and you know that," I said to her.

"You and I aren't mated, Izra! That's the whole fucking point! I'm marked but that doesn't mean shit if I can't have your pup. It's like being engaged and never having the chance of being married," Adika fussed.

"To make you happy I have to fuck another wolf?" I asked her feeling defeated. Adika thought that I didn't love her; she thought I only wanted pleasure. I loved Adika even though it didn't show at times.

"Don't say it like that because I don't want you to enjoy it. I don't want you to go down on her or bite her. I just want you to mate with her," Adika said.

"Only way I can mate with a wolf without biting her is if she is already in heat. If she is not in heat, I will have to mark her, so that her body can get ready for a pup. I can't believe I'm talking to you about this," I said pulling off, heading toward the house.

"I found a person that has connections to that, so all we have to do is give up half the money then the rest later," Adika said.

"What if her maternal instincts kick in? Once she breastfeeds the pup she becomes bonded with it. Where would that leave you and I? The mother would have to join our pack because it's tradition," I said to Adika.

"You let me put my magic to work with that," she said then kissed my face. I wasn't too thrilled about Adika's plan because it made me question our bond. I was starting to wonder if Adika loved me the same way I loved her. Since our pup died, she had been distant. When we got home Adika headed to our bedroom, while I headed to the cognac cabinet. I grabbed the bottle of Henny then drank it down.

"What's the matter with you?" Goon asked. He had blood all over his face. He used a towel to wipe it off.

"Bro, how many deer do you eat a day?" I asked Goon.

"Two because my appetite is growing. My beast is growing, too," he said.

Amadi came into the kitchen. "Elle has been distant since Camille died," he said. I took a swig of the cognac.

"Nigga, Camille was dead when Elle brought her here," I said not wanting to be bothered.

"Damn, bro, that was harsh," Amadi said.

"Life is harsh, Amadi, and you, out of all of us, should know that," I spat. Goon snatched the bottle out of my hand.

"Get some rest, Izra," he said to me.

"Is it possible to love someone you can't mate or have a spiritual bond with?" I asked him.

"Is Kofi in his room?" Goon asked us. I knew that they didn't know and couldn't answer me because neither one of them had ever experienced it. I wouldn't dare ask Elle because being in love with a human didn't exist to me. I walked out of the kitchen with my bottle of liquor. I wanted to be alone in the woods.

The cold, muddy dirt seeped through my paws as I walked through the woods. I stopped when I came across Adika's and my pup's gravesite. I lay over the site while my beast wept.

Two days later…

"What is this place?" I asked Adika as she rode on my back. We were at a cabin up in the mountains a few hours away from home. I was in beast form to get to our location faster.

"This is where they live," she said.

"Who is there?" someone called out from the back of the house. I growled. A man with long hair with a part in the middle stepped out of the shadows. He was dressed in regular clothing but he smelled like an animal.

"I'm Adika and I'm looking for Sosa," she said.

"I am Sosa, now what do you want?" he asked. I growled at him.

"Be careful with that tone, muthafucka," I said to him. He laughed.

"What do you want? This place is forbidden. Nobody comes here unless they are looking for something," he said to Adika.

"I want a female wolf," Adika said. I saw a girl peek around the corner of the house. Her hair was braided in two plaits with a part in the middle. Her skin was dark and her hair looked like silk. When she noticed me staring at her she hid herself.

"You want to breed?" he asked Adika. Our pack would never sell our females off to breed. I have noticed over time that every wolf pack didn't have the same traditions we did.

"Yes, how much?" Adika asked.

"You must be sure when you make a deal. I would hate for my females to get stuck with a pup. A wolf will not breed with a female if she has a pup already. That is bad for business," Sosa said.

"I'm aware of that, so how much is it?" Adika asked.

"Ten thousand dollars. I'd like five up front," he said. Adika reached into her sack then placed a small stash into his hand.

"Onya! Get your ass out here!" Sosa called out. The female that was peeking around the corner stepped out wearing nothing. She had black and red designs painted around her hips, wrists and ankles. She stood in front of us hiding her pussy. Her plaits covered some of her breasts and the rest spilled out on the sides.

"Onya is in heat. She went into heat a few days ago for the first time," he said to us.

"Where is her clothing?" Adika asked Sosa.

"Her purpose is to breed, so she doesn't need any," Sosa spat then I growled at him. I wanted to rip his throat out.

"This wolf has no manners, I see. He comes into my place and growls at me. He is disrespecting my territory and I want him out," Sosa spat. All of a sudden clothes and shoes appeared on Onya from Adika's magic.

"You have a witch, I see. Now you may leave and remember I will be back in a few months to collect my female and the rest of my money. As long as my female is within your territory we have a right to enter it, so don't try no funny business. I expect my female back here as soon as she has the pup. I'm only giving y'all two and a half months," he said then walked into his house.

"Are you hungry, Onya?" Adika asked. She shook her head no. Adika had lost all of her mind because we bought a female like she was property. Adika expected her to eat when I could sense how scared she was.

"Well, let's go," Adika said happily.

"We cannot take her to our home," I said to Adika.

"I know that and she will stay at my sanctuary," Adika responded.

Hours later we were at Adika's apartment building. I didn't know she still had it because she had been living in the mansion with the pack for months and had never spoken a word about it. Luckily no one was around to see a wolf walking in the building. After Adika unlocked the door I shifted back. Onya eyed me then turned her head. Adika tossed me my clothes out of her sack. "This is messed up. I cannot believe you just bought a piece of ass," I said to her.

"We agreed on it already," Adika stated.

"I don't give a fuck! Look at her. She is scared. She's never been with a male before. I would be the first to enter her when her first time should be with her mate," I fussed.

"We cannot give her back because, if we do, his pack will come and that would be too much. Goon has to deal with worrying about when Ammon is going to make his move and now this. We have to do it and get it over with," Adika said.

"How about you shift into a male wolf and you fuck her ass then," I spat.

Adika's eyes turned. "We had a deal," Adika said.

"You pressured me," I responded. Onya looked around the apartment as Adika and I fussed. Then she spoke up.

"I have to do this or Sosa will be upset," Onya said.

"I'll let you two get acquainted while I go get a drink," I said. Adika pulled me to the side.

"You have been drinking a lot lately," she said to me.

"Wouldn't you if I wanted you to fuck another wolf? This isn't going to bring our dead pup back. When will you understand that? Maybe it would be easier if this female wasn't like a sex-slave. Maybe it would easier if she agreed with it and wasn't forced by a pimp or whatever he is. This is not our tradition and you should know because you've been around wayyyy longer than I have," I said to Adika then walked out of her apartment.

****

The next day Adika and I sat at the table with the pack as we ate breakfast. Elle and Kofi were at what humans call a "Funeral" for Camille.

"I'm worried about Elle," Kanya said.

"He is all right. After Camille is buried he will be back to normal," Goon said.

Anik and Dayo were flirting with each other. Amadi was putting grapes inside Jalesa's mouth. I sat next to Adika growling at her. "Can you pass me the tray of steaks?" I asked.

"Get it yourself," she said.

"Simple-minded," I mumbled. I grabbed the raw pieces of steak and ate them. I started to choke then Arya patted my back.

"Are you okay, uncle Izra?" she asked me. A clump of something clogged my throat then I coughed it up. When I looked on my plate it was a big ball of cat hair.

"Meow," Adika teased.

"That was real fucking cute," I said then everyone else started snickering.

"I always knew he was pussy," Dayo said then laughed. I leaped over the table and attacked Dayo.

"Not again!" Amadi said out loud. Dayo punched me in the side then slammed me down on the table and it cracked in half. I shifted to my beast then bit his arm. Dayo burst out of his clothes then his wolf slammed me into the wall. I bit his neck then he howled; his howl made me bite him again harder than the first time.

"Stop it!" Anik cried as blood squirted from the side of Dayo's neck. Kanya picked Arya up then stormed out of the room before everyone else shifted. They tried to pull Dayo and I apart by sinking their teeth into our fur. Goon charged into the both of us, knocking us apart. Dayo flew into the wall; the wall cracked all the way up to the ceiling. When he got up his ears went back as he growled. Blood dripped from his neck and I tried to charge him again, but Goon's beast collided into mine. I felt my ribs crack as I landed on the marble floor.

"ENOUGH!" Goon's voice boomed inside my head. Adika ran to me but I snapped at her. She backed away

from me with worry in her eyes. I got up then limped into the hall where I shifted back. I collapsed as I tried to make it up the stairs but Amadi helped me up.

"That was not you back there," Amadi said. Amadi helped me to my bedroom. I lay on the bed. "Bro, this is going to hurt but I have to snap you back into place," he said. I grabbed my Henny bottle that sat next to my bed then guzzled the rest of the cognac down. I stuffed a pillow inside my mouth. *"Hurry up!"* I shouted inside Amadi's head.

Amadi felt my side where my rib was sticking out of place. If I was a human, I would've been dead. Werewolf bones are flexible most of the time because our body changes when we shift. Amadi used two of his fingers then pressed my rib bone back in. I howled as water filled my eyes. "There are two more sticking out," Amadi said, pressing them back in. Tears fell down my face. I knew how Dayo felt when we had to crack his spine back into place. Years ago Goon slammed Dayo on his back and he couldn't move afterward. Once Amadi was finished pushing my ribs back in, Goon came into my room. He gestured for Amadi to leave. Once Amadi was out of the room Goon growled at me.

"What was that, lil' brother?" he asked me.

"I don't know," I said. I pulled out another bottle of Henny.

"You got to talk about it, Izra," he said.

"There is nothing to talk about," I responded.

"It's your pup," Goon said then I took a swig.

“Have you ever seen a dead pup before? A pup that was connected to you? I wanted my pup, bro,” my voice cracked.

“I don’t know that feeling and I don’t know what to say, but I do know that we are a pack. If you ever feel like you’ve got nothing just remember you’ve got all of us. We all have temper issues and that will never change,” Goon said then patted my back. I winced in pain.

“Nigga, what the fuck is wrong with you?” I asked Goon. I didn’t think that Goon realized his strength at times.

“I keep forgetting you got bones like a baby pup,” he joked.

“I need me a fat-ass blunt and some strippers,” I said then Goon chuckled.

“You are back to normal already but is everything straight with you?” Goon asked.

“Yeah, bro, I’m good. Now let me finish this bottle,” I said. Goon got up then shut my door. I finished half of my bottle before I fell asleep.

****

“Wake up, Izra,” Adika said.

I blocked the sun out of my eyes. “What time is it?” I asked her.

"The next day, now get up and take a shower because you reek of alcohol," she replied. I got up and walked to the bathroom in my room. I brushed my teeth then relieved myself. Adika turned the shower on for me. I dropped my basketball shorts and stepped in. She stepped in with me. I let the hot water hit my face to wake me up. She massaged my back then reached down to grip my dick.

"I'm sorry, I don't want you to be mad at me. I just want us to do what we got to do and get it over with," she said.

"Whatever," I answered. She turned me around to face her. "Can't you just think of me when you enter her?" she asked as she massaged my testicles. Adika kissed my chest then my neck. I picked her up then held her above my head. I leaned her against the shower wall as she draped her legs over my shoulders. I nuzzled my nose into her sex, which caused her to purr. Her long, black tail wrapped around my dick like a snake. Adika did some very strange things to me during sex. Her love was an addiction; I couldn't picture myself entering another wolf.

I stuck my tongue inside Adika then she rotated her hips as she arched her back off the wall.

"Bite me! Oh, please, baby, bite me!" she shouted. I pulled her pussy lips into my mouth then slowly bit down. Her legs shook as she humped my tongue. I gripped her ass harder while my beast growled and sucked on her pink bud. Her nails dug into my neck. I reached up to grab at her full breasts. "Damn it, Izra," she purred. "Put it in," she said.

I slid her down the wall then she wrapped her legs around my waist. "And you complain on how much I like pussy. You want me to put in?" I asked teasing her. I bit her neck then she used her long, cat tail to force my dick into her.

"No cheating," I said. I pinned her arms above her head with one hand. I used my other hand to play in her sex. I clamped down on her grape-sized nipple, which caused her to moan. My middle finger slid in and out of her wet sex. Her pupils and her lips turned black. Black spots appeared on her body; her black, sharp fingernails curled over.

"You are so beautiful to me," I whispered in ear as I inserted another finger. I pulled my fingers out of her then she seductively licked my fingers. She purred from her taste then I kissed her. I turned the shower off then pulled her out. I picked her up, took her to the bed. I propped her up on all fours before her tail disappeared. I spread her cheeks then stuck my tongue into her.

"You are a nasty dog, shit! Ohhhh, Izra, don't stop," she purred as I licked her bottom. I growled as small drops of semen dripped from the tip of my dick. Adika's scent was driving my wolf insane. I hated cats, which was typical for our species, but Adika was different. Her cat was exotic, frisky and untamable.

"URRRRRRRRRRRRR," she purred, which caused me to stick my tongue further inside her anus. Adika's pussy throbbed from her orgasm.

I pulled my tongue out of her as I kept her cheeks spread, admiring her fleshy mound. I placed a sloppy, wet kiss on her cum-coated pussy lips. After I finished pleasing her with my tongue, I rubbed my dick between her slippery, wet slit. She arched her back like she didn't have any bones in her body. I slowly eased into her pussy. "RRRRRRREEEEEEOOOOWWWW," she screeched.

"Shut the fuck up before I burst early," I said. Adika's meows turned me on and caused my dick to throb.

"Fuck me," she purred. She wanted it long, hard and rough. I pulled my dick out then slammed it into her. A leash appeared around her neck.

"Bad lil' pussy," I stated. I gripped the leash wrapping it around my hand.

"My pussy is bad, baby, give it to me!" she shouted. I pounded into her as I gripped the leash and a fist full of her hair. I plunged into her, hitting her spot, which caused a wave to gush out of her pussy. Sounds of my testicles slapping against her inner thighs echoed through my room. Adika tried to climb the wall but I yanked her leash back.

"You want it then take all of it," I growled as I pumped into her. Sweat ran down her back as she clawed at my wall and mattress. I leaned forward then bit her as hard as I could and my nails dug into her hips, scratching her. The more my beast ravaged her body, the wetter she became. Her pussy gripped my dick, which caused my stomach to tighten up. I swelled up inside her, stretching her open. She screamed, purred and clawed as I poked her sensitive spot. I rocked back and forth inside her, causing her body to buck forward.

"It's so fucking big," she moaned, slamming down onto my length. I stopped moving as I watched her wet pussy coat my dick and squeeze it. I could see how tight her pussy was gripping my width. Thick, white cream coated my dick as she bounced her ass against my pelvis.

"GGRRRRRRRRRR," I growled. My veins thickened as a sensation traveled through it, exploding into the tip of my head. I howled as she continuously slammed down on me. I gripped her leash then pumped into her, shooting inside her like a machine gun.

I collapsed on top of her then she rolled me over. She climbed on top of me, digging her nails into my chest then her cat tail wrapped around my neck. She slid down onto my dick then rode me until Amadi knocked on the door telling us we were too loud.

****

"What's up, nigga?" Derrick asked when I stepped inside his barbershop. I walked to the back of the shop and he followed me. Derrick was a human I did jewelry business with. He copped something from me every month.

"You got them for me?" he asked. I sat the black velvet bag down on the desk. He opened it then pulled out the black diamond and yellow grillz I had made for him.

"I don't know where you get these diamonds from but this shit here is legit," he said. He went into his safe in his office then pulled out a few stacks. I counted the money. "Okay, hit me up," I said before I stuffed the eight grand in my pocket.

"Wait a minute, nigga, what are you doing tonight? Are you trying to roll with us to the strip club?" Derrick asked. He was cool but he wasn't that cool.

I will have a few of my niggas rob this muthafucka for my money back. I'm behind in paying child support and this lil' nigga hasn't cut me a deal since I been copping from him, Derrick thought. I chuckled.

"Naw, I don't mix business with my personal life. That's how muthafuckas get killed," I said then walked out of the shop. I dropped my business cards down at the front desk, where a light-skinned woman sat popping popped her gum with colorful hair.

"Hold on, girl, let me call you back," the woman said then hung up the phone.

"Excuse me, handsome, what's yo' name?" she asked me.

"Izra," I stated.

"How old are you with your fine ass?" she asked me.

"One-hundred and twenty years old," I stated then she laughed.

"You are funny," she said.

That bulge in his sweatpants is all I'm concerned about. I like them young, she thought.

"I want you to take my number so we can hook up," she said.

"I have baby mama drama and she is crazy, too. She will fuck your whole life up. That hair on your head will be gone by the time she finishes with you. So, I have to decline but in the meantime you might want to take care of that itch," I said to her. I was too familiar with the scent of a yeast infection.

"What itch?" she asked me.

"There is a CVS across the street," I went into my pocket and pulled out a twenty. I put the twenty in her hand. "Monistat will help that," I said then walked out of the shop. She called me every word she could think of.

I had to stop past Adika's apartment to take Onya some raw meat. I unlocked the door then walked in. I headed to the kitchen to put the meat in the fridge.

Onya came into the kitchen, dripping wet, wrapped up in a towel. She had a pretty face and even a nice scent, but I still had no attraction to her.

"Adika wanted me to bring you by some food," I said. I walked around her. She grabbed my arm.

"When will we mate? I want to get this over with," she said.

"I need an erection to enter you. I'm soft around you and your scent doesn't harden me," I said to her then she growled.

She wrapped the towel tightly around herself. "What I am supposed to do?" she asked.

"Run away," I told her.

"He is dangerous. He has a pack behind him that is rich and they live like humans with fancy jobs. They have connections all around and if I run away I will be killed," she said.

"Do you think you can have a pup and not bond with it? The pup will not be with you. It will be with me and my mate. What kind of wolf willingly neglects her pup?" I asked her.

"I need to do this for my freedom. Once he makes a certain amount off me then I will be free," she said.

"Have you seen a dick before?" I asked. She shook her head no. I pulled down my sweatpants then showed her. "You see this?" I said holding my dick in my hand.

"This is going to get hard then split your pussy in half. I'm going to swell inside you and may even get stuck. Now, if you really want to do this then let's go. I have to watch a porn or something first to get aroused," I said as I put my dick back in my pants. Onya didn't budge. "Call Adika if you need something else," I said then walked out of the apartment. When I got into the hallway I breathed a sigh of relief but when I looked down I had an erection.

"Oh, hell no!" I shouted then hurriedly ran to my car.

****

When I arrived home there was a full house. I wanted to talk to Kofi about my problems because he knew a lot. I hated to sound selfish but I was glad that he was back, although it was under different circumstances. I walked to his room but his door was cracked. Before I pushed it open I heard him and Adika talking.

"It's just so hard for Izra and I. All I want to do is give him a pup. You know what's it like to lose a pup. Remember when I lost our pup? You turned to Opal after that and she gave you so many of them. It makes me feel empty inside," Adika said to Kofi.

"That's not why I mated with Opal. I mated with Opal because she and I are made for each other. I know what Izra is going through because I felt the same way when our pup came out of your womb dead. He is a young wolf like I was back then, and soon he will learn to cope with it. It's all new to him, so don't put the pressure on him. Izra can be very unpredictable at times, so just be patient," Kofi told Adika.

"You think I should tell him about us? I know it was years and years ago, but I just feel awkward. Once upon of time you and I shared something special and you were the first male to enter me," she said. I stepped back. I didn't want to hear anything else. I felt betrayed because Kofi was like my father and to find out he was once with Adika did something to me mentally. Both of them kept that secret from me. I growled as images of him fucking her the same way I did filled my head. I went into the kitchen to grab a bottle of Henny.

"Is everything okay with you?" Kanya asked while holding her twin pups.

"Yeah, I'm good," I answered her.

"Are you sure? You have been going through liquor like it's water," she said with concern.

"It's either that or kill a muthafucka," I said then walked out of the kitchen. I headed straight to the woods so that my beast could roam freely. Life as a beast was stress free until I shifted back to my man form. When I was my beast I didn't think about mating or anything else. All I cared about when I was my beast was hunting. Liquor and my beast were the only two things in my life that gave me balance.

"Where are you? We are supposed to go on a date tonight. I just want to tell you that I'm ready," Adika's voice came inside my head.

"Fuck you," was all I could say then for the rest of the night I ignored her.

****

Two days later…

I snuck in the house after being in the woods for two days as my beast. I headed to my bedroom to shower then to get dressed. I made sure Adika left for work before I came back in the house. I was headed back down the stairs and Kofi was standing at the end of the staircase.

"Is everything okay? Everyone was trying to reach you but you didn't respond to us," Kofi said.

"Yeah, I'm straight," I answered bluntly then he stared at me.

"When did you start lying to the old man?" he asked me. I chuckled.

"Have you ever lost a pup before?" I asked him.

"Yes, and I understand how you feel but there's something else going on with you. Would you like to talk about it?" he asked.

"We just did, bro," I said to him then he growled at me. Kofi didn't like when we referred to him as bro because he took on a role as our father. He said that was disrespecting his position as our guardian. I walked away from him then out of the door. I hopped on my motorcycle then sped away from the house.

I stopped at the store to grab Onya a few things. She needed to go and I didn't care where she went. Adika had to figure something else out because I wasn't doing anything for her. If she wanted a pup she needed to steal one. I was damned if I did everything she asked for when she couldn't be honest with me. There was no telling what else she had hidden from me. I took trust very seriously because I gave it to those I cared about. I never lied to Adika and held nothing back from her, and I expected the same in return. Once I pulled up to the building, I grabbed the bag from the back of my bike then walked up the stairs. I used my key to unlock the door. When I walked inside the apartment, I heard laughing coming from the living room.

"What's so funny?" I asked Onya.

"This show is funny. I think it's called the *Maury* show. Humans are very different from us," she said sitting in Indian style wearing only a shirt. Her hard nipples poked against the material and the scent of her being in heat filled the apartment. I dropped the bag on the floor.

"I got you some clothes since Adika doesn't have much clothes here. Here is your ten grand, five for Sosa and the extra is for you. I don't care what you do with it but you are free to go," I said to her then a sad look appeared on her face.

"I can't leave until I do what I came here to do. Sosa will never accept money from my hand. You will have to give it to him and that's after we mate," she said then stood up. My eyes drifted down her brown thick and shiny thighs then traveled up to her wide hips. Her breasts were nice and round because her body wanted to carry a pup.

"That's between you, Adika, and Sosa. I'm out of it, so if you want to stay here, that's cool with me. Just know that I will not be stopping by to bring food or anything else anymore. You are Adika's problem from now on," I said to her. I turned toward the door then she pulled me back. "Wait, let me come out with you. I want to see your city. I just need to get some air then afterward you can leave and never come back," she said sweetly. I turned around looking down at her because my height towered over her by more than a foot. Onya had an innocence to her and maybe it was because she'd never been with a male before. Her body was untouched and pure. I growled at the thought of that, but I didn't want to have those thoughts. Her full lips looked soft and I could picture them wrapped around my dick. It was her scent that was giving me intimate thoughts. The urge of me entering her body was becoming unbearable.

"You've got five minutes to get dressed, and if you don't, then I'm leaving you," I said then sat down on the couch. She smiled and grabbed her bag. She went to the back to get dressed. I have been around females for a very long time. I knew their body measurements without seeing them. Onya was around a size twelve.

When she came from the back room my mouth almost dropped. Her jeans hugged every curve and the shirt made her full breasts look fuller. Her hair was up in a bun and she even wore a pair of hoop earrings. She turned around flirtatiously in the heels she wore. As she showed herself off my beast almost growled. Onya's ass and Adika's unicorn were running a race. My dick stood straight up and pressed against my jeans.

"Do I look okay?" she asked me.

"Yeah, now bring your ass on," I said then stood up.

"What is this?" Onya asked as she eyed my bike.

"A motorcycle," I said. I got on then pulled her toward me. I threw her behind me and she giggled.

"You are very strong," she said holding onto me because she almost fell off. I gave her my helmet.

"Put this on and hold on tight. I'm going very fast, so if you get dizzy, close your eyes," I said, revving up my engine. Dayo and I were the only two that were fascinated with bikes.

"Where are we going?" she asked.

"You will see," I said then pulled off.

****

“What is this place?” Onya asked as the loud rap music blared through the speakers.

“It’s called a strip club,” I said. She held my hand tighter as we walked through the crowd.

“Where the hell are you?” Adika’s voice came through my head. She sounded past angry but I ignored her. I figured out a trick about Adika. She only knew where I was and what I was doing if I answered her. If I didn’t answer her then she couldn’t see my vision. Witches were complicated but I was starting to learn her capabilities. Every witch has their own ways of magic and spells. Adika couldn’t fool me like she thought she could.

I paid for our section then a waitress brought out a few bottles of Moet and Hennessey. The Moet was for Onya, of course.

“What is she doing on that pole?” Onya asked curiously. I could tell she wasn’t used to this type of environment.

“She is performing and getting paid to do it,” I said.

“Isn’t that bad?” she asked.

“Isn’t Sosa your pimp? In this generation, what you do is called prostitution. You sell pussy and Sosa takes your money from it,” I said. A sadness came over her. I poured her a glass of Moet. “Drink this and relax. When a stripper comes over here, touch her ass and throw her some money. It’s like an escape,” I said to her.

“What is your escape?” she asked me.

"Stop being nosey, Onya. I didn't come here to be questioned. I came here to think and maybe you should, too," I responded. A red bone stripper came into our section and she was phat. She leaned forward, clapping her ass in my face. I could see the look on Onya's face as her glowing eyes changed to gray. She wasn't too pleased with my reaction toward the stripper but she wasn't my mate. She didn't have a reason to show that emotion. I tossed some bills at the stripper and Onya started growling. The stripper worked her way over to Onya then Onya rolled her eyes. The stripper picked up on Onya's attitude then whispered in my ear.

"When you ditch your jealous girlfriend come and see about Vanilla Cream. I won't charge you because it's on me, sexy," she said as she rubbed on my dick. "You are packing heavy weight," she said then kissed my cheek. She looked at Onya then rolled her eyes after she collected her money from the floor. Onya growled at her as she walked out of our section.

"Yo, what the hell is wrong with you?" I asked her.

"I don't know!" she yelled at me.

"Your marbles aren't too tight, are they?" I asked her.

"What does that mean?" she asked.

"Your simple ass is crazy or something," I replied. She sipped her champagne as she ignored me. I sat back and watched the strippers while Onya sat back and drank until the club closed.

****

I had to leave my bike and catch a cab. Onya was so drunk that she couldn't hold onto me on the motorcycle. After I paid the cab driver, I picked Onya up to carry her into the building. She giggled as her head flopped back. "You are very handsome," she said but I ignored her. When I got into the apartment I lay her down on Adika's old bed.

"Help me with my shower, please. I feel nasty being in that place," she said.

"You've got to be kidding me," I said. She stood up then wobbled to the bathroom. She started to sing one of the rap songs the strippers were dancing to. I fell over laughing for the first time in days.

"Yo, your ass is off-beat," I called out to her. She walked out of the bathroom naked. She stood in front of me, wobbling side to side with her grayish beast eyes. Her canines hung out of her mouth.

"You want to see my beast?" she asked but I said nothing. Her bones started to crack, which caused her to crouch over. I sat and watched her morph into a white wolf. She had a gray stripe going down the middle of her back. Her snout was narrow, indicating that she was a female. The male snouts are much wider. Her beast was smaller than mine but she was so beautiful. She almost reminded me of a bigger version of an Alaskan Husky.

She walked over to me with her bushy tail raised. The scent of her being in heat was even stronger. A howl almost escaped my throat as pre-cum oozed out the tip of my head. She shifted back then looked at me with lust-filled eyes. Her body needed to be penetrated. I could see it in her eyes that she wanted me to enter her. Her beast didn't care that she was a virgin because in our nature we are supposed to mate.

"Please," she said as her trembling hands reached out to me. She nervously straddled me. "You are very hard to resist. Even my beast feels that way," she said. Her breasts were pressed against my chest. Her arousal filled my nostrils, which caused me to growl. Her wetness seeped through my jeans as she sat on my lap. She was dripping in heat. Sweat beads formed on my forehead as I eyed her swollen breasts and hardened nipples. I pulled her closer to me then took her nipple into my mouth. She gasped then moaned as I hungrily sucked on her swollen nipple. Her nails extracted as she pulled me closer to her chest. I laid her down then licked from her chest down to her stomach. I pinned her legs up then inhaled the enticing scent of her wetness as it pooled from between her slit. I kissed her pink pearl then sucked on it. Onya's body lifted from the bed as I tasted her. I hardened my tongue then slowly entered it inside her tight hole. She howled then burst into a fit of moans as my tongue went in and out of her. Her wetness seeped from the corners of my mouth. I growled as my nails grew then sank into her legs. I had the urge to mark her because my beast wanted me to. My teeth slowly went into her skin but not all the way; just enough to bring her pleasure. My finger entered her anus then she gasped. I know it was a new feeling to her but her beast wanted pleasure and I was going to give it to her.

Her pussy contracted around my tongue pulling me. My head thrashed around between her legs.

“OOOOOOOHHHHHHHHHH!” she screamed as her body trembled. I sucked on her pearl harder then she howled as she climaxed. I flipped her over then positioned her on all fours. I spread her cheeks then went diving back in as I ate her from the back. My hands gripped her cheeks as I brought her down on my hard tongue using it like a dick. Her wetness ran down her legs as she climaxed again. I stuck my middle finger inside her pussy while massaging it with my thumb.

“ARRGGGHHHHHHHHHHHHH! GGRRRRRRRRRRRR!” she moaned then growled. I latched onto her pussy which brought her an intense orgasm. She came harder than before as she squirted. Her body jerked as she kept coming. Once she was finished she fell over onto the bed. I got up then washed my face and hands. When I walked back to the bedroom she was breathing heavily.

“Goodnight,” I said to her then left.

****

“Nigga, you are in trouble. Big fucking trouble,” Dayo said to me when I came into the house.

“What?” I asked.

“Kanya, Jalesa, Anik and Adika were talking about your ass. They had to calm Adika down, nigga. What was you doing?” he asked me.

“None of your business, but I was out at the strip club,” I said to him.

"Where have you been?" Adika asked floating in the air with her cat eyes staring a hole into me. When she floated around like that, it made me nervous.

"What are you doing all of that for?" I asked. I was ready to shift just in case she caught me off guard.

"I haven't seen you in two days!" she screamed and it rang inside my ears. The glass in the mirrors shattered and the windows flew open.

"I'm tired," I said as I headed toward the stairs. She used a force, which yanked me by the back of my neck. I stumbled backward on the stairs.

"Wait a minute, Adika. You are doing too much. Let him go!" Dayo said then growled at her.

"This doesn't concern you," she said to Dayo.

"That's my little brother and you are hurting him. You ain't a part of this pack! You are only here because of him. So let him go," Dayo said as I was being choked. Adika let me go then came down on her feet. Dayo helped me up as I gasped for air.

She crossed her arms then looked at me like what she did to me didn't bother her.

"You are real lucky. You are hurting me, too, Izra," she said then disappeared.

"That bitch is crazy," I said to Dayo.

"All witches are. Damn, nigga, she was about to kill your dumb ass," he said. After I caught my breath I headed up to my room. Kofi was playing his orchestra music and it took everything in me not to go into his room and kick it over. When I walked into my room Adika was coming out of the bathroom. She had on a silk robe and her face seemed to be angelic, but I knew that would change once she was pissed off.

I pushed her face-forward into the wall. I put all of my weight on her. I bit her neck as hard as I could then she gasped. I lifted up her robe, exposing her bottom. I undid my pants then let them drop down to my ankles. I released my dick then entered every inch I had to give into her. I gripped her hair roughly. "Is this what you want?" I gritted as I pounded into her. She moaned then purred as she scratched at the wall.

"I love you so much," she cried but I didn't want to hear that. She loved me but she wanted to give me to another wolf. She loved me but she didn't tell me that she carried Kofi's pup at one point in time. That wasn't love to me because I felt like a tool. I felt like she was using me to get what she wanted. Images of Onya's pussy dripping into my mouth caused me to go deeper inside Adika. She moaned louder as I grinded into her spot. Her pussy squeezed me, making it harder for me to thrust into her. I bit her again. *"Loosen up!"* Once she loosened I turned her around. I picked her up then slowly moved her up and down on my dick. She looked down, watching my dick slide in and out of her. She opened her robe, grabbing at her breasts.

I took her breast into my mouth as I pulled her all the way down to my testicles. Her eyes rolled to the back of her head as her legs shook. When she screamed she was coming I swelled inside her. She screamed louder as I pumped my seeds into her. Once I was done I stood her up and didn't say a word to her. I headed straight to the shower. I wanted to lock the door but I remembered that wouldn't stop her.

I wonder what Onya is doing, I thought.

Ammon

I sat in what my pup called a "conference room" inside one of Sosa's establishments. Dash and his comrades discussed ways to take over the area. They wanted to kill off male wolves so that Sosa could have more access to the females. Sosa wanted power the same as I did. He had what it took to be an Alpha. His pack was strong and vicious almost like my warriors. Most of my warriors were dead, a few left trapped inside the portal. I needed to make my move and fast.

"We need to be very cautious because Goon's pack is strong and he is the son of a witch. He is able to protect his warriors and make them stronger. We need to find a weakness then take them down. He can sense everything, so we have to be careful and unpredictable. This isn't just a pack of werewolves. These werewolves are descendants from strong, ancient Egyptian roots," Dash said. I was surprised of his knowledge because he seemed not to have any. Earth wasn't as complicated to me and I even learned their language in a short amount of time.

"Onya will take them down. She is trained to trick anyone with her cunning and innocent ways. She knows how to think without giving anything away. They can try to read her mind and won't figure out a damn thing. Once she has the pup then she will be sworn into the pack. Once she is sworn into the pack we will know everything about all of them. Onya will break the pack down and then they will lose focus on Naobi. Without the pack's defense, Naobi will be easier to capture. She is a strong witch, so we will have to ambush her with a lot of wolves. She will use spells to keep the gang of wolves off, but that will weaken her. Big spells take a lot from a witch, so you all keep that in mind. The harder we make her work the better and the easier for her to be captured. Ammon will get what he wants and so will I. I want the females inside Goon's pack. Without their males in the way they will become vulnerable. They will need male protection and that will drive them to me," Sosa said.

"That will take months!" Dash shouted then the other wolves growled at him.

"When you want everything in the palm of your hand then patience is the key. Only a dumb muthafucka thinks carelessly. Now, I know all about witches and warlocks. I know a witch doesn't see what it doesn't feel. If they don't suspect anything then they won't sense it," Sosa said.

"Strength of a warrior," I said then Dash growled at me. Once Sosa and his pack left the room it was just Dash and I.

"We don't have time. Musaf said that he could only shield us for a small amount of time," Dash said.

"You should've been a female wolf that breeds pups. No pup of mine will have a heart of a coward. This is no longer about Musaf. It's about my grand prize and that's Naobi. I don't fear Musaf or his spells. The only thing I fear is not having power. You need to learn from Sosa because he is a wolf that fears nothing. He thinks and make sacrifices to get what he wants. That, my son, is what you call power," I said to him.

"How is it working out for you? If power is meant for you to have, then you will be able to reach out and grab it. But you need a bitch to make you stronger," he spat.

I stood up from my seat. "Use your tongue against me again and you shall see how it will make a good meal to the pigs," I said to him then walked out of the room.

****

I sat in Dash's temple that he called his apartment. I wanted my mate back. I often asked myself was it the power because I was really starting to miss her. I had urges to be with Kaira because of her scent from being in heat but then it went away. I wasn't going to stop until I had Naobi back in Anubi.

"Come back to me!" I shouted inside her head.

"Go back to Anubi and I will meet you there. As long as you are on Earth I will not come to you. I know all about Musaf shielding your location. I will not play any games with you," she said.

"I'm going to kill your mate!" I shouted at her.

"You tried that but it was me who told my mate not to kill you. Be careful how you speak, my king. This is Earth and not Anubi. You don't hold any clout here! You are not strong here, and the sooner you see that, the better off you will be at home. You look weak on this planet! Dash is stronger than you and he is so stupid he doesn't know. Go back to Anubi where you belong! Jalesa is protected by a pack that is very strong. How is Musaf and your deal going to work? Jalesa is marked by Amadi. I believe that he isn't

going to want her after that but I bet you won't tell him that. Don't worry because I will! See you soon in Anubi and believe me when I tell you that my visit isn't a friendly one," Naobi spat.

"You will die if you go against me!" I replied then she laughed. I punched a hole in the wall then howled. I was defeated and didn't know what else to do. I wanted my mate at any cost but I needed to get back home.

"*I need to get back home. Can you open the portal at dawn?"* I asked Musaf.

"What will I have in return?" he asked.

"*Dash will bring you the witch,"* I said.

"*He has until the next full moon or else I will strip him of everything, including his strength. I made a deal with you and your pup, and I would like to see to it that it is sealed,"* Musaf said.

Dash walked into his temple with Sosa.

"Sosa has a friend he wants you to meet," Dash said then a woman appeared on the side of them. She was dressed in all black, her pupils black as well. Her skin was a deep brown and her hair was wrapped in a silk scarf. There was something familiar about her but I couldn't make it out though I knew she was of Egyptian roots.

"What is a wolf like you doing with an ancient witch?" I asked Sosa.

"This is Ula," Sosa said.

She looked at Sosa. "I can speak," she spat at him. Her accent was a little different than Egyptians because she sounded more like the humans.

"I finally get to meet Ammon the wonderful wolf god. The strongest immortal to rule Anubi. Do you know who I am?" she asked me but I didn't respond.

"Isn't magic wonderful? It was able to turn a dying human into a wolf," she said as she walked around me.

"What do you want?" I asked her.

"What makes you think I need something from you? You can't help me. You can't even help yourself," she said as her black eyes glowed. My body slammed into the wall with snakes going around me. Her eyes turned red like the color of blood. "I'm Ula, the daughter of Saka. My father was very dear to me and he kept me hidden, and when Naobi casted him away it set me free. I have lived on Earth with the humans for many years. This is my home and you are not welcome," she said then a long black snake came from her mouth and wrapped around my neck.

I shifted then charged into her. She disappeared. A dozen small snakes slithered across the floor. Sosa shifted then growled at me as he circled me. I charged into him then sank my teeth inside his throat. I slammed him into the wall then leaped on him to bite him. Dash stared at me.

"Finish him off," I said to Dash then he laughed.

"You do it! You are the king of Anubi, remember?" he replied.

"You are a traitor!" I said as Sosa attacked me along with Dash. I slammed them both onto the floor then leaped out of the window into the deep woods but a force yanked me back. There stood Ula, looking at me.

"The party just started," she said.

I shifted back to man form. "What did you do to my pup, Dash?" I asked her.

"He saw the coward that you really are. Saka created me to be his messenger. I know all about you and what you have done. I know about Naobi turning against her father. I know everything! When Sosa told me about our special visitor, I was shocked. King Ammon decided to visit Earth, so why not pay him a visit? Sosa gave you up and so did Dash because I have more to offer than you do. I will fix all of what my father wanted me to fix. I have you and now all I need is Naobi," she said.

"Naobi will catch you," I said. She laughed.

"If she can see me, her pure heart won't allow her to see evil. My father created me from the darkest magic. He knew that Naobi was going to become stronger and then put him away. He had a vision of it all and now his dream may come true. I've waited many years for this moment. He knew of her mate and how she was going to come to live on Earth. Why do you think he kept me here on Earth?" she asked.

"I will rip your heart out if you touch her!" I growled.

“You don’t even love her! Who are you fooling? Saka showed me everything! I know more about your beast than you do. What you did to her father will forever be a pain on her heart! That is not love! It’s greed and pure evil,” she spat. I was ready to shift.

“When I take the soul of your beast I will see all of what no one else has seen. I will do what my father sent me to do and that is to show Naobi the truth. Even if it kills her she will know the truth. If she forgives herself for what she did then I will kill her myself,” Ula said. She kissed me then sucked my soul out of my body.

Anik

"Wake up," I said as I shook Dayo. He sat up then looked around.

"Damn, my back hurts," he said. Dayo and I spent the night in the woods making love. I was still in heat and each day that passed the sensation was worse. Dayo spotted a deer then shifted. He tore into the deer without suffocating it first. His beast dragged the deer to me then laid it down by my feet. I shifted into my beast then bowed my head over my kill. After I was done praying to the spirits of the afterlife, I went for the deer's stomach. Dayo growled as he pulled the warm, bloody flesh away from the deer. After we finished eating, we cleaned each other's faces off. We shifted back then got dressed to head to the house. As soon as I got in the house, I showered then got dressed for work. Kanya took Arya to school because I was running late.

When I closed the bedroom door, Izra was coming out of his bedroom half asleep. He rubbed his eyes. "Ay yo, Anik, did you see Adika?" he asked me.

"Not yet I just came home a few minutes ago. She might be at the store," I said to Izra. I walked down the stairs and he followed me. Adika and Kofi came into the house laughing.

"Where the fuck you been at?" he yelled at Adika, startling her.

"Kofi and I went hunting. I tried to wake you but you were in a deep sleep. But what's new because all you did was drink yourself to sleep last night," Adika said to Izra.

"You and Kofi went hunting, huh?" Izra asked. I knew in his tone he wasn't too pleased with the situation. I wondered where his mood came from because the rest of the pack was fond of Kofi.

"Is something wrong with Kofi and I hunting?" Adika asked Izra.

"Read my fucking mind and you will know what's wrong with it," he spat. I was running late for work but I couldn't leave. I had a feeling something was going to break out and I didn't want that to happen.

"You don't talk to your mate like that!" Kofi said to Izra.

"Look at this shit. Go on ahead and defend your baby mama. The both of you ain't shit but some lying muthafuckas. Go ahead and tell the whole pack how you two ancient dinosaurs were intimate and having pups and shit," Izra said. Adika burst into tears.

"I wanted to tell you but it was too hard. We didn't want to hurt you," she said.

Izra growled as his eyes turned. "Well, it's too late for that shit, isn't it? We are supposed to be a pack that can trust each other. Well, that's what you taught us anyway, right?" he asked Kofi.

"It was a very, very long time ago. I didn't mean for it to be like this. I have a mate and Adika loves you very much," Kofi said to Izra.

"This shit is for the birds," Izra said then walked away. Adika was ready to follow him but Kofi stopped her.

"Let him cool off because he is still drunk. He isn't the best person to talk to when he is mad," Kofi said sadly then walked up the stairs. I hugged Adika then she cried on my shoulders.

"I'm losing him, Anik. I felt it a couple of nights ago when he came home late. I shouldn't have brought that wolf into our life. I have a feeling it's her. I sent him to take her a few things and since then he has changed," Adika said to me.

"Wait a minute, what?" I asked.

"I did what you told me to do and found a wolf to carry his pup. He didn't want to do it and that's where our problems started. I kept asking him and asking until he finally gave up. I cursed him," she said sadly.

"You cursed him?" I asked her then she pulled me to the side.

"The wolf is in heat and Izra wasn't attracted to her scent until I cursed him. I wanted him to impregnate her but my curse backfired. I was hoping when he took her the meat he'd sleep with her. But I think he ended up feeling something for her. The only way the curse rubs off is after he mates with her," Adika said. I started to growl but I caught myself.

"I was for the idea if he was willing to do it for you. But once he said he didn't want too you should've left it alone, Adika. I don't know what to say because I feel bad. I'm starting to feel like it's all of my fault," I said.

"It's not your fault and you are right. Once he said no I should've left it alone. I brought a female into our relationship. She is even staying at my old apartment," Adika said. She was ready to tell me something else until Izra walked past us fully dressed.

"Where are you going?" she asked Izra. He chuckled. At first I thought maybe Izra was going through something but I could tell he was cursed. He didn't have the same attitude and he just wasn't himself. I could tell by the way he looked at Adika that his love for her was slowly drifting away.

"OUT!" he said then left the house. The door slammed and echoed through the halls.

"I have got to fix this, but whatever you do, please don't tell the pack. Goon might even ban me from everyone. Even though it was a harmless spell it's still a spell," she said. After I promised her I wouldn't tell anyone I left for work. I guess I wasn't the only one with a secret, which made me feel even worse about it.

Two hours later…

"So, do tell why you were late for work," Anastasia said to me.

"She was getting some dick," Kanya said then laughed. I blushed with embarrassment.

"My heavens that sounds good right about now. A big, pretty, black cock," Anastasia said.

"So, how was Club ROAR? Adika and Kanya told me you went. I love it! You need to see the show when two guys fuck one girl," Anastasia said then fanned himself. He was very, very animated. I couldn't believe humans acted that way.

"We should go tonight," Kanya said.

"Ummm, I don't know about that," I said.

"We close late tonight so we can go when we leave from work. I want to see what Anastasia is talking about. I've never seen a sex show up-close before," she said excitedly.

"Let me call Dayo and tell him I will be home late," I said. I sent Dayo a text letting him know I wasn't coming straight home. He texted me back stating that if I came home too late, he was going to let me suffer on the night he and I mate.

"What did he say?" Kanya asked.

"He said it was cool," I answered because Anastasia was listening to us.

"He said if I come home late, he will let me suffer on the night we mate," I said into her mind and she laughed until tears filled her eyes.

"I can actually picture him doing that to you," she replied.

“Where is Jalesa?” I asked after I noticed she hadn’t come to work. Adika was supposed to be working also but I knew she had business to take care of.

“Jalesa has been locked away with Amadi in the bedroom. Adika was supposed to show up but she isn’t answering my messages,” Kanya said. The store started to get busy and it stayed busy until it was time for Kanya to close. After closing the store we all got into Kanya’s new Range Rover then headed to the club.

****

“What on Earth is he supposed to be? A tiger?” Kanya asked as the same guy Dayo and I saw eat raw meat sat inside a cage.

“A wolf,” I said.

“What a disgrace to our kind,” she said then laughed.

Anastasia got down on the ground. He brought his leash with him. He had on a spiked collar with a leather and fur leash attached to it. A man walked up and openly rubbed Anastasia’s ass. “Whoa,” Kanya said.

“It gets worse,” I said. I ordered two shots of Patrón from the bar. Kanya ordered a bottle of wine.

“I think I need something stronger. I thought that maybe you were exaggerating a little bit and now Anastasia is in his own world, so I didn’t believe him either. This place is like a big den of horny people,” she said before she sipped her wine from the bottle. A White man walked up to her then playfully bit her neck while gripping her bottom.

He smoothly started humping her leg. "My god Goon doesn't even do that and he is always horny," she said to me. She gently pushed the guy back.

"Work it, hunty," Anastasia screamed while sitting on a big man's shoulder. He reminded me of a small child as he sat up there. I regretted going to the club without Dayo because he made it seem more exotic. The guy left Kanya alone once she bit his arm with her sharp teeth.

Seconds later, Kanya dropped her bottle of wine when she jumped up, startled. "Are you okay?" I asked her.

"Goon popped into my head scaring the crap out of me. He is not happy about that man rubbing on my bottom and kissing my neck," she said nervously.

"You want to leave?" I asked her.

"Umm, yeah, because I'm really not about this life. I love sex but this shit here is creepy. Oh my god, is Anastasia eating raw meat?" Kanya asked. When I looked Anastasia was being tossed around the crowd as he howled like an animal with a raw steak in his hand. Blood was smeared all over Anastasia's face. I couldn't believe how hard he partied—he was the center of attention.

"I guess he isn't coming to work tomorrow," Kanya said. I started to sweat and my stomach started to cramp. The room was spinning. I grabbed Kanya's arm.

"What's the matter?" she asked.

"I don't feel too good," I said as another cramp shot up my spine. It caused me to double over.

"Let's walk to the bathroom," she said pulling me through the crowd. She pushed open the bathroom door and it was empty, which wasn't a surprise. Everyone was busy acting like animals. I frowned up my nose when I pictured them going on the floor like animals instead of using the bathroom.

"I wouldn't be surprised if those crazy assholes out there pissed on the dance floor. Have you ever seen a club bathroom this clean?" she asked. I went into the stall.

"I was thinking the same thing," I said as I pulled down my black dress pants.

"AHHHHHHHHHHH!" I screamed as blood seeped through my panties.

"Kanya, I'm bleeding. I'm bleeding, what should I do? Oh my god, blood is coming from my vagina," I said.

"Your body is preparing itself to carry pups. Your uterus is expanding before you get pregnant," she said.

"I'm going to be carrying pups?" I said still not believing it. "I'm scared," I said then burst into tears. Kanya gave me wet paper towels to clean off with. "Dayo, calls this a hoe bath," I said then chuckled a little.

"I'm not surprised at all but look on the bright side. Tomorrow night or maybe sooner, he will impregnate you and those cramps will go away," she said. I trashed my panties then used a paper towel as panties until I got home. I washed my hands then walked out of the bathroom. There was a woman onstage and she had the same markings of a Chippewa wolf. I stopped as I watched two men sexually touch her. One was entering her body as the other man sucked on her breasts, which was odd because Chippewa wolves didn't sleep with humans or believe in engaging in sex without a connection.

Kanya pulled me through the crowd as my eyes never left the stage. When we left the club we walked down the long hall in the tunnel, then climbed up the ladder and out of the pothole. As soon as I got inside Kanya's truck I put my seat belt on. "Are you okay? Did you see something?" she asked.

"I'm fine," I said to her.

"Are you sure? I feel like you aren't. Are you running from something?" she asked me.

"No, I'm just nervous about having pups, that's all," I said.

"It's a beautiful feeling, Anik, because your connection with Dayo will be so much stronger after you mate. It's like a love that you never knew existed in the real world. It's almost like a fantasy come true," she said as she pulled out of the parking lot. She turned up the radio as she sang along with the song that played. I looked out of the window. My cramps came harder then I burst into a heap of sweat.

"Please get me home," I said as my hands started trembling. Kanya sped up then slammed on the brakes.

"What the fuck is that?" she asked. When I looked there were five wolves blocking the small road. Yellow eyes glowed at me. The pack leader stared at me with his white and gray fur. He had a red dot in the middle of his forehead. I had a feeling he was around me when I spotted the Chippewa woman at the club. He was who I had been running from as well as Arya's father.

"He looks like your wolf with the red paintings," Kanya said then growled. Her eyes turned gold and so did her nails as her teeth sharpened.

"I don't think so," I said because I didn't want to be kicked out of the pack. Sosa jumped on Kanya's truck and the impact shattered the windows. Glass flew into my cheek; I was in too much pain and my body wouldn't allow me to shift.

His sharp teeth snapped at me as his pack howled. Kanya's beast charged into him through the windshield. I slowly began to shift again as I blocked the pain out. When I finally shifted I charged into the wolf that had his teeth into Kanya's hind leg. I heard howling and I knew that loud hoarse howl from anywhere. It was Goon, he saw visions of Kanya being attacked.

I was attacked by two wolves as they clawed and bit into me. I tackled one of them—my teeth pierced through the thick fur around his neck. Blood squirted into my mouth as my beast shook him down. The other wolf bit my shoulder to slow me down. Kanya's jackal howled out from Sosa's strong bite. The wolves that were on me tried to kill me. They were ordered to kill me because I ran away with Arya. A bolt of lightning came out of the sky then cracked the ground. Goon's beast eyes glowed as he tore into Sosa and the other wolf. Dayo's and Amadi's beasts charged into the wolves that were trying to rip me apart. An eighteen-wheeler came speeding down the dark road. Dayo dragged me by the back of my neck to avoid me getting hit. He laid me down in the woods on the side of the road. My body transformed back slowly as I coughed up blood. Dayo's beast whimpered as he licked the open gashes on my body.

"I'm going to bleed out and die. I'm getting cold," I said to him as blood filled my lungs. I closed my eyes as I suffocated.

Dayo

Goon, Amadi and I were hunting when he told us he saw Kanya and Anik being attacked by a pack of wolves. Goon teleported, bringing us with him. I saw five wolves attacking Kanya and Anik. Kanya's beast was stronger than Anik's, so she held her own. Kanya heal just as fast as Goon. My mate was covered in blood as two big wolves savagely tore into her like a meal. I snapped the wolf's neck in half that was trying to kill . He died instantly. An eighteen-wheeler was speeding down the small, back road then I hurriedly pulled Anik to the side. Blood was pouring out of her and her pretty face was no longer recognizable. I licked her, hoping it would stop the blood draining from her body. A river of blood flowed underneath my paws.

"I'm going to bleed out and die. I'm getting cold," she said. I shifted back then cradled her.

"Hold on Anik, you got to hold on," I said. Kanya's beast ran over to us. Goon killed another wolf; three of the wolves were dead. The eighteen-wheeler slammed on breaks, sending Kanya's Range Rover into the air as it jack-knifed. Goon and Amadi ran towards us.

"We have to go before humans arrive," Amadi said. The wolf with the red paintings on his face watched us from the other side of the road then he and the other wolf disappeared.

"We will fight them again but we have to save Anik," Goon's voice came into my head.

******

I paced back and forth by our bed as the pack worked on her. I still had her blood on my skin. I didn't know what to do because I'd never felt for another the way I felt about her.

"Calm down, bro," Amadi said to me. I punched a hole in the wall.

"I can't calm down until I find out who that wolf is that attacked her. You saw how they attacked her! I've never even attacked a deer that way when I hunt. They know her, bro; I saw how that nigga looked at her. He wanted her to die," I said.

"I'm going to bite her neck until her pulse stops after I give her my blood. She will heal quicker but you have to step out of the room," Goon said.

"Nigga, step out of the room for what?" I asked.

"He is going to kill her then his blood will pump through her veins. If he heals her while she is in this much pain, it will send her into shock. The healing hurts worse than anything, it burns," Amadi said.

I looked at Anik and she was barely holding on. "I'm not stepping out of the room," I said.

"Muthafucka when I bite her your beast is going to want to challenge me. It won't understand that I'm trying to save her. You think I feel like fighting you right now? Now, step the fuck out of the room!" Goon shouted, his eyes turning blue. Kanya and Jalesa stormed into the room with towels and more blankets. Amadi pulled me out of the room. Anik's blood was all over him, too.

"This blood is giving me flashbacks," Amadi said to himself. The door slammed behind us and moments later I heard the sound of Anik's neck being snapped by Goon's jaws. Amadi winced then I growled.

"Calm down, Dayo," Amadi said to me. A heatwave ran through my veins as my body started shift. "He is only saving her. Your beast needs to know that!" Amadi said.

"Where is all of this blood coming from?" Arya asked wiping her eyes from sleep. Relief overcame me. "What's the matter Dayo? Why are you crying?" she asked me. I didn't know tears ran from my eyes because it took a lot for a beast to cry. I have never cried before because I never had a reason to.

"Dayo is just upset right now, Arya," Amadi answered for me.

"Where is my mother?" Arya asked. I picked Arya up then walked her back to her bedroom. I stepped on something.

"What the fuck was that?" I shouted out and when I looked down it was some object that she called a "Barbie".

"Kanya said that you have a very bad mouth," Arya said after I lay her back down in the bed.

“Your lil’ bad ass knows every curse word there is so don’t act surprised,” I replied.

“My mother is in heat, isn’t she? Aren’t you supposed to be making pups with her so she can stop sweating all the time?” she asked me. I grabbed a Teddy bear then shoved it in her arms.

“This is what your grown ass should be worried about,” I said. I stood up then she laughed.

“That’s where the blood came from. My father used to tell me, when I see blood that means I’m ready to mate,” she said.

“What happened to your father again?” I asked Arya.

“He was killed. Can you tell me a bed-time story?” she asked me. I sat back down next to her.

“Once upon a time there was this little girl and she was grown before her age. One day she came home pregnant because she let this little boy touch on her in school. She told her mama she was pregnant and her mama whipped her ass. The little girl never looked at a boy again,” I said.

“What happened to the baby?” she asked.

“It was raised as her sister because the little girl was too young to be a parent,” I said then she frowned up her small face then growled at me. Her little canines showed, which caused me to chuckle because it was somewhat adorable.

“That wasn’t a story!” she said.

"I know but it was a warning. Now take your little grown ass to sleep," I said then walked out of her room.

When I walked into the hallway, I heard Adika and Izra's voices. They were arguing. "Shut the hell up, Adika, before I throw you out of the window to see if cats can really land on their feet," Izra said to her.

"I will make your dick disappear," she shouted back at him.

"Good! That way I won't have to fuck your sneaky ass with it again," he said. Izra paused then looked at me. "Damn, nigga, what happened to you?" he asked. Izra and Elle wasn't with us when it happened. He didn't know what was going on.

"Anik was attacked," I said to him.

"Where is she?" Adika asked.

"In our room with everyone else. I'm not allowed to go in," I said then Adika disappeared.

"You know out of all the times she disappeared this will be the one time I hope her dumb ass stay where she's at," Izra said. I shook my head.

"Who attacked Anik?" Izra asked me.

"I don't know," I said to him then he patted my back, "Be easy, bro," he said then walked down the hall to my room. Kofi came up the stairs with something hot in a cup. He went to my room too; everyone was there but me.

An hour later I walked into our bedroom after I showered in the hall bathroom. Anik was sleeping peacefully. She looked like she'd never been in a fight; her face glowed like never before. She reminded me of a sleeping angel. I got into bed with her then pulled her close to me. I swallowed her frame up in my embrace, feeling the warmth of her body. She slightly moved then growled. "You are squeezing me," she whispered then I let her go.

"I was afraid," I said to her then she smiled with her eyes still closed.

"You must have been because you are not an emotional beast. You fight your feelings like they are your enemy," she said. "ARRGGHHHHHHHHH!" she screamed.

"What happened?" I asked as I jumped up.

"These darn cramps are killing me!" she said as she clutched her stomach. "I'm being punished for something. I was attacked and now this," she said. I gently pushed her back then climbed out of the bed.

"Who was that nigga, Anik? And don't lie to me," I said to her.

"I don't know," she answered.

"I saw the way he looked at you!" I shouted which caused her to jump.

"Why are you yelling at me?" she asked.

“I want to know what is up with my soulmate. If you got some things with you then I need to know. You could’ve died on me and you need to take this seriously,” I said to Anik.

“I’m telling you the truth,” Anik said to me.

“At first it was a witch who tricked me and lied to me and now it’s my soulmate. My luck with immortals isn’t good and I’m pissed off,” I said to her then she reached out to me.

“I’m telling you the truth. I was at the club Roar and they followed me. I’m in heat and they could’ve picked up my scent,” she said. It was possible but there was something about her story that didn’t sit well with me.

“A wolf attracted to a scent isn’t going to kill you. Maybe rape you if they can’t control their beast, but not kill you. You were ambushed and those wolves didn’t give two fucks about the scent that dripped from your pussy,” I said to her. Anik pulled away from me then laid down. She turned her back toward me. I walked out of the room.

****

“My mate is lying to me, bro,” I said to Goon as we lifted weights.

“Of course she is but for what reason? We all know that she lied. The real question is what she is hiding from? Her thoughts are normal, so whatever it is she isn’t trying to think about it,” Goon said.

"She'd better tell me or else I'm not knocking her up. She wants me to give her pups when I don't even know who the fuck she is now. I don't like secrets, bro. I've been a caged animal for months behind Keora and now this shit. I can't deal with this right now," I said.

Elle walked into the gym room. "What's up, bro?" I asked him.

"Nothing," he said. I wasn't used to seeing Elle that way. Elle was the older brother that took on the father role at times. He was no longer himself. Elle picked up a fifty-pound weight then hurled it into the wall.

"What the fuck," I said. Elle paced back and forth with his eyes changing as he took deep breaths to calm down. He growled then picked up another weight. He hurled the second weight into the wall; the weights made two large holes inside the wall.

"Yo, you need to chill out!" I said to him then Goon shook his head telling me to keep quiet.

"Let him vent," Goon's voice came inside my head. I sat still and watched as Elle paced back and forth, messing up the gym room.

"That's enough! I can't take this shit no more, bro. What is wrong with you?" I asked him.

"I wasted my time for a human, is what is wrong with me. I watched her live her life when I could've been living mine," he fussed. Camille died days ago and Elle still couldn't get over it.

"Nigga, we live for like, almost ever. What time did you waste?" I asked him.

"That's beside the point," he said.

"I'm not following you right now, bro, it's not too late. Camille lived a loonnggggg life and it was time for her to go," I said to Elle. Anik walked past the room with her scent lingering. I followed her into the kitchen. Sweat seeped through her robe and her skin felt clammy when I touched her. Her eyes were the color of her beast. Her fangs were sharp and her lips were black because she was stuck in mid-shift. Mid-shift is when the human form is trying to shift but the body is fighting with its beast to be released.

"My cramps are getting worse," she said with tears in her eyes.

"ELLE!" I called out to him because Kofi had left the house. He came running into the kitchen.

"What's going on? Are you okay, Anik?" he asked her then felt her forehead.

"Her cramps are getting worse," I said to him.

"She will need to mate tonight," Elle said to me.

"Not until she tells me what she got going on. I'm not giving her pups until then. She doesn't understand the meaning of this pack and that we don't keep secrets," I said to Elle.

“You are not playing fair,” Anik said to me then her body collapsed. I hurriedly ran to her and she was burning up. Her temperature rose and it was higher than ever before.

“Tonight during the full moon she will be ready to mate. You have to take her upstairs and wrap her up in ice-cold towels. She will sleep and when she wakes up it will be time,” Elle said.

“Is everything good in here?” Goon asked when he came into the kitchen. He froze when he saw me cradling Anik.

“She has blood dripping from between her legs. Is that normal, Elle? Kanya didn’t bleed that much,” Goon said as he stared at the blood dripping on the floor.

“All female wolves bleed differently,” Elle responded. I hurriedly rushed Anik inside our bedroom then ran the shower. The water was ice cold when I stuck her in, she slowly opened her eyes...

Anik

I knew Sosa was going to find me but it wasn't me I was worried about. Sosa cared less about me because it was Arya that he wanted. After Dayo carried me out of the shower in his strong arms he laid me down in our bed. Elle and Goon brought me cold towels. Amadi came in with herbal tea then I smiled at him. "I haven't been seeing much of you lately," I said to him then he smirked.

"That's because he been getting some pussy. About damn time, nigga," Dayo teased then patted his back. Kanya and Jalesa came in to check on me after they came home from work. Arya was out with Adika; Izra and Kofi were missing. I started to get sleepy and everyone left the room except for Dayo. I hated that I lied to him but I was ashamed of where I came from. I was ashamed that I was a slave to a wolf that only wanted me to raise his daughter. I was ashamed that Arya was only ten years old and was already preparing to carry pups.

Dayo rubbed my stomach with his strong hands. "Are you scared?" he asked me.

"No, are you?" I asked him.

"I'm scared of losing you, Anik," he admitted then I squeezed his hand.

"I love you, Dayo. I felt it when I first laid eyes on you. I will always be in your heart," I said to him.

"You sound like you are ready to die on me or something," he replied. He kissed my lips then I closed my eyes as the wet, cold towels soothed my body. Moments later, I fell asleep.

******

When I woke up I got back into the shower; I felt much better. I would've been doomed if I went into heat alone because Arya wouldn't have known what to do. I dried off then oiled my body with Amadi's oil that made my skin glisten. I took the two braids out of my hair then fluffed it out. The thick tendrils fell down my shoulders then, afterward, I applied my make-up. I wanted to take Dayo's breath away. I sat in the middle of the floor naked with my legs crossed then said a silent prayer. I prayed for my family that Sosa killed and the new beginning of life that Dayo and I were going to create.

Moments later, Dayo walked into our bedroom with a slab of raw meat on a tray and my favorite part of the deer, its heart. It was fresh and still warm. I instantly picked it up then bit into it. The tangy taste of warm blood filled my mouth, which caused my stomach to growl. It felt like I hadn't eaten in months.

"Arya is asleep," Dayo said to me. He did a great job making sure she did homework and chores. He stayed on top of her and corrected her when she was wrong. He did it in his own way but she listened to him.

"Thank you," I said to him. After I was finished eating, I had a glass of wine to relax my nerves. The bright moon started to peek over the night clouds. I felt the wave come over me like a burst of energy that traveled down between my thighs. My pussy throbbed and ached, which caused me to growl then moan. It was a feeling that I had never felt before and the wetness started to drip from between my slit. I touched myself then squeezed my breasts.

"Ummmm, Dayo, it aches," I moaned. He picked me up then laid me down on the bed. He spread my legs then nuzzled his nose into me then growled loudly. His fingers spread my pussy lips apart; he looked at me as his eyes changed color. He stuck his tongue inside me, which caused my lower body to rise up from the bed. I gripped his strong shoulders then howled as his tongue moved in and out of me. He laid his tongue flat across my swollen bud then sucked on it.

"SHAT!" I shouted as my body trembled. I toyed with my hardened nipples. I squeezed them and pulled on them as another force took over my body. He pulled away from me then laid down on the bed. I straddled him then he lifted me up by my hips like I was a feather. He placed me on his face then turned me around. He pushed me forward. "You know what to do," he said to me as I stared at his huge black dick. My hand gripped around half of his width. His tongue went back into me as his nails dug into my ass cheeks. I licked the tip of him, tasting the sweet serum that dripped from his dick. I kissed the tip of his head then it throbbed. He smacked my ass then stuck his tongue further into my hole. He growled as he slurped and sucked on the essence that dripped down my inner thigh. He thrust himself further into my mouth and down my throat. I almost gagged as his girth filled my throat. He pushed more into my mouth then smacked my ass.

"Relax your mouth," he moaned against my pussy. Spit ran down my hand as I sucked his thick member. The harder I sucked the more he ate me out. When he sank his teeth into my vagina lips, I sat up then rode his face, screaming as I climaxed. He jerked himself off as I rode his face faster. His tongue never missed a beat as my pussy swallowed his lips. I grabbed my breasts as I came again. Dayo's nut shot straight up into the air then drizzled down his shaft. He pushed me forward so I could taste him. I cleaned him off as he moaned my name. He was harder than before. The veins in his dick thickened as he grew. I positioned myself in the doggy-style position, which was our mating position. I wanted it badly as I leaked from between my legs. Dayo positioned himself behind me then spread my cheeks.

"This is going to hurt, Anik, I swelled up badly," he warned. I howled when he pushed his dick inside me; it felt like he was tearing down my walls with pressure shooting up my spine. I lost control when he squeezed all of himself inside my tight center. His beast howled loudly, which pained my ears. I felt every ridge of him.

"GGRRRRRRRRRRRRRRRR!" he moaned as he slowly pushed himself in and then out of me. Tears fell from my eyes because I felt like I was being split from my ass. I gripped the sheets, tearing them. My nails grew out then my teeth sharpened. His nails dug into my scalp as he pulled my hair then pounded into me.

"Damn, this pussy is wet. SHIT!" he groaned slamming into me. I was grabbing everything in front of me as he slammed into my spot. The pain mixed with pleasure caused me to scream. I arched my butt higher to take more of him.

"Is it in your stomach yet?" he groaned turning me on even more. I squeezed my breast while my other hand gripped the bed post. Sweat dripped down my cleavage and down my butt-crack as Dayo showed no mercy on my pussy.

"UUMMMPPPPHHHHHH!" I moaned, taking his beast. He slammed into my spot again then howled, gripping my hair tighter. He throbbed inside me then got stuck as his width expanded. He howled for a long time as his voice grew hoarse. His nails dug into my back, which caused my skin to open. He was stuck against my spot and it caused warm, thick liquid to gush from between my legs. I fell forward, sprawled out, as my body jerked like I was being riddled with bullets. My eyes rolled to the back of my head then he took my breath away. I felt like I was being suffocated as he pumped his wolf serum into me. Wolf serum doesn't stop until the cervix closes, and after it closes the mating is over. He howled again as it continued to squirt from his dick into my womb. I could no longer endure the pleasure; my body gave up on me, sending me into a coma-like sleep.

******

The sun beamed down into my face as the curtains blew away from the opened window. A small blue bird sat on the windowsill. The warm breeze brushed across my skin. I held my hand out then it hopped on. "Hey, little birdie," I said to it. It chirped then my stomach growled. The bird was no longer cute anymore, it looked like a delicious snack. I prayed over it before I tore its head off.

"Good morning," was all Dayo said as he watched me chew the small bird like bubble gum. I snapped the bird's small bones between my jaws.

"What the fuck," he said. I swallowed the bird then spit out a few feathers I couldn't digest. I climbed out of bed then Dayo's eyes got big. I looked down and my stomach was swollen. He looked nervous as he stared at me. "ELLLEEEEE!" he called out.

"What happened?" Elle asked when he burst into our room. I only had on a T-shirt. Dayo must have put it on me while I was asleep.

"Her damn stomach, bro," he said then Elle chuckled.

"She's carrying pups," he answered.

"Already?" Dayo asked him.

"It happens fast, bro. In two months she will be pushing them out," Elle said.

"I need to eat," I spat. Another bird landed on the windowsill then I snatched it. I tore into it as Dayo and Elle winced then gagged.

"She needs to eat; she's been asleep for four days," Elle said. Amadi came into the room with a tray of meat then I tackled him; the meat flew to the floor. I grabbed the meat off the floor then stuffed it inside my mouth as I growled. Izra and Goon came into the room. They all looked at me as I licked the blood on the floor from the meat. When I stood up I was a bloody mess. I growled at them as they stared at me in disbelief.

"What?" I asked them.

“That shit was gross. I thought Kanya ate like a pig but you just ate bear meat like it was candy,” Izra said. Goon pushed Izra into the wall.

“Shut the fuck up, muthafucka!” Goon spat. My stomach growled again then I shifted. I leaped out of the window and headed straight toward the woods to hunt for a pregnant deer.

****

Hours later, I sat in the living room full and bloated while Kanya, Adika and Jalesa rubbed my stomach. Arya was playing with Akea and Kanye while they sat in their bouncer. Everyone laughed around me and sipped their wine as we celebrated. Dayo’s pack brothers took him out to celebrate.

“Are they moving yet?” Kanya asked me.

“Yes, I feel little flutters,” I said.

“I’m so jealous right now,” Adika said then I squeezed her hand.

“Don’t be, because you can always share them with me. We are all like family,” I said.

“Yup, one big, hairy, mean family,” Kanya giggled. She was a little tipsy.

“Goon wants more pups,” Kanya said.

“Are you serious?” Jalesa asked.

“No, his naughty behind just likes the process we have to go through to get them,” she said.

“What’s the wolf serum like? I think I passed out when Amadi gave it to me,” Jalesa said.

“The best dick in life. It’s like a drug or something because when Goon and I mated I stopped breathing. His dick swelled up so big, it got stuck against my spot. I came over and over again. He was in his ancient form when we mated. He was all black and around eight feet tall. His face was like his wolf but his body was like a man. Just remembering it makes me want to give him more pups,” Kanya said then fanned herself. Adika fanned herself, too.

“I think I need to change my panties. There is something about wolf dick that makes you go crazy,” Adika said then downed her shot of liquor.

“I think we are scaring Jalesa,” Kanya said.

“I think I might be pregnant,” Jalesa said then Adika spit her liquor out.

“Goddamn it. You, too?” she asked with sarcasm.

“It was bound to happen, Adika. She isn’t a beast, therefore, she doesn’t have to wait for a specific time to get pregnant. Besides, Amadi marked her, so I’m not surprised if she is. It’s also a good thing, that way Ammon won’t have to take her,” Kanya said.

“Ammon has been very quiet. I haven’t heard from him since the big fight,” Jalesa said.

“I have a feeling it’s not the end because it’s too quiet. But we have another issue. We need to figure out who attacked Anik, and why,” Kanya said. I looked over at Arya to see if she could hear us but she was on the other side of the room playing with the twins. I didn’t want her to know what happened at that moment. If she knew Sosa had found me, she would’ve told the pack about him.

“Are you having symptoms?” I asked Jalesa to avoid the conversation about Sosa and his pack attacking us.

“I’m very tired and I don’t feel the same. It could be from lack of sleep and the amount of pleasure he gives me. He had me stuck in the room for a whole day just giving me all of his beast,” Jalesa said then blushed.

“All of this talk got me aroused,” Kanya said then stood up.

“I’m going to go to my bedroom and see if my husband can mind-fuck me. His visions are so real that I can actually feel him inside me,” she said then all of our mouths dropped open.

“Are you serious?” I asked.

“Very much so. My Goonie is fully loaded with everything. I’m one lucky mate,” she said then rushed off.

“HOT ASS!” Adika called out then we all burst into a fit of laughter.

****

Dayo came home drunk and high from being out with the pack. He fell right to sleep as soon as he hit the bed. I undressed him then tucked him in underneath the sheet. I hurriedly got dressed then snuck into Arya's room. I wrapped her up in a blanket then snuck out of the side door. I put her inside the van. I hurriedly went back into the house to grab our two suitcases that I had hidden inside the hall closet. As soon as I got back inside the van I pulled off. I didn't want to leave but I had to. Sosa was going to find me and take Arya away from me. I had to protect her even if it meant leaving my mate behind. I didn't want my problems to become theirs. They welcomed me with opened arms and they didn't deserve Sosa's reign. Sosa was my problem and I had to deal with it. It was selfish of me but I couldn't run away while in heat because that would've caused a lot of attention from the male wolves. I had to concentrate on protecting Arya and my twin pups.

I drove and drove without a destination. I had the money I saved up from working at the jewelry store but I had to be careful how I spent it. I heard Arya moving around in the back.

"Where are we going?" she asked, looking out of the window.

"We are going far away," I said to her. She burst into tears, which caused my tears to fall from my eyes.

"Why are we leaving? What about our new family? They loved us!" she screamed.

"Sosa's pack was the one who attacked me," I said to her.

"The pack will protect us. We have to go back! What about my school and my new friends? What about Dayo and the pups that you are pregnant with?" Arya cried.

"I don't know right now!" I said

"Take me back! I want to go back!" Arya screamed. I swerved because she started to shift in the back seat. She burst out of the back window then ran into the woods. I pulled over and almost hit a car. I got out then jogged into the woods. "Arya, please don't do this to me! I'm pregnant and can't run as fast," I yelled out to her. I heard her small howls. She was deep in the woods. Her young beast was very fast and could outrun the whole pack.

"ARYA!" I called out but she didn't answer me.

"Get your ass out here this instant! I am still your mother and you will listen to me!" I shouted. I stayed in the woods looking for Arya until the moon went down. My pregnant body couldn't shift into my beast until I gave birth. The pups took a lot from their mothers, which slowed down the shifting process.

I walked out of the woods to my van. Once I got in, I broke down. I didn't know what to do because if I went back they wouldn't had been too pleased with Arya roaming around. It was my fault she ran away. She was a young wolf and I prayed a lone male wolf couldn't find her. Someone tapped on my window with a light shining in my face.

"Is everything okay, ma'am?" a Caucasian middle-aged officer asked me.

I put the window down. “Yes, I’m fine,” I said wiping my eyes.

“I got a call stating that a dog jumped out of a van and a woman ran into the woods behind it. I’m just making sure that everything is fine,” he said to me.

“Yes, I’m fine. I lost my dog,” I said. He looked in the back.

“It’s a fine to drive around like this. Do you want me to give you a lift? If not an officer will pull you over and give you a ticket,” he said. I grabbed my bags out of the van. I was going to go back for Arya but I couldn’t risk her coming out of the woods in beast form. Humans feared animals, especially a wolf, because she was still bigger than an average dog. Arya’s beast shifted back to human form when it wanted to. She couldn’t control her beast and would attack if she thought I was in harm’s way.

“I’m going to call a tow truck,” the officer said then walked to his car after he grabbed my suitcases. I got into his car then my stomach started to growl. It was time for me to eat. “Are you hungry?” he asked. He heard my stomach growl when he got into the police car.

“No,” I lied.

I looked out of the window as he pulled off. We drove a few miles until we got to a market. He pulled into the parking lot. It was six in the morning and sleep started to take over me.

“I’m going to grab a cup of coffee and I will be right back. Are you sure you are okay, ma’am?” he asked.

"Yes, I'm fine," I answered. I was thinking of a way to find Arya. I couldn't risk driving the van and getting a ticket because I didn't have a license. I was thankful that he didn't ask me for one. When he came back he had a pastry with him and a soda. The smell of the pastry made me gag and I didn't drink soda. He tried to give it to me but I declined.

"I'm fine, thanks anyway," I said then he started up the car.

"What is a young, pregnant woman like you doing roaming around at night?" he asked. I looked down at my stomach; I looked to be around four months pregnant.

"I was visiting a family member," I said. He drove me to the police station minutes later. He parked in the back of the building. I stayed put until he tapped on the window.

"Come on, ma'am, a cab is going to take you to your destination. My shift is over," he said. I got out of his car then he grabbed my suitcases. I walked through the parking lot then froze. I smelled a scent that I was too familiar with, followed by a growl.

"My dear Anik," Sosa said to me. I hid behind the officer. "Thank you officer for finding my mate," he said to the officer. The officer looked at me then smiled wickedly.

"My pleasure and send a pretty young wolf to my home in an hour," the officer said.

"You sided with the humans?" I asked Sosa then he laughed.

"Who do you think pays the big bucks to screw an exotic female wolf? He is a paying member," Sosa said.

I hit the officer in his face. "Son-of-a-bitch! How dare you!" I yelled, hitting him again. He pulled his gun out then pointed it at me.

"I will shoot you if you don't stand back!" he yelled at me then I growled at him. Sosa wrapped his arm around the officer's neck then snapped it. The officer dropped to the ground then I took off running, but I wasn't fast enough. Sosa leaped over four police cars then tackled me down to the ground. I hurriedly twisted my body before I fell to protect my pups.

"Get up!" he said pulling me up by my hair. He sniffed the crook of my neck then slapped me because I smelled like another wolf.

"You took my daughter away from me," he spat as he dragged me out of the parking lot then back into the woods.

"You mated with a wolf outside of your tribe? Shame on you! Those are supposed to be my pups!" he yelled at me as he dragged me across the ground. We ended up on the highway where a pick-up truck was parked on the side of the road. I tried to get away but he yanked me by my hair. He bit my shoulder as hard as he could; tears stung the brim of my eyes.

"Please, stop!" I said to him. He licked around his lips to taste my blood.

"You are sick!" I yelled at him. His eyes turned a golden-yellow with a tint of red in the middle. His shoulders grew broader.

"I will kill you then cut those mutts out of your stomach. You resist me again and I will make good on my word. You had no business taking Arya away from me! You put your nose into something that didn't concern you. Now, you either get in the truck or get your neck snapped. The choice is yours, so choose wisely," he said to me. I cradled my stomach as my pups started to move. The small flutters brought a sense of relief over me. I got into his truck then he laughed. "My wife is finally home," he said to me. I was married to Sosa but we didn't have a wedding. In our tribe we didn't have weddings but we had spiritual ceremonies. We had to drink an ounce of each other's blood. Sosa's pack wasn't spiritual Indians; he had a cult. He made up his own sick beliefs and rules. Sosa wasn't a full Chippewa wolf, so his way of living was different. He was a just a loner who took advantage of the weak in our small town. My kind wasn't violent and only fought to protect the young. We believed in peace and Sosa took it all away. The older wolves that ran my small and hidden town accepted Sosa, and in return, he turned against them. His pack ambushed the town and killed the majority of my tribe. The males and older females were killed, and he let the young females live to mate with his pack.

"You are having female pups," he said to me.

"How do you know?" I asked him.

"The markings on your body from your tribe indicates the sex of the pups that you will have. You breed nothing but females," he said to me. I looked at him then he smiled. He rubbed my face. "You owe me," he said then touched my stomach. I burst into tears because he was going to keep me until I gave birth then kill me.

****

“What place is this?” I asked when he pulled up a long driveway to a big mansion. It was almost the size of Goon’s mansion.

“My new home. The home I bought for us before you decided to run away. Now get the fuck out of my truck because you stink! You smell just like that wolf, and when I see him I’m going to rip his damn teeth out!” he yelled at me. I was scared of Sosa because he was very evil. His face was so handsome but underneath it all he was wicked. His skin was the color of honey and his eyes slanted, showing some of his Indian traits. His hair was braided going down on the sides and his tall, muscular body attracted women of all kinds.

“You were going to give up your daughter!” I yelled at him then he laughed.

“Simple bitch! Do you really think Arya is my daughter?” he asked me.

“WHAT?” I yelled then he laughed.

“Arya isn’t my daughter. I was just grooming her to become one of my females inside my operation. I lied to you, Anik. You were young and naïve then, but I see how much you have grown now and I do mean physically,” he said as he grabbed my breast. I smacked his hand away.

“Who are Arya’s real parents?” I asked him then he chuckled.

"Don't worry about that," he answered then yanked me toward the house. After he unlocked the door, he pulled me in; the inside his home was beautiful. In the foyer on the wall there was a picture of Sosa and I. He had his arm wrapped around my waist and I was smiling, but behind my smile you could see the sadness in my eyes. I wasn't physically locked away but I was emotionally.

"I think about you every day," he said.

"You killed my family! I will always resent you!" I yelled at him.

"One more outburst like that and I will bite a clump out of your face. This is your home now and we will raise those pups together. I was thinking about killing you but now I've changed my mind. You are a strong female and you will make even stronger females after I breed with you. Now, follow me because I want to show you something," he said sternly. I slowly followed him up the spiral staircase.

"Hurry up, Anik!" he yelled. I caught up to him and he was standing by a set of big wooden doors. The carvings in the door were of wolves and Indians. He pushed the floor-to-ceiling doors open and it was a computer room. He pulled me in then pushed me down into a chair. He did something on the computer until Dayo and I appeared on the screen inside the club Roar.

"Did you enjoy his pleasure?" he asked as he watched Dayo play between my legs while the sex show went on in front of us.

"What is all of this?" I asked him.

"Sex sells with humans. That club was a big investment. I was going to go into business with a guy named Xavier but your wolf friends killed him. I was going to go into business with Dash because he was going to get a lot of jewelry that he was promised by Keora. But then your wolf friends went to war with his pack and he never got the jewelry. We were going to use the money from the jewelry to open the club. I was desperate, so I made a deal with a witch named Ula. I walked into a bank to see if they would give me a loan for my club. It was just my luck that the loan officer was a witch. She gave me everything I wanted right in the palm of my hand. Do you know how much money humans spend on having sex with a female wolf while she shifts? They spend thousands! That's why I need all the females I can get to be groomed to give pleasure to humans," he said then tears ran down my face.

"How did you end up with Arya? You told me she was your daughter and forced me to raise her. Who was that man that showed up and wanted to take her the day I ran away with her?" I asked Sosa.

"Her real father. He owed me a debt! He got one of my females pregnant and didn't pay me, so I took his pup. He didn't have my money for the female he mated with. The female didn't want the pup, so I took her and decided I would make better use of her when she got older. I wanted you to take care of her while her mother made me a lot of money. The money that the male couldn't come up with," he said.

"You sell your females without an ounce of guilt," I said to him.

"I was going to sell you until I figured out how special you were to me. I don't just sell female wolves; human females are a little valuable, too. You saw it for yourself the first time you came to my club. You were aroused, I almost smelled you through the computer. I could've had your mate killed then but I wanted to see how well he knew your body. I had one of my humans follow you two when y'all left my club. He put a tracking device on your van when you went to work the next day. If I would've used a wolf, then you and your mate would've smelled him. Humans really do come in handy. They are very hard to detect," he said.

"If the humans sell our species out, then what?" I asked him.

"Money is what matters and it gives you the ability to do everything that our beast can do, plus more. I have a circle of business partners who are millionaires that invest a lot of money into this, and they aren't thinking about selling our species out," he said.

"You don't make a deal with a witch without giving something in return. What did you have to give her?" I asked him.

"It's simple, don't you think? Ula had a vision that Ammon would come to Earth for Naobi. I only became friends with Dash because he is Ammon's son. Ula wanted me to lead her to Ammon through Dash. So, in the meantime make yourself at home. Oh, and that golden jackal is very feisty and she can make me millions!" he said.

"Goon will not allow that to happen. He is more than just a beast!" I said to him.

"That he is, but too bad I can't say the same about his father," a voice said from behind me. When I turned around I jumped up. There stood a woman with black eyes holding a snake in her hand. The snake was long and black and had red eyes. A thick cloud covered her then she disappeared. When she came back she no longer looked wicked; she was a beautiful woman with long braids and nicely done make-up. She wore a pair of ripped jeans, a cropped, white top with a pair of red pumps. She looked to be only twenty-three but I knew she was older.

"I just love that scary effect but how do I look now?" she asked posing like a model. "I'm Ula by the way, sorry I'm late. I had a date with the devil," she said then laughed. Sosa's eyes roamed over her hips and a light growl escaped his throat. I could see how bad he wanted her and I didn't blame him. Even though she seemed wicked she was still stunning and her figure was perfect.

What did I get myself into? I thought to myself.

Elle

A woman jumped in front of my car then I slammed on my brakes. I was in deep thought because I had a feeling something bad was going to happen. It was too quiet and peaceful. I pulled over then got out of my car.

"Excuse me, Ms. Lady, I didn't mean to do that," I said to her.

"Watch where the hell you are going next time!" she spat then walked off.

"Fuck it then," I shouted back at her. If only my pack brothers were there to hear me sound like them. I got back into my car then drove around the corner to the mall. Once I parked, I headed straight to the Footlocker.

After being in the store for an hour, I had a few jogging suits and tennis shoes in my hands. I saw that my brothers wore a lot of comfortable clothes and I decided to try it out. I lived my life on a schedule and have been since I could remember. I had to dress a certain way because it was a certain day and I was getting tired of it. I wanted to live freely like the rest of my brothers. Even Amadi was happy and laughing more. I was the only one whose life wasn't interesting. I missed out on a lot just sitting and waiting for something that never was going to come.

After I paid for my items, I walked out of the store. As I walked past a hair salon, a young woman came out. She had a pretty, nutmeg complexion with a short haircut. The soft curls framed her gorgeous face. She wore a jogging suit and her face was clear of make-up. When she walked past me, I turned around and so did she. She rolled her eyes at me then kept walking with a sway of her hips. I realized it was the wolf at Camille's house. She looked different because she wasn't in the process of shifting and she cut her hair off. I didn't recognize her until her stank attitude started to show.

I went into an urban store and looked around. Goon, Dayo and Izra wore a lot of urban clothes. I grabbed a few pairs of denim-washed jeans and collared shirts. When I turned around she was behind me looking through a clothes rack. I towered over her, more than a foot. She looked at me again then rolled her eyes at me.

"Are you following me?" I asked her.

"No, I'm not following you. Perhaps you are following me. If so then I suggest you to cut it out," she said. Her scent filled my nostrils, her scent was inviting. She growled at me low enough so only I could hear.

"That's very cute by the way," I said to her.

"And what do you mean by that?" she asked then cracked a smile.

"Your inner beast is beautiful," I whispered into her ear. Her scent rose something in me that had been dormant for years. I felt my erection press against my jeans. I stepped back from her as a low growl escaped my throat.

"Are you hitting on me?" she asked.

"Naw, your beast isn't appealing. I call all females beautiful. It's a respect thing. But we need to talk because I have some questions to ask you. I couldn't formally introduce myself the other night. I want to know how you know Camille?" I asked. When Kofi and I went to Camille's funeral, we stayed outside of the church. I watched her burial a few feet away. I thought it was a ceremony just for her family. I didn't feel comfortable being around her husband's family, either. Her family didn't know me and I wanted to avoid questions.

"She saved my life years ago. We have been friends since then. What she saved me from is none of your business, just know that she was the only human I held close to my heart," she answered.

My eyes roamed her breasts but I didn't mean for them to. I tried not to look at a woman's body without looking into her eyes. Kofi told me that a woman's body is like the finest gem. He said that the gem value is worth more than meets the eye.

I cleared my throat. "Have a nice day, beautiful," I said to her then walked away. She stood in the same spot as she stared at me.

After I paid for my items, I headed out of the mall and back to my car. When I turned around she was standing on the sidewalk in front of the entrance to the mall. She had two small bags in her hand as she flagged down a cab but it kept going. I put my bags in my trunk then walked over to her.

"You need a ride?" I asked her.

"No, thank you, I don't deal with strangers. I still don't know you like that," she said.

"Your beast can handle her own," I said then she smiled.

"Charming," she answered.

"What's your name?" I asked her.

"Fabia," she answered then her stomach growled.

"Do you want to walk to the restaurant around the corner?" I asked her.

"I don't know if that will be a good idea," she said.

"Don't worry, beautiful, if I bite, you can bite me back," I said to her then she blushed.

"You are so different from the others," she stated.

"How so?" I asked her.

"The male wolves that I have run into are very aggressive but you are different. I hope you don't think that I'm being nice. I can somewhat see why Camille was taken by you," she said smartly. I chuckled because Fabia wasn't as mean as she appeared to be; I could tell she didn't trust others much.

"I'm from ancient Egyptian roots. Our kind is a little bit different," I explained.

"Maybe some other time, Elle. I have to get going," she said. A cab pulled over then she got in. "Meet me here in two days at four," she said then closed the door. I waved her off then headed toward my car.

******

When I walked into the house, Dayo was in an uproar. Between him, Izra and Goon that was normal. Dayo punched the wall. "Calm down, bro!" Amadi said to him. Dayo pushed Amadi away from him.

"What is going on?" I asked as I sat my shopping bags down.

"That bitch left me and took Arya with her. I thought maybe she took Arya to school then went to work. But when I went to get dressed, I noticed some of her shit that was in the closet was missing. I checked Arya's things and some of her shit was missing, too. I'm going to bite her fucking face off. I mated with her then gave her pups and she left me. I think this was a set-up," he said then punched the wall again. His body shifted into his beast and his beast howled. Amadi and I took a step back away from Dayo as he ran down the hallway then jumped through the window.

"He is hurting, bro. Arya meant a lot to him. To all of us," Amadi said. Goon walked into the house.

"What's up?" he asked with the pups in their carriers.

"Anik left Dayo and took Arya with her," Amadi answered.

"WHAT!" Goon shouted which caused the twins to cry.

"Maybe she is coming back," I said.

"She is hiding something and didn't want us to know. I bet it involves that other pack that attacked her. She could've left Arya here," Goon fussed. I took the twins from him. "I'm going to go find Arya. Anik can stay where ever her dumb ass is! If that pack is after her then that means Arya is in trouble," Goon said then walked back out of the house.

"I'm going to go and look for them, too. When Jalesa comes downstairs tell her that our date is cancelled. She doesn't know about Anik being missing yet, so tell her for me," Amadi said then shifted. His large beast ran out the door behind Goon.

****

A few days had passed and there was no sign of Anik or Arya. Kanya located the van and it was at a tow truck yard. The window was busted out with specs of blood on the back seat.

"Can't you locate them?" I asked Goon as we all sat in the kitchen thinking and drinking. Izra and Dayo were smoking weed. Dayo passed the blunt to me but I declined.

"I can only locate Kanya because she and I are mated. I can't see visions of Anik or Arya. I can feel that they are alive but that's it," he said.

"Ask your mother," Kanya said to Goon.

"No, I'm not asking her anything. This is my damn pack and it's my responsibility. This is not Naobi's concern and I will not make it. Besides, they aren't of Egyptian roots. She doesn't have a connection to them," he answered then took a shot of Henny.

Jalesa and Adika appeared at the table. "Welcome back, Jalesa, but I wish you would have left Adika where she was at," Izra said then growled at Adika.

"Go to hell, punk!" Adika shouted at Izra.

"I'm in hell as long as you are in my presence," Izra said.

"Y'all need to shut the fuck up!" Dayo said to Izra and Adika.

"Wait a minute, nigga, you can't talk to her like that," Izra said standing up. Dayo growled at Izra.

"Just stop it! Anik is out and possibly in danger while pregnant along with a child. We have to do something about it like figuring out who those wolves are and what they want. I know Anik, and she wouldn't do this to hurt anyone. She did it because she thought we wouldn't accept her," Kanya said.

"It doesn't matter what her simple ass thought, Kanya. I mated with her and if she wanted to leave she should've done it as soon as Goon healed her. She's being a bitch about the situation and when I catch her, you know what I'm going to do? Stick my foot up her ass. She took my damn pups away from me and possibly put them in danger," Dayo spat.

The sound of glass shattering startled us then we all ran to the living room. In the middle of the floor laid Arya with a broken arm. Shards of glass were embedded in her body, which caused Kanya to scream. Dayo hurriedly ran to cover her small, naked body up.

"It hurts," Arya cried. I hurriedly ran to get some wet towels. Her scream pierced my ears when Goon healed her. Everyone surrounded Arya as she cried. Her wounds weren't too bad but it was enough for a wolf her age.

"Who did this to you?" Goon asked her after she was completely healed.

"I was hit by a car on my way back home. I was lost in the woods for a few days. When I leaped out of the van, Anik called after me, but I kept running. I should've went back to her but I feel safe here," Arya cried.

"Who is after y'all?" Dayo asked.

"My father and his name is Sosa. Anik told me that he was the one that attacked her and that's why she left. She didn't want to bring harm to the pack," Arya replied. Adika and Izra looked at each other suspiciously.

"Where does he live?" Dayo asked.

"I don't know. I was never to leave the house and Anik wasn't allowed far from the house. She knows where he lives," Arya answered.

"I thought he was dead," Jalesa said.

"He is dead to us," Arya responded. Everyone followed Dayo as he carried Arya upstairs to her room.

"Izra," I called out.

"What's up, bro?" he asked me.

"If you know something you will tell the pack right?" I asked.

"Yeah, why you ask me that?" he lied.

"Are you lying to me, bro?" I asked him.

"Naw," he answered then walked off. When I turned around Adika was standing behind me.

"Is everything okay?" she asked me.

"I hope so," I said then walked up the stairs. When I looked at the clock, I noticed that it was past four in the afternoon. I missed my date with Fabia but I had a feeling it wasn't the last of her.

****

I noticed something was off about Izra and Adika. They seemed quiet and to themselves. I'd been around the pack long enough to know when one was lying. Izra was hiding something and I wanted to know what it was. When he left the house, I followed him. I covered myself in a lot of cologne and Amadi's oil to fade out my sent. If I hadn't, Izra would've known that I was following him. His motorcycle weaved in and out of traffic. My car wasn't as fast but I managed to keep up with him. Whatever was on his mind must have taken him off focus because several times he almost hit another vehicle. I followed him for about twenty minutes until he pulled up to a building. Seconds later a woman ran out of the building then hugged Irza. He got off his bike then picked her up. She kissed his lips.

"What the hell! Wolves don't step outside of their mate!" I said out loud. Well, at least that's what I thought. Something strange was going on because Kofi taught us to love our mate. We were taught to never desire another female and at the point I was confused about our tradition.

That's probably why Adika and Izra aren't getting along. He is having an affair, I thought to myself but there was more to it. I saw the interaction between them when they mentioned Sosa. Goon usually picked up on those things but he was focused on Arya at the time.

Izra openly grabbed the female's bottom then she blushed. He gave her his helmet then she hopped on his bike. He pulled off then I followed them. I stayed a few cars behind until I noticed I wasn't the only one following them. The car sped up on their tail, almost cutting them off. Izra took a back road because he noticed he was being followed. I sped up to get a better look and almost crashed when I noticed it was Fabia following them. Izra popped a wheelie on his bike then the female leaped off his bike turning into a wolf, which took me by surprise. Izra drove his bike into the woods then the car pulled on the side of the road. Fabia jumped out in her beast form and I followed. I ran into the woods then burst out of my clothes, turning into my beast. I ran until I heard growling.

Izra was in beast form as he tried to pull Fabia's beast off the other beast. Fabia's beast tore and clawed at the other beast then slammed her into a tree. Izra's female friend bit Fabia's face, which caused her to howl out. I pulled Fabia off the other beast, then laid my large beast on top of hers until she shifted back. When she came to she screamed and cursed. "I'm going to kill that bitch when I get to her! She and that devil she works with ruined my life," she screamed. I shifted back then pulled her away as she kicked and screamed. Izra's female yelled back at Fabia.

"You have been stalking me! I know that you've been watching the building where I stay," she screamed. Izra shifted back then looked at me.

"What are you doing, Elle?" he asked me.

"We will talk about that later," I said with my arms around Fabia. Izra growled at me.

"No, nigga, let's talk now! Why were you and that bitch following us?" he asked me then I growled at him.

"Watch your mouth, bro!" I said to him then his eyes turned. He wasn't the same Izra and I couldn't put my finger on it. Something was going on with him and I needed to figure it out and fast.

"Why were y'all following me, and why did she attack my female?" he asked. The female he was holding on to smiled and I knew she was up to something. She was no good for Izra and I didn't understand what he was doing with her.

"I was following her to kill her! You don't know what she is capable of. She is a conniving bitch and I trusted her! She lured me into a sex slave ring where these humans had their way with me. She is a scam and she isn't shit but a whore!" Fabia screamed then Izra growled.

"Elle, I don't know what that bitch you got over there is talking about, but she doesn't know shit! Onya is not the type to do something like that," Izra fussed.

"Bro, what happened to you? You have never been this naïve or one to fall for someone so easily," I said to him.

"Let's go, Izra!" Onya called out to him then he followed her. I was ready to charge into him but Fabia pulled me back.

"No matter what you say or do, he won't believe you. Onya is a manipulator and was trained to manipulate a male's mind. She puts on an innocent role and will have you feeling sorry for her. She is Sosa's head female and she is just as evil as him, if not more. I bet your friend Izra thinks Onya is a virgin and she isn't. She's got pups scattered all around," Fabia said as she walked back to her vehicle. I followed her as cars honked at us as we stood on the side of the road. I realized that she and I were still naked; we ruined our clothes when we shifted. Fabia popped the trunk open to her car then hurriedly got dressed. She gave me a pair of sweatpants.

"Seriously, I can't fit that," I said to her. She tore the pants apart with her sharp teeth.

"Wear them like panties," she said. She had bite marks on her arm and neck. The wound on her neck bled profusely and I started to worry about the amount of blood she was losing.

“I need to look at that. How long does it take for you to heal?” I asked her.

“A few weeks, depending on how bad it is.” She winced as the blood started to run down her neck. Her adrenaline was going down and I could see the look on her face as her body started to get weak.

“Elle, I don’t feel so good,” she said then fell into me. I hurriedly rushed her to my car then sped off.

****

Dayo, Amadi, Goon and Kofi all stared at Fabia as she slept in the guest room. Goon was beyond angry when I brought Fabia to the house.

“You just found a stray animal on the side of the road and decided you wanted to bring her home? Like seriously, what the hell is going on, Elle? I think you’ve lost your mind since Camille checked out,” Dayo said still angry behind Anik’s disappearance.

“She is a friend of Camille’s,” Kofi said.

“Elle’s smashing friends now? And what was Camille doing being friends with a wolf?” Dayo asked then Amadi growled at him.

“Shut up, Dayo! You talk too fucking much,” Goon said to him.

“So you mean to tell me it’s okay to just bring a stray home? What if she got rabies or what if she turns into Kojo and starts fucking shit up?” he asked Goon.

“She is one of us,” Amadi said.

“She is a wolf, but what kind of wolf is she? She doesn’t have markings on her like Anik, and she isn’t an Egyptian wolf, so who is she?” Dayo asked and I didn’t answer. I didn’t know what tribe Fabia came from. I barely knew her but I knew she knew something that we didn’t regarding Sosa.

“All I know is that she knows Camille and she knows Sosa. She also knows the wolf Izra is creeping around on Adika with. The wolf he is creeping with is tied to Sosa. I was following Izra and Fabia was following the wolf that was with Izra. We ended up in the woods on the side of the road. She and Izra’s female were fighting. Something is wrong with Izra. His eyes aren’t the same. It’s almost like he is cursed or something. Has anyone noticed how weird and off he has been acting? He doesn’t think the same, and his mind is all over the place,” I said.

“I figured that out but I thought it was because he lost his pup. There’s too much going on and I’m about to just go out on a hunting spree. Ammon is on Earth, Izra is acting weird and then you have this wolf Sosa that just came from out of nowhere. Izra is sleeping with a wolf that is connected to Sosa. Oh, and Anik is still missing. Everything is tied somehow because it doesn’t make sense for all of these events to be going on at the same time. I’m going to figure this shit out,” Goon said then left the room.

“I’m with Goon, too, bro, something is connected to all of this. It’s like one big puzzle with a lot of connecting pieces missing,” Amadi said then Kofi agreed.

"So, if Fabia knows this Sosa nigga then she knows where I can find him to kill him. What he and his pack did to my mate will forever be unforgettable," Dayo said.

"It sounds like this Sosa wolf has another agenda besides Anik. He wants something else and he is using that female that Izra is with to get it," Kofi said. We all agreed.

****

Fabia had been asleep for two days after I drugged her and gave her some herbs so that she could heal. Goon refused to heal her, which was understandable because he didn't know her. I barely knew her. I was in the kitchen drinking a pitcher of water when Adika walked in. She had bags around her eyes and dragged her feet when she walked. Maybe it was because of the news about Izra. She waited up all night for him and he never came home. She knew he was with another female.

"Is everything okay?" I asked Adika.

"My mate is with another wolf," she answered.

"Are you hiding something?" I asked her.

"Yeah she is, and she'd better get to talking," Goon spat when he came into the kitchen.

"Don't start no shit with me, Goon!" Adika screamed at him.

"Izra told me how much you wanted a pup and how you wanted him to mate with someone, but I brushed it off.

I knew he wouldn't do something like that. But that wolf he's with wouldn't be that wolf, now would she? Izra loves you very much and I can't see him just going off with another female. I know how conniving you witches can be. Now, what the fuck did you do to my lil' brother? He never ignores me when I enter his thoughts," Goon said.

"You're accusing me of something all because he didn't answer you?" Adika asked.

"What's going on? Why are you yelling at her like that?" Kanya asked in Adika's defense when she came into the kitchen.

"Kanya, I don't have time for your ways of thinking right now because your judgment is always off. Keora was coming around our pups as Adika and you swore up and down that I was trying to control your life. I kept warning you about it, and you still didn't believe me. I know she is your friend, but just stay out of the way when I'm trying to get to the bottom of shit. She knows what's going on with Izra and she'd better talk now. He didn't start acting different until she started pressuring him about a pup," Goon said.

We all looked at Adika then she broke down. "I cursed him," she said then burst into tears.

"Adika, why would you do that?" Kanya asked.

"He wasn't interested in Onya's scent. I wanted him to get her pregnant and he didn't want to. All I wanted was a pup, but it backfired. Not only did he pick up her scent, but he fell for her quickly. The last time he and I made love he was thinking about her. I heard his thoughts when he entered my body. He wished that I was her," Adika said.

"Okay, so undo the spell," Kanya said.

"She can't undo it. You cannot undo that type of spell; it has to run its course until the reason you casted the spell is completed. Izra will be brainwashed until he gets that wolf pregnant," Goon said.

"I got Onya from Sosa," Adika said then Kanya slapped her, slicing Adika's cheek.

Goon yanked Kanya back. "Cut that out!" Goon yelled. Kanya's eyes turned gold.

"Years of friendship is gone down the drain. From the moment I found out about you being a witch, everything is always happening around you. Your evil sister, and now it's you. You brought someone in our backyard. Elle just told us earlier that Onya is sided with Sosa. No wonder Anik ran away with Arya. Izra is falling in love with an enemy and there isn't shit we can do about it. Once he marks her, that's it, and it doesn't matter if the spell wears off. She will be carrying his pup and their connection will build. Izra is going to protect her and that just means that he will go against us. You turned my brother against us, Adika!" Kanya yelled at her.

"I will leave," Adika said then Goon's face softened up after Adika disappeared. I could tell that he felt sorry for her.

"We need to get to Izra and Anik before we figure out anything else. Anik is carrying pups and I'm sure Sosa found her. Nothing else matters to me until they return home," Kanya said then walked out of the kitchen.

“Once they return home, I’m putting a tall, iron gate up around the property. Every time someone leaves the house it’s some shit. This is starting to be too much,” Goon said feeling defeated.

I patted his back. “It’s time for us to step out of tradition, bro,” I said to him then he crossed his arms.

“What do you mean?” he asked then smirked.

“You already know,” I said then passed him the Henny bottle.

“I like the sound of that. Step out of tradition because that shit isn’t working for us. No more rules; we have to fight dirty. Enter every wolf territory in this town. Everything we are against, we will do. I bet they will know that we aren’t just some traditional muthafuckas. We have to think how everyone else thinks now. It doesn’t hurt to play tit for tat anymore. Sosa will come out, I bet. Thinking with tradition is starting to make us easy targets,” he said then passed me the bottle.

“What will Kofi think?” I asked Goon.

“Kofi is our father but he isn’t the Alpha. I am, and what I say goes. No more rules, Elle. If you fight a wolf and he surrenders, kill him anyway. This isn’t Anubi and we shouldn’t continue to live like it. Only the strongest survive on this planet and that’s the only rule,” he said then his eyes turned blue. He took another sip of his cognac.

“These muthafuckas about to see some wolves they have never seen before,” Goon said then growled.

****

“WHAP! GRRRRRRRRRR!” I was awake from my sleep. I fell asleep in the chair in the guest room where Fabia slept peacefully. I jumped up then growled, ready to shift, until I saw the frightened look on her face.

“Did you touch me? I heard other male voices in here? Did someone touch me while I was asleep?” she asked with tears in her eyes.

“No, I brought you back to my home to help you,” I said to her. She checked between her legs then sniffed her fingers. “What are you doing?” I asked her.

“Making sure a male didn’t leave his scent in me,” she said.

“We are not like that! You have to learn how to trust,” I said to her. She sat down on the end of the bed wrapped up in a sheet with tears falling from her eyes. “I’m so sorry, Elle. If Camille trusted you then so should I. My body has been used as a tool by too many males. I was a young wolf when I was separated from my mother. I was roaming the woods alone when Onya found me. She told me a man would help me find my mother but that same man killed my mother. He kept me in a cage underground in a tunnel with other young wolves. You don’t know what it’s like to be a sex slave to a human. They threw stuff at me and entered every hole in my body,” she said with tears falling from her eyes.

“Is that how you met Camille?” I asked her.

“I had enough one day. I saw an opportunity to escape and I did. Sosa had his pack attack me and do things to me no female wolf should ever endure. They left me for dead on the side of the road. I used every strength I had to stand up and flag someone down. I was so battered I couldn't even shift to my beast to ease my pain. Camille stopped for me and she was so loving. I hated humans because of what they stood for, but she was different. She said I had eyes like a beast and she told me she knew we existed. She put me in a hotel room and nursed me back to good health. After I healed she sent me to Africa where I'm really from. She said that she knew of a beast that was from there. Her and I kept in contact for years and I came back when she told me she was dying," she said then wiped her eyes.

"Sosa knows that you are here now," I said to her.

"He thought I was dead and you interfered with that. I was going to kill Onya but I'm sure she will tell Sosa that I am here," she said.

"How did you find Onya?" I asked her.

"I was in a cab the day I ran into you at the mall. The cab driver rode down the street she is staying on. I saw her walking into the building. I rented a car so that I could watch her. I have been watching her for a few days," she replied.

Arya burst into the room. "Jalesa told me you had a pretty lady friend in here. I want to meet her," she said.

"Get your grown ass out there Arya!" Dayo's voice boomed. Fabia stared at Arya and Arya stared back.

"Uncle Elle, why is your friend staring at me like that?" she asked then hid behind Dayo.

“That’s her,” Fabia said.

“Who?” I asked.

“That’s one of Onya’s pups. She looks just like her. She has her mother’s wolf scent,” she said.

“My real mother is dead and my other mother ran away with with Uncle Dayo’s pu—” was the last thing she said before Dayo tapped her mouth.

“What I tell you about that, Arya? Mind your business! Now go downstairs and clean the kitchen,” Dayo scolded her. He seemed bothered but I knew he was relieved that Arya returned home.

“Okay,” Arya said then walked out of the room. Dayo shut the door after she left the room.

“Where can we find Sosa?” I asked Fabia.

“I don’t know. He is very well hidden and he blends in with the humans. All he used to talk about was a club where humans and wolves could have sex freely. A club where humans could live out their fantasies as beast,” she said.

“You said you were kept in a tunnel, right?” I asked her then she shook her head. “I heard Dayo talk about a club like that in a tunnel. It looks like Sosa got his dream after all,” I said.

“Yes, he didn’t have the money for it then. But that was his next step. Sosa is very smart, I will say,” she said.

“What do you think he is using Onya for?” I asked her.

"To break up the pack after she has a pup. She will be his eyes inside the pack. Once she knows everything, she will report to him. His wolves will use that information and attack the pack. He will kill all males and older females and let the young females stay alive. Young females need a male's protection. The females will turn to him because they will become vulnerable. Sosa will use that then brainwash them. Once he does that, he owns you," Fabia said.

"That son-of-a-bitch must die!" I spat angrily.

"I hope his whole pack dies," she said.

"What kind of wolf are you? You almost look like Kanya's jackal but your face is shaped differently. Your structure is very unique and stunning," I said to her then she blushed.

"I'm of Ethiopian roots. My tribe back home are all golden wolves. We all look the same but the males have a white streak on their chest and they are bigger. But we all do look similar to the golden Jackal," she said.

"What do you want to eat?" I asked her.

"Raw meat, of course," she said.

"Would you like wine with that?" I asked her then stood up. Fabia smiled at me.

"What are you up to, Elle?" she asked me.

"We owe each other a date, remember?" I asked her.

“It wasn’t a date. Just two people having dinner at the same place,” she said.

“Two people are going to have dinner at the same place right now. Now, let me get going. I have to make a good expression on a lovely beast,” I replied then she blushed.

“You are not charming,” she said then smirked.

“Your beast thinks that I am. I can hear the low growls coming from the pit of your stomach,” I responded then walked out of the room. Fabia was interesting, very interesting, and my beast didn’t seem to mind.

Naobi

"I can't hear his thoughts anymore," I said to myself as I paced back and forth.

"Let me out so I can help you," Keora said to me.

"Shut up! Ammon is too quiet and that isn't good," I said to her.

"You need my help!" Keora said. I heard a bell ringing then I looked around.

"What is that noise?" I asked annoyed.

"The doorbell. Someone is here to see you," Keora said. I disappeared then reappeared by the door. I opened the door and it was Adika. She stood before me with a tear-stained face.

I opened the door then she walked in. She sat on the couch and I sat down across from her.

"What troubles you?" I asked her.

"I have a feeling you know," she said to me.

"I will once I look inside my globe but I promised Akua that I would let everyone live their lives. I haven't been watching to give you all privacy," I said to her.

"I did a terrible thing," she said with her head down.

"No, my child. You will hold your head up when you speak to your mother," I said to her. She wasn't my blood daughter but she and Keora are my creations. Keora disappointed me many of times but I still loved her.

"I cursed Izra and now he is falling in love with a wolf who disguised herself in sheep's clothing," she said.

"The wolf in sheep's clothing is you, my dear. You betrayed your mate. Now tell me why you casted a spell on him," I said to her.

"I wanted him to get a wolf pregnant so he and I could raise it. He agreed just to make me happy, so I paid a man who controlled women. The man that gave us his wolf is a man with a plan, and he is using the female to get closer to us. Izra wasn't into her scent, so I cast a spell with a string of her hair then mixed it inside his alcohol. I wanted him to mate with her but he fell out of love with me. I lost him and he also found out about Kofi and I," she said.

"So, what are you going to do?" I asked.

"I can't uncast the spell," she said.

"Will you love him the same if you never got the pup that you wanted?"

"Yes, I will still love him the same," she replied.

"So, you don't need a pup. What you can't have is not as important as what you do have," I said then stood up.

"What can I do? I haven't practiced a spell to get him to fall back in love with me," she said.

"Only wicked witches can cast a spell for love. It's considered cheating fate. We don't belong with someone who we aren't meant to be with. So you can practice all you want and you will never find one because your heart is not wicked. But, if you love him that much, a spell is not needed," I told her.

"He won't look at me," she said.

"Fight for him, Adika. You find him and you fight for him until you can't fight anymore," I said to her.

"His mind is blocked," she said.

"Follow me," I said then headed down to the basement.

****

"Aren't you going to speak to your sister?" Keora asked Adika.

"Go to hell," Adika fired back.

"I've been there already," Keora said.

"Cut it out," I said. I pulled out a small globe then chanted until Izra came up. Adika put her hand over her mouth as she watched him give oral pleasure to another wolf.

"Where is the popcorn?" Keora asked then Adika turned her into a tub of popcorn.

"I will fix her later," I said.

“He pleasures me that way. That sneaky bitch isn’t as innocent as she seems. She is screwing his face while his tongue is inside her. Virgin, my ass!” Adika screamed.

“Where is he?” she asked me.

“He is at a place called the Four Seasons. It’s a hotel, whatever that shall be,” I said to her.

“I know exactly where that is located. He and I spent many nights there when we wanted to have our privacy away from the pack,” she said. A feeling came over me then I placed my hand over Adika’s stomach.

“Are you carrying a pup?” I asked her then she burst into sobs.

“I just found out. Must’ve happened the last time he entered me. I can’t think about the pup because I know my powers will eventually suck the life out of it. I don’t have any attachment to it,” she said then disappeared. I turned Keora back to normal then she coughed popcorn out of her mouth.

“I hate being in this cage!” Keora screamed then the cage disappeared.

“You are free,” I said to her. She looked around then looked at me.

“At what cost?” she asked me.

“Your life,” I said to her.

“What? Adika will die too,” she said.

“Not death but your life. Do you know why witches can’t carry babies? The power stops its heart because it doesn’t turn immortal until the age of five. At five they become strong and notice their power. But if a witch is inside a womb as a witch then it will be strong enough to withstand the power inside the womb,” I said to her.

“What are you saying?” she asked me.

“I want you to be reincarnated through your sister’s womb. If you are as pure as you say you are then you will do it. If you are still selfish then you can be forever locked up. It’s your choice; your life for the life inside her womb,” I said to her.

“How will that work?” Keora asked.

“Let me work my magic. But just know that your memories will be gone and your looks will be gone. You can start off a new life but with Adika and Izra as your parents, of course,” I said to her.

“That’s a favor for me, but what shall I give you in return?” she asked me.

“I thought you’d never ask,” I replied.

****

“How was your day, beautiful?” Kumba asked me when he walked into the kitchen. He took off the thing he called a tie along with his suit jacket.

“It was interesting,” I replied then he kissed my lips.

"Have you heard from that punk, Ammon?" Kumba asked me with his eyes turning green.

"No, he has been quiet lately, which is different," I said to him.

"I still can't believe he pulled the shit that he did. He had a whole war going on in the woods behind my house. Damn, it pisses me off when I think about it. I could've killed him; I wanted to kill him," Kumba seethed. I floated up to reach his broad shoulders. I rubbed them then he relaxed. I took his mind to another place. Someplace far in a jungle with pretty waterfalls.

"This is nice. It must be wonderful to be in control of magic," he said as the tropical birds flew through the sky.

"It's a temporary escape even though we are still in our kitchen," I answered him.

"When are you going to come to the restaurant with me? I talk to my staff about you all the time and they want to meet you. What are you scared of?" he asked then turned around to face me.

"Will I do good interacting with humans? My English is still a little rocky. When I speak English, I don't even understand myself at times," I said then he chuckled.

"My lovely Naobi," he said then opened up my robe. I stared into his green eyes then slowly unbuttoned his shirt. I rubbed my hand across his muscled stomach with the black stripes etched across his skin.

"So beautiful," I said to him then he picked me up. He wrapped his strong arms around my waist then captured my left breast inside his wet and warm mouth. His tongue gently flickered across my swollen nipple.

"Kumba," I moaned his name then his teeth gently bit into the flesh around my nipple. I wrapped my legs around him as his mouth explored the upper half of my body. My wetness seeped through my slit onto his dress slacks.

"Your pussy smells so good," he said. He leaped through the waterfall with me still in his arms. It was a small-like cave behind the waterfall with pretty pink and yellow flowers growing out from it. He undid his belt then his pants. He stepped out of his pants then pulled me down onto the floor of the cave. My body trembled underneath his large frame as he kissed me. His hands groped my breasts as he sucked on them. He kissed down my stomach then he spread my legs. He opened my lips then stuck his tongue inside me. I cried out as my back arched from the ground. His tongue flickered across my pink pearl as his head thrashed around between my legs. My sex throbbed like a heartbeat, as warm liquid seeped out of me. Kumba latched on then sucked harder as my legs trembled.

"OOHHHHHHHHHHHHHH!" I moaned. He pinned my legs up until my knees touched my forehead. He hungrily licked the essence that drizzled down my rear end.

"Pretty fat pussy," he said. A tear slid out of the corner of my eye when Kumba stuck his tongue inside me. My muscles squeezed the tip of his tongue as I squirmed underneath him.

"Move your hips against my tongue. You will come harder," he said. I wasn't too familiar with the technique,

but I was learning. It was a different pleasure than what I was used to but I enjoyed it. I slowly moved my hips against Kumba's tongue like the Egyptians did back home when they danced. A hoarse cry escaped from my lips as the sensation grew stronger. I wanted to scream but I knew if I did, a bolt of lightning probably would've struck something. I moved against his tongue faster and harder as my legs began to tremble tremendously. My body jerked then everything started to spin. I chanted his name then lost my breath when his thick and long shaft entered me. I closed my eyes and let him take me away. He grinded into me then pulled out of me.

"Touch yourself," he said to me. I touched my arm and didn't know what the reason was for.

"Touch your pussy. Rub that pink, little pearl as I move in and out of you," he said. My hand slowly reached down between my legs to touch myself in a sexual way. I'd never touched myself that way before. Kumba lowered my hand further down between my legs.

"It's our pussy. Don't be afraid to touch it. I want you to touch it and pretend that it's me," he said. I touched then rubbed myself. Kumba started moving back inside me.

"It feels too good. I don't know what is ready to happen," I said to him.

"You are coming on my dick," he said then moaned. His large size stretched me open wider. He was so hard as he plunged in and out of me. With each thrust, my body bucked backward as loud sounds came from me. I sounded like an animal but I couldn't help it. Kumba was giving me magic. His teeth latched onto my breast then he grabbed a fist full of my hair. He hungrily licked and sucked on my

neck as he made animal-like grunts. He raised his body up then came back down inside me and a fluid gushed out of me. It reminded me of the very same waterfall that we laid behind. He bit my neck then squeezed my breast as he sped up, slamming his hard-on inside me, continuously causing my body to jerk then shiver.

"I'm about to make you come so fucking hard. Umph! PRRRRRRRRRRR! FUCK, NAOBI!" he shouted, going deeper inside me until he swelled up then pumped longer and harder, which caused water to fill my eyes. He was so deep it hurt, but my body convulsed from every stroke until a big wave came again then squirted out of me as I screamed. He collapsed on top of me. When our vision was over we laid sprawled out on the kitchen floor.

"I guess that's what you call stamina," I said then Kumba roared into laughter. He rolled off me then clutched his stomach as he laughed.

"What humored you?" I asked him then he kissed me.

"You said that in clear, damn English," he said then he looked at me with a serious expression.

"Where is Keora? She is too quiet and I know she isn't sleeping," Kumba said.

"She is taking care of something for me. It's time for me to sit back and watch the chips fall," I said to Kumba. He pulled me up then wrapped his arms around me. "You deserve it and I deserve you. I got you all to myself now," he said. Something ran down my inner leg. It was thick and white.

"Why is milk dripping out of me?" I asked Kumba then he smirked.

"You don't want to know what we call that on Earth," he said.

"What do you call it?" I asked then touched it. It felt thick and creamy.

"I think it's bad milk," I said then he shook his head.

"You've really got a lot to learn. That is the after math of the pleasure you gave me, also known as nut. That is how you got pregnant with your son," he said to me.

"I didn't know it comes back out," I said.

"Don't worry, beautiful. You let me worry about that and all you need to do is enjoy it," he said.

Izra

"Stop it, Izra!" Onya giggled as I ticked her stomach with her legs thrown over my shoulder. I playfully growled at her then bit her inner thigh. Onya's pussy glistened from the oral pleasure I gave her. I held my hard dick, dripping with pre-cum. Her scent had me ready to explode. All I wanted to do at that moment was thrust my dick so far into her, she howled. I wanted her beast to bite my neck as I thrust inside her. The urges were getting uncontrollable. Adika was no longer on my mind. Elle following me along with that other wolf wasn't on my mind, either. I blocked everyone out as my mind focused on one thing and that was mating with Onya. Her scent caused beads of sweat to form on my forehead. My teeth expanded from my gums then I howled inside the hotel room. I'd been with Onya at the hotel room for days. I knew Elle was going to tell the pack where he found me. I didn't want to be bothered. I had a feeling they went to Adika's apartment for me.

"Izra, I have to tell you something. It's really important. It's about what Fabia said," she said but I wasn't trying to hear it. I flipped her over then dug my nails into her bottom as I spread her cheeks. I nuzzled my nose into her pussy then hungrily licked between her lips again.

"Ohhhhh, Izra!" she screamed. I slapped her on the bottom then pushed her head further down on the mattress. My adrenaline started pumping as I slowly entered her. Her pussy sucked me in then I howled as I dug my nails further into her cheeks. Even if I wanted to pull out I couldn't.

Onya growled then wailed as I slammed myself all the way into her.

"AWWWWWWWW! FUCK!" I howled out when she and I were struck by some type of lightning. Onya's head went crashing into the headboard. I went sailing onto the floor as the painful shocks traveled through my body.

I heard purring and I knew that noise from anywhere. Adika stepped out of the dark corner in mid-shift. Her yellow cat eyes looked at me and black hairs covered her body. Onya tried to get up but Adika slammed her into the wall again.

"How did you find me?" I asked Adika. I tried to get up but I flew up against the ceiling and was stuck. Long vines with thorns grew up the wall, causing it to crack. The vines wrapped around me and thorns pricked into my skin. I tried to shift but I couldn't.

"Did I ruin your romantic evening?" Adika asked then picked up the champagne bottle out of the ice bucket.

"Moet? Very classic, Izra. How does it feel to stick your dick inside a loose wolf? She's supposed to be a virgin and you just slid right in," she said. Adika used a force again to slam Onya into the wall for the third time. Onya's head started to bleed. A lamp went sailing at Onya, but she moved.

"Let me down, Adika! I don't have time to be playing Carrie with your evil ass!" I seethed. I wanted to rip her throat apart.

"This is all of my fault and I'm here to fix it," Adika said to me.

"Fix what? You and I are done. Where is Kofi? Go fuck with him and leave us alone. I swear when you let me down I'm going to bite your fucking face off!" I yelled at her then she laughed.

"Yes, daddy, bite me!" she said then slapped her ass.

"Crazy damn female. I swear I'm not sticking my dick into another cat," I said as another thorn entered my neck.

"Leave him alone," Onya said then stood up.

"We know all about you and Sosa! We know everything and I bet you thought Izra was really falling for you. But let me let you in on a secret. I cursed him so that he could find your scent appealing. He didn't like your scent at first but I was desperate for a pup," Adika said.

"YOUR SMALL BRAIN, OLD ASS DID WHAT?" I yelled at her and she jumped.

"Not now, Izra. We'll talk about this when we get home," she answered.

"You'd better cast a spell or whatever it is that you do. That's the only way you will get me to go home with you. I told you at first I didn't like the bitch and you did this to me. Onya, stand back and away from her. She is crazy as hell. Adika, let me go!" I yelled at her. The vines disappeared then I fell to the floor.

Adika looked at me with an intense look on her face. I knew I hurt her, but I just couldn't be involved with her anymore. The spark was gone.

"I love you and I'm not giving up," she said to me.

"Bitch, you heard him, now leave!" Onya said to Adika.

"Both of y'all, just shut the hell up. Onya, if I were you I would just chill out. Out of all my years I have never seen a beast that wasn't aggressive. I mean, you seriously fight like a toy dog. That cat right there will fuck you up. I'm only telling you this because I care about you," I said to her. Onya backed away then Adika hissed at her.

"Oh, shit!" I said when Adika shifted into her large cat. She charged into Onya but Onya was already in beast form. They collided into each other then knocked over the nightstand and lamp. Growling and hissing filled the room. Onya's fur flew everywhere as Adika clawed and bit her. Adika's cat was faster and more aggressive than Onya's wolf. I shifted into my beast then charged into them. I tried to pull them apart but Adika scratched my face. I growled at her then she hissed at me. She backed up into the corner with her back humped up and her long, black tail puffed out. Her sharp, white teeth sparkled then her eyes started to glow. She lifted up her paw then came down onto Onya's face. Onya's wolf whimpered in pain as blood dripped onto the white carpet.

I shifted back to human form. "Stop this shit now before I owe the hotel more money," I shouted. Onya's beast burst through the door then tipped over the cleaning lady's cart. The humans in the hallway screamed as a big wolf being chased by a large, exotic cat ran down the hallway. I shifted then ran after them. Onya burst through the door to the stairwell. Adika's cat leaped down the flight of stairs onto Onya's back. Onya howled as Adika bit her. Adika's tail wrapped around Onya's neck then slammed her wolf into the wall. A few hotel workers came down the stairs then screamed when they saw our beasts. I collided into them to break them apart.

"There are no pets allowed in this hotel!" someone shouted.

"Those aren't pets! You see how big those damn animals are? Someone in this hotel is into animal smuggling. Those are wild animals!" someone shouted as they ran past us. Onya got away from Adika then ran into the dining area. There looked to have been a special occasion for the humans. Adika jumped on the table then everyone screamed as they ran out of the dining room. Onya burst out of a window. Adika and I landed on the sidewalk following Onya. When I looked around, Onya was gone then Adika and I disappeared. When we reappeared we were in a different place, we were at Adika's apartment. I shifted back to my human form then stared at her. Tears ran down her face as she stood in front of me naked.

"Muthafucka!" she screamed then slapped me as hard as she could. She tried to hit me again but I caught her by her neck. I lifted her up then growled at her as her feet dangled off the floor.

"You did this shit to me! I'm not a fucking lab rat! How are you going to practice spells and shit on me? I was your mate!" I yelled at her then dropped her onto the couch.

"I didn't think it was going to be like this," she said.

"Well, it is because I don't feel shit for you even when I try to. You are full of surprises; you know that? I had to find out about you and Kofi, and now this spell shit.

Suppose what you are saying about Onya is true. I was eating an enemy's pussy and I stuck my dick in her. I betrayed my fucking pack, Adika!" I said to her.

"Stop yelling at me! I know what I did and I'm going to fix it. All I want is for you to dig deep down into your heart and forgive me. I'm willing to wait until you do if you can't right now. I know how stubborn you are but I'm not giving up, Izra. Kofi was before your time in another life. A life where we lived on Egypt's land. I can't remember his touch or what he even feels like. I want my eternity with you. I don't care about having a pup. All I want is you," she said. I sat down next to her then she laid her head on my shoulder. "I'm so sorry," she said.

"What are we going to do, Adika?" I asked her.

"You stay away from Onya," she said then went into her bedroom. She came back out with shopping bags. "You took her shopping, too?" she asked throwing the bags at me.

"She didn't have nothing here and your shit is a little too big for her," I said to her. She crossed her arms.

"What are you trying to tell me, Izra?" she asked me.

"Nothing, Adika, damn. How mad is the pack at me before I return home?"

"You are staying here until we work us out. I don't you want you running into Onya," Adika said to me.

"I don't know my mama but I for damn sure know your old ass isn't her. I'm not staying here," I said to her. She stood up.

"You can't get out unless you are a warlock and got some type of magic going on," she said to me. I opened up her apartment door and there was a brick wall in front of it.

"No, Adika! Hell no!" I said. I opened up all the windows and all of them were blocked.

"How am I going to hunt or make my jewelry? Kanya put an order in for more bracelets by the end of the month," I said then she snapped her fingers. In front of me on the table was all of my supplies to make my jewelry and a tray of raw meat.

"That meat isn't USDA approved," I said to her then she giggled.

"That shit ain't funny," I said to her then cracked a smile. She picked the meat up then stuffed it inside her mouth.

"So, you don't have to hunt for meat? Why were you hunting with Kofi then?" I asked her.

"I hunt with the rest of your pack brothers. Why does it matter with Kofi? He is a mated male and he doesn't think about anyone else but Opal. I can't believe you are accusing me of something. You don't miss me?" she asked me. She was touching my heart all over again. I never stopped loving Adika; it was the trust that drove me away. The spark was gone but I still loved her.

"I don't know," I answered then grabbed a piece of meat. Adika's stomach started to growl even after she ate half the tray meat. I looked at her then she stood up but I grabbed her hand.

"Why does your stomach sound like that? I know you aren't hungry because you almost ate a whole tray of meat," I said to her.

"Maybe I was just hungry. I'm getting tired so are you ready for bed? I hope you take a shower and wash her nasty scent off you," she said to me then I growled at her. I got up then headed to the bathroom to shower. After my shower I dried off then headed to Adika's bedroom. She changed the bed and the rest of her room.

"I saw you give her pleasure with your mouth on my bed through a vision," Adika said, which angered me.

"You brought her here and you wanted me to give her pleasure. How else was I going to get her pregnant? You think a wolf just smells a scent and not crave it? I couldn't help that I wanted to taste her and it's your fault. I don't want to think about it anymore. You made a fool out of me," I told her.

"You want to vent then let's vent. I've been fighting hard for you and you don't see that! Everyone is saying it's my fault. I know it is but look at the bigger picture! I did all of this for you! I wasn't thinking about nothing else but making you happy. I wanted a baby but I wanted to feel connected to you even more. I was desperate for a stronger bond with you, but don't think I haven't noticed how you changed after you realized I couldn't carry your pups. I wanted to be normal. I always wanted to be normal but there is nothing normal about me. I have been with many males throughout my life but NONE of them made me feel the way you do," she said to me. I felt something fall from my eye and it was a tear again.

"What are you doing to me, Adika?" I asked her.

"I'm expressing what real love is and the dumb shit we do because of it. I made a horrible mistake and I need you with me. I won't bring up pup talk anymore. I'm complete with just you and I," she said then hugged me. I wrapped my arms around her waist then squeezed her as hard as I could.

Anik

"I'm not going to your party!" I screamed at Sosa. It had been over a week since I'd left Dayo and the rest of the pack. Every day Sosa made me regret it more and more. My stomach was a little bigger than before but not too much. My appetite was uncontrollable, and at times I found myself being nice to Sosa just so he could feed me more.

He grabbed me around my neck. "You will do what I say before I make you starve. Wear this pretty dress and comb your hair. You look like a wolf," he said then walked out of the room.

"I am one, asshole, and you are, too!" I yelled behind him after he slammed the bedroom door. I was trapped inside the house because there were wolves roaming around his property. They were ordered to attack me and kill me if I left the house. Sosa had more of a wicked heart than Ula. I grabbed the dress then held it up to me in the mirror. I wasn't even sure I could fit it.

"Pretty dress," a voice said from behind me. When I turned around it was Ula dressed in an all-black gown that clung to her curves. Her make-up was beautiful and her hair was styled in big, loose curls that fell down her shoulders.

"No snakes?" I asked her. One slithered across the floor then up my leg with red, glowing eyes. I smacked it off then it disappeared.

"Watch it, darling, before you get on my bad side. I find you quite interesting," she said to me.

"Sad I can't say the same about you," I said to her then she walked around me. She eyed my body then smirked.

"The male you mated with must be very strong, like one of those warriors with nice muscles and strong shoulders. I bet he is very tall and beautiful. A strong male makes his woman's body more profound after he marks her," she said to me.

"He is very strong and I miss him. Why are you friends with Sosa? You don't have to be this way," I said to her then she smiled.

"You really do see the good in everyone, don't you? But that's in your nature, of course," she said. She waved her hand in front of me and a black, beautiful dress covered my body. Around my stomach area the extra material sagged down. My hair was pinned up in a bun and diamond earrings draped from my ears.

"Beautiful," she said. I didn't understand Ula. She was wicked but it didn't show unless someone pissed her off.

"Thank you," I said then she looked at me.

"Why are you being nice to me, Anik? I'm wicked with a black heart," she said.

"You are not fooling me. I fear Sosa before I will fear you, and you are more powerful than him. Without you he wouldn't have all of this, but for some reason his heart is blacker than yours," I said to Ula.

"Don't try to figure me out. What you need to do is be on good behavior so that Sosa can stop his rants," she replied.

"You had your heart broken before," I said to her.
"You can't break what's not there. My father created me to be his messenger and that's it," she told me.

"Your father isn't here. You can change the purpose of your life," I replied.

"Close your eyes. I want to show you something, and after I show you, we will never speak on it again," she said to me.

"What are you going to do to me?" I asked.

"Chile, I can turn you into a heap of dust in just zero-point-five seconds and that's with your eyes opened. Close your eyes and just look at what I'm about to show you," she spat. I sat down on the bed then closed my eyes…

I walked into a barn where the light from inside shined underneath the old, wooden barn door. I opened up the door then walked inside. Ula was dressed in a long, white lace dress with a flower behind her head. She danced as her sweet voice carried a melody.

"Come on, get up! Dance with me!" she said happily. I didn't see who she was talking to until she pulled him up. I stood in shock as Amadi gazed into her eyes.

"Your father will hear us," Amadi said.

"They are not my real parents. They found me in the woods where my father left me. I don't care what they think. Let's runaway together," Ula said to Amadi.

"I can't leave my brothers," he said then moved the thick, kinky hair back that fell down into her face.

"Come on, Amadi. I love you and you love me. Let's just go away and forget this place. You see what they do to Black folks here," she said.

"I don't fear any man," he said then picked her up. He spun her around then she giggled freely. Tears filled my eyes at how innocent Ula was. Amadi and Ula fell into the hay then he stared into her eyes before he kissed her. A growl escaped his throat as his hand slid up her thigh then he pulled it back.

"I want you, too," Ula said to Amadi.

"I haven't done it before," Amadi said then sat up. Ula pulled him back down.

"Neither have I, but it can be our first," she said then took off her dress. She pulled her white panties down then stood before Amadi naked. He nervously undressed himself. After he was naked, she looked at his hard-on then gasped. He looked down embarrassed because it hung down his leg.

"I might hurt you, Ula," he said to her.

"It doesn't matter. I want you to be my first," she said to him.

"You don't know what I am," he responded.

"And you don't know what I am, but we love each other and nothing else matters," she said. He lay her down then kissed her passionately. She moaned as he sucked on her neck. A louder growl escaped from Amadi. He slowly eased himself into Ula then she tensed up.

"I've got to stop," Amadi said.

"No," Ula said then wrapped her arms around him. I saw the look in her eyes as he worked himself into her. She was in pain but she gave it up to him because she loved him. A tear slid out her eye when he went further in, taking her virginity. A scent of fresh blood permeated the air because he broke her hymen. Amadi started to speed up as he started to shift inside her.

"NO, AMADI!" I yelled out. His nails grew out, cutting her skin. He pumped in and out of her, he couldn't control it. His beast wouldn't allow him to. Ula cried, "Amadi, it hurts! Stop, it hurts!" Ula screamed but he didn't stop. Ula cried in pain then I ran toward them but they seemed far away.

"Stop it, Amadi!" I yelled but he didn't. His teeth expanded then he bit Ula's neck. Blood squirted into her face as she gasped for air. I screamed and cried because Amadi's beast tore into Ula's neck. Moments later, he pulled out of her then looked down at her. Tears fell from his eyes as she reached out to him.

"I'm okay," she choked out then coughed up blood, but Amadi didn't hear her. Ula's blood saturated the hay underneath her. She closed her eyes seconds later then Amadi picked her up. He wrapped her up in her dress then stormed out of the barn. I followed him into the woods. He used his sharp nails to dig a hole.

"She is not dead! Stop it! She is not dead!" I yelled into his face but he couldn't hear me. Once the hole was big enough he laid Ula in it then covered her body up with dirt. Ula's father called out to her then Amadi shifted. He climbed up a tree then disappeared into the night. I tried to dig Ula up but my hands went through the soil as if I was a ghost. I sat down by the tree and cried.

"I will stay with you," I said to her.

"Open your eyes, Anik," she said bringing me out of my dream. My face was drenched with tears.

"I'm so sorry," I said to her. A black tear escaped her eye then disappeared.

"I haunt him every chance I get. For days I waited by the hole he buried me in. Those days turned into years. I wanted to see if he would come back but he didn't. He left me to rot in the ground. I could've killed him then but I'd rather watch him suffer. Do you see why I'm so mad? I forgot about what Saka wanted me to do when I met Amadi at a fair. I was in love and it warmed my heart to the pits of my soul. I forgot all about spells when I was with him. I was free from everything, but that night proved to me that you can't lose focus. It showed me that I have one purpose and that is to fill Saka's request. He saw a vision years and years ago of Naobi coming to Earth to stay. I have been waiting for her and now she is here," Ula said.

"You are helping Sosa sell females," I said to her.

"Sosa has been doing that before I met him. I have no concern for weak women. Those females let Sosa ruin their families then turn around to work for him. Why should I care about that? All I do with Sosa is keep track of his money and invest in properties for him. What Sosa does on the side is not my concern. But you are different, Anik, very different from the rest. Unlike them you see the real beast that he is. The other females look up to him like he is god until he puts a price on their pussy and then they want someone to pity them. I have no respect for women like that. If someone can brainwash you then your life is pitiful in the first place. But you are what draws me here. Be patient, chile, it will all come to an end," Ula said but I didn't understand what she meant by that. We were interrupted by a big boom and glass shattering. Ula disappeared then I opened the door. I looked down the hall and prayed that Dayo found me. A naked woman walked down the hall with scratch marks all over her.

Sosa followed her. "What are you doing back so soon?" he asked the woman.

"Fabia is alive and she blew my fucking cover. It's over now! They know everything, I'm sure. Izra's mate came to him and told him everything then she attacked me. A fucking cat attacked me!" she screamed.

"What did you do? WHAT DID YOU DO?" I asked then charged into the woman. I knew the cat was Adika she was talking about. Sosa grabbed me.

"You stay out of this!" he yelled at me then grabbed me by my neck.

"Nice to see you back home, Anik. I know a lot about you but you know nothing of me. I appreciate the care you have been giving my pup, Arya," she said then smiled. I hulked up a clog in my throat then spit in her face.

“Shame on you! Shame on you!” I yelled at her.

“You are going to hurt my pups,” Sosa said to me.

“You all are sick! I hope you two get ripped into tiny bits of pieces. I’m going to take those pieces and burn them. A bunch of scammers, liars, manipulators and murderers,” I screamed as Sosa dragged me down the hall.

“We have a limo that will be here shortly. Get yourself together before I tie you to a tree in my backyard,” he said to me.

****

“Hold your fucking head up and greet the people,” Sosa whispered in my ear. I was at an event with both werewolves and humans.

“I have over twenty wolves inside here who are at my beck and call. If you go near a door they have the authority to attack you,” he said to me. He even went as far as blindfolding me to make sure I didn’t know where I was going in case I escaped. I knew I couldn’t be lost while carrying pups. I wouldn’t be able to hunt. I would’ve been stranded and starved.

“You are a piece of shit,” I whispered to him. He was ready to respond until a White man walked toward us.

“Lovely evening, isn’t it? And who might this be?” he asked lustfully staring at my swollen breasts. My nipples were pressed against my dress but I couldn’t help it due to my pregnancy.

"Don, this is my wife Anik. Anik, this is Don; he is one of my partners. Don, I suggest you keep your eyes off of her or else I will slice your wife's pale and plastic face open," Sosa spat with his eyes changing. The man held up his hands.

"Whoa now, buddy. I didn't know you had a wife," he said.

"Onya has returned. I will send her to your cabin tonight," Sosa said to Don. Don smiled then patted Sosa's shoulder.

"She is my favorite," he said then walked away. I looked at Sosa then growled.

"Shut up. You should be lucky that I don't give you away," he spat.

Ula walked through the crowd with her long dress dragging the floor. A lot of the men gawked at her but she kept walking, ignoring everyone that talked to her. Sosa lustfully growled at the sight of her.

"Why don't you try to pursue her? And let me go home," I said to him.

"I lust her, there's a difference. In some strange way it's you that I want," he said.

"You are a filthy dog," I said then he roared with laughter. I wanted to take a chunk out of his face.

"Tonight when we get home you will dress in your sexy lingerie. Tonight I shall get rid of that stench that pores out of your skin. You smell just like him," he said. My hands trembled because he was going to force himself on me.

"I'm carrying pups," I said to him.

"Orgasms are harmless," he said. A tear threatened to escape my eyes. "Hold it in, Anik. Smile at the guests and greet them. This is your new family now, so get used to it," he said to me. I walked around the ballroom smiling and waving like I'd won a beauty pageant. Sosa mingled right in with the humans. He was laughing and smiling and even invited a few of them out to play golf. Sosa sickened me. At that moment I wished he was human because he would've been easy to kill.

****

"Your lace lingerie is on the bed. I expect you in my room in ten minutes," he slurred then grabbed my breast. He got drunk at the party and I could've made my move, but ten other wolves escorted me back to his house. After he walked out of my room I cried. I had to figure out something because I couldn't give myself to another male. After I got out of the shower, I got dressed in the lingerie he had out for me. I stood in the mirror by the bed and just stared at myself. I hated myself at that very moment. I thought staying with Dayo was betraying the pack but I realized leaving was the betrayal.

I walked out of my room then down the hall to the big wooden doors of Sosa's room. I pushed the door open then covered my mouth. Sosa had Ula sprawled out on the bed licking between her legs. Ula moaned loudly when Sosa pinned her legs up. His long tongue entered her then her legs trembled. She grabbed at his hair as he growled. Sounds of him slurping up her wetness echoed through the large apartment-sized room. Ula moaned as her body raised off the bed. Sosa undid his pants as he continued to eat between her legs. His pants dropped to his ankles. He ripped open his button-up dress shirt, revealing muscles all over his strong and broad back. His long and wild curly hair fell down his back. He picked Ula up off the bed then ripped her dress off her. She wrapped her legs around him then threw her head back when his teeth sank into her breast. I covered my mouth to keep from howling; I was more than aroused. Ula reached down to grab Sosa's dick, which dripped with pre-cum. He was long and hard, ready to burst. I could see the veins thicken in his dick. She slowly jerked him off as he licked and sucked on her breast.

"Awwwwwww, Sosa!" Ula screamed. Sosa growled and his ears grew upwards and pointy. His beast wanted to come out. Sosa's dick was pointed at the entrance of Ula's opening. She wrapped her legs tightly around him as he gently eased her down onto him. His hands palmed her ass harder as he pushed his full girth inside her. Sosa moved Ula up and down on his dick. Her essence dripped down his length like a water slide then down his testicles.

"Your pussy is so wet," he growled. He slammed her down until his dick disappeared inside her. A slight moan escaped my lips. Sosa's strong legs stood firmly as he held Ula up. He moved her up to the swollen tip of his dick then brought her back down. Her nails dug into his shoulders as he savagely pumped into her. Ula's scream pierced my ears and I knew what kind of scream that was; he swelled up inside her. Ula's lips quivered but Sosa didn't stop; he crouched down going further inside her. Ula's pussy gushed as she came then her body went limp. Sosa walked to the bed with her then laid her down on her stomach. He spread her cheeks apart and stared at her swollen vagina lips that were smeared with her gooey and thick substance. He nuzzled his nose into her then sniffed her. He growled as he jerked himself off. His tongue entered her from behind and Ula's body trembled.

"ARRGGHHHHHHHHHH!" she screamed as her body shook from another orgasm. Sosa smeared her wetness over her ass cheeks then spanked her. He gripped her hair, pulling her head back then bit her neck. I had an orgasm as I watched him roughly make love to her. He pulled her up then pressed her lower-back down into the doggy-style position. He held himself as he entered her again. He grabbed her hair then howled as he pumped into her. Ula's pussy gushed again as her legs shook and sweat beads dripped down her back. Sosa howled again as he continued to pump in and out of her. Each time he entered her, he gave her all of his size. Ula gripped the sheets and cried as he tore into her pussy like the beast he was.

"GRRRRRRRRRRRRRR!" he moaned then his body jerked. He came inside her then collapsed on top of her. I hurriedly went into my room then took a cold shower. I moaned from the times it felt like Dayo's dick ripped me apart. After I showered, I climbed into my bed. When I turned over, Ula was looking down at me then I jumped up. I almost fell on to the floor but a force yanked me back.

"How did you like the show?" she asked me but I said nothing.

"When this is all over just remember I cared a little bit," she said then disappeared. I lay in bed then it hit me. She only slept with Sosa so that I didn't have to. I was going to find a way back home. I couldn't deliver my pups in Sosa's care. I would rather die before he touched them.

Amadi

Jalesa snuggled underneath me as she slept peacefully. She thought she was pregnant and so did I. I was for certain I gave her a pup. Jalesa being pregnant would've stopped everything, but I wasn't sure of that anymore. It seemed as if Ammon had disappeared. I got up to use the bathroom.

"Can't sleep?" she asked me then I jumped.

"When will you go away?" I asked her then she laughed.

"I can't go away, handsome. It's your guilt that keeps me around you. When you are truly sorry, I can forgive you," she said to me.

"I am sorry! What more do you want me to do?" I asked her then she looked at me with sad eyes.

"Saying sorry isn't the same as being sorry. You say it but you don't mean it," she said to me. I closed my eyes.

"This is not real," I said to myself. When I opened my eyes, I was no longer in my bedroom. I was in the woods next to where I buried her. She walked around me wearing all black. Her skin was clear and she no longer looked dead. "What is this?" I asked her.

"Dig me up!" she said then tossed me a shovel.

"Don't make me do this," I said to her. The belt around her waist turned into a snake. Its red eyes glowed then it hissed at me.

"Dig me up and I will go away," she said. Her eyes turned black then she floated up in the air.

I picked up the shovel then started to dig. As the hole got bigger I realized I should have already come across her remains.

"They're not here," I said to her then a force sent me sailing into a tree.

"Do you know why I'm not there? I never died! I'm a witch, Amadi. I healed moments later after you buried me. I know what you are and I know you didn't mean to hurt me. But what I didn't know was that you were going to just let me rot! You never came back!" she yelled at me. I stood up then touched her face.

"All this time you've been here," I said to her. A black tear dropped from her eye then burned her face. "Are you an evil witch?" I asked her.

"I have always been until I met you," she said then stepped away from me. "I thought you loved me," she said to me.

"I did love you. I couldn't face what I did to you, so I never came back. I wanted to pretend I didn't do it," I said to her. Her beautiful face held a hurt expression. I reached out for her then pulled her into my embrace. "I'm so sorry, Ula," I said to her then she pushed me away.

"Do you love that witch?" she asked me.

"Yes, I do," I responded. Then the scent of another wolf filled my nostrils. I looked around then growled. "What's that smell?" I asked out loud. I started to smell Ula then she backed away.

"I smelled that scent when my pack attacked another pack," I said to her. The night Anik and Kanya were attacked by Sosa and his wolves, I smelled the same scent.

"What beast marked you?" I asked her.

"Jealous?" she asked then chuckled. I growled at her.

"What beast marked you?" I asked then she smiled.

"You already know," she said then disappeared. After she disappeared I ended up back in my bed next to Jalesa. Ula was alive and I didn't know how to feel about that, but a part of me was curious.

****

The next night…

"Are you sure about this?" I asked Dayo. Elle, Dayo, Goon and I walked down the tunnel in our beast form to a club.

"Yeah, nigga I'm sure. This is the club Fabia told Elle about," Dayo replied. A man stood in front of the door at the end of the tunnel. He tried to get on his walkie-talkie but Goon's beast tore into him, splitting him almost in half. Dayo burst through the door then we all leaped through the door and into the crowd. Everyone started screaming. I

smelled a few wolves in the crowd then our pack howled. The humans ran out of the club, falling over each other. The man on stage shifted to his beast and a few more other beasts came out. I leaped onto the nearest one, biting into his neck. One leaped from the top floor onto my back but I shook him off. I charged into him then slammed his beast into a table. I jumped on him then tore into his neck as he howled. When I yanked away from his neck, I pulled a chunk out, which killed him instantly. Our beasts continued to attack the other beasts as more came from out of the back. Dayo's beast climbed up the wall then leaped down onto another beast's back. Dayo's teeth snapped the beast's neck instantly. There was blood everywhere but we didn't stop.

A man stepped from behind the curtain on the stage wearing a suit. His eyes changed then he growled. "This is my territory!" he yelled.

"Fuck your territory! Where is Anik?" Dayo asked then he laughed.

"She is at home enjoying our pregnancy. Don't worry about her because she is being taken care of. You should see how much her breast has swelled," he said. I sniffed the air and there was that scent again. The same scent that lingered on Ula. A huge wolf jumped from the upper level then landed on the stage. It was Goon's brother, Dash. Goon and Dash charged into each other. Dayo and I went after Sosa at the same time. Elle was fighting off the other wolves. We started to get outnumbered but his wolves weren't as strong as us. Dayo caught Sosa by the back of the neck then tossed him into the air. Sosa shifted into his beast in the air. I leaped into the air then caught him by the throat. He and I landed on a table. Dayo jumped on him.

Dayo and I sank our teeth into Sosa's neck. A shot rang out then a few more. A few bullets hit Dayo in the back twice. They couldn't have been normal bullets because they didn't do anything to our kind; the bullets had to been specially made to be used against us. Another one rang out then hit Dayo again. I hurriedly ran up the wall onto the upper level where the bullets were coming from. Four human men had large guns aimed down at the pack.

I hurriedly jumped onto one, tearing into his face as he screamed out. My teeth tore the flesh clean off his cheek. A bullet flew past me. I looked up and three of them had their guns aimed at me. A large, black snake slithered past me then wrapped around the three men. One man tried to shoot but he couldn't, as the snake squeezed them, crushing their bones. The snake's eyes were red, the color of blood.

More men came out with their guns drawn.

"If I were you, boys, I would drop them!" Ula said as she walked past me.

"What are you doing, Ula?" one of them asked. She knew them.

"Drop your guns or else," she said.

"Shoot the crazy bitch!" one of them side. A bullet pierced through Ula's stomach. Her wound immediately closed up; she spat the bullet out of her mouth.

"Your wife is going to need a closed casket for you," she said then the shooter's body caught on fire. More wolves ran from the back. I was surrounded by wolves and humans. I attacked the closest one to me then snapped his neck. A wolf jumped on me then he and I fell over the rail, crashing down onto the stage. I got up then charged into him but Elle got to his neck before I did.

Goon and Dash rolled around on the floor, biting each other. I rushed to Dayo who lay on the floor with blood coming from his mouth. His eyes looked cloudy and foam came out of his nose. The bullets had poison in them. Sosa's wolves started to close in on us. I stood in front of Dayo, ready to die to protect him. Dash's wounds closed up as soon as Goon bit him. His strength came from Musaf's spell. An army of humans guarded Sosa as they escorted him to the back. Screams came from the upper level; I knew Ula was behind it.

Goon's beast slammed Dash into the wall then he evolved.

What the hell, I thought to myself. Goon transformed into a tall, black beast with a body like a man. His snout grew out and his teeth were sharper. A gold plate covered his chest; he was in his ancient form. He picked Dash's big beast up by the back of its neck. Goon opened his mouth then tore Dash's head off. Bullets started flying at Goon but they bounced off of him. He picked up three men at the same time then bit into them. Another bullet flew at him then he turned the human into ashes that shot at him. Once they saw that they couldn't kill him they ran. Some got away but a few turned into ashes. After the coast was clear, Goon walked over to Dayo. Elle and I stood back as Goon howled. He picked Dayo up then sucked the poison out of his wounds. Moments later, Goon's body fell then he turned back to his human form.

"His ancient beast weakens him. It took a lot of his strength," Elle said. Dayo shifted to his human form, too.

Elle put Dayo on his back then I put Goon onto my back. We headed home but I knew it was far from over.

The day after…

"How do you feel, bro?" I asked Goon. Kofi was in the room giving Goon an herbal drink to take the weakness away.

"You wolves know that you aren't allowed to enter another pack's territory. You all went looking for trouble," Kofi said.

"You'd rather for trouble to come to our front door? I'm glad we killed most of them muthafuckas anyway. I promised myself that Dash was going to die by my beast," Goon spat.

"That is not our tradition!" Kofi yelled. Goon threw his cup against the wall. It would've hit me if I hadn't moved.

"Fuck our tradition. It's not my tradition! It's yours and the people in Anubi. This is Earth and we are surrounded by other wolves who have agendas to fuck with us. If a wolf isn't from this pack then his life to us holds no value," Goon said then got out of bed.

"I can't believe this! That wasn't smart thinking!" Kofi said to Goon.

"What's smart thinking, Kofi? I don't think you even know because you are stuck here when your home is in Anubi. You let a piece of shit control y'all's lives back home and you do nothing about it. Ammon is a coward and you stood behind him for many years!" Goon said to Kofi.

Kofi growled at Goon and was ready to charge into him but I jumped in the middle.

"Can we not do this right now? Anik is still missing. Izra is missing and Adika is nowhere to be found. We need to bring everyone back," I said.

"Fuck Izra! He isn't missing and that's why I'm not looking for him. He sided with that bitch he was running behind, so he is as good as gone!" Goon yelled. Kofi yanked away from me.

"If you know what you are doing then be my guest. Just know years of tradition just went down the drain because you all wanted to act like a bunch of untamed beasts," Kofi said.

"Beasts are not tamable creatures and that's what makes us beasts," Goon said to him. Kofi walked out of the room then Goon shook his head. "Where is my mate?" he asked.

"I'm right here," Kanya said. She walked in then kissed him on the lips. "How are you feeling?" she asked him.

"Fine now that I see your beautiful face," he said, his mood softening. I chuckled then he looked at me. "What's funny, bro?" he asked me.

"You are bipolar, bro. I will chat with you later," I said to him then walked out of his room. Jalesa went to open up Kanya's store and I needed peace of mind. I headed to my oil room then locked the door.

"What bothers you?" the voice asked. I turned around then pushed Ula into the wall.

"You are against our pack?" I asked her.

"Is that the way to talk to someone who saved your life?" she asked me.

"What are you to Sosa?" I asked her.

"I work for him, and not like that. Although I'm immortal I still work as if I'm human. I keep track of his money and things of that nature," she said. I growled at her.

"How is it that you can enter this house and nobody can detect you?" I asked her.

"I'm not really here but I'm here, almost like a hologram. Meet me at the park in an hour by the beach," she said.

"And if I don't?" I asked then she shrugged her shoulders.

"Then you just don't," she said then disappeared.

Anik

I sat still as I watched Sosa and Ula argue.

"Where were you when my club was being ambushed?" Sosa asked her.

"None of your fucking business! Who are you to question me? I'm not in your pack, nor do I care about your pack. I gave you wealth in exchange for access to Ammon and that's it! You hired me to keep track of your money, nothing more! That weak bitch, Onya, you got working for you, got your cover blown. Someone you thought was dead gave away all your dirty little secrets and now the other pack knows about you. Give it up, Sosa," she said to him then he slapped her as hard as he could.

"You are a worthless bitch!" he said to her. Ula's eyes turned black then Sosa flew into the wall, which caused the ceiling to crack.

"I guess you forgot that all I gave you I can take it away," she said to him.

"Fuck you!" he said then got up. He stormed out of the room angry. He had been angry because Goon's pack ambushed his club. I ran and hid from him when he came home because I was scared. I hid inside the closet until he calmed down.

Ula grabbed my hand then she and I disappeared. We ended up at a playground by a beach.

"This isn't over, Anik. I still have to settle my score with Naobi, but Sosa will not come after you again. I have nothing against your pack but I must do what my father wanted me to do. I could've brought you home sooner but for my selfish reasons I couldn't. I was drawn to your aura because you reminded me of my old self. You see something in me that no one else does," she said then disappeared.

"I don't know where I am," I said out loud.

"Anik!" a voice called out to me and I wanted to scream. It was Amadi. I ran to him then hugged him for dear life. He pulled away from me to look at me. "Are you hurt? Did he touch you?" he asked me.

"I'm fine. Please, just take me home to Dayo," I said.

****

The house was quiet when we came home. Amadi pointed his head toward the gym room. I walked down the hall and my palms started to sweat. I hadn't seen Dayo in over a week. Amadi told me that Arya came home a few days after I left. I had a feeling she found her way back home. It was early and she was in school. I couldn't wait to see her when she got out.

I walked into the gym room and Dayo angrily lifted the weight. He slammed it down then grabbed his pitcher of water. His back was turned toward me. I was quiet as a mouse as I snuck up on him. I reached out to touch his back then he turned around. His eyes looked down at my stomach then back at me. He pulled me into him then squeezed me. He lifted me up then kissed my stomach. "I'm happy to see you, too," I said.

"I'm only being nice because you are carrying my pups. You don't know how bad I want to throw you across the room," he said to me then hugged me tighter.

"Where were you? Did Sosa really take you?" he asked me.

"Yes," I answered him.

"That punk-ass nigga! Did he touch you? He didn't rape you, did he? What did he do to you?" Dayo asked me then checked my body. He lifted up my shirt then checked my stomach then my breasts.

"I'm fine," I said to him.

"Did he touch you?" he asked me again.

"No," I lied.

"That muthafucka is dead. Where did he keep you?" Dayo asked me.

"I was in a big house, almost like a mansion in the woods, but I don't remember where. It was in an area that I have not been before," I said to him.

"Don't you ever pull that shit again! I'm serious, Anik. We didn't know where you were. We searched every day for you and came up with nothing," he said.

"I'm here now, that's all that matters," I said.

"How did Amadi find you?" he asked me.

"Someone brought me to him," I said.

"Amadi knows someone that knew where you were?" he asked me.

"Ula brought me to Amadi," I said.

"Who is Ula?" Dayo asked me. Amadi didn't tell the pack about Ula. I felt like I was betraying him by telling Dayo about Ula.

"She is a witch and she is also Naobi's sister. She has been living on Earth for many years waiting for Naobi to come. She wants to finish her father's unfinished business," I said then put my head down. I felt bad because Ula saved me but I knew if the pack knew I was holding information they would've been upset.

"Let me get this right. There is a witch who is Naobi's sister that possibly wants to kill Naobi but somehow she ends up at Sosa's house to free you and she knows Amadi? Amadi ain't never tell us about a witch named Ula. Hell, if he would've mentioned that name I probably would've shifted then bit him. What type of name is Ula?" Dayo asked.

"Amadi did something very bad to her and it made her evil. She wasn't always that way. Sosa was going to force himself on me but she slept with him instead. She brought me back home, Dayo. I don't want anyone to hurt her," I said then he snatched away from me.

"She is against our pack!" he yelled at me.

"It's not the way it seems. She never said she wanted to kill Naobi and she is not against this pack," I said to him.

"Did she brainwash you? Are you really Anik? Witches play more games than NBA Sports and I don't trust none of them," he said.

"Ula just needs Amadi to show her that he cared about her. I don't believe she really wants to hurt anyone," I said then he shook his head.

"I don't care if Amadi writes her a damn letter with smiley faces all over it. She is still an evil witch. Let me guess, she is behind Sosa's operation. She is the reason he has that much power," he said.

"Yes, she works for him, but not in that way. She is not connected to his dirty work. But her bringing me back home should mean something," I said to him.

"No, it doesn't, Anik. If she wasn't that bad, then she wouldn't try to take down her own sister. Saka is gone, what reason does she really have? I will tell you what reason she has, she doesn't have any but she doesn't care because she is an evil witch," he fussed.

"I'm going to help her," I said to him then he growled at me.

"You aren't going to do a fucking thing but stay home and rest your body. The pups will be here soon and all of this Dr. Phil bullshit you got going on is dead!" he said to me then walked out of my face. I heard him call for Amadi and I knew it was about to be something.

"What's going on?" Amadi asked Dayo.

"Who is Ula and don't lie to me, bro?" Dayo said to Amadi. Amadi looked at me then I looked away.

"She is an old friend," he said.

"No shit, nigga. I know she is old; she is a witch. How is she your friend when she is sided with Sosa?" Dayo asked Amadi.

"It's not like that, bro. She saved my life last night," Amadi said.

"Do y'all two muthafuckas think I'm going to believe an evil witch saving lives and shit? She is after Naobi and you know Goon isn't going to allow someone to come after his mother. When Goon goes to war it's never by himself, so therefore, we are against her. Did you know she wanted to kill Naobi?" he asked Amadi.

"No, I didn't know that. All I know is that Sosa marked her," he said.

"I will be the first wolf in history to take a Tylenol PM. So you are cool with Sosa's mate?" Dayo asked him.

"I don't think that's his mate," Amadi said.

"He marked her! If she isn't his mate, then what the hell is she to him and to you? You attacked him as soon as you saw him. Are you in love with her or something?" he asked Amadi.

"I was in love with her years ago but then I killed her. She started haunting me afterward," Amadi replied.

“Oh, I get it. Y’all think because I smoke a lot of weed then I’m a little behind, right? Y’all two just saying shit and think I’m supposed to believe it? Arya tells better stories than this. At least her ghost seems real. So, she’s been haunting you? Are you sure that isn’t Camille’s old spirit?” Dayo spat then I pinched him.

“She wasn’t dead when I thought I killed her. I buried her alive and she’s been pissed off since then,” Amadi said.

“Bro, if you were on *The First 48* they would’ve caught you in ten damn seconds. You buried someone and didn’t know they was alive?” Dayo fussed.

“He panicked and it was his first time. His beast took advantage of her. He was afraid that word got out that he’s a wolf. She saw him change and he felt like he had to protect you all,” I explained. Dayo looked at me with yellow-brownish eyes. His beast was beyond angry.

“How do you know?” Dayo asked me.

“I was there,” I responded.

“Were you even born when this happened? Your wolf is younger than Izra’s. You are only twenty years old in wolf years, if that,” Dayo said.

“I wasn’t really there but she showed me a vision of it happening,” I explained then sadness came over Amadi’s eyes.

“You saw everything?” he asked me then I nodded my head.

“I was a monster,” Amadi said then I hugged him.

"You didn't mean it and she knows that," I said to him. Dayo stood next to us with his arms crossed.

"So, Amadi is a rapist?" Dayo asked then Amadi pushed him.

"Don't say that anymore!" Amadi yelled at Dayo.

"Say what? That's what your story sounds like. No offense, bro, but what you need to do is fix this shit you got going on in your personal life. If she is after Naobi, I hope you stop her before she strikes. We can't keep battling muthafuckas over shit that has nothing to do with us. Goon's beast is getting stronger but the power it has makes him very weak afterward. Ammon is here to take your mate, and your scorned lover is against us. That's too much shit, bro," Dayo said to Amadi.

"What do you want me to do?" Amadi asked defeated.

"You worry about Umbrella and the rest of us will worry about Sosa and Ammon. Dash was with Sosa last night and Ammon came to Earth with Dash. Ammon has got to be tied to Sosa, too. Let us worry about that and you fix whatever you got going on in your life," Dayo said to Amadi.

"What will Jalesa think?" Amadi asked us.

"She loves you so I know that she will understand. You and Ula need to make peace, and maybe she will forget about her plans with Naobi. Ula isn't this way and you and I both know it," I told Amadi then he shook his head.

"Are we going to tell Goon about this?" I asked then Dayo looked around to make sure Goon wasn't nearby. He growled at me.

"HELL NO! Don't tell that angry muthafucka nothing. I saw his ancient beast last night. I thought Kanya was lying when she said how tall it is. That nigga turned into a transformer then bit Dash's head clean off. If Kanya took that ancient beast, I don't understand how she got any walls," Dayo said then my mouth dropped.

"DAYO!" I yelled at him.

"All I'm saying is don't tell him nothing yet. Let's try to fix it first. I'm not trying to see him turn to that again. I'm glad bro was able to save my life, but that beast Ammon and Naobi created isn't right. Kanya is just as crazy because there is no way a little jackal should be turned on about something like that," Dayo said then Amadi stifled his laugh.

"Let me get to it then," Amadi said then walked away.

"That nigga's relationship is doomed. If Jalesa lets him go to make everything right with Uno then she needs to take her ass back to Anubi," Dayo said then shook his head. I rolled my eyes at him.

"Her name is Ula," I spat.

"I forgot," he said nonchalantly.

"When are you going to start thinking before you speak?" I asked him.

“I do,” he said then pulled me to him. He gripped the back of my head then kissed my lips. He slipped his tongue into my mouth. His nails massaged my scalp as he hungrily kissed me. He seductively bit my bottom lip. “I missed you so much, Anik,” he said to me then I blushed.

“How much?” I asked him. He pulled me into the hall closet then closed it.

“I can barely fit in here,” I complained as I looked down at my stomach.

“That’s even better,” he said then slid my pants down. He ripped my panties off then tore open my shirt. His sharp teeth clamped onto the middle of my bra then he pulled it away from me—my bra was ripped away. I stood in front of Dayo naked; he hungrily eyed my swollen breasts then growled. His yellow-brownish eyes glowed in the dark closet. I reached out to touch his broad chest and sculpted abs. Dayo’s body was carved from the richest dark chocolate. His eyes looked down at me as his beast lustfully growled; he turned me completely on.

His warm and wet mouth seductively traced the outline of my breasts as he massaged my nipples.

“That feels so good,” I moaned. My hot sex throbbed and I just wanted him to hurry up.

“Please, just enter me,” I said pushing his hand down between my legs. He smeared my wetness over my sex as his hand palmed my pussy. He bit my nipple gently, which almost caused me to howl, but he covered my mouth.

“Damn it, Anik. I don’t want them to know that we are fucking in the coat closet,” he said as he thumbed my clit. I pulled his head down by the back of his neck then bit him. Dayo moaned out as his erection pressed against my leg. I bit him again then he moaned louder. "FUCK!" he said as he picked me up. He leaned me against the wall then slowly entered me. My stomach was in the way but he held me up as if I weighed nothing. My back was pressed against the wall as he slowly worked his way inside me. I was a little tighter than usual and Dayo grew frustrated.

"Open it up before I bust early," he panted as he tried to squeeze the rest of himself into me.

"I'm trying to," I said.

"Stop tensing up," he growled.

"I can't help it. You are too thick," I said. Dayo's finger slipped inside my rear end then I gasped. My pussy muscles relaxed as my body concentrated on his finger, which was in the wrong hole. He started moving in and out of me.

"That's it, baby," he moaned.

His finger went further into my other end and I almost screamed from the combination. I didn't know what he was doing but the wetness that pooled out of me was proof of how much I enjoyed it. He entered another finger into my rear end then sucked my breast. I slowly humped him back, my hips moving in a circular motion. Dayo grew harder and longer. I smacked his face.

"Fuck me harder," I said to him. I didn't know if it was the pups that caused my arousal to be so intense or because of how much I missed him.

"Anik, don't tell me that if you don't mean it," he said then I bit his neck harder than I ever did before. My ears grew out, pulling the skin back on my face. My teeth expanded further out of my gums. Tiny hairs pierced through my skin like little needles. I was in mid-shift and I wanted his beast.

"I want your beast, Dayo," I said to him.

"You know how intense it gets. I might bite too hard," he said then my beast bit him.

"I want your beast," I said to him again. His breathing sped up as I felt his body go through mid-shift. A growl escaped his throat and his beast's eyes lit up the dark closet. His nails dug into my skin as he held me up against the wall. His dick swelled then I tightened around him.

"ARRGGHHHHHHHHHHHH!" I screamed as his beast pumped viciously inside me. He growled as he slammed me down onto his length, filling me up each time. He clamped down on my neck, which caused my nails to scratch his chest. The smell of sex and fresh blood filled the closet. My scent filled Dayo's nose then he howled as he slammed into me. He held my legs over the crook of his arms with my back pinned against the wall. I was pinned with my pussy open and spread for him to enter. He grinded into my spot then slammed into it. My legs shook as I came hard. His dick throbbed inside me, causing him to go harder and faster. He wasn't making love to me; his beast was fucking my beast. It wasn't loving strokes; each stroke was angrier than the last. I came again but harder than the first few times. Dayo pulled my hair then bit my neck again. His teeth sank further into my skin. The pressure started to build then shot up to my head. The blood then came rushing back down through my veins; it was like a drug. My head started to spin when he did it again as his dick tore into my tight hole. He jerked then pumped harder into me. I stopped breathing and my body went limp as the wind felt like it was knocked out of me. For a human that wouldn't be a good thing, but to my beast it was like heaven. I squirted onto him as he howled. He swelled up against my spot and I could no longer take the pleasure. A tear slid out of my eye as my body felt the need to burst. Dayo came, and when he did, his beast almost caused me to go deaf from his howls. I closed eyes then drifted off…

****

As soon as I opened my eyes Arya jumped on me. Kanya hugged me then Jalesa kissed my face. I sat up and realized I was in bed.

"You are back! Thank the heavens, you are back." Kanya squeezed me.

"I can't breathe," I said but she didn't hear me.

"She can't breathe," Jalesa said to Kanya. Kanya let me go then rubbed my stomach.

"We were worried sick about you," Kanya said.

"I'm home now," I said happily.

"Did Sosa hurt you?" Arya asked me. I pulled her closer to me.

"No he didn't hurt me," I said then she wrapped her small arms around my neck.

"So you just come home and get fucked inside a closet then pass out. Dayo was carrying you up the stairs with a winter coat on you when I came home. Goon had to calm me down because I thought you were dead. But he told me how you and Dayo mid-shifted and had sex. You know that's dangerous," Kanya said to me then laughed.

"I needed it and it was amazing. I felt like I was high off something. Where is he? I'm still aroused. Is that normal?" I asked Kanya.

"Yes, those pups are going to have you raping Dayo in his sleep. But trust me, he will not mind. Goon loved it," she said.

"Where is Adika?" I asked everyone.

"Adika and Izra have been gone for days. Nobody can get in touch with either of them. Naobi told Goon that Adika and Izra are locked away together to focus on their relationship. Goon was bothered by Izra's disappearance, so Naobi finally told him. I kind of went overboard with her. I feel so bad because it has been eating me up since she disappeared," Kanya said.

"What did you do?" I asked her.

"Aunty Kanya pimp-slapped her," Arya said. Kanya tapped Arya's mouth.

"What I tell you about that language?" Kanya asked Arya.

"That's what Dayo said," Arya said then I shook my head.

"Your mate needs help," Kanya said to me then laughed.

"Make a long story short, Onya is working with Sosa. I saw her at the house and she told Sosa that some woman named Fabia blew her cover and that Izra left with Adika. It's good to hear that they are focusing on each other because when I heard that from Onya, I got worried," I said to her.

"I know about her. Adika paid Sosa for Onya to carry Izra's pup. It was a setup from the start," Kanya said.

I didn't want to tell them about Ula at that moment. Knowing about Ula was only between, Dayo, Amadi and I. We didn't want to start something that could've been fixed. I had a lot of faith in Ula.

"I'm glad Adika and Izra are together, too. I think everything going on around them would've made their situation worse. They were starting to become enemies," Jalesa said. I looked down at Jalesa's stomach to see if she was pregnant. Before I left home she thought she was but her stomach was flat.

"I'm not carrying a child," she said to me.

"You will soon," Kanya said to her.

"I don't want to," Jalesa said then Kanya told Arya to leave the room.

"Why not? I thought that's what you wanted," I said to her.

"Amadi needs to let go of everything that he is holding on to. I hear him talking to a woman from his past when he thinks that I'm asleep. I even tried to get inside his head and there's nothing, which tells me that something evil is lurking around him. I can't see evil but I can feel it," Jalesa said.

"I'm sorry to hear that," I replied. I knew that woman was Ula.

"How can you prevent yourself from getting pregnant?" Kanya asked Jalesa.

"I use this potion that I made from old Egyptian days. After we make love, I drink it," she said. Kanya looked at Jalesa with a disturbed expression. I thought it was disturbing, too, but I didn't know how Jalesa felt on the inside for her to do something like that.

"You have Adika that can't have babies but you drink a potion that prevents you from having them?" Kanya asked.

"You two wouldn't understand. You don't have a force hovering over your mate all the time. You don't know what it feels like to have a mate that doesn't open themselves up. Amadi keeps everything to himself. He goes into his oil room and just stays there. There's more behind that oil then what he is letting on," Jalesa said.

"I'm not judging you, but do you think that is a good thing to do without him knowing? Just because he is secretive doesn't mean you need to be. Why not just stop having sex with him until you figure out what it is he is going through?" Kanya asked.

"He marked me! I can't help that I get aroused," Jalesa yelled, which took us by surprise. I hated to be in arguments that didn't concern me.

"I feel sorry for Amadi. He is so sweet and quiet, and if he has all of that going on then I can understand why he doesn't say much," Kanya said then Jalesa left the room.

"Did I say something wrong? Her drinking that potion is like an abortion," Kanya said.

"What is an abortion?" I asked her.

"When a human gets pregnant and they don't want the baby. They go through a surgery to stop the baby's life from progressing. Jalesa was having pregnancy symptoms and now she doesn't have them because of some potion. What does that sound like? I hope she wasn't pregnant and just tired from the sex. That will hurt Amadi even more, especially if he is dealing with something. I just wish everyone was happy, that's all," Kanya said. Elle came into the room with Kofi.

"There is my mood reader," Elle said smiling. Kofi gave me a hot cup of tea but it was really some kind of grass that he grinds up himself. The herb was very refreshing even with its bitter taste.

"I'm finally back home," I said then Elle hugged me. He kissed my forehead and so did Kofi. I still didn't know much about Kofi, but he reminded me so much of Elle and Amadi.

"Where is Goon?" I asked everyone.

"He is visiting his mother. He said it was something important," Kanya said. Her twins started to cry then she hurried to her room. Dayo walked into the room with a slab of meat. He laid it across my lap then I dug into my tray. Kofi, Elle, and Dayo just stared at me.

"I find that to be rude," I said with blood dripping down my chin and onto my night shirt.

"I'm sorry, baby, but it just amazes us that you can out-eat Goon," Dayo said then I laughed. Goon did eat a lot and his appetite was bigger than everyone else's in the house.

"I'm so happy to be back home," I said then my eyes watered. "It was so stupid of me. I should've just told you all what was going on but I was embarrassed," I said then Dayo kissed my forehead.

"Everyone has a past, Anik. There are a few things I should've told Izra," Kofi said. I was there when Izra blasted Kofi and Adika but I didn't think anyone else knew about it, so I kept my mouth shut.

"What happened between you and Izra?" Dayo asked.

"Years and years ago Adika and I shared a bed. It was way before I found out that Opal was my soulmate. I should've told Izra but I didn't. At one point in time, Adika carried my pup. Izra heard us talking about it. I don't think he cares for the old man anymore," Kofi said sadly.

"Adika smashing the homies," Dayo thought then I growled at him.

“We will figure it out but I’ve got to go because Fabia and I are going out to dinner,” Elle said.

“I’ve got to meet this Fabia,” I said to Elle then he smirked. I noticed something different about Elle. His dreads were pulled back and he had on regular clothes. He wore a long-sleeve shirt that clung to his muscled, but lean, frame. He wore a pair of denim-washed jeans and Timbs.

“Don’t you look handsome,” I said to Elle.

“About time this nigga got with the program. Every day he walked out of here like he was dressed for Camille’s funeral,” Dayo said.

“One more outburst, Dayo, and that’s your ass,” Elle said getting mad. Kofi pulled Elle back then laughed.

“He is just excited his mate is home. Let’s give them their space,” Kofi said then he and Elle walked out of the room.

“Are you ready for round two?” Dayo asked. He slid his hand between my thighs then I moaned.

“Lock the door,” I said to him then got undressed. We had a long night ahead of us.

Naobi

"He isn't dead," I said as I stared at Ammon's body. He was in a very, deep sleep. Keora found him for me. She knew of Dash's routine and found Ammon's body behind Dash's building in the woods. I touched Ammon's hand then closed my eyes and got nothing from my vision.

"His beast isn't inside his body," I said.

"Good, now we can throw him in the river," Akua said.

"He is still your father," I said to him.

"He is a wolf serum donor," he replied then Keora giggled. Akua looked at Keora then growled. "You trust her?" he asked me.

"Yes, I believe she is worthy of it now," I said to him.

"I'm like your sister, Goon," she teased him.

"Then that makes you incest because at one point, you wanted me to plug you," he answered.

"Would you two hush!" I yelled at them.

"Where is Dash?" I asked Keora.

"I killed him," Akua answered nonchalantly.

“You killed your brother?” I asked.

“Bit his head off. Musaf did a good job at shielding him because it took too long for him to bleed out. I had no other choice but to take his head off. My pups could’ve died from that ambush he pulled and Keora needs to be dead, too,” he said then his eyes changed.

“Keora has a purpose and she will fulfill it when all of this confusion is over. I’m getting tired of battles. I’m an old witch and I don’t feel like fighting anymore. I just want to enjoy my mate,” I said.

“What purpose does a no-purpose serve?” Akua asked me then Keora’s mouth dropped open.

“I will fight your big ass,” Keora yelled at Akua then he smirked.

“Only a witch can do something like this to him,” I said as I looked down at Ammon. I made a bed appear then his body rested on it. I covered him up with a blanket.

“Kumba isn’t going to want this man in his house after Ammon sent an army after him,” Akua said to me.

“Ammon has an enemy that we don’t know about. You might not like it but he is still a part of me. Just because I’m with my true mate doesn’t mean I will see your father suffer. Anubi needs their king otherwise you will have to go. You have to get over it because this will break up your pack if he remains this way,” I replied.

“If Kumba comes home pissed off at you I will not just stand by and watch,” Akua said to me.

"What am I going to do with him? He was just lying in the woods under a bush," I said.

"Goon can take his father home with him," Keora said.

"Mind your damn business. This doesn't have shit to do with you," Akua said to Keora.

"Send him back to Anubi," Akua said to me.

"The portal isn't opening any time soon. Why do you think Kofi is stuck here?" Keora asked him.

"Why does she have any existence? What a waste of life," Akua spat.

"You wasn't saying that hundreds of years ago. You were all up in my life if you know what I mean, my prince," she said.

"Bitch," Akua mumbled but I heard him.

"Akua, just go home. I will figure this out," I said to him. He kissed my cheek then walked up the basement stairs. It was just Keora and I.

"I found him for you and now I'm free. How will my spirit get inside Adika's womb?" she asked me.

"When her pup's heart stops beating you will no longer exist. Your spirit will breathe a new life inside her pup," I said to her.

"How can you do that?" she asked then I smiled.

"An old witch never tells her secrets. Now, get some rest while I figure out what to do with Ammon," I said to her.

"Thank you, Naobi," she said to me then went into one of the rooms inside the basement. I grabbed my spell book to see what was going on with Ammon. I'd never seen a spell like that before—someone took his soul without killing him. His heart was still beating, his body still warm; he just couldn't wake up.

I closed my eyes then squeezed Ammon's hand, so that I could see a vision, but I still got nothing. I tried again but it was blank. I threw my spell book across the room.

"I'm not doing this for you! I'm doing this for our son so he wouldn't have to go to Anubi," I yelled at him but he couldn't hear me. The door upstairs opened and it was Kumba. I could hear his heavy footsteps entering the house. I put a stone wall up behind the door to the basement then disappeared.

"There is my queen. Why aren't you dressed? A car is coming to pick us up in an hour. The grand opening of my newest restaurant downtown is tonight, remember?" he said to me.

"Akua came over to visit. I will shower now," I said then headed upstairs. I needed to find a cure for Ammon and fast because, if not, Akua would've been sucked into the portal to take Ammon's spot.

****

“We finally get to meet the lady in Kumba’s life,” one of his associates said to me.

“Yes, and you must be Mr. Kenneth?” I asked with my hand out. He shook my head.

“That would be me, and that dress is very stunning. Don’t be surprised if my wife asks you where you got it from. Speaking of my wife, I think I should check on her. She is pregnant and about to pop,” he said then walked off.

The dress I wore was gold and it wrapped around my curves. It gave my hips more of an expression. The sleeveless dress draped down at the neckline, showing a small amount of cleavage. The front of the dress stopped at my knees and the back of it dragged the floor.

“I got this dress from magic,” I said to Kumba then he smiled.

“Can you magically make it disappear when we get back into the limo? If I didn’t have a party to host, you would’ve been in trouble. I would’ve sampled every treasure you are hiding underneath it,” he said to me. A warm feeling came over me, which caused me to fan myself.

“There he is! The best cook in town! I must say that this restaurant is beautifully decorated,” a middle-aged White man said to us. I could tell by his expensive-looking threads that he was wealthy. He was a very attractive man with blond hair and pretty blue eyes. He had a nice physique and he walked around the restaurant like he owned it.

“What’s happening, Don? How is it going?” Kumba asked him as they shook hands.

"I'm doing great. This is a lovely place you have here. I have to bring my business partner here for our meetings," he said to Kumba.

"Anytime, just call me ahead of time, so that I can make sure you have your own section," Kumba said. He interacted with humans very well. You would've never known that he was an immortal by the way he lived his life.

"Will do, and who is this lovely lady here?" Don asked Kumba.

"This is my fiancé, Naobi," Kumba answered. Don reached out to shake my hand.

"Nice to meet you. That is a remarkable dress you are wearing," Don said to me.

"Nice to meet you, too, and thank you," I replied.

A young, pretty woman walked toward us with her hair braided. Her long, black dress clung to her body and she seductively swayed her hips as she walked. Her brown skin glistened under the lights. When she got closer she reached out to Don. Don wrapped his arm around her waist. "Kumba and Naobi, I would like for y'all to meet Onya," he said to us. I looked in Onya's eyes then realized she was the wolf that I saw through Izra's vision. Onya shook Kumba's hand then she reached out to shake my hand.

"Nice to finally meet you, Onya. Hopefully this will not be the last time we run into each other. I have learned how small circles are around here," I said to her. She snatched her hand back then looked at because I burned it.

Kumba and Don walked off to talk, leaving Onya and I standing next to each other.

"What are you?" she asked me.

"You will see as your soul will slowly drain from your body to the pits of hell. I will come to collect soon, but in the meantime, enjoy your night," I said to her then she growled at me.

"Your beast isn't as threatening as you think, my child," I said to her.

"You will see once I bit your head off," she said angrily then I laughed when she started to choke. Onya grabbed at her throat as she tried to breathe. She fell onto the floor, gasping for air. Don rushed to her then a crowd surrounded them. A human pressed down on her stomach and another one opened her mouth.

"She's choking!" someone screamed as I watched. Kumba looked at me with confusion on his face.

"Not now, my love," I said into his thoughts.

"I see something in her throat!" a White woman called out as she held Onya's mouth open. She reached inside her mouth then pulled out a black Egyptian scorpion. The crowd gasped.

"What the hell is that thing?" someone asked then the woman threw the scorpion across the room. They helped Onya up then Don gave her a cold glass of water. I looked at Onya then smiled. *"my gift to you,"* I said into her thoughts.

Don took Onya to the corner of the room. As she talked her eyes changed into her beast and not once was he frightened.

"What was that?" Kumba asked me.

"Me being nice. Why is that human not afraid of that beast? Something is wrong, don't you see? If he is not afraid of her that means that he knows immortals exist. Humans knowing of our existence is not good," I said to Kumba. Don looked at me then I waved at him. He hurriedly escorted Onya out of the restaurant.

"We have to protect our kind," I said to Kumba.

"We will figure that out later, but for right now, let's dance," he said to me.

"Yes, my king," I said to him then his handsome face lit up.

"I'm not your king, Naobi. I'm your mate," he said to me.

"You are still my king," I replied.

Izra

"I've been here too long. My beast needs to run loose in the woods for a few days," I said to Adika when she came out of the bathroom. She didn't look too good and her skin was pale. She wobbled a little when she walked. I rushed to her. "What's the matter with you?" I asked her.

"I'm fine. I must have eaten some bad meat. I just need to rest for a little bit," she said.

"We need to get the fuck out of this cramped apartment because, soon, I will be sick. I need to get back to the house. My brothers are looking for me, I'm sure. But then again, they might think that I've switched sides. Come on, Adika, just let me go," I said to her.

"You might run into Onya," she said.

"So, what! I'm not thinking about Onya," I spat. I felt like I was in a cage. I missed seeing the sunlight from outside.

"I see now how humans feel when they are on death row. This isn't shit but a life sentence," I said to her then she threw-up on the floor.

"We need to go back to the house and have Elle, Amadi or Kofi look at you. Is that a hairball, though?" I asked as I looked at the thick chunks of food that was splattered across the floor.

"I just ate something bad, that's all," she said.

"You are a witch, Adika. You can't predict shit like that?" I asked her.

"Would you shut the hell up?" she asked me.

"Let me go home then! I left my cell-phone at the hotel room. Don't you think my pack is trying to get in touch with me? Bad enough you blocked them out of my head! I can't get in touch with nobody," I said to her.

"You cannot leave here until Onya is dead! I'm going to find her once I feel better enough to kill her," she said to me.

"So now you are a wicked witch?" I asked her.

"I'm a witch who is in love with her beast!" she yelled then threw-up again. Adika fell onto the floor then I rushed to her. She looked sick, very sick. Her lips looked pale and her skin felt clammy.

"We need to get out of here and go home. You are sick and you need help," I said to her. She screamed as she clutched her stomach. I lifted up her baggy shirt and that's when I noticed. Adika hid her body underneath baggy clothes so that I couldn't see her stomach. I was locked away with her and not once did she come onto me. She didn't want me to know she was pregnant.

"I'm so sorry," she said clutching her stomach. I picked her up then walked to the door.

"Unblock the door, Adika! Do it now because there is no way in hell I can be locked up in an apartment with a dead pup," I said to her. I felt in my heart the pup was dead. Adika was sick the last time she lost our pup.

Adika closed her eyes then the brick wall that blocked the door slowly disappeared, but using her magic drained her even more. Once the door was unblocked, I took off down the stairs then out of the building. I ran with her in my arms into the woods. I shifted into my beast then she slowly got onto my back.

"Hold on tight! I'm going to be very fast," I said to her. She squeezed me around my neck as tight as she could as I ran through the woods, headed toward our home.

****

"Where have you been at, nigga?" Dayo asked me after I burst through the door with Adika on my back. Adika climbed off my back but her legs wobbled. Dayo hurriedly caught her before she hit the floor. He picked her up then ran her upstairs as I shifted back. When I got to my room, I hurriedly put on a pair of shorts. Dayo lay Adika on our bed then went to get Kofi and Elle. Seconds later, they ran into the room. "What happened to her?" Kofi asked as he rushed to her. He felt her forehead. "She doesn't feel good," he said then Adika whined.

"Just get it out! Please, get it out of me!" Adika screamed as she clutched her stomach. My eyes stung as water filled them. I hated to see her go through that again, and I hated that I had to go through it, too. Elle came back in the room with his leather doctor bag. He was going to cut her stomach open to take the pup out of her or else the pain wouldn't go away. Elle was the one who cut our first pup out of her stomach. Dayo rushed in with towels and a big metal bowl filled with ice-water. Elle pulled out his stethoscope then placed it on Adika's stomach.

"There's no heartbeat," Elle said to us.

"You've got to get out, Izra," Dayo said to me.

"Where is that punk-ass muthafucka? I heard his voice," Goon said when he walked into my room. When he saw Adika he froze. "She lost the pup again?" he asked me then I shook my head. Goon patted my back. "Come out here and talk to me. Let them help her," he said to me but my feet wouldn't move. Elle grabbed his sharp cutting knife; blood seeped out of the cut as he traced it across her lower stomach. She squeezed Kofi and Dayo's hand as Elle cut her. "STOP!" I yelled out.

"I've got to get the pup out!" Elle said.

"NO! Don't do it!" I said. A small vision appeared into my head of Adika giving birth to our pup.

"Son, I know this is hard for you, but we've got to get it out," Kofi said to me.

"Our pup isn't dead!" I said ready to attack Elle but Goon grabbed me in a bear hug.

"Elle, if you cut her open I'm going to kill you! I'm going to forget that you are my brother and bite your throat out! My pup ain't dead, bro, but if you take her out now she will never survive," I said to him.

"Adika just passed out from the pain! The pup is not alive and that's why she is sick!" Elle yelled at me.

"Listen to me, bro, that is my pup and you'd better not fucking touch her," I said then growled at him. Dayo looked at Elle.

"It's his mate, bro, and what he says should go," Dayo told Elle.

"This is not the best decision to make, Izra. Look at her!" Kofi said.

"I swear on this pack, I will kill a brother if my pup is taken out of her womb," I told them. Kofi looked at Adika then stood.

"Her life is in your hands, son. Whatever decision you make there is a consequence. You must blame no one but yourself," he said then walked out of the room. Elle grabbed his stethoscope then placed it on Adika's stomach. A look of confusion came over his face as he rubbed the stethoscope around her stomach.

"This is unbelievable!" Elle said.

"What happened?" Goon asked then went over to Adika. He placed his hand over her stomach. "This pup is alive and kicking," Goon said.

"It was dead," Elle said in disbelief.

"Congrats, baby bro! Now come over and give us a hug, nigga! I don't like your ass but I did miss you," Dayo said to me. Elle, Amadi, Goon and Dayo pulled me into them.

"Adika's cut is closing already. She is sleeping peacefully, so let her rest," Elle said to us. I walked out of the room and my brothers followed me. As soon as I closed the door, Goon started to growl at me.

"Where is that wolf you were creepin' with, bro? She is against this pack," Goon said to me.

"Adika came to the hotel room and caught me fucking Onya. They fought then Onya just ran off and I haven't heard from her since. I don't know what I was thinking. When I was around Onya, I was like a little lost puppy, bro. I didn't know Adika put a spell on me until she showed up at the room. I should've known something wasn't right because Onya's scent wasn't all that appealing to me. Adika had me locked up inside her apartment, away from everyone. I just found out she was carrying my pup. Where is Anik and Arya?" I asked.

"They are home but the females went shopping for the pups Anik is carrying," Goon said. I looked at Elle and there was something about him that was different. I looked at his gear.

"I almost thought this old nigga was a rapper now. Elle, you grew up, didn't you?" I asked him then he chuckled.

"I'm just relaxing that's all," he said.

"Who was that wolf that was following Onya and I?" I asked him then he smirked.

"She was Camille's friend and she worked for Sosa," Elle answered.

"What is she to you because, nigga, you never had swag," I said to him then Dayo laughed.

“I told this nigga he looked too thugged out,” Dayo said then they we all laughed.

“That’s because Elle getting him some wolf pussy,” Dayo said.

“Naw, I don’t think Elle is hitting that yet,” Goon said.

“Would y’all stay out my business?” Elle asked.

“Where is Amadi?” I asked them.

“He went to the store. But I will holla at y’all later. I’m ready to run out real quick. Welcome back home, Izra, but I’m not fucking with you tomorrow, so don’t say shit to me,” Dayo said then walked down the hall.

“Fuck you, too, nigga! I wasn’t going to say shit to you anyway!” I shouted behind him.

“Damn, I hate that nigga,” I said.

“Where did you get Onya from? You’ve been to Sosa’s house, right?” Goon asked me.

“I don’t think that was his house. It was a cabin and since he was already plotting, I doubt if that was where he slept. Sosa seems a little smart, so I’m sure he doesn’t know want us to know where he lives,” I answered.

“Anik said it was a mansion, and we found Ammon,” Goon said.

“I almost forgot about that nigga,” I said.

"Yeah, me too, but his body is inside Kumba's house in the basement. A witch got to him and took his beast away from him. He isn't dead but he is sleeping," Goon said.

"Well, good!" I replied.

"That isn't good, little brother. A witch with his beast can destroy this whole pack except for Goon, but it would still a challenge Naobi might even have a problem defeating it. That isn't a good combination. Whomever that witch is has an agenda," Elle said.

"Why can't these ancient immortals let us be? It's like the old against the young. What witch is powerful enough to take Ammon's punk-ass beast?" I asked.

"That's what we are trying to figure out," Goon said.

"I need a drink," I said then headed to the kitchen. When I got into the kitchen there was papers all over the island. I picked one up. "What the hell is this?" I asked as Elle and Goon walked into the kitchen behind me.

"Arya had pictures of your beast in her little camera. Dayo told her to print them out and place them all over town," Goon said. I looked at the picture and read the words. The words under the picture read, *Lost German Shepherd*.

"I'm going to fuck that nigga up! I don't look like no punk-ass cop dog!" I fussed then Goon laughed until water filled his eyes.

"Arya was convinced that you will see it and come home. Dayo did it so that she wouldn't be so worried," Elle said. I trashed the papers but Goon hurriedly grabbed one. "I'm sorry, bro, but I have to keep this. You talk too much shit, it's only right. You do look like an extra-large German Shepherd, though," he said putting the paper in his back pocket.

"Your beast even posed for the picture," Goon said then Elle fell over laughing.

"So what! Fuck the both of you! Arya was bored and I shifted for her. She wanted to take it to her school for 'show your pets' day!" I shouted at them.

"But, bro, you were chewing on a toy in the picture," Goon said.

"It had to look believable," I said then Elle roared with laughter.

"I told Arya not to show anybody that," I said then laughed myself. I was happy to be back home. I grabbed a bottle of Henny from the liquor cabinet.

"Are you going to roll up?" I asked Goon.

"I guess so. You smoking, Elle?" Goon asked him. Elle thought about it.

"I guess I can celebrate Izra's return home," Elle said then I patted his back.

"Elle is officially on the other side," I said then he shook his head.

"Now all we need is for Amadi to convert his ancient old ways," I said.

****

Adika was asleep then all of a sudden she jumped up then looked down at her stomach. “Get it out of me!” she screamed.

“It’s not dead!” I said to her. She placed her hand over her stomach then tears flowed down her face.

“What happened? This is not possible,” she said as she got out of bed.

“According to the vision I had it is possible and it’s going to happen,” I said to her.

“What vision?” she asked me then I told her the vision I had when Elle started to cut her stomach.

“I must be cursed!” she panicked.

“Sit down, Adika! If you are cursed, then it’s a good curse, now enjoy the pregnancy. This is a do-over for us,” I said to her then she wrapped her arms around my neck then kissed me.

“Oh, Izra, I must be dreaming,” she said.

“Can I smack you to wake you up?” I asked her then she rolled her eyes.

“Where is Kanya? She isn’t too fond of me. I don’t feel comfortable being here,” Adika said.

“This is family, Adika. Kanya will get over it,” I said then the door flew open.

“Uncle Izra!” Arya screamed then leaped on me. She wrapped her arms tightly around my neck. Wolf pups are also strong because it felt like a teenage boy squeezing me. I hugged her back then pulled her off of me.

“I thought we had a secret? Why did you show them the picture of my beast playing with a dog toy?” I asked her then Adika giggled.

“It was a cute picture, Izra. You looked like a well-behaved house pet,” Adika said.

“You saw it, too?” I asked her.

“I been saw it,” she said then Arya hugged her.

“Everyone is home now,” Arya said. Kanya ran into the room then squeezed Adika.

“I’m so sorry! Please forgive me,” Kanya said then Adika hugged her.

“It’s forgiven, but the next time I’m slapping you back,” Adika told Kanya. Kanya placed her hand over Adika’s stomach.

“Miracles happen, I told you,” she said to Adika. Anik wobbled into the room.

“Damn, Anik! Who did you eat, Dayo?” I asked then Adika slapped my arm.

"Very funny, but that does sound good right about now. They had me in the mall for hours and I'm starving," she said then sat in the chair. "I'm glad you two are back. I would love to give you two a hug but I can't make it over there. My feet are killing me," Anik complained.

"Where is crackhead, Jalesa at?" I asked them then Kanya growled at me.

"She is talking to Amadi," Anik answered.

"What is a crackhead, Uncle Izra?" Arya asked him.

"A person who is cursed and it causes them to steal. After they steal they disappear. You see them for a second then, when you blink your eyes, they disappear," I said to Arya.

"Jalesa does disappear a lot. I'm ready to ask her if she can turn me into a crackhead, too, that way I can disappear in my class," Arya said then skipped out of the room. Kanya, Adika and Anik's eyes glowed as they looked at me. Kanya and Anik also growled at me.

"What? There is nothing wrong with multitasking," I said to them.

"That's my cue to leave. I'm ready to get dinner ready and have a glass of wine. I need to take in everything Izra just told Arya and he actually thinks it's multitasking," Kanya said then hurriedly exited the room.

"Kanya! Help me out of this chair!" Anik said trying to get up. Kanya came back then pulled Anik up. Anik looked at me then rolled her eyes before she followed Kanya out of the room.

"It's okay, baby. I still love you," Adika said to me then purred.

"Then let me taste you before we go downstairs for dinner," I said slipping my hand into her panties.

"Now you want to touch me? We've been locked away with each other for over a week and now you want to get hard?" she asked me as she slid her panties down. Her arousal permeated the air.

"My beast was on bad behavior. I think you should do something about that. I want you to slide down onto my hard-on and ride that shit until I howl," I said to her then she purred. Adika was turned on and so was I. She hurriedly took her shirt off then undid her bra. Her breast sprang out, which caused my beast to growl. I hungrily took her swollen breast into my mouth.

"Oh, Izra!" she moaned as she pulled my head closer to her chest. She grinded seductively onto me; her wet sex brushed against my dick. I slid my finger into her wet, tight and dripping cave. I smeared it across her lips to her mouth then hungrily kissed her to taste her. A leash appeared around my neck then the door slammed and locked.

"You must be ready to do some magic," I said then squeezed her juicy and round bottom. She pushed me down onto the bed. Her yellow eyes glowed then her lips turned black. Her jet-black hair grew out long and bushy, it reached her hips. Her sharp canines hung out of her mouth. Her body turned black with shimmers sparkling all over her body.

“Damn, you are so beautiful,” I said staring at her as she sat on top of me. She was a beautiful creature and guilt came over me. I tasted another wolf and even entered her to mate with her. My dick went limp as I thought about everything I did, although I couldn’t help that I felt that way because she cursed me.

“Are you thinking about her?” Adika asked me.

“Yes, but not in that way. I feel bad for what I did and the things I’ve said to you,” I said to her.

“I did that to you, Izra. I want to feel you,” she said to me. She slid down my body then grabbed my dick.

“Don’t panic,” she said then milk started to pour out of my dick.

“What are you doing, Adika? I think this is too kinky!” I said to her as she purred. Her cat hungrily lapped up the milk that drizzled down my length like a milk waterfall.

“Damn it, you are freaky,” I said then growled as she stuck my length into her mouth. She hungrily sucked on me as her arousal filled my nose. I growled louder then grabbed a fistful of her hair. I slowly pumped down her throat as she sucked on me. She took me further into her mouth as she hungrily drank the milk. My nails dug into her scalp as I started to move in and out of her mouth.

“Suck it harder! Jerk it off! Yeah, just like that,” I growled as my stomach muscles started to tighten up. I almost howled as she grabbed my testicles to massage them. She popped me out of her mouth then kissed my swollen head. I moaned then growled because of the intense pressure her warm and wet mouth gave me.

"I'm about to explode," I said gripping her hair with both hands. My beast pumped roughly into her mouth and she never once gagged. She relaxed her throat and let me fuck her mouth as her spit mixed with my pre-cum, and milk ran down my shaft. I howled out as my dick jerked then exploded to the back of her throat. She hungrily swallowed everything I fed her. She wiped her mouth off then laid on the bed with her legs spread. Her pink, shiny pearl sat between her black and shimmering pussy lips. I sat up then she yanked me by the leash she had around my neck. I fell between her legs then she pushed my head down into her sex.

"Sniff it like the beast you are," she moaned. I hungrily sniffed her then she slowly grinded onto my lips. Something sticky got on my lips. I ran my tongue across my lips and it was sweet.

"Is that honey?" I asked her.

"Yes," she moaned.

"You really got some tricks I see," I said then pinned her legs up. Honey drizzled from between the slit of her pussy then down her ass crack. I had to tell my pack brothers about that because it was mind-blowing.

I stuck my tongue into her honey pot then let it drizzle down my tongue to the back of my throat. I sucked on her hole then kissed it. She arched her back up from off the bed as she grabbed the sheets.

"Come on my tongue."

She grinded her hips harder as she continued to moan. I hardened my tongue then stuck it inside her. Her pussy responded by squeezing the tip of my tongue. I slid my finger into her anus then she cried out in pleasure as her legs started to tremble. She bucked forward onto my mouth until my teeth gently sank into her pearl. She squirted inside my mouth as I drank her essence mixed with honey. I growled as my appetite grew stronger. I turned her over then laid down underneath her dripping-wet pussy. I pulled her right down onto my mouth.

"Fuck my face, Adika. My beast is still hungry."

She gripped the leash she had around my neck as she rubbed her wet pussy across my lips. I gripped both of her ass cheeks then squeezed them. She slowly rode my tongue as the honey dripped down the sides of my mouth. The honey was good but her essence tasted better. I smacked her plump cheeks so that she could ride my face faster.

"I don't need the honey."

"Oh, Izra, I'm about to come!" she screamed as she bounced on my hard tongue as it entered her. I slid my finger inside her anus again then she trembled as she screamed my name. I howled as she came inside my mouth. My beast wanted to take her. He wanted to roughly fuck her. I was going to make it up to her later but I needed to slam into her wetness.

"I need to fuck, Adika."

She got up then held my swollen dick up with her hand. She slowly slid down onto my erection. She sucked me in until all of me was planted inside her.

"Damn it, Izra! It feels like you are about to burst through my stomach."

"Just ride me before I attack you. My dick is so hard it aches!"

She planted her hands firmly onto my chest then slowly slid up until just the tip was inside her. She slowly slid back down but I didn't want it slow. I flipped her over, landing on top of her. I pinned her legs back until her pussy sat up in the air. Her knees were planted against her forehead. I slid my dick up and down between her wet pussy lips to get it even wetter. My entry was going to hurt but I needed it. My swollen head pierced through her tight opening then she dug her long, sharp nails into my forearms. I slid in until all of my length disappeared. I pulled out then slammed back into her. She moaned as I filled her up with my beast. Her wetness drizzled out like melted chocolate as I pumped into her. I gave her long, hard strokes as I growled. I thumbed her pretty, fat pearl then squeezed it.

"Hold your legs up!" I said to her because she was trembling. I braced myself on both arms then straightened my body. I slammed into her over and over again until she yelped. My skin slapping against her sweaty skin echoed through the room. I pulled out then tasted her; I sank my teeth into her pussy lips as she creamed on my tongue. I entered her again, sliding all the way in until I came to a hilt. I was planted against her pleasure spot. I stayed in that position until I swelled and couldn't pull out. I was stuck inside her and she continuously came on my swollen dick, screaming and clawing at my face and arms. I felt my skin tearing but the pleasure shielded any pain she was afflicting on me. I howled then gripped her hair. I bit her neck as I pumped viciously into her until her eyes rolled back into

her head as her body shook from back-to-back orgasms. Adika cried out with tears running down her face. The pleasure was unbearable but my beast couldn't stop until he was satisfied. I pumped and howled inside Adika longer than I ever had. I gripped a fistful of hair as my beast rammed inside her. Both of our bodies were covered in sweat. Hairs pricked through my skin and I felt my ears pulling the skin back on my face. I was in mid-shift while inside Adika's pussy. I bit her breast then she came. Her body was getting weak and I knew I had to hurry up and explode before she passed out on me. I pumped into her as her breasts bounced.

"GGGRRRRRRRRRRRRRRRRRRRRRRRRR!" I growled as my semen spilled inside her, pumping into her like gas. I howled then she closed her ears as my body jerked then slammed into her spot one more time before she and I passed out.

****

"She did what?" Goon asked me as he chewed a cube of meat left over from dinner. Adika and I missed dinner; when I woke up I went downstairs to get us something. Goon was going the through the fridge, which was normal.

"She had milk coming out of my dick and had honey leaking from her pussy. I thought when she turned into a unicorn it was sexy but, bro, what she did screwed me up. I have a beautiful witch who turns into a cat and anything else she wants to. I went chasing behind a basic werewolf who couldn't do shit, but look at me," I said then Goon chuckled.

"That is interesting but next time, tell her to duplicate you," he said then I spit my water out.

"You did that to Kanya?" I asked him.

"It took me a while to study it out of the spell book but I did it. She walked into the room out of the shower one night and there were two of me standing there naked. Bro, you should've seen her face. I almost attacked him because he was eating her out, making her scream," he said.

"You are one jealous nigga. That was yourself, fool," I said in disbelief.

"Shut the fuck up, bro. But, anyways, I had to remind myself that it was fake and it was all a mind thing. While he was eating between her legs, she was sucking me off. Myself and I took turns fucking her. She even took me in the rear end while the other me entered her from the front. Kanya slept for three days after that. She wants it again but I was pissed off at myself," he said then chuckled.

"Bro, she took the both of you at the same time?" I asked.

"At the same time, bro. I tried to duplicate her this morning and it lasted for only two minutes because she was jealous. She almost bit me when she watched herself give me head," he said.

"Y'all are crazy. Where is your spell book? I need to let Adika borrow it," I said to him then he laughed.

"Witches are amazing but I'd rather become my beast. The magic brings great pleasure inside the bedroom, though," he said.

"You are one lucky, big muthafucka. How do y'all do it?" I asked Goon.

"I don't know, bro, you have to study it. Witches have this energy that surges throughout their bodies. Almost like electricity and that is what gives us the power to practice these spells. Once you practice a particular spell you don't have to anymore. My body can make another me appear in the blink of an eye without me looking in the book. Almost every spell we practice sticks with us. You read it then collect it then you keep it," he said but I didn't understand.

"I don't get it," I said.

"You don't have all the brains to understand, bro," Goon said to me then shook his head. Amadi came into the house. His chest had blood smeared across it and he was only wearing shorts. "You went hunting this late?" Goon asked him.

"Yeah, I couldn't sleep," Amadi said then grabbed a bottle of liquor. He popped the cap off then guzzled it. Amadi wasn't much of a drinker. He sipped occasionally with the maximum of two glasses.

"What's going on with you and Jalesa?" Goon asked with his eyebrow raised. Amadi let out a deep breath.

"Jalesa and I have been making love since the first time I entered her. She has been ovulating and still there is no pregnancy. She is fertile, yet, my pup still isn't in her womb," he said.

"Does your wolf serum work?" I asked him then he growled at me.

"Yes, idiot, it works! I stay inside her every time until the swelling goes down, and still, there isn't a pup. She showed signs of pregnancy at one time then one day she no longer had them. I was for certain that her cervix closed after I mated with her. I think I'm losing my mind," Amadi said to us.

"Jalesa is a crackhead, bro. You can't trust that type of species," I told Amadi.

"What in the hell is a crackhead?" Amadi asked me.

"A different type of species that steals and just disappears," I said to him.

"Do they shift?" Amadi asked then Goon shook his head.

"Amadi, if you listen to this fool, you are just as lost as him. Crackheads are humans that get high off crack," Goon said.

"This nigga thinks he knows everything," I said.

"I got to know everything with a dumb-ass muthafucka in the pack," Goon spat back. Dayo came into the kitchen half-asleep.

"It's hard sleeping with a pregnant female," he said then yawned. He looked at Amadi. "What's up with you?" Dayo asked him.

"Jalesa is having an affair," I said then Goon punched me in the chest. I slid off the barstool then into the wall. I coughed as I held my chest. “Have some respect, Izra,” Goon said to me then Dayo laughed.

“All right, damn, y’all can’t take a joke,” I said.

“Maybe Jalesa is having an affair with someone from Anubi. What if she and that old nigga, Musaf, was kicking it or something?” Dayo asked then Amadi scratched his head.

“You might be onto something,” Amadi said then took another sip.

“If you listen to these idiots, you will lose your mate. Maybe she just doesn’t want to have a pup,” Goon said to Amadi.

“Well, maybe I shouldn’t have marked her. I love Jalesa but I wasn’t ready to enter her, but she thought it would help me,” Amadi said.

“You let her pressure you?” I asked him.

“Yeah, because I wasn’t ready but she insisted. I’m over that now. I’m upset because she isn’t carrying my pup and something is wrong with that,” Amadi said.

“Ask her,” Dayo said then took the bottle from Amadi.

“I asked her and she said that her body wasn’t ready. She lied to me. When you mark a female you are connected to them. I know for a fact she was ovulating,” Amadi said.

“Maybe she put a spell on herself so she wouldn’t carry your pups,” I said to him.

“I think this jackass is onto something, Amadi. Witches can be very sneaky,” Dayo said.

“He ain’t lying,” I agreed with him.

“She loves him; so why would she do that?” Goon asked then looked at Amadi. “You got something you want to share with us?” he asked him.

“Not at the moment,” Amadi answered then Dayo looked at him. They knew something that Goon and I didn’t.

“What is the real reason, bro?” I asked Amadi.

“I don’t know,” he answered.

“Yes, he does,” a voice came from behind us. It was Jalesa standing behind us and, like always, she appeared from out of nowhere.

“Can you warn us or something when you sneak up on us? We are having brother talk,” I said to Jalesa.

“I can see that, but Amadi was missing from our bed. It’s late, Amadi,” Jalesa said to him.

“I know that, beautiful. I will be in the room in a few minutes,” Amadi said without looking at her.

“Tell them the truth. Tell them how you still think about another woman. Tell them how you still talk to her when you think I’m not listening. Tell them how she died years ago but you won’t let her go. I have to share you with someone who is dead,” Jalesa said.

"Between you and Elle, I don't know who likes dead people more. Isn't that called necrophilia?" I asked Amadi.

"That is probably the biggest word in your vocabulary," Dayo said to me.

"That is not true!" Amadi yelled at her, causing her to jump.

"Then what is the truth? You only feel comfortable entering me when your eyes are covered," Jalesa said to him.

"Well, maybe you need to do some freaky witch shit instead of just lying there," I said then Goon growled at me but I could tell he wanted to laugh.

"This isn't any of your concern," Jalesa said to me. Her accent was strong. At times I couldn't understand her.

"Chill out, bro. She is still my mate," Amadi said to me then I shrugged my shoulders.

"Can we talk about this later when I come to bed?" Amadi asked her.

"No, I want to talk about it now. In our bed you don't share your thoughts, but you'd rather sneak out to share them with your brothers," she spat.

"Why aren't you carrying my pup? I marked you and we mated. You should have a swollen belly already," Amadi said.

"And you should leave the past in the past," she spat.

"How can I when you give no reason to?" he yelled. Amadi's body went soaring into the kitchen wall then a bolt of lightning struck his chest. His eyes turned then his snout grew out of his face. Dayo hurriedly grabbed him.

"You can't shift on your mate, bro," Dayo said to Amadi.

Jalesa's feet raised off the floor then her hair started blowing as the windows opened. The sound of thunder echoed through the sky.

"Oh, hell nawl," I said then lightning came through the window. It split the kitchen island in half, which caused our drinks to fall onto the floor. Goon's eyes turned blue, and black hair covered his face.

"Respect our house, Jalesa," Goon warned her.

"Crazy witch," I said then my body went sailing into the wall. I shifted then charged into her but she disappeared. I howled then everyone came running down the stairs.

"What is going on?" Kanya asked half-asleep.

"Jalesa went coco on Amadi and Izra," Dayo said then smirked. Amadi was a little weak but be managed to stand up on his own.

"She is just going through something," Goon said as his face went back to normal. I took my hind leg then scratched behind my ear. Kanya patted my head then scratched behind my ear. I was ready to go to sleep.

"This nigga is really a dog," Dayo said then I growled at him.

"I like him better this way. His beast can be so loveable," Kanya said.

"I'm going to my oil room," Amadi said then grabbed another liquor bottle on his way out of the kitchen. I shifted back then hurriedly grabbed a pan to hold it over my dick because Anik and Kanya were in the kitchen.

"Hold on to that pan like your life depends on it, bro," Dayo said to me. I sat down in the chair with it still covering my dick.

"It's Dayo's turn to roll up," I said. Goon fixed the kitchen island back to normal.

"I want to hit it," Kanya said then grabbed a chair.

"Good night, Anik," Dayo said. She rolled her eyes at him then wobbled out of the kitchen.

"I'm ready for the pups to come," Dayo said.

"What happened to Jalesa?" Kanya asked Goon.

"We'll talk about it later, beautiful," Goon said to her then she kissed him.

"Y'all are just too mushy," I said.

"You need help," Kanya replied.

"Don't say nothing to her that will get you fucked up, baby bro," Goon said to me.

"If he hits you, Izra, then I will jump on him. We will have to jump that big muthafucka. Have you seen his ancient beast?" Dayo asked me.

"What ancient beast?" I asked.

"Nigggggaaaaaaa, you done missed a lot of shit chasing that wolf. We ambushed Sosa's pack and there were a lot of them. Sosa even had humans shooting at me with poison bullets. But this nigga turned into a wolf version of the abominable snowman. He tore Dash's head off like Godzilla. I haven't looked at the nigga right since," Dayo said then Goon fell over laughing. Kanya laughed until she screamed.

"I love his ancient beast. I think it's remarkable," Kanya said then blushed. Dayo looked at her then looked at Goon.

"Can I ask y'all something and, nigga, if you hit me it was well worth it. I really need to know if Kanya really mated with your ancient beast," Dayo said.

"Yes, I took all of him," Kanya answered.

"No wonder he needs to duplicate himself to fit inside you," I mumbled. Goon faked a cough then patted his chest. Dayo cleared his throat but I knew he wanted to laugh.

"You told him about our sex?" Kanya screamed at Goon.

"Naw, not really," Goon answered.

"So, Dayo and Izra must think I don't have any walls," Kanya said.

"Well, do you?" Dayo asked then Kanya stormed out the kitchen.

"I'll see you in a few, beautiful," Goon called out to her. Once he heard the door slam he laughed until tears filled his eyes. Dayo and I just stared at him until he stopped. "She is always uptight," he said then passed the blunt to Dayo.

"Well, are you going to answer for her? Izra and I are waiting for it," Dayo said.

"Kanya is tighter than a keyhole," Goon answered seriously.

"No wonder she got you acting bipolar and doing human-like shit like getting married," I said.

"Pussy whipped," Dayo said.

"Aren't we all," Goon answered.

"When is Kofi going back home?" I asked Goon.

"Come on, nigga, don't start that shit. Let it go because Kofi isn't thinking about Adika. He is like our father and you buggin' on the real," Dayo said.

"I know that, yah bitch. I was going to talk to him before he left. Kofi likes to leave without saying anything," I said to them.

“That’s because it’s hard for him to say good-bye to us,” Goon said.

“How is Adika feeling?” Dayo asked me.

“Better than ever,” I answered.

Amadi

"You are late," Ula said when I walked into her house. I was surprised that she kept the house her adopted parents lived in. She fixed it up then turned the barn into her sanctuary. She had a fence put up around the land, which was shielded to keep other immortals from finding her.

"I've been meeting with you for the past few days and still you give me nothing. Are you going to leave Naobi out of this and give Ammon his beast back?" I asked her.

"Why would I do that, Amadi?" she asked me.

"Because this isn't you. I'm not convinced that you are some wicked witch," I said to her then she smiled.

"That's because I'm not wicked. I'm hurt and have been for a very long time," she spat. She stood up then walked over to me. Her long, black, lace see-through gown dragged the floor. She stood in front of me then slid her hands up and down my chest. "So big and so strong," she said as she looked at me. I pulled away from her.

"I have a mate," I said to her.

"You know the difference between me and Jalesa? I've loved you for many years and she loves you for the moment," she said to me.

"You don't know what you are talking about," I said to her.

"But you know what I am talking about. I only haunted you because you allowed me to. If you weren't thinking about me then I wouldn't have ever been on your mind. You couldn't let me go and that's what hurt me, Amadi. You held on to me for many years and not once did you come back. That's what made a part of me hate you," she said to me.

"It's too late," I said to her.

"Perhaps, you are right. You know I can curse you and have you kissing my feet and serve me the finest wine. I can turn you into my slave, but I'd rather have the real thing than a façade," she said.

Her phone rang. She held out her hand and her phone floated to her. She answered the phone. "What is it, Sosa?" she asked him.

"I need to see you again. I'm sorry at how things have gotten between us. I've been craving you since the night I entered you," I heard him through the phone.

"I am no longer working with you, so find another person to look over your money. I made you rich and you led me to Ammon! The only reason I stayed around your home was because of Anik. Our dealings are done! I could've killed you when you put your hands on me, but I saw a better vision of your death," Ula spat into the phone.

"I will have you again! I marked you and the way I made you scream is all the confirmation I need! You belong to me and you will see that," he said to her. I snatched the phone from her then crumbled it inside my hand.

“How dare you not show me any respect. You answered for another beast in my presence,” I said to her.

“Why does it matter to you?” she asked me.

“It doesn’t,” I spat. Her finger traced the outline of my jaw.

“You are so handsome to me. Your love was so delicate, it made my heart warm. How can I forget you?” she asked sadly but I couldn’t respond. She walked away from me then sat in her black chair with the high back and gold trim around it. She seductively crossed her thick, smooth legs. “I like this little game of yours. You want me to change my mind about Naobi before the pack catches onto me, huh?” she asked me.

“Why do you ask me questions that you have the answer to?” I asked her.

“Make love to me then I will leave Naobi alone,” she said.

“You want me to relive what I did to you?” I asked her.

“You can’t kill me, Amadi. Maybe my spirit but not my presence, which is all you left me with anyway,” she said then a glass of wine appeared in her hand. She took a sip as she eyed me from my shoes to my head. She craved me—I could tell by the way her nipples poked through the fabric. Although she was in lust, I could see the love she had for me in her eyes.

“You smell like another wolf,” I said to her.

“Who taught you how to make those fragrances? I taught you how to make them. Don’t worry, I soaked all morning in a tub full of special herbs,” she said to me.

“I have a mate,” I said to her.

“What you have is wasting time, our time. How was she when you entered her? Did your beast go crazy or were you able to tame him?” she asked me.

“I was able to tame him,” I said to her. She slowly lifted her gown then opened her legs. Her hairless sex was spread open and the scent that poured from between her legs was desirable.

“When you entered me you couldn’t control him. Your beast craved me. Your beast stared into my eyes. I was the beauty in your eyes. Unlike your mate, you can’t even stare at her when you enter her. That is why you can tame your beast, your eyes are always covered. I see visions of you and her. I’m still connected to you, Amadi,” she said. I turned around then headed toward the door then she appeared in front of it.

“If you tell me that you no longer feel something for me then I will let you be. If you tell me and mean it, I will let you walk out of that door and you will never hear from me again. I will let you live your life and I will move on. Tell me you don’t want us,” she said. I stared into her eyes and flashbacks of me and Ula popped up into my head…

“Let’s go to the fair,” Elle said to me.

"Kofi doesn't want us around humans," I replied.

"We can say we went hunting," he said as we walked through the woods.

"Okay, but we can't stay long," I said to him. It was 1945 when Elle and I went to an all-negro fair. A Black family had the fair every year on their land. It was the talk of the town and Elle wanted to go. It was the first time I'd ever been around a lot of humans.

"Try this," Elle said handing me a brown paper bag of popcorn. I stuffed a handful inside my mouth then I started to gag.

"What is that?" I asked then spat it out.

"It's human food. How can they eat that?" Elle asked me then I shrugged my shoulders. A sweet fragrance filled my nose. I hadn't smelled anything like it before. I followed the scent until I ended up at a table with small glass bottles lined up on it. Behind the table sat the prettiest human I had ever laid eyes on. She looked at me.

"Five cents a bottle," she said to me.

"I 'on know what da me," I said to her. It wasn't clear English like the way she spoke but she understood me.

"Five cents a bottle or you don't want any?" she asked me.

"No," I said to her.

"Are you shy? What's wrong with you, boy?" she asked me. I turned to walk away but she called out to me. "I can give you one," she said to me. I walked back to her then she grabbed my hand, placed the bottle inside my hand.

"I made this oil, it is very good for your skin. Drop a few drops into your bath and your skin will be very smooth," she said to me. I opened the small bottle then sniffed it—it was this scent that drew me to her table.

"Smells good," I said to her.

"Thank you. I sit in that barn over there and make them all day. I can show you how to make them if you like," she said to me. Elle called out to me then I waved her good-bye.

"Was that a human?" Elle asked me.

"Yes, she is very beautiful," I said to him.

"We will not tell anyone about this," he said as we headed back home to our small house deep inside the woods.

The next day I snuck back out then headed to the barn where she said she made her oils. I snuck in through the back of the barn. "I know it's you," she called out. I stepped out from behind a stack of hay.

"Come and sit with me," she said. She had a lot of pots and bowls in front of her. The bowls that sat in front of her had different types of flowers inside them. She crushed

the flowers up with a small stick. I sat down next to her. "What's your name?" she asked me.

"Amadi," I answered her.

"My name is Ula. I don't talk to many people, especially boys, because my father will be mad," she said.

"My fada will be mod, too," I answered her.

"How old are you?" she asked me.

"Seventeen," I lied.

"I am, too," she answered then stared at me. She grabbed a bowl of flowers. "Now crush these up and I will tell you what to do from there," she said to me...

I traced my finger down her neck where I bit her. I leaned forward then kissed her neck. She wrapped her arms around me when I slowly licked her neck. I traced my tongue up her chin until I landed on her lips.

"Tell me to go away, Amadi," she said.

"I can't," I replied then picked her up. She wrapped her legs around me then I lay her down on the kitchen table. I slowly ripped the thin material gown off her. Her plump, brown nipples stared at me. I leaned down then captured one into my mouth. My other hand slid up her leg then between her legs. I toyed with her sex as she slowly grinded onto my hand.

"I know you want to explore me but I need it now," she begged. I undid my pants then pulled down my boxers.

Ula pulled my shirt over my head then kissed my chest. I had to remind myself that she had been with other males and she was more experienced since our first time. I pushed her back then slid her down to the edge of the table. She squeezed her breasts with one hand then played in her sex with the other. She moaned loudly as she pleasured herself.

"Watch me," she said then stuck a finger inside her pussy. She pulled her wet finger out of herself then stuck her finger inside my mouth. She stood up then pulled me down on the floor. I laid on my back as she climbed on top of me. I grabbed at her breasts then she slid down my length. She moaned. "SHIT!" When all of my dick disappeared inside her, I growled. It felt like I was home as her walls gripped me. She slowly rocked back and forth then rotated her hips.

She leaned forward then gripped the back of my head. "Bite me, Amadi," she said to me.

"No," I said. She lifted up then slammed herself down onto me.

"Bite me and fuck me!" she said. My sharp teeth bit into her neck. I thrust upward inside her until I couldn't go any further. I grabbed her hips then pumped upward. Ula's body bounced up and down as I slid in and out of her. She screamed my name as her pussy came on me.

"Oh, shit, Amadi! Baby, don't stop!" she screamed then I sat up. I sucked on her breasts as I continued to bounce her up and down on my length. I lifted her up from under her legs, her legs rested over the crook of my arms. She wrapped her arms around me as I slowly slid her up and down my swollen dick.

"DAMN IT!" she moaned. I looked down and watched her come drizzle down my length. My dick stretched her open with each thrust. She rotated her hips on me then I bit her again, harder than the first time. Her legs trembled as her breasts pressed against my chest.

"It hurts like hell but it feels so good," she screamed as she bounced on me, which caused me to howl. She pushed me back then turned around. Her back faced me as she planted her knees on the floor. She leaned forward to grab my ankles. She bounced her round bottom on my dick. I watched as her tight pussy gripped all of my size as she rode the life out of me. My nails palmed her ass then I slammed her down onto me. Ula's body trembled then jerked as I continued to bring her up and down on my dick. My nails put three long scratches down her back, opening her skin.

"Fuck me harder!" she screamed. I pulled her back then turned her over. She lay flat on her stomach, her wetness was smeared across her round bottom. I spread her then slid back in. She scratched at the carpet as I rammed myself into her.

"Harder, baby, harder! I'm about to come again! OHHHHHHH, AMMMAADDDIIIIIIIII!" she screamed. I turned her over then slid back into her. Her legs wrapped around me then I kissed her. I slowed down because I swelled even bigger and didn't want to hurt her again.

"I'm not afraid of your beast," she said then sucked on my bottom lip.

"But I am," I said to her.

"Don't be. I'm the beauty in the eyes of your beast. He won't hurt me because he craves me too. Go inside me until you reach my spot. I want you to swell up. I want to feel all of your beast, Amadi," she said.

I sucked on her lip as I slid further inside her. Her body tensed because of the pressure I caused. When I reached her mushy soft spot, she dug her nails into my back as she creamed on me harder. Her upper body rose from the floor then her eyes rolled to the back of her head. I howled out as my semen squirted inside her. My beast clawed at the carpet as he came inside her. I bit her breast then she cried but not because of the pain. She cried because my beast gave her an unbearable pleasure. I lay down on top of her until I was able to pull out without hurting her.

****

"You got my hair wet," Ula fussed when she stepped out of the shower. I stepped out behind her then picked her up. "You were always playful," she said then giggled. I tossed her up then caught her over my shoulder. I smacked her behind. "Put me down, Amadi!" she laughed.

"What's the magic words?" I asked her.

"Ughh, you still remember that?" she asked.

"I love Amadi," she said then I dropped her onto her bed. She pulled me down next to her then lay on my chest. "We had the best picnics. I always brought you a sandwich but you would never eat it. You made up every excuse in the book so that you wouldn't eat it because you didn't want to hurt my feelings. I used to make them for you anyway," she said to me.

"Wolves don't find peanut butter and banana sandwiches appealing," I said. I rubbed my fingers through her hair.

"I missed when you used to do that," she said to me.

"I'm sorry, Ula," I blurted out.

"I know," she said then giggled.

"Can you give Ammon his beast back?" I asked her.

"I guess so. He was an asshole," she said then sat up. "Let's go out on a date," she said then jumped up. Right before my eyes she was dressed in black leather pants and a red leather jacket. She wore a pair of red heels and her hair was pinned up.

"Witches amaze me," I said.

"You know, Amadi. You are still a young wolf. You look to be around twenty-five. You don't need to dress so casual all the time. You need to get with the program," she said to me.

"My brothers tell me that," I said then stood up.

"You have a nice physique, very tall and muscular like a male model. You will look good in a pair of jeans and a nice, fitted shirt," she said as she walked around me.

"You want me to dress like a human?" I asked her.

"Baby, we live like humans. This is our world, and we have to blend in. I lived on Earth for many, many years and

I always followed the times," she said. My eyes roamed over her hips and the way her pants hugged her curves. She blushed. "Naughty boy," she said. When I looked down I was fully dressed. I looked at my shoes. "Those are Jordan tennis shoes. You will love them," she said. She pushed me in front of her mirror. I wore a fitted gray shirt with a hoodie on it and a pair of stylish jeans.

"My tribal marking is showing around my neck," I said to her.

"It's sexy!" she said then rubbed her hands up my arms. "It still amazes me how perfect you are," she said.

"This is the real you, Ula. You are not an evil witch. I know you were supposed to be but it wasn't meant for you to be this way," I said to her.

"Truth is I don't know who, or what, I am. I only know what I am when I'm with you. Without you, I'm lost," she said sadly. I pulled her to me then hugged her.

"I was the same way, too. When I buried you a part of me went with you. I have not been the same since then," I admitted.

"Let's go," she said then pulled me out of her room.

****

"I thought we were going out on a date. This isn't a date," I said to Ula then she smiled.

"It is for me. I always wanted to do this," she said as she held a pair of pants against me.

“I don’t like shopping,” I said to her. She stormed to another clothes rack. Ula was the center of attention inside the store. All the human males stared at her as she sashayed in her high heels.

“I didn’t think you came to the mall,” a voice said from behind me. Kanya and Adika stood behind us. Kanya had the pups in a double-seated stroller.

“It’s a long story,” I said to them.

“Amadi, try this on!” Ula called out. Kanya and Adika peeked around me. Kanya growled at me then Adika smirked.

“Are you creepin’?” Adika asked me. Ula walked over to us. “Damn, she is beautiful,” Adika said then Kanya nudged her.

“Umm, Ula, these are my sisters. Kanya and Adika, this is Ula,” I introduced them. Adika waved but Kanya didn’t.

“I’m sure they are Jalesa’s friends,” Ula said.

“You know about Jalesa?” Kanya asked.

“I know about everything that involves Amadi” Ula said.

“I think we should stay out of this,” Adika whispered to Kanya.

“They don’t cheat. It’s not in their tradition,” Kanya whispered back to Adika but Ula and I heard her.

"It's not in his tradition, but I was with him many years ago. When a beast loves, he loves for eternity," Ula said.

"She knows a lot," Adika said.

"I know EVERYTHING about Amadi. It was nice to finally meet you two," she said to them. She kissed my lips. "I will be over in the shoe section," she said then strutted off.

"WOW! She is a bad bitch," Adika said then Kanya growled at her.

"What? I'm sorry, but she is. You see her body? I'm so jealous right now. It's almost as if she was created to be perfect. Is she a wolf?" Adika asked.

"She didn't smell like an animal. I'm assuming she is a witch," Kanya said.

"They make witches like that?" Adika asked then Kanya rolled her eyes at her.

"Would you stop it? He is with Jalesa," Kanya whispered.

"I know but she just said she was with Amadi years ago. If that is true, then Amadi's heart was never meant to be given to anyone else. Look how he looks at her. They have an unfinished love," Adika whispered back.

"I'm standing right here," I said to them.

"I'm staying out of this. We love Jalesa like a sister and I just hope you tell her before it's too late," Kanya said.

"Ms. Jalesa struck my man with a bolt of lightning," Adika fussed.

"Do you blame her?" Kanya asked.

"Don't nobody use witchcraft on Izra but me," Adika spat then Kanya rolled her eyes.

"Where is Jalesa?" I asked them.

"She went to lunch with Naobi," Kanya said.

"Okay, I will see you two at the house," I said then walked off.

****

I put my shopping bags in the closet inside my bedroom.

"We need to talk," Jalesa's voice said from behind me. When I turned around, she stared into my eyes. Guilt filled my chest but I couldn't help who I was in love with. I thought I'd killed Ula and knew I had to move on, but she wasn't dead.

"I know," I said.

"I'm sorry for what I did to you the other night," she said then guilt really hit me.

"I'm sorry, too, Jalesa. I never meant for any of this to happen," I said to her.

"I knew you weren't ready but I kept pressuring you. I thought maybe if I gave myself to you then you would forget about her. You still talk to her, Amadi, and she is dead," Jalesa said.

"She isn't dead," I said to Jalesa.

"That's what makes me mad! In your mind she is alive but she really isn't," Jalesa said.

"She isn't dead. I thought she was, but she isn't," I said then tears fell from Jalesa's eyes.

"That's why I can't give you a pup. You don't love me the same way you once loved her," she said.

"What did you do to our pup, Jalesa? You want me to give you answers but you can't give me one! The one answer that means a lot to me. What did you do, because I know for sure that you had one inside your womb," I yelled at her.

"In Anubi, it is forbidden to have a pup by a male who belongs to another female," she said then wiped her eyes.

"This isn't Anubi, Jalesa. What did you do to it?" I asked her.

"I drank a potion to make it disappear from my womb," she said.

"There are witches with hearts darker than yours and they would never do some shit like that. You killed our pup? That's why I lost a connection to you," I said to her.

"That's it, Amadi. Our connection was never really there," she said.

"Bullshit, and you know it! I felt something for you and you will not stand there and tell me I didn't. Despite what you thought, I did feel something for you. Did you not see what Izra and Adika went through when she lost their pup? You turn around and do the same shit to me?" I asked her.

"It's my tradition, Amadi. Those are the rules that I have known all my life. You and I are from two different worlds," she said.

"I'm from the same world as you but I don't believe in what you believe in. This pack takes life very seriously. Our pups are not just made from passion. We make our pups with females that we love. That pup was connected to me! Our bond with our pup is strong even if we never get to see them. I knew you were pregnant and you lied to me," I said to her.

"I'm going back to Anubi when the portal opens," she said to me.

"That would be for the best," I said to her then hurt filled her eyes.

"I'm sorry, Amadi," she said.

"I don't think I will ever forgive you for that. You don't know how bad my beast wants to rip your face apart.

I'm starting to think that Anubi isn't shit but a world full of heartless immortals. I have not seen one innocent immortal come from there, not one!" I said to her then she disappeared.

"What are you yelling for?" Elle asked me after he knocked on my door.

"Jalesa killed my pup." I said to him.

"Are you sure?" Elle asked not believing me.

"What the fuck I got to lie for, Elle?" I asked him then he held his arms up.

"Calm down, bro. I just didn't think as old-fashioned as she is that she would do something like that," he said.

"That's why she did it. She is too old-fashioned," I replied.

****

"I don't know about this, Amadi," Ula said as we stood in front of Naobi's house.

"You've got to give Ammon his beast back," I said to her. I rang Naobi's doorbell. The door opened and Naobi stood in front of us dressed in a gold dashiki with a gold scarf wrapped around her head. She wore jewels around her neck that a human would kill for.

"Who is this witch you bring to my home?" Naobi asked me.

“I’m Ula and I have something to give you,” she said.

“What do you have to give me, and you’d better tell me quick,” Naobi said.

“Ammon’s beast, although I don’t think he needs it,” Ula joked. Naobi stepped aside to let us in. Naobi looked at me then at Ula.

“You must be wicked if you took his beast. You wanted to use it against someone?” Naobi asked.

“Ammon’s beast doesn’t interest me enough to use it. He was in the way of what I was trying to do. Besides, I hate immortals from Anubi. Anubi isn’t nothing but the VIP for hell,” Ula said to Naobi.

“You don’t speak of my world like that,” Naobi seethed.

“I speak on how I see it,” Ula said.

“You speak like someone I know,” Naobi said.

“Saka, he is my father. He created me to give you a message. He wanted me to show you, and tell you, all about the world you speak of,” Ula said then Naobi laughed. Anik, Dayo and I worried that Ula was going to hurt Naobi, but all she wanted to do was show Naobi who Ammon really was.

“Poor Saka must be in an uproar in hell knowing that his daughter isn’t as evil as he is. I couldn’t see a vision of you. I can’t see evil; so how come I couldn’t see you?” Naobi asked Ula.

“I’ve been practicing for years. I know how to shield myself from even you. He taught me how to shield myself from you,” Ula said.

“I can turn you into a pile of dust right now,” Naobi said to Ula.

“I’m not afraid of you. I just want to do what Saka wanted so that I can have my life back peacefully with Amadi,” Ula said. Naobi placed her hand over Ula’s heart then closed her eyes. I didn’t know what she was doing but a white light beamed from Ula’s chest then it went away.

“Love made you pure? You really love him?” she asked Ula.

“Don’t be surprised,” Ula said then Naobi laughed.

“I find this witch amusing. She has a very slick tongue even when she knows I can cut it out,” Naobi said then held her hand out.

“Where is his beast?” Naobi asked. Ula snatched off a necklace from around her neck. The charm that hung from the necklace was shaped like a spear. A black cloud swirled around inside the charm.

“Follow me,” Naobi said.

“For what?” Ula asked.

“You did the curse so you shall do it again,” Naobi said to Ula. Jalesa came down the stairs.

“My queen, I’m heading out to Kanya’s store,” Jalesa said. She froze in her tracks when she saw Ula and I.

“Who is she?” Jalesa asked.

“I’m the dead girl. Nice to finally meet you,” Ula said to her.

“You were telling the truth?” Jalesa asked me. A force started to choke me. I growled as I felt my body shifting. A snake slithered across the floor then wrapped around Jalesa’s throat. Naobi turned the snake into ashes.

“Cut it out!” Naobi yelled.

“One more time, Jalesa. I have been very calm with you but that will be the last time you use that witch shit on me,” I said to her.

“She used it on you before? I haven’t used any on you, and yet, you killed me. She is very bold,” Ula said.

“Cut it out, Ula,” I said to her then she rolled her eyes.

“Where is Ammon’s body?” Ula asked.

“You did that Ammon?” Jalesa asked Ula.

“Of course, I did. I didn’t like him. He thought he was going to walk around here playing king when his throne is in another world. I had to show him that this isn’t his world and he doesn’t belong. I believe that Anubi needs to be separate from us. The two separate worlds don’t mesh well. You all just come here, but the immortals on Earth are forbidden from there. You tell me if that is fair or not,” Ula seethed.

“We are always welcome on Earth,” Jalesa said.

“Well, let’s give out passes to the immortals on Earth to go to Anubi. Have you seen the wolves from here? They are vicious and they care for no one. The packs they travel in are just packs without meaning behind them. The packs here don’t have tradition or the same beliefs as you all. But you all come from Anubi and flaunt your royalty into the poor immortals’ faces. I never knew how bad the wolves were, until one came into the bank I work at for a loan. Sosa is one of those many wolves,” Ula said.

“Sosa has an evil heart,” Naobi said.

“That may be true, but he has the heart of a wolf who would do anything to survive. His pack was poor and could barely eat. I know this doesn’t concern you, but you all need to learn what it is like to not have the finer things in life. You can’t come to Earth and call someone evil because their struggle was different than the struggles in Anubi. I bet the youngest pup in Anubi has gems around his or her neck,” Ula said.

“She speaks like a demon,” Jalesa said.

“No, she speaks of an immortal who cares about other immortals. You have so much hate for Anubi but this wolf that you are in love with was born there,” Naobi said.

“He was born there but his heart is on Earth. Saka wasn’t always heartless. Ask Ammon what he did to him before his heart filled with hate. Ammon had Musaf turn Saka that way because Saka refused a favor for him. Musaf poisoned Saka with demon snake blood for Ammon. You think Saka took the innocent souls from Egypt just to do it?

He took pure souls so that his heart could become pure again, but that demon he was possessed with was too big to fight. Musaf gave Ammon what he wanted in return for a life in Anubi. How do you think an old witch who does evil voodoo got into Anubi?" Ula asked.

"She isn't speaking the truth," Jalesa said.

"What reason do I have to lie? I already got what I wanted," Ula said then grabbed my hand.

"My father took me from my mother," Naobi said.

"Your father knew that your human mother's village would've burned you. You think people don't get scared when they hear the name, witch?" Ula asked.

"I didn't see those visions," Naobi said.

"Even the strongest witch can be brainwashed. My father always told me that. I never knew who he was talking about until now," Ula said.

"My father never told me what Ammon did. He had a chance to tell me when I begged him to give me strength to give birth to Akua," Naobi said.

"Saka tried to tell you but because he was evil, you did not listen," Ula replied.

"Musaf got rid of Saka's soul," Naobi said sadly.

"To cover up Ammon's filthy trash! Are you sure you want me to give him his beast back? Hell, Anubi needs to thank me for doing them a favor," Ula said then chuckled. A bolt of lightning struck Ula from Jalesa.

"Don't speak of my world with so much filth," Jalesa said. Ula got up.

"The world that you were a peasant in? Which one were you? The bitch that served grapes or do you fan the king and queen's faces when they got hot? I bet you did all of that," Ula said. A big wave of red electricity slammed into Jalesa, sending her into the wall.

"What on Earth is this shit?" a deep voice roared. When I turned around Kumba stood in the middle of his living room with green eyes.

"Take me to Ammon's body," Ula said then Naobi put her head down. I remembered that Naobi didn't want Kumba to know about Ammon being locked away inside his house.

"Who is she and what about Ammon's body?" Kumba asked as he undid his tie.

"I'm Ula, Naobi's sister," Ula answered.

"Where is Ammon's body, Naobi?" Kumba asked.

"In the basement," Naobi answered.

"Your old mate is in my basement?" Kumba yelled at Naobi.

"We are here to pick him up, bro," I said to Kumba.

"Why is that muthafucka in my basement is all I want to know," Kumba seethed.

"Do I have to spill the tea all over again?" Ula asked. I pulled her back.

"Not now, Ula!" I warned her.

"Is he going to attack her?" she asked me.

"No, he is just angry. I think he will attack Ammon instead," I answered her.

"His body was found in the woods. I brought him here to figure out a way to wake him. Ula took his beast from him and now she is returning it," Naobi answered calmly.

"What the fuck is going on in Anubi now?" Kumba asked.

"Stop yelling, Kumba," Naobi said to him.

"Stop yelling? You have a mess in my living room like a storm has been through it and you have your old mate inside my house. Yet, you want me to stop yelling?" Kumba asked. Kumba walked out of the living room toward the basement. He snatched the door off but there was a metal wall blocking the doorway.

"I hope like hell you didn't touch him. Remove this wall, Naobi," Kumba said but Ula moved it out of the way.

"Sorry, but Amadi and I have plans. I'm kind of in a rush, so we need to hurry up," Ula said then headed down the stairs. The basement looked like it belonged in Anubi. The walls were like red clay with hieroglyphics sketched on them. Naobi had candles lit everywhere. In the corner of the basement, Ammon lay asleep on a bed.

“Hurry up and wake him up so I can mess him up. I would be less of a man if I attacked my prey while it slept,” Kumba said.

“That will not fix anything! No matter what you do to Ammon, it won’t fix anything. All I want is for him to return to Anubi, so that Akua doesn’t have to. I want peace, Kumba. That’s all I want. Is that so hard to ask for?” Naobi said then Kumba calmed down.

“The only thing that is keeping me away from that jackass is the love I have for you. But once he wakes his ass up, he is out of here. I don’t even want him to take a breath inside my house,” Kumba fussed.

“What made you put Ammon’s beast inside that charm? It would’ve made you more powerful if you had used it,” Naobi said.

“When I took his beast, I saw a lot of his demons. I saw things that I shouldn’t have seen. Saka told me a lot but Ammon’s beast showed me even more. I could no longer tolerate him,” Ula said.

“I don’t believe her,” Jalesa said.

“I believe her and I have no idea who she is,” Kumba spat. Ula put the charm to her lips then inhaled the black cloud in. She put her lips to Ammon’s lips then blew his beast back inside him. A growl slipped from my lips as I watched her kiss Ammon. Moments later, Ammon’s eyes fluttered then he coughed. When he sat up he charged into Ula with his hand around her throat.

“You evil witch! I shall seek that you will never breathe again,” he shouted. I charged into Ammon then slammed him against the wall.

“You don’t put your hands on a female,” I said to him then his eyes turned. He pushed me off him then fixed his shirt.

“What is all of this chaos?” he asked as he looked around. Kumba roared but Naobi put her hand on his chest; he calmed down.

“Get this sucka’ out of my house, now!” Kumba shouted. Ammon growled at Kumba.

“You want to challenge me? No immortal will live after challenging the king of Anubi,” Ammon spat.

“Can I take his beast back? I know an antique shop that I can sell the necklace to right around the corner,” Ula said then Kumba chuckled.

“Hush up, jezebel,” Ammon said to Ula.

“Bro, watch your mouth,” I warned Ammon then he laughed,

“You let these immortals brainwash you? You have Anubi roots! You watch your tongue or I will punish you,” Ammon said to me then looked at Naobi.

“You will leave now! Enough of this and that feline. You belong in Anubi with me. This is not your world and you will not live here,” Ammon said. Kumba charged into Ammon but a force pulled him back then held him down. A lot of nasty words spewed from Kumba's mouth as Naobi held him down with her magic.

"I need answers, Kumba," Naobi pleaded with him. Ammon smiled at Kumba.

"My beautiful queen, come back where you belong. I care nothing about your sins. I just need you back next to me," Ammon pleaded then Kumba roared. Ula and Jalesa covered their ears.

"What did you do to my father?" Naobi asked Ammon.

"I will not answer anyone who isn't my ruler. I'm my own ruler and I will not answer to you," Ammon replied.

"Wow," Ula mumbled.

"Let's go to Anubi, my king," Naobi said.

"Are you going to leave with him?" Kumba asked hurt.

"Yes," Naobi said. She grabbed Ammon then disappeared into a gold bright light.

"The portal isn't open. She must have used a spell," Jalesa said. Kumba was free to stand up, his eyes glowed then he punched a hole in the cement wall.

"What just happened?" Kumba asked.

"Naobi went back to Anubi," Jalesa said. Naobi's arm reached out of gold light. She pulled Jalesa inside the light then it disappeared.

"Anubi is so rich that even their portal shines gold," Ula said.

"I don't think Naobi left to go home," I said to Kumba.

"She is alone with that punk," Kumba seethed.

"She left Anubi with unfinished business. I think she is going to fix what she can. I know that she will be back," I assured Kumba.

"I hope like hell she does because I will find a way to get her back! I don't know how but I will find a way there," Kumba said.

"I don't think Ammon is really the problem other than the fact that he wants power and can't seem to keep his dick inside his pants. The real problem is Musaf, the voodoo cat warlock," Ula said.

"How do you know of Ammon's affairs?" I asked Ula.

"You will see. Let's just say that if Ammon dies, Goon will not be the one to rule Anubi. The oldest son has to be the ruler," Ula said then she checked her nails. The broken nail grew out long and pointy. The color turned from black to red on all of her pointy, witch nails.

"How do you think this color looks on me?" she asked then held her hand out.

"Not now, Ula. Who is Ammon's oldest son?" I asked then she smiled.

"If I tell you now then the bomb won't explode when it drops," Ula said.

"I need a drink," Kumba said.

"Great, dinner is on me," Ula said to him.

"Where is Keora?" I asked as I looked around.

"I can longer keep up with these witches," Kumba said as he noticed she was missing too.

Ula picked up a spell book. Her hand swiped over it then it opened. The pages flipped by itself then stopped. "It is telling what was last read. It looks like someone did a reincarnation," she said.

"It's always something," Kumba said.

"I'm hungry so can we go now? Then tonight I can rub my beast down with some oil and listen to him growl. I'm in a rush, so let's go," Ula said then hurried up the stairs.

"You must've really bit the hell out of her. She is very smitten by your beast," Kumba said.

"You don't want to know the whole story," I said to him then we followed Ula.

Elle

"I often wondered what animal is really a shifter," Fabia said as we stood in front of a lion's cage at the zoo. Fabia was a breath of fresh air. She was beautiful inside and out, and had a smile that could brighten up the whole room.

"My plane leaves in a few days. I will be heading back to Africa. I only came for Camille. I hate this city. It is filled with so much pain," Fabia said. I didn't want her to go but with a past like the one she had, I couldn't stop her.

"I will miss you," I admitted then she grabbed my hand.

"Come with me for a month. My village is filled with a lot of spiritual beliefs," she said.

"I know, I've been there plenty of times," I said to her.

"I want you to come to the village I am from. It is sacred and I'm sure you haven't been there. They will welcome you with open arms. A nice, tall, toned wolf like yourself would draw all of the attention," she said. I wrapped my arm around her shoulder then whispered into her ear.

"What if I just wanted attention from a beauty like yourself?" I asked her then she blushed.

"Are you flirting with me, Elle?" she asked me.

"Don't I always?" I replied.

"Are you always arrogant?" Fabia asked me.

"Yes, my beast can be," I said then stared at her. "What were Camille's intentions? She told me to call you before she died. Do you think about that?" I asked Fabia.

"Camille had different beliefs. She believed that if two beasts came into her life then it was a sign. I told her it wasn't a sign because she was in love with you, and you belonged to her," Fabia said.

"My tribe believes in fate. We believe that every purpose has a cause. Sometimes we might fall in love so that it can lead us to our soulmate. I think Camille coming into our lives meant something. It's not every day a beast falls for a human, a human that will eventually die. Beast soulmates mate for life. We all are destined to be with someone who will live for eternity," I replied.

"Are you telling me that our lives are already mapped out?" she asked me.

"In our tradition that's what we believe in. Our ancestors have visions of us and they drew it on the walls inside their temples," I answered.

"That is a beautiful belief," she said then looked at the lion.

"The belief isn't as beautiful as you. Now, let's go see the monkeys because they amaze me. They are between being human and animal at the same time, unlike our beasts. When we shift we become something else. They are just stuck," I said then she laughed.

“I never looked at it that way,” she said. I looked down at her lips that had something over them to make them shine. I traced the outline of her full, plump lips with my finger.

“Can I kiss you?” I asked her. Fabia and I went on several dates but we’d never touched each other. I couldn’t help the way I was feeling and I knew how she felt about males. As bad as I wanted to kiss her I waited because I knew it would’ve made her uncomfortable.

“Yes,” she answered. I leaned down then captured her bottom lip into my mouth. I gently sucked on it then she moaned. The scent of her arousal filled my nostrils, my growl unable to be heard by the humans because of the roar coming from the lion. I pulled away from her then she wiped off my lips. “You had lip gloss all over your face,” she said. She grabbed my hand. “Let’s go see the monkeys,” she said.

****

We walked up to the hotel where she stayed.

“I had fun with you today,” she said to me.

“I will see you tomorrow,” I said then she stared at me. “What’s the matter with you?” I asked her.

“I was wondering if you wanted to come up and have a glass of wine with me. I don’t sleep good at night because I have the urge to hunt. I would rather eat store meat then hunt in this city alone at night,” she said.

"You want to go hunting?" I asked her.

"Not really," she said.

"A beast always needs fresh meat, Fabia. Let's go hunting. I know a spot where there is a lot of deer meat," I said to her.

****

I watched as Fabia's beast snuck up on a large buck.

"Be very quiet. If you make a noise it will run, and then you will have to fight with it," I said to her.

"I have not hunted in a long time. The wolves in the village go and seek food for the females," she replied.

"Leap on it," I shouted inside her head. Fabia's beast leaped onto the buck's back.

"Avoid his antlers, they can be very sharp." Her beast dodged the buck's head as it almost slammed into her side. She rolled the beast over then clamped down on its neck.

"He is too strong!" she panicked.

I ran into the buck then sank my teeth into its throat. I jerked his neck inside my mouth, snapping it instantly.

"Show off! That's only because your beast is twice the size of mine," she said. She tore into the buck's stomach hungrily, chewing through it's flesh. Fabia growled as she ate and I watched. She lifted her head with blood dripping from her snout.

"Are you hungry?" she asked.

"No, that meal is all yours. I went hunting with my pack this morning," I replied. After she was done, I licked her face then she nuzzled against me.

"Let's run wild. I hear a water running somewhere close," she said then took off through the woods. I ran after her but her beast was fast. When I caught up to her, I playfully bit her bushy tale.

"Cheater!" she yelled then ran faster until she came to a lake that was deep in the woods. The half-moon and stars brightened up the dark night.

"This is so beautiful, Elle. Nature is amazing and we get to explore the beauty of it. We can run wild inside the woods and let our beasts take us over.

"We have the best of both worlds," I replied.

Fabia slowly shifted back then stood in front of me naked.

"I want to sleep here tonight and watch the sun rise," she said then sat down, snuggled beneath my beast. Fabia looked like a little girl compared to my wolf. Her small hands grabbed my face. "Your beast has eyes like a human. Camille was right," she said. My beast laid out for Fabia so that she wouldn't sleep on the ground. She climbed on my back then got lost inside my fur.

"This is even more comfortable than the bed inside my hotel room," she said.

"Get some rest, Fabia. Once the sun rises my beast will awake to hunt." Moments later, light snores echoed through my ears. I didn't sleep because lone wolves always moved around in the deep, dark woods at night.

****

Fabia climbed down off my back then stretched out. My eyes roamed her naked body and the mound between her legs. Her sweet scent filled my nostrils. My beast wanted to take her but I had to resist. I slowly shifted back to human form then she eyed me. Her eyes roamed over my body then stared at what hung between my legs.

"Is everything okay?" I asked her.

"Ummm. Yeah. Uh-uhmm," she stuttered then cleared her throat. "I'm sorry, what did you ask me?" she asked.

"Our eyes never deceive us. It's all there if you want it," I flirted then she blushed.

"What makes you think I'm interested in that part of you?" she asked with her hands on her hips. I sniffed the air then growled.

"Your morning arousal is driving me crazy," I said to her.

"That is just rude how you male wolves can invade our privacy," she said then laughed.

"Scent is a part of animal instincts. I'm a man, beautiful, but I'm still all animal and your scent is driving it crazy," I said to her.

"You make everything sound so perfect even telling me that the scent from my pussy is driving you crazy. Very classic, Elle, but I have to take a rain check," she said then walked past me. Her round bottom jiggled and her nipples poked out far enough for me to capture between my lips.

"Down, boy," she said then I grabbed her hand. I pulled her to me then kissed her. She didn't fight it, she kissed me back with the same amount of passion I had for her. My hand slid between her legs and she was dripping. The scent became even stronger, which caused blood to travel down to the tip of my dick.

"Your body is ready to go into heat," I said then pulled away.

"That's why I need to hurry back home before I get into something that will force me to stay here," she said.

"Are you running from Sosa? If so, I promise you that his time is limited," I said to Fabia.

"It's not Sosa I'm running from, it's you," she said then walked away from me. "Let's find our clothes so we can leave," she said. I wanted to ask her what she meant by running from me but I decided not to. Falling for Camille had taught me not to force something that should come naturally.

****

"What's the matter, bro? You've been quiet," Dayo said to me as we worked out inside the gym room.

"I'm almost afraid to tell you. Talking to you is like getting a tooth pulled," I said to him then he growled at me.

"Very funny, Elle. You've been really acting all thug on us since you stepped foot inside pair of Timbs for the first time," Dayo said to me.

"This nigga is always talking shit. Beat him up, Elle. I will help you out," Izra said when he came into the room.

"Now I'm stuck with you two," I said then shook my head.

"What does that mean?" Izra asked.

"Nothing," I said then continued to bench-press the six-hundred pounds of weights.

"It's that Fabia wolf, isn't it?" Dayo asked.

"Naw," I said then Izra laughed.

"We already know it's her, bro. What are you lying for?" Izra asked then I sat up.

"Okay, damn. She is going back to Africa in a few days and I'm going to miss her. A part of me feels bad because, since I've been kicking it with her, I haven't thought about Camille. It's like Camille is this distant memory," I replied. Dayo and Izra looked at each other then fell out laughing.

“Bro, seriously? Camille’s old ass didn’t want you to think about her. Hell, why would you want to? She was all old skin and bones, bro. Like, I bet our mummified ancestors look younger than Camille. I mean, bro, she looked like a distant memory. I don’t know, Elle. I think you might need to get checked out. I thought you was going to tell us that Fabia was going into heat and you couldn’t resist her. You know, something of that nature,” Izra said then Dayo popped him on the back of his head.

“Nigga, you didn’t even let him finish!” Dayo said to Izra.

“Finish for what? As soon as he said Camille, I stopped listening. I see if she was old and sexy but, bro, she looked like she got ahold of some black magic,” Izra said then Dayo burst into laughter. Dayo laughed until he howled because he couldn’t catch his breath.

“Stupid muthafuckas,” I mumbled.

“Chill out, Izra,” Dayo finally said.

“I’m trying to school our older brother,” Izra answered.

“Bro, don’t listen to this fool. His woman had a spell on him and he didn’t even know it. Then he got caught red-handed eating another wolf’s hot box,” Dayo said.

“I bet you didn’t tell Elle about the human diapers and baby food you bought for Camille. The only reason you didn’t give it to Elle is because she died. If you go into the hall closet you will see all of that shit is still in there, Elle,” Izra said then Dayo pushed him.

“I was helping him out. I didn’t want her crapping all over the place. Old humans are not potty-trained. They go everywhere like animals,” Dayo said.

“Have some respect for human life,” Kofi said when he walked into the room.

“I’ll get up with y’all later. I have to make a run to drop something off at Kanya’s store,” Izra said then walked out of the room.

“My youngest pup doesn’t want anything to do with me,” Kofi said.

“Izra doesn’t know how to apologize when he is wrong. I can see that he is no longer mad. I think he is avoiding the issue because he knows he reacted in a way that he shouldn’t have. He will come around,” I said to Kofi.

“I hope he does before I go back home. Izra is very stubborn when he doesn’t have to be,” Kofi said.

“Why don’t you and your mate come here?” Dayo asked Kofi.

“I’m an old believer. I think we need to be separate from others. Our beliefs and the way of life isn’t the same as the immortals and humans on Earth. I’m stuck in my tradition and I want to live it freely,” Kofi said.

“Anubi isn’t living,” Dayo said.

“It isn’t the place I’m interested in. It’s the meaning behind it that keeps me going back. Anubi was created for the greatest immortals to live. It is a beautiful place that anyone would want to live in. You know the book *Wonderland* that Arya reads? Anubi is like that. The river sparkles because of the diamonds that flow through it. Everything you will ever need is in Anubi. It's like my *Wonderland*," he said.

"Ammon shouldn't be king," I said then Kofi chuckled.

"Ammon was a great warrior who served his people. But he became obsessed with having more than he needed. He is king and he still needs more power. Ammon was never that way until he became the ruler of Anubi. He loved Naobi so much. You could see it in his eyes when he looked at her, but Naobi became stronger as the years passed and Ammon became power-hungry. Greed is a disease of all species. Greed for women and power. It can get the best of us, even after many years of tradition, it can still get us. It takes a strong warrior to not give into the greed and lust. A wolf in heat can walk past Goon and he wouldn't even smell her. Dayo loved many women but when he met his soulmate, he hasn't looked at another female. Izra refused to mate with another female even though Adika wanted him to. She had to curse him for him to even smell another female. You loved a woman for years and watched her fall in love with another man. You stayed with her in her final moments. What you all experienced is what Anubi stood for. Don't let one power-greedy wolf stop you from believing because the tradition flows through our veins," Kofi said.

"Damn, that was deep," Dayo said then patted his chest.

"Are you about to cry, bro?" I asked him.

"I was ready to catch an Anubi holy ghost," Dayo said.

"Holy ghost?" I asked him.

"I went to church with a human woman before. I just wanted some of her goodies. But you got to go one Sunday. The preacher talks then some old woman will stand up. She starts moving like she is trying to dodge a bolt of lightning. She screams, 'hallelujah' then she dances harder. When her hat falls off she has caught the holy spirit," Dayo said then Kofi chuckled.

The door opened then closed. The sounds of heels clicking echoed throughout the hall. Amadi came into the gym room with a beautiful young woman.

"I need to tell y'all something and it's a lot," he said.

Dayo and Kofi looked at the woman. "Bro, I don't think Jalesa is going to like this," Dayo said.

"She and I agreed to part ways because we believed in different traditions. This is Ula," Amadi said. Then Dayo choked on his water.

"That's the evil witch?" Dayo asked.

"Can you people come up with another name besides evil witch? It's so old-fashioned, so fairytale-like," Ula said.

"Where is Goon and Izra? I want everyone to hear this," Amadi said.

"I don't know where they are at but we are listening," Dayo said.

Amadi told us everything about Ula haunting him and her being Naobi's sister. He also told us about Naobi going back to Anubi and taking Ammon and Jalesa with her. I couldn't believe it when Amadi told us that Ammon was the reason for Saka being wicked.

"So, Dayo and Anik knew but didn't tell anybody?" I asked.

"I didn't say anything because I trusted Amadi. He told us he was going to fix it before it blew over. I wasn't worried about anything, but I would like to know where Sosa lays his head. I have a right to know where he kept my mate. He needs to suffer more for what he did to her and Arya. That fight at his club wasn't good enough. I want to see him take his last breath," Dayo spat angrily.

"If I show you where he lives, what do I get in return? Favor for a favor," Ula said.

"Ula, tell Dayo where Sosa lives so that he can make sure Anik, his pups and Arya will remain safe. The games are over, Ula. You got a chance to talk to Naobi and now you have a chance to make all of this nonsense right," Amadi said to her.

"Okay, I will show you," Ula said.

"I think this witch is dick-whipped, bro. You saw how easy that was? This nigga has her in order," Dayo said inside my head.

"She loves him, bro, that's all it is. I don't think she is the push-over type. I think she will do anything to make him happy," I replied to Dayo.

"My wolf brother is too gone. I have known Ammon for years, but in reality, I didn't know Ammon at all. I don't know this beast he has become. I think he died a long time ago," Ammon said then left the room.

"How can you trust her, Amadi?" Dayo asked.

"I will take full responsibility for anything that happens from here on out," he said then I smiled.

"So, you been in love all this time with another woman?" Dayo asked then shook his head.

"Kofi said that once you fall in love nobody else can replace them. That's the true meaning of our tradition, bro. Wolves love their soulmates forever," I said then Dayo stood up.

"I will take care of Sosa myself. That nigga had no business taking my mate while carrying my pups. I won't be happy until he is dead," Dayo said then walked out of the room.

"And you all call me evil. Everyone wants to kill someone from Anubi. You think Naobi can bring me back a necklace from there? Is there a way someone can call her? She owes me for giving her Ammon's beast back," Ula said.

"Bro, how did you end up with a female version of Izra?" I asked Amadi then he shrugged his shoulders.

"Good luck, bro!"

Naobi

I sat at the festival table as I watched Ammon laugh and smile. Jalesa served the wine and grapes. I wasn't happy about what she did but I didn't fault her. Ammon made those rules and everyone had to follow them. A female couldn't carry a child inside her womb if the man wasn't rightfully hers. I wanted Jalesa to be happy and I knew it was going to come for her. I realized why Ammon made those rules; he wanted to sleep with females freely and not have them carry his pup. I could've easily known but like Ula stated, "Even the strongest witch can be brainwashed."

"I want to thank Baki for taking my place while I went to Earth for my mate. He is a great warrior and this feast is for him," Ammon said then held his gold cup that was filled with wine up in the air. Everyone cheered and patted Ammon's back to welcome him home.

"Where is my son?" Kaira asked.

"He is on Earth where he will remain. He betrayed his world and he isn't welcomed back," Ammon said.

"His pups are here!" Kaira yelled.

"Send them back to Earth. I don't want anything to do with them! They cannot live here and you know that!" Ammon roared.

"You animal!" Kaira yelled then growled.

“Throw her in the dungeon until she gives birth. Once she has that pup, send it to Earth so that a human can find it,” Ammon said.

“Are you going to let him do this to me?” Kaira asked me with tears in her eyes.

“He is your king and you should obey his rules,” I said to her.

“When I get my day, this world will be shamed! Every one of you will turn to dust!” Kaira spat as Ammon’s warriors took her away.

“Let’s welcome King Ammon back! Where is the music?” I asked as I held up my cup of wine. Ammon looked at me with admiration. My eyes turned black then the smile on his face disappeared.

“Where is Kofi?” Opal asked me.

“He will come back once everything is settled. Kofi is safer with my son’s pack until I finish what I came to do,” I said to her.

“What are you going to do?” Opal asked then I smiled.

“I’m going to show that son-of-a-bitch how to rule Anubi. By the time I’m done, this will be a new world. Have some wine and enjoy this feast, my sister. Tomorrow the sun will shine over the crystal lake and give this temple the light it has never seen,” I said then got up from the table. The Egyptians danced and feasted as I watched. Baki walked over to Jalesa then whispered something in her ear. I watched Baki and the way he walked. I watched his smile and the way he laughed.

“Have fun, my queen,” Ammon said then wrapped his arm around me.

“Tell me something, my king. Why does your head warrior remind me so much of yourself in your younger days? He even throws his arrow the same way you do. Musaf must have really outdone himself with that spell to disguise Baki as your son. He is quite stunning but he doesn’t look anything like you. Never trust a wolf in sheep’s clothing,” I said to Ammon.

“What are you speaking of? Baki isn’t a pup of mine!” Ammon shouted.

“Who is Baki’s mother?” I asked Ammon.

“You trust an evil witch over your mate?” Ammon asked me.

“Tell me the truth, Ammon, for once in your demonic life. Who is his mother, and what did you and Musaf do to her?” I asked him.

“His mother was poisoned,” he said.

“Are you his father?” I asked him.

“What does it matter?” he asked me.

“Your life,” I said to him then he chuckled. His traced his finger down my cheek.

“Everything I did, it was for you. Your father wanted me to lose you,” Ammon said.

"My father knew what you did and tried to warn me, but Musaf got to him before he could tell me. How did my father know about you and Baki's mother?" I asked him. What Ula had said started to play in my head, the pieces coming together.

"He wouldn't get rid of her even after I told him it would hurt you. He kept telling me that I didn't deserve you," Ammon said then his eyes turned blue.

"You hurt me so much," I said to him.

"Your father told me about your true mate. He told me that you were going to leave me. I knew about Kumba for centuries. Why do you think I bedded other females? I needed your power but I didn't need you," he spat.

"Is that so, my king?" I asked him.

"You can have a better life here. All the diamonds, gold and gems are right here. What are you going to do on Earth? Be someone's peasant and work? The best life is here, and I can give you that in exchange for your magic. Your magic is a gift that can make Anubi so much better and stronger. You waste your magic on nonsense. How about bigger and stronger wolves? Wolves that can take out ten warriors at a time. How about wolves that can use the same energy as Akua?" he asked then I laughed.

"You speak like a rotten and filthy fool. Do you hear yourself? Your imagination is pathetic just like your sex. All that equipment and it's worthless. How about asking for magic for down below, because that's where you really need it. You think I care about jewels? I can make my own jewels and diamonds and more. How did you think our son and his pack have so much of it? The jewelry Akua has is better quality than the jewelry here. I bet you didn't know I could do that, did you? I can do a lot, but what I won't do is be a slave to your filthy ass any longer. I came here to collect your soul and serve it to the hell you came out of," I said to Ammon.

"You wouldn't," Ammon said.

"Akua isn't your oldest son. He will not be the ruler of Anubi. I'm very thankful for the fun you had with your jezebels. It gives Akua a whole new life, which isn't here. That wine you drank at the feast will kick in very soon. I shall watch you take your last breath," I said to him. I pulled him closer to me then whispered in his ear. "When you take your last breath you will beg for me to give you life. And when you do, I will set your body on fire," I said then my hands burned his skin. He backed away from me.

"You don't scare me. I'm a warrior and I faced death many times. My death should be victory," he said then walked away.

"Come and have a glass of wine with me until death comes, my queen," he said, his eyes still blue.

****

I paced back and forth inside my old sanctuary in Ammon's temple.

"Why does Ammon want to die?" I asked Jalesa.

"I don't know. Do you think he is tired of living?" she asked me.

"No, that arrogant donkey is up to something. I must admit, Ammon knows everything about me. If he was a warlock, he would have all my magic. He isn't as much of a fool as we think he is," I said.

"Where is Musaf?" Jalesa asked me.

"I don't know. His mind is shielded and I cannot see his visions. Something is going on, I can feel it. That wine is slowly poisoning Ammon," I said to her.

"Ammon made a deal with Musaf. Musaf made Dash stronger in exchange for me. Ammon didn't keep his end of the deal. That will make him owe Musaf a favor. Musaf will not just leave if someone owes him a favor. A witch never backs down from a favor," Jalesa said.

"Musaf is an old warlock. He is the oldest warlock out of all the warlocks. His strength is becoming weak. He needed you so that you could give him a strong witch child," I said to Jalesa.

"So he could live through the child. Musaf wanted to reincarnate himself through a baby," Jalesa said.

"He doesn't have the baby," I said then it hit the pit of my stomach.

"Musaf's soul is in Kaira's womb. Ammon knew all along what he was doing. He purposely got Kaira pregnant," I said to Jalesa. The bell inside the temple rang, meaning there was an emergency. Jalesa and I disappeared then reappeared inside the main chamber where Ammon held his meetings. Everyone rushed in as Jalesa and I waited. Ammon opened the door then walked in. Everyone bowed down to him as he walked down the golden silk rug. Once he sat down in his chair, everyone stood up.

"Centuries and centuries ago I was once a human. I was hunting for my village one night and came across a beast. The beast was big and black, with eyes the color of the Nile River. He bit me and I died. My mate, who is a witch, saved my life with her magic. The magic she used turned me into the beast that killed me. I died centuries ago, my soul leaving my body. I was a man who protected his village. I was a man who fed his village. I had markings of a true warrior. I was a great man and I lived a great life until the day that beast took my life. I am not Ammon anymore. I am the wolf god! I am the king of Anubi. Ammon doesn't exist to me anymore. Tonight, when the full moon peaks over the river, I will be all beast and man. I will be my ancient beast from here on out. What you see in front of you will not be anymore. I will become stronger and I will rule with my long, gold spear," Ammon told his people and they cheered. Ammon looked at me and said, "In the prophecy that was written thousands of years ago, it said that the wolf god will rule amongst his people as his beast. It said on the night Anubi marks two thousand years that the ruler will change and his beast will become stronger. No magic will kill him and he will become undefeatable," he said.

"Well, that's why Ammon didn't care about dying. He knows that he can't," Jalesa said.

"Now, let's celebrate this new beginning for the king of Anubi!" Ammon shouted.

"I think Akua will have to defeat his father," I said then Ula's words came into my head again. "Even the strongest witch can be brainwashed."

“What have I created?” I asked Jalesa.

“A wise witch once told me that we will all face our biggest opponent even if we are stronger. You taught me that many years ago,” Jalesa said to me.

“I can defeat him but the stronger his beast, the more power I will have to use. The more power I use then the weaker I will become. I’m not a young witch anymore. I have so many years on me that I lost count. I can fight him but I won’t last long,” I said.

“Goon is very strong. Ammon only has his beast but Goon has beast and magic. I know you don’t want to hear this, but Goon is Anubi’s only hope. He is the only one who can defeat Ammon. Once Ammon becomes this beast, Anubi will turn to hell. We must save our people,” Jalesa said.

“You will make a great queen one day. I saw a glimpse of your future earlier. I hope that you forgive Amadi because your heart will heal and you will fall into a greater love,” I said to her.

“I forgave Amadi as soon as I set foot back in Anubi. This is my world and I belong here,” she said. Ammon turned over his hourglass.

“When all of the sand is gone, Anubi will have a new king. I will not accept Ammon as my name, I will be called by my last name Uffe. Uffe means ‘wolf man.’ The body of a man with a head like my beast. If the name Ammon slips from anyone’s lips, there will be a punishment. Your tongue will be cut from your mouth. Your mate will be taken away from you,” Ammon said.

“I must hurry back to the portal to warn Akua. Keep everyone safe until I get back,” I said to Jalesa then hugged her before I rushed off. The sand was going to run out, and fast. Akua’s ancient beast came from me. What Ammon waited thousands of years for, Akua was born with it. Akua was born a beast and Ammon was turned into one. Akua is stronger than his father and Ammon knows it.

****

I reappeared inside Akua’s mansion. The kitchen light turned on and a naked Izra stood in front of me.

“What are you doing?” I asked him.

“Hi, Naobi,” Adika said as she hid behind him. I could tell that she was naked too.

“We were celebrating,” Izra said. Adika popped Izra on the back of his head.

“Cover yourself up! Your dick is still swinging,” she spat. Izra grabbed a plate then covered himself.

“I’m sorry about that, but, ummm, is everything okay? It’s late,” Izra said to me.

“Where is my son?” I asked.

“He is in his room, but I would knock before I go in. He and Kanya been howling all night,” Izra said. I disappeared then reappeared in front of Akua’s door. I knocked then heard growling followed by moaning. I knocked again.

“WHAT!” he yelled.

“It’s your mother!” I yelled from the other side of the door.

“Oh, shit,” I heard Kanya spat. Moments later, the door opened. He had scratches all over his chest and he wore a pair of sport shorts.

“Is everything okay?” he asked concerned.

“We need to help Anubi,” I said to him. He growled then his eyes turned blue.

“No disrespect, Mother, but Anubi can burn. My family is here, on Earth,” he said.

“Listen to me, son. Your father is about to rule as his ancient beast. His man form will be gone! Do you understand that if Anubi goes down then those immortals will come to Earth? We cannot have the worlds collide that way. You might not have a connection to Anubi because you are mad with your father, but that is still your home!” I said to him.

Kanya came to the door wearing a robe. Her hair was all over her head and she had bite marks on her neck. Goon looked at her then smirked. “I apologize, Mother, but we got a little wild, excuse our presence,” he said. My heart warmed because of his manners while his father had none.

“If he goes, what about his pups and wife? He will have to rule Anubi if Ammon dies,” Kanya said.

“Ammon’s beast has been very busy. He has an older son that Musaf covered up for him,” I answered.

"So, I can kill him? Blood isn't supposed to shed in Anubi," Goon said.

"The rules must be broken to protect our world. It's the only way. We have to hurry because I'm using all my strength to take us back through my portal," I told him. The doors opened and the pack came out into the hallway.

"What's going on?" Elle asked.

"I'm going to Anubi to kill Ammon," Akua answered.

"We are going with you then," Dayo spat.

"I can't take all of you through the portal. I only can take Goon and Kofi," I said then Amadi growled.

"We can't let him fight alone. What if he gets ambushed by Ammon's warriors?" Amadi asked.

"That's what I want to know," Elle said.

"I'm going!" Izra said as he came out of his room. He was no longer naked.

"Goon's ancient beast can defeat Ammon's warriors. His warriors aren't strong," I replied.

"I will be okay. You all just handle Sosa because he will not get away with what he did to Anik. I will go to Anubi and defeat my father," Akua said.

"But, bro, your ancient beast takes a lot of strength from you," Dayo said.

"Not while battling, but, yes, I will be weak afterward. Don't worry about me," Akua said.

Anik came out of a room. "Is Jalesa in Anubi?" she asked me.

"Yes, she is back home," I said. Anik handed me a pretty, purple rock with orange specs inside it.

"This is for good luck. Tell her to keep it. I will miss her," Anik said sadly. I put the rock inside my sack.

"I will tell her," I told Anik.

"Wait, she isn't coming back? Does this have to do with Amadi and that Ula chick?" Kanya asked.

"Mind your business, Kanya. Amadi and Jalesa agreed on her returning home," Akua spat then Kanya rolled her eyes at him.

"Where is Kofi?" I asked.

"Down the hall where he is listening to that bull crap," Dayo said then howled. Kofi stormed out of his room. "What happened? What's the emergency?" he asked.

"We are going to Anubi. I will tell you later, but we must go now," I said to him. The pack embraced Kofi—well, everyone did except for Izra.

"You're not coming back?" Izra asked Kofi.

"I will watch you all from up there. I only came back because Ammon brought his warriors with him on Earth. I will be home with my mate and I will help build Anubi back the way it should be," Kofi said.

"I apologize for my behavior. I know you would never hurt me intentionally," Izra said. Kofi pulled Izra to him then kissed his forehead.

"My youngest pup. It takes a lot of courage for a man to admit his true feelings. You are growing up, and when your pup is born, you will grow even more," Kofi said to him then took a step back. Water filled Kofi's eyes.

"My five pups, many years of teaching. You are the strongest pack I have ever seen in all my life. I had to break up many fights, but you all still love each other. Never let anyone pull you apart," Kofi said.

"We are going to miss you," Kanya cried. Kofi hugged her.

"I will still be here in spirit," he said then walked over to Anik. "I just met you but you have a beautiful heart and much patience. Dayo isn't the easiest beast to get along with," Kofi joked then hugged her. When Adika came out of the room, he wished her farewell.

"I will be back," Akua said then stood next to me before we disappeared. I went back then grabbed Kofi's arm after I sent Akua through the portal. It was time for Ammon to die.

****

When we arrived back inside the temple people were running for their lives.

“What in the creation is going on?” Kofi asked.

Screams filled my ears then Akua growled, “I smell blood,” then ran down the hall of the temple toward Ammon’s feast room.

When I got there, bodies lay sprawled out. His warriors stood guard and watched Ammon’s tall wolf god slice people into half.

“If you don’t obey me then you will die!” Ammon shouted. I sent a bolt of lightning into his chest and he laughed.

“Ouch, that stung,” he said then his warriors laughed.

“What have you done?” Kofi asked.

“My dear brother, this is power. Look around you and tell me what you see. You see pointless immortals who live in Anubi. Anubi is for those who possess strength and power. If you don’t have it then your life is forever pointless,” Ammon said. Kofi shifted then charged into Ammon’s beast. Ammon’s beast threw Kofi into the wall. I looked around for Jalesa but I couldn’t find her. Ammon’s wolf god was able to speak in the same way his human form spoke. His wolf god’s voice was deeper and louder.

Akua’s black wolf growled, “You, my son, have everything it takes to gain the whole world. You waste it to live a life like a human?” he asked Akua. Thunder shook the temple then Akua howled. His ancient beast appeared from the dark cloud that circled his body. His ancient beast stood tall, very tall. A gold shield covered his chest. The gold skirt around his waist was like a shield. Gold bangles covered both of his arms and the gold helmet on his head had a blue gem in the middle of it.

"What is this trick? Kill him!" Ammon shouted to his warriors. They charged into Akua but they turned into a pile of ash. Baki stood next to Ammon, looking confused.

"Ammon is your father. He had your mother killed. He is not the king that you think he is. You just watched him kill innocent people, and for what? These are your people and you watched him take their lives," I said to Baki.

"A great warrior follows his king even if it's into the pits of hell," Baki said.

"He brainwashed you. You are not like him," I said to him.

"You turned one pup against me and now my oldest one?" Ammon asked. I knew at that moment that he actually cared for Baki.

"You are my father?" Baki asked.

"What do you think? I turned you into the greatest warrior in all of Anubi. It was I who gave you shelter when you could've lived on Earth. I showed you everything and now you question your king?" Ammon roared. Akua charged into Ammon then they fell over a few statues, cracking them in half. Ammon sent a punch into Akua's ribs then Akua choke-slammed him.

"If you are truly a great warrior and for your people then you will let Ammon die. It's his fate. Your fate is to rule and fix the world your father destroyed," I said to Baki. He backed away from me then ran to help Jalesa carry out the few innocent people who were still alive but injured.

Akua's beast pushed Ammon into the wall and pieces from the ceiling fell to the floor. Jalesa charged into me because a big piece almost fell on top of me. We stood and watched Akua and Ammon bite, slam and punch each other.

"Goon's beast is beautiful! He has the body of an ancient warrior. How did Kanya take all of him?" she asked me.

"His mate was made for it. Kanya's body is built for him. If she were smaller then it wouldn't have worked," I said as I watched Akua take a bite out of Ammon's neck. Blood dripped from Ammon's neck onto the temple floor.

"You will not defeat me!" Ammon yelled.

"I will have your head and put it right next to Dash's," Akua said then slammed Ammon to the floor. The floor cracked then spread across the room. I looked down between my feet and noticed the floor starting to open.

"The temple is going to collapse," Jalesa panicked.

"It's going to collapse either way if Ammon doesn't die," I replied. Akua's blue eyes glowed then lit up the room.

"What is that? What's happening?" Jalesa asked.

"Akua is getting agitated," I replied. Ammon swapped his big hand at Akua's face. His face opened from the three long scratches. Akua rammed his father's head into the wall then took a chunk out of his shoulder. Ammon howled then was slammed to the floor. Akua's heavy, clawed foot came crashing down onto Ammon's face. Ammon kicked Akua's leg then Akua's leg snapped, which caused him to howl.

"NOOOOOO!" I ran toward them. Ammon's big hand came across my face, knocking me into the wall. I couldn't defeat him. I used my strength to open the portal and keep it open so that Akua and I could return back to Earth.

Akua howled as he snapped his leg back into place. He charged into Ammon then picked him up by the throat. He used both hands to squeeze Ammon's throat. Akua's long, sharp nails pierced Ammon's neck. His blood ran down his son arms as he squeezed harder. Blood poured from Ammon's mouth. Ammon looked at me and a tear fell from my eye as I had flashbacks of the times he made me happy. The man he was before he became immortal. The man who I feel in love with and gave my body to. That man was gone for many years, I cringed at the sound of his neck snapping. His head dangled over then Akua threw him into the wall then howled, causing the temple to shake like an earthquake. Debris fell from the ceiling then collapsed on top of Akua. I screamed as I watched the heavy clay fall on top of his body. When I screamed, Jalesa hurriedly covered my mouth.

"The whole temple will collapse if you scream," she said as tears poured from my eyes. I walked to the pile of debris that covered my son.

"I don't have any more fight in me. I'm so weak that I can just die," I said then a large, black, clawed hand came through the debris. The debris rolled down then Akua's bloody beast crawled out of the pile. I couldn't pull him or help him because he was way bigger than I. His body slowly started to change back. He lay in front of us bloody and weak. I hurriedly kneeled down next to me.

"Make sure you tell my pups, mate and pack that I love them. I'm too weak, Mother, I can feel life leaving my body," he said.

"Don't talk that way. Just hang on till I get strong enough to heal you," I said as I covered his open wounds with my scarf. Jalesa tried to heal him.

"He's lost too much blood," she said then cried.

"I will join you. If you die, I will go with you. I brought you here. It's all of my fault," I said then pulled him close to me. I rocked him back and forth as a river of blood ran across the floor. Seconds later, I was being pulled back. Baki kneeled down next to Akua.

"I am a fast healer. He can have some of my blood. He needs blood with the same type as his to heal immediately," Baki said. Akua coughed up blood before he spoke.

"I don't want any more parts of Ammon," he said.

"Think about your family. Kofi said that nothing should ever break your pack apart. We all have a great deal of pride but right now it's not needed," I said to Akua. I was going to shove Baki's blood down his throat myself. Baki took out a sharp knife then cut his wrist. He grabbed a metal cup that lay next to us on the floor. He drained his blood into the cup until he became weak. Baki handed me the cup then I put it to Akua's lips.

"Drink it!" I yelled. Akua gagged as he drank the cup full of blood down to the last drop. Once he finished, he gagged then howled. His wounds closed just enough to stop him from bleeding out. Baki leaned over then Jalesa caught him.

"All you need is rest," she said to Baki.

****

Akua's eyes fluttered as he lay on the bed. It was morning and we had to go back to Earth.

"He's up," one of the female servants said. The other one washed him as she blushed.

"He is the strongest warrior I have ever seen. Look at his structure and long legs," she told the other one. She pulled the cover back from around his waist then gasped.

"You don't have to wash that. He has a mate," I spat. Akua sat up then looked around at all the beautiful women that surrounded his bed. She stuck a grape and a cube of raw meat inside his mouth. They giggled and whispered, amazed by his presence.

"Is he staying?" one of them asked.

"No, we are leaving shortly," I answered.

"But he is the son of Ammon. He is the king," someone said.

"He isn't the oldest one," I replied. Akua stood up with the silk sheet wrapped around his waist.

"Kanya isn't going to like this shit one bit," he said then I laughed.

"It's tradition. Strong warriors get special treatment. They don't even dress themselves here," I said to him.

"Kanya needs to visit Anubi to learn some of this," he said as one of the females touched his chest.

"What in the hell is wrong with them? They've never seen a beast before?" Akua asked me as he pried their hands away from him.

"At least I know that you are a faithful man," I answered. I snapped my fingers. "You all may go now," I said to them.

"We must wash him. It's tradition to treat a warrior with such royalty," one of them said.

"That isn't needed," I said to them. They left the room disappointed.

"Whew! I can breathe now. The scent of their arousal was everywhere," he said.

"Get dressed. I will meet you in the hall," I said then walked out of the room. Once I left, I almost screamed from excitement. My son healed well and was back to normal.

I looked out of the glassless window at the other side of the temple. It had fallen out right after we helped Akua and Baki up. The other side needed to be rebuilt anyway to fit the new king of Anubi. I had a good feeling about Baki.

I did what I had to do to help my people. Anubi is now in Baki's hands and it's his job to protect his people. I hope he learned what Ammon couldn't teach him. I hope he learned how power and greed could destroy a life.

"My queen," Jalesa said from behind me. I gave her a hug.

"My daughter, I'm going to miss your presence," I said to her. I went into my sack then handed her the stone Anik gave me. Jalesa's eyes lit up.

"I'm going to miss them even though I didn't fit in there," she said.

"You are very stubborn," I said.

"I got it from you. You would strike someone quick with a bolt of lightning," she said. Kofi walked down the hall with a slight limp.

"I'm getting old. One swipe from Ammon's beast knocked the shit out of me," he said then chuckled.

"We are all getting old. It's time for a new beginning. I'm interested in the pups that will meet their mates," I said.

"What do you know?" Kofi asked.

"A wise witch never tells her visions. We just watch it happen. Akua's pups will be very strong and so will their mates. I guess Keora will find love after all," I said.

"Wait a minute, what?" Jalesa asked.

"Keora will find the love she always wanted. We just have to sit back and watch how it will happen," I said.

"You reincarnated her but you never said how," Jalesa said then Kofi smiled.

"You never cease to amaze me. I've been wondering how Adika's pup came back to life because we knew it was dead," Kofi said.

"Big things come in small packages," I said then Akua came out into the hallway. Kofi patted his back.

"Your ancient beast almost scared my beast," he joked then Akua smiled.

"Before we leave, I need to make a few stops," I said to Akua. I headed down to the dungeon of the temple where they kept prisoners. Kaira sat on the floor with a bulging stomach. She growled at me. "There is no need for animosity. I am here to tell you that the pup you are pregnant with is going to carry on Musaf's soul," I said to her.

"Nobody is going to take my daughter! I don't care what soul she has or what she may become. My other pup is dead because of your son," Kaira spat.

"Your son is dead because he was like his father. Don't blame anyone but yourself. You bedded a man that didn't want you. Ammon is dead now but I'm sure you already heard. I guess Baki can free you now. But I'm warning you of your pup. Usually in reincarnations the memory is gone. The existence of them is forgotten, but that is only when they are reincarnated without vengeance or a pure heart. If you go into a new life wicked, then your soul will remain wicked. I doubt if his heart was pure before he got inside your womb," I said to her.

"Musaf is a male! You think I'm going to believe he is inside my daughter?" she asked.

"You fool, Kaira. It doesn't matter the sex! It's the life itself. She will be a woman, talk like one and look like one, but she will possess Musaf's witch," I replied.

"Good! I hope she sends you straight to hell," Kaira spat.

"I'm going to let you in on a secret," I said then got closer to her cage. "That witch is going to kill you when you give birth to her. That witch has the soul of an ancient warlock. When she comes out of your womb, your life will drain. I guess you can finally be with Ammon after all," I said then walked away. She yelled and screamed at me but I kept walking and never looked back.

The guards that stood by Baki's door let me in his room. He sat up in his bed when he saw me. "Anubi's new king," I said to him.

"I don't think I can do this. I'm a warrior not a ruler," he said.

"Which will make you an even better king," I said to him.

"I watched those innocent people die last night. I stood and did nothing. I watched Ammon do many things over the years, and still, I never did anything," Baki said with hurt in his voice.

"That doesn't make you a monster. It just means you loved Ammon. When we love someone we don't see any wrong. I can see visions of the future but couldn't even see what was in my face. I loved Ammon, that is why. He showed you how to be a great warrior and you cared for him because of that. The connection you had with him was because he was your father and not just your mentor. Now you have the chance to make a better life here," I said to him.

"Dash's pups are still here. I will care for them and not send them back to Earth," he said.

"You are changing Anubi already," I said to him. Akua walked into the room then stared at Baki.

"That's my little brother," Baki said.

"I appreciate you saving my life last night," Akua said to Baki then held his hand out.

"What is that?" Baki asked then looked down at Akua's hand.

"It's a gesture that is used on Earth. You shake his hand," I said.

"Kaira's pup has Musaf's soul. I will do everything I can to keep this place safe, but I can't get rid of the pup. All pups are innocent," Baki said.

"That's your call. My work here is done. I don't have to come back anymore," I replied. Jalesa walked into the room with a tray of grapes and raw meat. Baki's smile lit up the room. "We will always be in touch," I said to Jalesa then walked out of the room. Akua said his good-byes then followed me.

"Keora's soul is inside Izra's pup?" Akua asked me.

"Yes, as soon as we get back, Adika and I will talk. Keora realized her wrongs and decided to sacrifice herself to give her sister happiness," I replied. He shook his head.

"I'm Keora's uncle? I slept with her ages ago," he said.

"That was another life. Besides, really isn't Keora anymore. She won't remember anything and she will not look the same. She will just have Keora's magic," I replied.

"I've got to be around when Izra finds this out," Akua said.

****

I sat in the corner of our bedroom and watched him sleep. His large chest sat up like a mountain with light snores coming from his mouth. I got up then climbed into our bed. I sat on top of him. "My love," I called out to him. His eyes popped open then he held his arm up in front of his face to block the sun. He sat up then squeezed me as he hugged me. I placed kisses all over his handsome face.

"I haven't been gone long," I said to Kumba.

"It felt like eternity all over again. I thought you went back to him," Kumba said.

"Ammon is dead," I blurted out.

“How do you feel about that?” he asked me. He tilted my chin up so that I could look into his eyes.

“I’m relieved. I finally feel free. I feel like this is a new life, like I was born yesterday. The weight that was on me is gone,” I said to him. Kumba kissed me liked he’d never kissed me before. He climbed out of bed, still holding me. His strong hands massaged my bottom as he kissed me. He sucked on my neck as he walked me to the bathroom. He sat me down on the sink then ran the shower. I stared at his strong and wide back. I reached out to him.

“Make love to me, Kumba,” I said to him. He slowly slid my long, silk skirt up to my waist, exposing my bare skin.

“All of this greatness and it belongs to me,” he said then licked my lips. Kumba made love to me all that day. He was buried so deep inside me, my face was flooded with tears. It was a beautiful feeling, and I was going to enjoy it for the rest of my life.

Izra

"SHE TOLD YOU WHAT?" I asked Adika.

"Why are you yelling? You should be happy that Keora did this for us. Naobi said that she will not have her memory or even look like her. She will be a totally different pup," Adika said. I sat down in the chair in the family room. I had just walked in the house from hunting.

"My pup slept with two of my pack brothers. Keora was with Goon ages ago and she slept with Dayo. They swelled inside my daughter? I'm about to fuck them niggas up," I fussed.

"Calm down!" Adika yelled at me.

"I can't calm down, Adika. Our pup smashed the homies and she isn't born yet. She is going to be born not a virgin. What if our pup is pregnant?" I asked as I paced back and forth.

"Stop making all of that noise! Anik is asleep!" Dayo yelled at me when he came into the family room.

"You are a sick son-of-a-bitch!" I said to Dayo then he growled at me.

"Stop it, now!" Adika said to me.

"What is his problem now?" Dayo asked.

“Naobi told me earlier that Keora’s soul is inside our pup. She is strong enough to stay inside my womb until it is time for me to have her,” Adika said as she rubbed her stomach.

Dayo gagged then threw-up inside the plant next to the couch. “That’s sick, bro,” he said to me then threw-up again.

“Anik is going to be pissed. She brought those plants back to life,” Adika told Dayo. Dayo sat down on the couch.

“I feel bad, bro. I’m having twin daughters and then we got Arya. I know how you must feel knowing Keora took Goon’s ancient beast. Bro, no homo, but his ancient beast’s dick is bigger than mines, I’m certain. So, if you want to be mad, be mad at that nigga,” Dayo spat. Adika put her hand on her head.

“I think I’m about cry. I’m standing here next to two morons who don’t know shit about reincarnation,” Adika spat then stormed out of the living room.

Elle walked past the living room. I called out to him since Kofi wasn’t there.

“What is it, Izra? I’m taking Fabia to the airport,” he said.

“Adika is pregnant with Keora,” I told him. He just stared at me.

“She’s being reincarnated through the pup that died inside Adika’s womb?” Elle asked me.

“Yes,” I replied.

“Okay, and? Bro, please don’t tell me you are ranting about Keora being with Dayo, Goon and plenty of other males. Your pup is still your pup, and she will be born a virgin. I know you, little brother, and sometimes you don’t use your mind. All that pup has of Keora is her strength,” Elle said. Goon came into the living room with the twins in his arms. He sat them down on a mat to roll around on.

“I don’t want to hear any shit from you. I can see it in your face that you know about Keora,” Goon said to me then I waved him off.

“Why are you letting Fabia go back home, Elle?” Dayo asked him.

“I’m not trying to force her into anything,” he replied.

“But you like her, she likes you. Your guardian angel led you to her. I don’t get why you would let your soulmate leave like that,” Dayo said.

“Elle is a virgin, bro. He doesn’t know what to do with all of what Fabia is working with. Fabia might spread her legs and Elle will grab his doctor bag like he’s a gynecologist. He doesn’t know where to stick it,” I said.

“He’s been with Camille,” Goon said as he played with the pups on the floor.

“Naw, bro. Camille doesn’t really count. Elle is still a virgin,” Dayo replied.

"I'm not listening to this shit. One is dumber than the other. Izra doesn't know shit about reincarnation, which is part of our religion. Dayo smokes so much weed he can't even tell a deer from this jackass," Elle pointed at me then Goon laughed.

"Are all the women in Anubi weird and cracked out like Jalesa?" I asked Goon.

"NO! HELL, NO! The women in Anubi seem freakier than the women on Earth. Bro, I woke up and ten of them was feeling on me. They gave me a massage, fed me and bathed me. I think almost all of them were in heat. A few of them grabbed my dick. I'm telling you now, my brothers, Anubi is like a playboy mansion. The women who are servants act that way while the mated women are not allowed near any males but their own," Goon said.

"I've got to go. I will be back later," Elle said then walked out of the living room.

"Where is Amadi?" Goon asked.

"Up Ursula's ass crack," Dayo replied then stood up.

"I'm ready to pick Arya up from school. I will holla at you two later," Dayo said then walked out of the room.

****

Dayo, Amadi and I ran through the woods headed to Sosa's home. Ula told Amadi that he finally came back home. Sosa went into hiding after the pack ambushed his nightclub. When we got to his home, a pack of wolves were around his house. The full moon lit up the sky. The house he lived in was almost the size of our mansion.

"We are outnumbered," I said to my brothers.

"Y'all couldn't wait for us? I told y'all that all I needed was five minutes to calm Kanya down. She didn't want me to leave," Goon said from behind us. His blue eyes lit up the woods along with the moon. Elle's beast stepped out of the woods with a scowl on its face.

"Is it just me or does Elle's beast seem sexually frustrated?" I asked them.

"Shut up, Izra. It's beast mode, bro. I can taste that nigga's blood on the tip of my tongue. I've been patiently waiting for this," Dayo said then growled. We hid in the dark as we watched the other beasts walk around Sosa's house. Sosa lived on a land that sat behind millions of trees. I didn't understand how someone could drive to his house because there weren't any roads nearby. Dayo howled then the rest of us howled, scaring the bats out of the trees.

The beasts that surrounded Sosa's home came toward us. There were about nine wolves.

"You've got to be kidding me! These are all females! I'm really going to kill him because of this. I'm not feeling this," Dayo said.

"Sosa isn't as dumb as we think. He knows that we wouldn't battle a pack of female wolves but if one of them aims for my throat then I have to kill her," Goon said.

"Amadi wouldn't mind killing a female wolf," I said then he growled at me. I stepped back. *"Damn, bro I was just kidding,"* I told him.

"Not now, Izra they are closing in on us," Elle said.

"I'm going to fuck him up myself," Dayo said.

"What do you all want? This isn't your territory!" one of them said. The rest of the females stood behind her but they were all frightened. They didn't want to battle a pack of oversized male beasts. Their wolves were small and very feminine and could easily distract a male pack because they were all in heat.

"This is really sad, bro. They are young females and he put them out to guard his home. They probably don't even know how to fight," Dayo said. Goon stepped forward.

"I*f we kill him then you all will be free. This is not the way a female wolf is supposed to live."*

"We have no choice. We have no home or money. We are safer here," the head female spoke.

"I will give you all very expensive pieces of jewelry if you leave, but if you stay and fight us, our beasts will attack and it will be out of our control," Goon told the female leader.

"How can we trust you?" she asked.

"We would've killed you all by now. Our beasts can take your whole pack out within a few minutes. We are trying to help you, but if you stay and fight with Sosa, all

bets are off," Goon said. The other wolves backed away from the female leader because they didn't want to fight.

"Inside his home, there is a pack of male wolves. There are two humans who have poison in their bullets on top of the roof. The poison is created by Sosa to stop immortals. Attack the humans first because the poison will slow you down and Sosa's pack will ambush you," she said.

"Wait for us in the woods," Dayo told the pack of females. They ran off then disappeared into the dark woods.

"Izra look out!" Dayo said as a bullet flew past my head. It had come from on top of the house. Wolves came out of nowhere growling at us but my pack immediately started to tear into them. I leaped onto the house, my beast climbing until it landed on the roof. Two humans dressed in some special type of gear had their guns aimed at me. I jumped on the one that was closest to me. My teeth tore into his stomach. A bullet from the other human flew past my head as I continued to tear into the human until he stopped breathing. I slung the dead human over the roof then jumped onto the other human. His gun slipped out of his hand.

"Let me go!" he yelled. My sharp teeth punctured the skin on his neck, instantly snapping it like a twig. I kept the human inside my mouth as I leaped down from on top of the house. I dragged his body across the yard then lay him down on the front of Sosa's doorstep. The pack killed most of the wolves. Only three out of twelve wolves were still living. The three wolves ran into Sosa's house. They went crashing through the window.

"There's more wolves inside, I'm sure," Goon said. Dayo's beast looked at the dead human in front of the door then looked at me.

"You seriously brought him a treat? You have more dog tendencies than a wolf. Only dogs bring their masters their kill," Dayo said to me.

"Wolves are wild dogs, jackass. I can't help myself at times. Does Do cats and lions have the same tendencies?" I asked Dayo.

"I understand your beast is playful, bro, but now is not the time to play," Elle said to me.

"*I can't help it, damn it! My beast likes to play!"* I shouted. I could hear snickering inside their heads.

"We all went through that phase when we were younger. Every now and then I like to catch a tossed stick," Amadi said.

"Every now and then, I still like to piss in the backyard next to my favorite tree. That's all y'all are getting from me, and Izra, don't you dare say a word," Dayo said. We looked at Goon and Elle as we waited for their confessions.

"Aren't we in a middle of a fight? Why are we having beast talk?" Goon asked.

"As soon as you and Elle tell us, we will go inside his home. They aren't coming out, trust me. They are waiting for us," I said.

"I can't believe you muthafuckas right now. I like when Kanya rubs behind my ear and when she brushes my fur after I shift," Goon said.

"I have a water bowl next to my bed and that's all you are going to get from me!" Elle shouted. Goon used a force to shatter Sosa's thick, wooden door. We stepped inside the house. We heard growling coming from upstairs.

"Izra, is that you?" Onya's voice called out to me. She didn't look too good when she stepped in front of me. Her skin looked pale and she had dark circles around her eyes. A patch of her hair was missing.

"You went against Adika for that? No amount of witchcraft can make me look at her! Plus, her scent is burning my nose, bro," Dayo fussed.

"She was beautiful. I don't know what happened. Maybe Adika cursed her and made her look like this, but her scent is about to drive my beast wild," I replied. Adika's curse was still on me. I had the urge to taste Onya again.

Onya stepped closer to me as the pack growled at her. She reached her hand out to touch my snout.

"In that short amount of time we spent together, I fell for you. You treated me the way a female is really supposed to be treated," she said.

"With the way she looks, it looks like you treated her bad, bro," Dayo said. I knew what I had to do to make the spell go away. I attacked Onya. I blocked out her screams as my teeth pierced through her neck. The sound of her blood gurgling inside her throat echoed throughout the

foyer as my teeth ripped her throat out. I snapped her neck then her body fell onto the floor.

Five wolves came down the hall, the one in front was Sosa. Dayo growled at him before he leaped. Their beasts knocked down the walls in the hallway as they rolled around. Sosa's wolves tried to attack Dayo then the pack jumped on them. More of Sosa's wolves came out into the hall. Blood and fur flew everywhere. A few of them got struck with lightning from Goon. I chewed into one wolf's throat as another wolf sank his teeth into my throat. Amadi killed the wolf that had my throat. The wolf that I had my teeth in stopped breathing then I snapped his neck. Dead wolves lay in the hallway. Amadi, Elle and I were bloody. It was our blood mixed with the other wolves' blood. Sosa and Dayo rolled around, fighting each other. Dayo slammed Sosa's beast onto the floor then bit his face. Sosa's hind legs kicked at Dayo but Dayo's beast overpowered his. Dayo went for Sosa's throat then shook him as Sosa whimpered in pain. I heard growling from behind us, and when we turned, there was the pack of females.

"If they want to die, then let them!" Goon shouted. We stood in front of Sosa and Dayo, ready for battle. The lead female leaped over our heads and the rest of females followed. When I turned around they were ripping Sosa's wolf apart. Sosa was already dead but they didn't care. Hurt and anger filled their beasts as they tore him into shreds.

"That is beautiful," Goon said as his blue eyes glowed.

Elle

My body ached from fighting Sosa's pack from the night before. I slowly got out of bed then headed to my bathroom. I showered then got dressed in my Nike sweat suit. I found sweat suits to be very comfortable. When I walked into the kitchen, everyone was sitting at the table, laughing and telling jokes. The pack had no worries. Ammon was gone, Anubi had a new king and Sosa couldn't sell females anymore. All of our problems were solved.

The doorbell rang and Amadi went to answer it. Seconds later, he walked in with Ula. Everyone got quiet as they looked at them.

"Goon and Izra, this is Ula. Ula, these are my two brothers you haven't met yet. You met everyone else in the pack," Amadi said. Ula waved at everyone and they waved back.

"That's the evil witch, bro? I thought you were going to show us an old witch with gray hair and a big zit on her forehead," Izra said then sipped his orange juice. Adika pinched him then told him to behave. Izra's face turned green then his nose grew out. A big zit appeared on his forehead.

"Now you've got the witch you are looking for. I might be a lot of things, but don't insult me. Those evil witches in those fairytales have nothing on me," Ula spat then everyone laughed.

Adika turned him back to normal. "I don't like her," Izra said.

"You don't like nobody that you can't bully," Kanya said.

"I think what Izra was trying to say is that is he surprised in Amadi's taste," Dayo said.

Everyone talked and laughed and got to know more about Ula. Everyone had happiness with someone, but I wasn't mad about it. I just wanted to experience the life that I missed out on when I waited for Camille. I left the house then drove three hours away to the mountains where I rented a cabin. Fabia told me before she got on the plane that she was going to write me as soon as she touched down in Africa. I didn't know what her purpose was when I met her, but I was glad that I did.

****

I sat in a small coffee shop as I read the newspaper. I didn't know why I decided to read it. Maybe because the other humans in the shop were reading it. It didn't interest me but the article about Beastly Treasures caught my eye. Kanya's store was attracting people from everywhere. The article mentioned how they'd never seen pieces of jewelry like that before. They mentioned that it looked like the jewelry King Tut and Nefertiti wore. After I read the article, I left the shop. I headed back to my cabin, which was only a few minutes away. When I pulled up, there was a car parked in front of my cabin. I got out of my car then sniffed the air.

"You really like sniffing," a voice said from behind me. When I turned around, it was Fabia.

"I went by your home and Goon told me where you went. I didn't think to ask if you were alone," she said.

"I'm here by myself. I love the smell of pine trees," I replied. She reached out to touch my face.

"My plane stopped in Florida when I decided to come back. I don't know what I'm doing here but I felt like I was leaving something behind. I'm curious to know about the beast who stays on my mind. When I slept on your beast in the woods days ago, I slept like I haven't slept in years. I felt protected and relaxed. Not even my village back home brings me that much peace," she said. I hugged her.

"You made a smart decision, beautiful," I said then kissed her. My hand massaged her scalp while my tongue explored the plumpness of her lips. She slightly moaned as she kissed me back.

"In my past, I've been with a lot of males."

"In your present and future, you will only be with one," I responded.

****

Fabia lay across the bed in a purple panty and bra set. My hand slid up her thighs then her body quivered. Her fingers played in my locks while I explored her body. Soft moans escaped her lips when I licked the outside of her panty line. Her body temperature had risen when my sharp teeth slowly slid down her panties. A breeze came into the open window, blowing her welcoming scent into my nose. Fabia unlatched her bra; her dark, round and full breasts bouncing from being released. My beast growled lowly as I had the urge to fill her up. I spread her legs then kissed her inner thighs. I slowly licked up her inner thigh until I got to her wet slit. When my tongue entered her, she gasped then clutched the sheets as she came instantly. I pinned her legs down as I slowly traced the outline of her center. My beast's eyes stared into hers as my tongue flickered back and forth slowly across her pearl.

"You taste better than molasses," I said to her. Her nails dug into my scalp as loud moans filled the room. Her sticky essence slowly drizzled out of her as I continued to please her. She yanked my locks as she screamed from another orgasm. My tongue parted down the middle of her slit; up and down, around and around, as I slowly made love to her with my mouth. Her hips bucked forward then she raised her upper body off the bed. The eyes of her beast stared at me as she growled in pleasure. Her sharp nails pierced my shoulders as she slowly humped my mouth. Her breathing picked up as she bucked harder before her body slammed back onto the bed as she trembled.

"ELLLEEEEEEE," she cried out in pleasure as she came again. Seconds later, she pushed me down onto the bed. She licked my chest then my abs. Her tongue traced every ridge on my stomach. Her hands slid up and down my chest as she worked her way down further. She slid my sweatpants down then my boxers. She grabbed my hard dick with both hands then traced the length of it with her tongue. My dick jerked in her hands as pre-cum drizzled from the tip of it then down her hands. She hungrily licked it up before her warm and wet mouth covered the tip.

"I might taste like molasses, but you taste even better," she said then her mouth slowly slid down my shaft. I massaged her head as my fingers moved through her scalp. My chest tightened as more of her spit dripped down my dick. Up and down she went as her hands slid up and down my dick. I growled then bit my bottom lip, my sharp teeth causing my lip to bleed. I didn't know what Fabia was doing but it was about to release my beast.

"GRRRRRRRR! AWWWWWWW!" I grunted as I swelled then exploded into her mouth. I pulled her up then lay her down on her side. I lay behind her in the spooning position. I lifted her leg as I kissed the crook of neck. I slowly entered her from the back. My dick had swelled and it felt like I was tearing her open.

"I'm okay, Elle," she moaned as she clutched the pillow. I gently bit her shoulder as I slid further in. She inhaled deeply as her body trembled. I moved in and out of her slowly but she was still too tight.

"Let me in. You are resisting me," I whispered inside her ear. She relaxed then I slid further into her wetness. The sensation from her tight walls squeezing me caused me to bite her harder. I grinded into her and palmed her breasts. I sucked on her neck then licked in her ear as I sped up. Fabia's thick and creamy essence coated my dick as I pulled in and out of her. I grabbed her hip then thrusted myself further into her. My hand slid up and down her side as I made love to her. She howled from the pleasure. Her sharp nails shredded the sheets. She moved along with my rhythm.

"Do you want more?" I asked her. I wanted to release my beast but I took my time so that I wouldn't hurt her.

"I'm not a pup, Elle. Don't be afraid," she replied. I turned her over flat on her stomach then lay down on top of her. I slid into her until I couldn't go any further. I pressed my body down onto her then grinded into the spot I discovered that made her wetter. I gently gripped the back of her neck with my other hand on her hip. I rocked inside her back and forth. I looked down and watched my dick stretch her completely open. The noise of her wetness mixed with the growls of her beast turned me on. I sped up my pace as I went further in until my dick disappeared.

"Damn you, Elle!" she screamed as I went harder, slamming my dick into her spot again. Her walls tightened around me as a big wave came splashing around my shaft. My nails scratched the back of her neck and it turned her on even more. She spread her buttocks, allowing me more access. I was far into Fabia that she couldn't move. Every powerful stroke and deep thrust I gave her body made her growl louder. I started to swell even more and I couldn't move in and out of her as fast anymore. I went further in then stayed inside her as I continued to swell against her spot.

"ARGGGHHHHHHHH! AWWWWWWW! ELLLLLLEEEEEEEEE! SHIT!" she cried out from me stretching her open and filling her. My breathing sped up then I howled as I burst inside her like a broken pipe. My nails opened the skin on her back as my dick violently jerked inside her. I couldn't hold my beast back. I pulled her hair, leaning her head back then bit her neck as hard as my beast could. Fabia stopped breathing as her body jerked then a thick substance exploded on my dick from her orgasm. She gasped for air as if she was drowning while she continued to come on my dick. I pulled away from her as the swelling went down then I closed my eyes…

****

I woke up to the sound of birds chirping. My eyes fluttered because of the bright sun beaming into the window. I looked to the side of me and it was empty. I looked around the room and there wasn't a sign of her.

"Just fucking great!" I spat as I climbed out of bed. Fabia had trust issues with males, so I figured she would leave me. She ran from being attached and was afraid that she would get hurt. I climbed out of bed then my stomach growled. I walked out of the room then into the kitchen. I stopped as I watched a naked Fabia standing in the kitchen cutting up steaks.

"I wanted to surprise you. I was hoping you slept longer," she said.

"You killed a deer by yourself?" I asked her.

"It took me a while, but yes, I did," she said. I hugged her from behind then snuggled my nose into the crook of her neck.

"Get back in bed, Elle!" she scolded me.

"I like this image better. A naked and curvaceous beast in the kitchen preparing a meal for her male," I said as my hands roamed her body.

"My male, huh? That doesn't sound too bad. I have something I want you to read on the table," she said to me. I grabbed the letter with my name written across the envelope.

Dear Elle,

If you are reading this letter, that means I'm dead and you have met Fabia. The day I met Fabia, for some reason, I knew she was meant for you. Not every day does a human run across two beasts of the opposite sex. I don't want you to mourn me because what you now have is even greater. Fabia is the link between you and I. My purpose has been served and I know my death will draw you two closer. I know my death will make you two more vulnerable and lean on each other. That's why I waited all these years to introduce you two. Fabia has been through a lot and you have a beautiful heart. You are just what she needs to mend all the missing pieces to her puzzle. I did love you but I knew I couldn't give you what you needed. You belong to your own kind. You belong with a mate who doesn't get old and die. You can now live, Elle. Be free and love! I'm watching down on you two. Sorry I couldn't see the pups be born. You watched me build a family and now from the heaven in the sky I will watch you do the same. Funny how life turns out. You just never know what fate has in store for us. You never know who comes into your life to stay or to leave, maybe even learn a lesson from. Take care, Elle. I don't have to tell you to treat Fabia right because I know you will. You are a great protector.

Love you always,
Camille

I folded the letter then put it back in the envelope. Fabia sat on my lap with the plate of bloody steaks. I wrapped my arms around her waist.

"My beautiful beast," I said to her as I stared into her eyes.

"And I'm all yours, now open up and let me feed you. I have to keep my male big and strong," she said then stuck a piece inside my mouth. I sucked on her finger before I chewed up the fresh meat. Her breasts swelled then her nipples hardened. I licked my lips.

"I'm no longer interested in the meat, beautiful. I have another appetite," I said then she kissed my lips.

"What am I going to do with you?" she asked.

"Stay here and never go back home so that I can swell your stomach up. I can give you a life that you won't have to run from," I said to her.

"That's why I came back," she said then kissed my lips. I swiped everything off the table then spread her legs. I slid back into her and welcomed the new beginning of my life.

Epilogue

One month later…

Anik

"Push, baby!" Dayo yelled at me then I squeezed his hand.

"Yank her out! Please, just yank her out! She is ripping me apart!" I screamed at him. The pack was crowded inside the room as I gave birth to my twin pups. I had one out already but the other one was too stubborn.

Kanya and Adika fanned my face then dabbed my forehead with a wet towel. My hair was stuck to my forehead and all I wanted to do was just die.

"I see the head! Push, now! Really hard like you are taking a big dump," Dayo said to me.

"Seriously, bro?" Izra asked him.

"Muthafucka, do you have a better idea?" Dayo yelled at him. I pushed harder as my pup stretched me open. Sharp pains went sailing up my spine. I cried like a big baby as Dayo pulled her out. Dayo cut the cord then gave the pup to Elle and Amadi so they could clean her up. Adika and Kanya helped me sit up then Fabia gave me the other pup. We named them Baneet and Chancy, both Indian names. I named them after my mother and grandmother. Baneet slept peacefully in my arms while Chancy was getting cleaned up. Dayo held her for a while then gave her to me so I could feed her.

"Welcome to fatherhood, bro," Goon said to him.

"Those are my little sisters!" Arya said excitedly. Dayo kissed my forehead. After a while the pack gave us our privacy.

"They look just you," Dayo said.

"With your beautiful dark skin," I answered. Baneet whimpered when she woke up. Dayo gently put my left breast up to her small mouth so that she could latch on. Chancy was already sucking away. I knew then Chancy was going to be a hand full.

"Goon's sons better stay away from my daughters," Dayo said then I smiled.

"You can't think about that now," I laughed.

"Like hell, I can't. They will not leave the house for nothing. There's some messed up beasts out there," Dayo said.

"We will have to wait and see. I love you even more for this," I said to him.

"I love you, too, Anik," he said then kissed my lips. I was relieved that Sosa was dead and couldn't hurt another female wolf. I appreciated what the pack did for the females they found at Sosa's house. They bought a big house a few miles away for them to live in. Fabia spent a lot of time there, preparing them for a new life. Kanya's store was very popular and stayed overcrowded. She was working on opening a bigger store to give the females jobs. Adika helped them with blending in better with society. Ula did something very big, she got rid of all their memories of Sosa. It was almost like Sosa never existed to them. Ula also got rid of every memory of the humans that were connected to Sosa. It all worked out for the best.

Amadi

"Can I open my eyes now?" I asked Ula.

"Yes!" she shouted. When I opened my eyes I looked around the big, empty warehouse. I was puzzled.

"What is this, Ula?" I asked.

"It's your warehouse. Well, our warehouse," she said.

"For what?" I asked then she handed me a packet of papers.

"This is ours, Amadi. Years ago you and I always talked about how we were going to sell our oil and body products across the world. Now, here is the chance. We will hire workers to ship the oils to the stores from this warehouse," she said then I picked her up. I tossed her up then caught her. I spun her around then kissed her lips.

"You play too much! I'm not trying to mess up my hair! It took six tries to get it right," she fussed then I laughed. I ran my fingers through her hair then one of her earrings turned into a snake. The snake snapped at me then I smacked it on the floor. My heavy boot stepped on it.

"I hate snakes," I said to her.

"But I love them, especially this one," she said as she grabbed me between the legs. She slowly unzipped my pants.

"You want it right here?" I asked as I caressed her face. I still couldn't believe that Ula was alive and how I abandoned her. She wasn't the easiest person to understand but I understood her pain. I neglected her and I hurt her. All she wanted was for me to love her. All she wanted was for me to understand the pain I brought her.

"What are the magic words?" I asked her.

"I love you, Amadi," she answered.

"I'm going to spend my life making up everything I did to you. I'm going to kiss you so much you get tired. I'm going to massage your beautiful body every night after I make love to you," I said to her then she smiled.

"Bring yo' sexy ass over here. You make me want to take a trip to Anubi," she said then I chuckled.

"Are you feeling that good?" I asked because she wasn't pleased with Anubi and the way it was.

"Yes, that damn good. Let's christen this place, baby. I want you to howl my name. I love you, Amadi, but your beast is what I want tonight. Don't hold back on me," she said. I ripped her shirt off then clamped down on her neck as her hands slid up my chest.

"Damn you!" she moaned as I roughly ripped her skirt off. She didn't have on any panties. I picked her then she wrapped her legs around my waist. I slowly slid her down on my dick. I slammed Ula up and down on my dick until her loud screams echoed through the large, empty space. I had another chance at loving her again and I wasn't going to let her down.

Izra

"My water broke," Adika screamed out while I was driving.

"Right now?" I asked her.

"Yes, right now!" she screamed.

"Stop yelling at me, Adika. I didn't tell your ass to leave the house in the first place. You are the one who wanted to do all of this stuff like going to mall and going to the movies. I knew when you couldn't get out of bed this morning we should've stayed home," I said to her. Adika screamed so loud it burst the windows in the car. I pulled over to the side of the road.

I pulled the passenger seat back, breaking it so Adika could lay flat. She lifted her long summer dress then placed her feet on the dash board.

"Put your hand down there and see if you can feel her," she said to me. I put my hand between her legs and it was mixed with fluid and blood.

"I feel her head. She is almost out!" I said. Adika screamed as she pushed then lightning struck the tree next to my car.

"If that tree falls, I hope you got some type of magic to catch it. That's a big tree and it will crush us," I said to her.

"ARRGGHHHHHHHH!" she screamed, pushing our daughter out. Small wails filled the car as I held her up. She looked just like me. Yellow flashed through her eyes then a small bolt of lightning struck my arm.

"Damn it! She struck me," I said to Adika. Adika took her from me.

"She was born with magic. Oh, Izra, look at her. We have a baby! I can't believe I'm holding my baby," she cried then I kissed her face.

"Miracles happen," I said to her.

"I'm going to name her Monifa. In Africa, Monifa means 'the fortunate one'," Adika said. I grabbed my hoodie from the back seat then tore the umbilical cord off with my sharp teeth. I wrapped our daughter up in my hoodie then sped home.

I carried Adika and our daughter into the house. Monifa cried then everyone hurried down the stairs to greet us. The house was full and it felt like home more than ever. The sounds of babies crying filled the night. The mates argued at each other over things that didn't matter but we were all family. Kanya and Anik took Adika and Monifa to get washed up.

I sat down on the bottom step then tears filled my eyes. I tried to hold it in but I wept like a baby. My brothers formed around me then hugged me.

"Come on, bro. You about to make us emotional," Dayo said.

"I cried too when Kanya gave birth. It's beautiful when your mate gives birth. I cried like a big-ass pup, bro," Goon said.

"I got one rolled up," Amadi said out of the blue then we looked at him.

"One of what?" I asked him. He pulled a fat blunt out of his pocket then held it in front of me.

"Awww, not you, too, Amadi. You are about to join dumb and dumber," Elle said then Dayo pushed him.

"Fuck you, too, nigga," Dayo said then Goon laughed.

"It's going to be a long night. The females are upstairs having female talk. I'm listening to Kanya's thoughts right now. How about we go in the backyard and celebrate?" Goon said. It was the happiest moment of my life. I was mated with Adika for eternity. She got what she wanted and so did I. They say a beast never smiles, but that's a lie, because my beast couldn't stop smiling.

****

We sat in the back of the house, drinking and smoking. Moments later, Kanya ran out. We hurriedly stood up because we thought something went wrong.

"Fabia passed out and she is burning up," Kanya said. We all looked at Elle.

"Well, looks like old man Elle got to go," Dayo said then Elle walked toward the house as he followed Kanya.

"Fabia's been having heat pains all morning according to Elle. Elle is about to have a pup, too," Goon said then stared at the house.

"We need a bigger house. A real big house," he expressed. Amadi blew the smoke out of his mouth.

"Ula can't give me any pups and I actually don't feel bad about it. You all have enough pups for me," Amadi said.

"This is to new beginnings," Goon said as he held his cup of Henny up. We all toasted to it.

"New beginnings, niggas!" I hollered then they laughed.

Naobi

I watched my globe as the pack lived happily. Anubi was doing better with their new queen and king. Jalesa found the old-fashioned love that she desired. Everything worked out for everyone, including me. I helped out with Kumba and his restaurants, interacting with the humans. I had a great life and it was filled with love. But every ending doesn't completely come to an end. I had a vision of all the pups. New love and more obstacles were to come. I wasn't going to interfere with fate. I was going to let everything fall into place the way that it should be. This was just the beginning…

Beasts: A New Chapter/New Beginning

Kanye

Twenty years later…

The sound of my alarm woke me up. I knocked it off my nightstand. I growled because I hated to wake up in the morning. I enjoyed my nights and rather sleep all day. I took a shower then got dressed for school. I didn't understand why Akea, my twin brother, and I had to go to college. We had all of our lives to go to college. I walked out of my bedroom then headed down the stairs. We lived in an estate far away from the city. The closest home to us was twenty minutes away. We needed the big house because seventeen people occupied it. The home had twenty bedrooms and only twelve were filled. The family is big.

I walked into the gym room where my father and his brother, Izra, were working out. My father sat the weight down then looked at me. "Partied hard on a school night?" he asked me.

Izra walked past me then patted my back. "Next time hide the liquor bottle," he whispered then walked out of the room.

"College isn't for me. Maybe for Akea but not for me. Why can't I just work in the family business? I'm a werewolf that lives for eternity. What purpose does college serve?" I asked him then he growled at me. His eyes turned blue when he stood up.

"College will give you knowledge. Do you want to be a dumb immortal? That knowledge will stick with you and then you can pass it down to your pups in the future. We need to learn about what is in the world that we live in," he said to me. Akea walked down the hall dressed in a button-up shirt, khakis and a tie.

"I guess Akea blends in well with the science geeks," I said out loud.

"Akea is on the Dean's List," our father spat.

"Did you forget your pocket protector?" I asked Akea. My father slapped me on the back of my head.

"Leave him alone, Kanye, and I mean it," he said then growled. Monifa walked past me then frowned her nose up.

"Good morning, Uncle Goon," Monifa said then kissed his cheek. She kissed Akea's cheek then looked at me.

"Where is my kiss?" I asked her.

"Wherever your common sense is. What did you do to my necklace? I know you came into my room because your scent was in there. You'd better get to talkin', Kanye, or else," she said.

"Or else what? I wasn't in your funky room," I said to her then she mushed me. Akea and my father laughed as they walked away.

I mushed her back then she growled at me. "I'm going to kick your arrogant ass if you step foot in my room again. Don't touch my shit," she said to me.

"With your ugly self," I said to her then she pushed me. I pushed her back. "Don't mess with me this morning, Monifa, and I mean it," I said to her.

"Where is my neckless that Yardi gave to me?" she asked me.

"I don't know. Ask his punk ass where it's at. You shouldn't be messing around with a human anyway," I spat.

"Don't you mess with human females?" she asked me.

"None of your business," I said then walked away from her.

"I can't stand you, Kanye!" she screamed at me.

"I can't stand your ass, either!" I shouted back at her.

"Watch your mouth!" my mother yelled at me. I kissed her cheek.

"Good morning, Ma. How are you feeling? You look beautiful," I said to her then she smiled.

"Good morning, handsome. Did you have fun last night?" she asked after her mood softened.

"It was aight," I said. I had a threesome for the first time with two college chicks and it wasn't as fun as I thought it would be. They cried every time I entered them and it made me go limp.

"You need to take college a bit more seriously. You are a very smart boy but you are just too stubborn," she said.

"I will, Ma, see you later," I said then walked out the door. I got into my black sports car with the drop top then revved the engine.

"So, you were just going to leave me, huh?" Zaan asked me.

"I thought you had a hangover," I said to him then he got in the car.

"I did until my father came in my room with some type of drink. Nigga, when I sipped on that drink it made me felt like a new wolf," he said.

"Uncle Elle always got something special," I said. The twins Baneet and Chancy walked out of the house, laughing and giggling.

"Baneet got some juicy legs. Juicer than a raw T-bone steak," Zaan said as he lustfully stared at her.

"Dayo is going to mess you up," I said.

"I will take one for the team. Look at her ass and hips," Zaan said.

"Come here, Baneet!" Zaan called out to her.

"I'm running late for school! Call me," Baneet said then got into her truck.

"You got it bad, bro," I said to Zaan.

"I can't help it. She is beautiful and her smooth, dark-chocolate skin be having me stuck," Zaan said.

"Dayo is seriously going to mess you up," I said to him

"You riding to school with us?" I called out to Akea.

"No, go ahead," he said. Akea and I weren't close because he always avoided being around me. I picked on him at times because that was the only way I could communicate with him. In school he'd walked past me like he didn't know me. He talked to Zaan more than he talked to me.

"Harry Potter muthafucka," I said before I pulled off.

"What did you do to Monifa's necklace? I heard you two arguing," Zaan said to me.

"I'm going to take it to Beastly Treasures and get real diamonds put in it. I can't believe her punk-ass boyfriend got her fake diamonds. I hope she ain't screwing him," I told Zaan.

"What if she is?" he asked me then I growled. I gritted my teeth as I clutched the steering wheel.

"She know better," I told Zaan.

“Y’all don’t even get along. Why don’t you tell her you feel some type of way about her?” he asked.

“Because I don’t. I just don’t want her messing with someone who doesn’t appreciate her enough to give her real diamonds. Even if he can’t afford it he still should’ve waited or got her something else,” I said to Zaan then he shook his head.

Monifa

I walked through the mall with Baneet and Chancy. The three of us were very close.

We entered an urban fashion store. There was a big college party after the football game that night. “Damn it, do they believe in size fourteen’s around here?” I asked out loud.

“Right. Only one who can fit this crap is Chancy,” Baneet said. Chancy was slim and curvaceous while Baneet and I were a little heavier.

“And I’m not even interested in none of this,” Chancy said as she popped her gum.

“We should get an apartment away from home,” Baneet said.

“Our parents are very old-fashioned. The pack must live together and blah, blah, blah,” I said.

“I like it home,” Chancy said.

“You just like being around Akea,” I said then Baneet laughed.

“Akea doesn’t pay nobody any mind,” Baneet replied as she looked through the rack.

"If I had a brother like Kanye, I would be mad at the world, too. Kanye is an arrogant asshole and he makes my skin crawl. He isn't nothing but a chick magnet," I said.

"Speak of the devil," Chancy said. When I turned around Kanye and Zaan walked into the store and I must admit that Kanye is borderline gorgeous. Kanye had to be around six-foot-two and had a very nice build. His skin was the color of copper. His arms and chest were solid, giving him extra sex appeal. He had markings all over his body that he inherited from his roots. We all had a few but Kanye's tribal markings were different like his father. He wore a sleeveless shirt and a pair of shorts and tennis shoes. His hair was tapered on the sides and the middle was very wavy. Everything on him was perfect. Zaan was attractive also, but he was more of a lean build, and taller than Kanye. Zaan had pretty dark skin and he wore his hair in locks like Elle used to before he cut them off.

Kanye's eyes flashed blue when he saw me. I rolled my eyes at him. "Why can't I get away from him?" I asked out loud.

"Because you want some of him," Baneet teased me. Zaan kissed Baneet on her cheek, which caused her to blush. Everyone knew they were low-key dating, all except for Uncle Dayo.

"I got enough of you this morning and now this?" I asked Kanye.

"Shut up. I just came in here to get something to wear for tonight," he said then walked past me. I stared at the tribal markings that wrapped around his muscular arm and neck. When he looked at me, I hurriedly turned my head.

"You know you can't fit shit up in here, Monifa," Kanye said to me then laughed. Chancy and Baneet giggled then I growled at them. I stormed out of the store with Chancy following behind me.

"He makes me sick," I said out loud. A group of cute guys walked past us. Chancy waved at them, she was a flirt.

"What are you two getting into?" one of them asked us. He wasn't nothing cute to look at. Kanye, Baneet and Zaan walked out of the store. Kanye had a bag in his hand. When he saw the group of guys, a scowl came across his face. He stood next to me.

"What y'all niggas want?" Kanye asked then put his arm around me. His body language was intimidating. Kanye looked like a "thug". The group of guys walked off then he unwrapped his arm from around me.

"I'll see you at home, big head," he said to me then walked off. Zaan kissed Baneet's lips then smirked at me before he left the mall with Kanye.

"Why am I turned on?" I asked them then faked a gag.

"You two need to stop it. Izra will get over it eventually. Adika is mad cool and I don't think she will trip over it," Chancy said.

****

The hot water wasn't working inside my room so I headed to the hall bathroom. I pushed the door open then jumped when I saw Kanye peeing in the toilet. My eyes darted to his dick and he just stood there unbothered that I invaded his privacy. He sniffed the air then growled as he stared at me.

"Are you aroused?" he asked me.

"You jerk!" I said then hurried out of the bathroom. I went inside my room then locked the door. I fanned myself then took a cold shower. Visions of Kanye touching me filled my head and a strong ache formed between my legs. His scent even drove me crazy because it was still in my room. After I got dressed I headed out the door with Baneet and Chancy.

Arya was getting out of her car when we walked out the house.

"Look at you three all dolled up. Where are all of you going and did your fathers see y'all leave out? Y'all clothes are squeezing everything," she said then laughed.

"No, they didn't see us, that's why we are trying to hurry up and leave. We are grown anyway," Chancy said.

"Our father doesn't seem to think that," Arya said to her sisters then yawned. "I'm tired. I had a long day at the warehouse," she said. Arya helped out with Ula and Amadi's skincare products.

"We will see you later. Don't wait up," I said to her before she went inside the house.

"Chancy, it's your turn to drive. We've been in my truck all day," I said to her then she sucked her teeth.

"Fine!" she said as we walked to her car. Yardi sent me a message telling me that him and his frat buddies were already at the party.

"We are having fun tonight!" I shouted.

"I know I am," Chancy said.

"Hot ass," Baneet teased.

****

"Where is that necklace I bought for you?" Yardi asked me.

"It's home," I lied. He pulled me into him then kissed my lips. I wrapped my arms around his neck then kissed him back. I pulled away from him then sipped my spiked punch. The party was crowded, Baneet and Chancy stayed on the dance floor. Chancy was really into the party as she danced seductively. I pulled Yardi into me then grinded on him. His arms wrapped around my hips. Yardi was handsome. He stood at six feet and had a football player build to him. We dated since my freshman year of college. I was his tutor then one thing led to another.

Kanye walked through the crowd with Zaan. The girls rushed to him. I made all of them fall on top of each other then the ceiling light blew out. I'm a witch and werewolf. I loved my beast but my witch is what I loved even more. My mother taught me a lot of spells and I'd been practicing them with her since I could remember. Kanye looked at me because he knew I was behind it. I gave him the finger then he smiled at me. He blew me a kiss then winked at me and I forgot all about Yardi and what he was talking about.

"Do you hear me?" Yardi asked.

"What?" I asked him.

"Are you coming back to my room with me?" he asked me.

"I'm spending a spa day with my mom and cousins tomorrow. It's an all-girls outing," I replied.

"When are you going to make time for me?" Yardi asked me.

"Next weekend, I'm all yours," I replied. Kanye looked at me then looked at Yardi while a female stood in his face wanting his attention. He ignored her. She turned his head so that he could face her. Her name is Jaysha and word around campus was that he was messing around with her. She is a human and was very popular on campus. Her parents are very wealthy and she was quick to let someone know. Rumor was that before she met Kanye, she got a boy locked up because he dumped her. I hated her with a passion. I blocked out Yardi so that I could hear Jaysha and Kanye's conversation from across the room.

"What is wrong with you, Kanye? You don't call me anymore and you have been standing me up lately," Jaysha said to him.

"I keep telling you that I'm not feeling you anymore. Why can't you see that?" he asked her.

"We were in love," she said to him.

"Yeah, until you got pregnant. I can't get you pregnant. That baby wasn't mine, so that just tells me that you stepped out. I'm cool on you, Jaysha. Stop calling my fucking phone. I'm not trying to hurt your feelings, but you are setting yourself up. You slashed my tires, keyed my car and got the police to pull me over. You are crazy and I don't want any parts of it," Kanye said.

"The baby was yours!" Jaysha said then Kanye laughed in her face.

"Human women are very difficult at times. I have never come inside you. I can barely fit inside you. I hope you don't think you can get pregnant by giving head," Kanye said to her. Jaysha slapped Kanye as hard as she could but I could tell that it hurt her more than it hurt him. A bat burst into the window then attacked Jaysha. The crowd ran out of the frat house while Jaysha screamed and cried as she tried to swat the bat away. The bat bit and scratched at her face then it disappeared.

"What was that?" Yardi asked.

"A bat," I answered. I no longer wanted to be at the party. Hearing Kanye admit he had feelings for Jaysha turned my stomach. I thought maybe he was just screwing around with her but he admitted that it was stronger. I kissed Yardi goodbye then promised to call him. I walked out of the house with Baneet and Chancy following me.

"What was that about?" Chancy asked me.

"I don't know! What is wrong with me?" I asked.

"You've been getting very jealous over Kanye. Yardi can't even keep your attention anymore," Baneet said. I had a slight buzz from the punch and I just wanted to go home.

"This party sucks. Are you two ready to go? We have to get up early tomorrow for our spa day," I said to them.

"I'm ready, hell, I been ready," Baneet said.

****

I stood in front of Kanye's room door then looked down both ends of the hall. I made sure nobody was coming before I disappeared then reappeared inside his room. Kanye slept peacefully on his back. I blushed at his growls mixed with light snoring. I found him to be fascinating, especially his beast. My eyes roamed over his sculpted chest and tight abs. I slid the covers back then quietly got into his bed. I didn't know why I had these urges but I couldn't help it. I had to be close to him even if it was just for a few seconds. I could see the outline of his dick print through the thin sheet. I had a strong craving for him. A growl almost slipped from my lips but I hurriedly covered my mouth. Kanye opened his eyes, his ice blue pupils staring at me in the dark.

"What in the hell are you doing in my room, Monifa? Your crazy ass better not have cursed me," he said then jumped up.

"I was looking for my necklace! I know you took it!" I yelled at him.

"I know you'd better calm your voice down before your father comes in here, wondering what you are doing in here. If I did take your necklace, what makes you think I would sleep with the cheap thing?" he asked me.

"I wanted to be sure," I said then walked toward his door. Kanye pulled me back then pushed me up against the wall. I pushed him back then he held both of my arms above my head. He growled but not an angry growl, his beast was in lust. Kanye ran his nose down my neck then kissed it. His sharp teeth grazed my skin then sent shivers down my spine. Kanye pulled away from me.

"Get the fuck out of my room," he spat. He opened his door then pushed me into the hallway.

"Asshole!" I screamed before he slammed the door in my face. I headed back to my room aroused and confused. Yardi was very sexual but Kanye did something else to me without touching me. When I walked into my bedroom, my mother was sitting on my bed. She was very, very old but she looked to be in her late twenties. Immortals started aging slowly once they hit eighteen. We, the offspring, still looked eighteen but we were a few years older.

"What's going on, Mother?" I asked. She patted the bed so I sat down next to her.

"Why were you in Kanye's room?" she asked me.

"I was looking for my necklace," I lied then she laughed.

"Who are you fooling, Monifa? That necklace is the least bit of your concerns. You have desires, perhaps, even urges to be with him. Do you sexually crave him, and don't lie because I can see your visions when I want to?"

"Yes, I do. I don't know why, but I do. I can't help it," I admitted then she laughed.

"Your father will kill me if I told you this, but Kanye is your soulmate. When you have those desires and feelings for someone that strong it just means that you two are meant to be," she said.

"Ewwwwwwww," I said.

"You are saying that now. Every day that passes it will become stronger. I just hate to see Izra figure it out. He will lose his mind. Let me get ready for the headaches to come," she said then stood up.

"It's not nice to lead someone on, Monifa. I know that you aren't into that human boy. It will never work anyway because you and him are so different. You might want to break it off before he becomes too attached," she said. She kissed my forehead then walked out of my room. I lay in bed and tossed and turned all night. I should've slept next to Kanye where it was more comfortable.

Akea

I sat at my desk in my room, studying for an exam for my Astrology class. There was a knock at my bedroom door. “What is it? I’m busy,” I said. The door opened and when I turned around it was Chancy.

“Do you want to go to the movies with me?” she asked me.

“I’m studying,” I said.

“Who cares? You need to come out for some air. I want you to go to the movies with me and I’m not leaving your room until you do. I’m going to sit right here,” she said then hopped up on my desk. She crossed her legs and arms. Her beast’s eyes turned yellow as she looked at me. I dropped my pen.

“Fine, I will go,” I said then she hugged me. I stood up then grabbed my jacket. She cleared her throat.

“Sorry, Akea. I said movies not school. I like the look that you go for, you know, the smart clean look, but you need to bring it down just a notch,” she said to me.

“You want me to change my clothes?” I asked her.

“Umm, yes, that would be nice. Wait right here,” she said then walked out of the room. Moments later, she came back with two shopping bags.

“What is that?” I asked her.

“I was doing a little shopping with the girls and I bought something that would look good on you,” she said.

“I don’t want to dress like Zaan and Kanye,” I said then she growled at me.

“You just offended me. I know that, and that’s what I like about you,” she said. She pulled out a pair of nice jeans with a stylish jacket that looked like a blazer with a hood on it along with pair of fashionable boots to match.

“I like this,” I said.

“I know. It’s between thug and school boy,” she said.

“Let me take a shower and I will be right out,” I said then she kissed me. Her kiss landed on my lips then she walked out of the room. I took a shower then got dressed. A half-hour later, I walked down the long, spiral case stairwell. My father came out of the kitchen dressed in business attire. My mother wasn’t good at keeping track of how much the jewelry stores made because there was too much money. My father stepped up and took over the accounts. He fussed about it at first because he had to get up early and go to work, but over the years he got used to it.

“Who is this young lady?” he asked me then smirked.

“Chancy,” I said.

“Now, son, you are about to cause an uproar in this house because your uncle Dayo is missing a few screws. I’m might have to kick his ass. Now, when you go out with Chancy, be on good behavior,” he said.

“I will,” I said.

“Come talk to me for a minute before you leave,” he said. I followed him into the family room. He took off his suit jacket then loosened his tie.

“I still have to get used to wearing that hot thing all day,” he said then poured himself a glass of the cognac that sat on the table behind the couch.

“It will make me much happier if you connected with your brother. I know you might think that you two are different but you two came from the same womb. You are identical twins and him being a beast and you being a warlock shouldn’t make a difference. I know that he teases you but it’s because he wants your attention. I know you like studying and I am a proud father because of that, but your family in this house is important, too,” he said to me.

“Kanye and I have nothing in common, Father,” I said. A displeased look crossed his face.

“You and your brother are going to get along and I don’t mind forcing it,” he said in a stern voice. He stood up. “Have fun tonight,” he said then walked out of the living room. Chancy came into the room with her face done up in make-up. She wore a jean one-piece with a pair of strappy-heeled sandals. Her thick hair was braided straight back into a style. Chancy was very beautiful. She had skin the color of a Hershey’s bar. Her eyes slanted in the corners and she had a pair of full, pretty lips. Her cheekbones were strong, showing off her Indian roots. She was slimmer than Baneet and Monifa but she was just as beautiful. She flirted a lot and was a bit wild, but her personality could light up the room. Anik had the same personality and so did Baneet.

They all had an aura about them that made everything seem peaceful.

"Let's go!" she said then pulled me out of the door.

****

Chancy sat in the passenger seat of my car, talking and giggling. I laughed at a few of her jokes.

"You have a beautiful smile, Akea," she said then I looked at her.

"You have one, too," I said to her.

"Are you a virgin?" she asked me. I almost swerved my car off the road.

"Ummm, no," I said. She looked at me then crossed her arms.

"You've been with someone?" she asked me.

"Yes, a girl that was in my science club," I answered.

"What is her name?" she asked me.

"Sarah, Sarah Baxter," I answered.

"What immortal has a name like that?" she asked.

"She is human," I replied.

We pulled up to the mall. I parked my car then got out to let Chancy out. She grabbed my hand then strutted toward the movie theatre. I paid for our tickets then went to the popcorn and candy stand.

"I didn't think I would run into you here," a voice said from behind me. When I turned around it was Sarah staring at me with her blue eyes.

"The movie is about to start," Chancy said. When she saw Sarah and I looking at each other she froze.

"You know her or something?" Chancy asked.

"My name is Sarah and we were in the same science club," she said.

"Ohhhhh, you are Sarah? Mrs. Sarah Baxter?" Chancy asked with an attitude.

"Yes, and you are?" Sarah asked as her friends stood behind her uncomfortably because of Chancy's attitude.

"I'm his girlfriend. Now, let's go, Akea," Chancy spat then shoved her popcorn and candy in my arms. I looked at Sarah then followed Chancy.

Chancy didn't say anything to me as we watched the zombie movie. All the other females in the movie theatre snuggled up under their dates. Chancy sat quietly with her eyes straight forward.

"Did I hurt you?" I asked Chancy. Her yellow-brownish eyes stared at me then turned back to their normal color.

"Is she the reason why you don't feel comfortable around me? Is it my skin?" she asked me.

"Why would you ask me that?" I asked her.

"Sarah is whiter than my damn popcorn, Akea," Chancy spat.

"It was just something that happened. I think your skin is beautiful," I said to her then she smiled.

"Kiss me," she said.

"Right now?" I asked.

"Yes, I want you to kiss me," she said. I leaned forward then placed my lips on Chancy's glossed ones. I kissed her then she slipped her tongue inside my mouth.

"Suck on my tongue!" her voice said inside my head. I gently sucked on her tongue then she pulled away from me. She lay her head on my shoulder. When I looked down the aisle, Sarah and her friends stared at me.

"That will teach them bitches not to stare!" Chancy said. I had a feeling that Chancy was going to turn my world upside down in a good and bad way.

Osiris

I lay in bed while one of the servants rubbed my back. My father had me training for a whole day to become a great warrior. I was the son of King Baki and Queen Jalesa of Anubi. My aunt Neda came into my room. She sent the servant away.

"What do you want, Neda?" I asked her. Neda is my father's sister. Rumor around Anubi is that an old warlock got inside her mother's womb. Neda's mother died when she gave birth to her and my father raised her. I was born a year after Neda was born. She was like my sister instead of my aunt. She pulled a globe out of her pocket.

"What is that?" I asked her.

"This is Earth. The place where your uncle Akua lives. He is Ammon's second son, the black wolf. He killed my father," she said.

"Ammon was a bad wolf and made Anubi a bad place. Watch how you speak!" I said to her then she laughed.

"You are brainwashed but I will not be. Ammon was a great warrior. Drawings of him are all over this temple," she said.

"That was before greed and power killed him. I don't care about Ammon or Earth," I said to her.

"I want to show you something," she said. I followed Neda into her sanctuary then she closed the door. She told me to have a seat so I sat down across from her.

"I have something that will make you stronger. You will not need to train so much," she said then sat a cup down in front of me.

"What is that?" I asked as I sniffed it.

"Water from the Nile River. That's the river Akua drank from and he became stronger. He is even stronger than your father's beast," she said. She sat the globe down in front of me then showed me a big, black beast with blue eyes. I picked up the globe and watched the black beast run through the woods. His beast was strong and had the strength of ten warriors.

"I have never seen anything like it," I said to Neda.

"His eyes are the color of the Nile River because he drank the water," she replied.

"I didn't hear that story," I replied.

"That's because Anubi doesn't want us to know everything. This place holds many secrets. Now drink the water so you can be strong like your uncle," she said to me. I pushed the cup away.

"I will do it the right way as my father did. He practiced every day and so will I," I said. I stood up then walked toward the door but she blocked me in.

"What are you doing?" I asked her when I turned around. Neda stared at me with glowing eyes.

“I didn’t want to force it but now I have to,” she said then a force held me down. I tried to shift but I couldn’t. My growls were muffled out. “You are such a fool,” she said. She grabbed a bat from her cage in the corner of her room. It made noises as she carried it over to me.

“Back in the dark times in Egypt, our gods were cat and werewolf people. Everyone worshipped the two but there was another god nobody spoke of. It was a god that sucked the blood out of a human’s life. The warriors captured him because they feared him. They thought he was the devil because he couldn’t stand daylight. He was very different from the other two gods because he didn’t shift into a beast. The warriors held him out in the sun where his body turned to ash. His ashes were kept in an urn and I found it. It was in the dungeon downstairs in this temple. I gave him life from those ashes through this bat. This bat will bite you then kill you. Your heart will not beat anymore and your beast will be no more. You will be reborn as a vampire. You will be casted away to Earth because Anubi will fear you. I wonder how your coward father will feel about his only son being a vampire. It’s nothing against you, my wrath is against your father and all that he stands for. He watched my father die and did nothing, and now he will watch his son hunt and feed on his own people,” Neda said to me. The bat latched onto my neck then sucked the life out of me until I stopped breathing…

Made in the USA
Middletown, DE
04 March 2021

34818905R00228